Cash's gaze traveled over her lingerie, and he grinned. With one finger, he hooked her bra strap, dangled it. "Very nice."

She snatched it from him and picked up the pile of clothes, hugging it to her chest. Heat radiated from her face, and she gave him her boardroom stare. "I like it."

"Bet you do." Unfazed, he snitched a cookie and took a huge bite. "Mmmmm, mmmm. Can't beat these, can you?" Then, scanning the cramped space, he asked, "You good to go now?"

"Yes. I think I have everything I need. Thank you."

"Lock up behind me."

Her brows rose. "Is there much crime here?"

"In Maverick Junction?" He laughed. "Nah. But just the same, when you're here alone, it wouldn't hurt to throw the lock."

She nodded. *Throw the lock. If he only knew.* Her everyday life revolved around elaborate security systems, video cams, and ever-present bodyguards.

Not anymore. She was on her own now. For the short term. But she would take his advice. No sense being stupid.

"Dottie doesn't."

"I know. She should. I've told her that."

After setting her laundry back onto the table, lingerie-side down, she followed him to the door. He opened it and paused to give her a quick, friendly peck on the cheek.

She turned her head at that instant, and his lips missed their mark, landing squarely on her mouth.

Both pulled away as if burned, and she stepped back. Their eyes met and locked. Heat swept through Annelise; her breasts felt heavy. The man was potent!

His voice gravelly, Cash said, "Night, Annie." Without another word or a second's hesitation, he hurried down the stairs and into the night.

Annelise laid her fingers over her lips. Her tingling lips. Innocent. Accidental. The kiss had meant nothing. So why was her heart racing?

Somebody
Like You

Also by Lynnette Austin

The Maverick Junction Series
Somebody Like You
Nearest Thing to Heaven
Can't Stop Lovin' You

Somebody Like You

LYNNETTE AUSTIN

FOREVER

NEW YORK BOSTON

Copyright © 2012 by Lynnette Austin
Excerpt from *Nearest Thing to Heaven* copyright © 2013 by Lynnette Austin

Cover design by Elizabeth Turner. Cover images © Shutterstock.
Cover copyright © 2016 by Hachette Book Group, Inc.

Forever
Hachette Book Group
1290 Avenue of the Americas, New York, NY 10104
forever-romance.com
twitter.com/foreverromance

Originally published as an ebook and as a print-on-demand edition by Grand Central Publishing in December 2012
First Mass Market Edition: October 2016

Forever is an imprint of Grand Central Publishing. The Forever name and logo are trademarks of Hachette Book Group, Inc.

ISBNs: 978-1-4555-6944-1 (mass market), 978-1-4555-2837-0 (ebook)

Printed in the United States of America

OPM

10 9 8 7 6 5 4 3 2 1

To Barbara Bent, a friend through life's ups and downs, who has shown me New York City the way it should be seen! I stumbled on a rare gift when the two of us met at one of the very first get-togethers of the Southwest Florida Romance Writers.

And to the memory of my brother Brian Duffy, who, sadly, lost his battle with leukemia.

Acknowledgments

Books don't write themselves, and this one has certainly been no exception. So many provided help, encouragement, and expertise, and I'd be remiss not to acknowledge them.

Thanks to my incredible agent Nicole Resciniti of the Seymour Agency who believed in both me and the Maverick Junction series. To say I'm blessed to have her in my life—and in my corner—would be an understatement.

Lauren Plude, editor extraordinaire, has gone above and beyond in helping me take this book to new heights. Thanks for letting me bounce ideas off you and for not considering any question or concern too small or unimportant.

My critique partners, Diane O'Key and Joyce Henderson, the other two-thirds of the Three Musketeers, have my eternal gratitude. We've shared laughter and tears, celebrated success, and persevered through frustration.

Most of all, I want to thank my husband. Dave has provided love, encouragement, and confidence throughout the entire trip. He's listened to me rejoice when the story was soaring and put up with my whining when it wasn't, assuring me that everything would be fine. And Dave, thanks, too, for the endless supply of coffee and Peppermint Patties.

Somebody
Like You

Chapter One

Y ou've got to be kidding me."

Annelise Montjoy motored her Harley along what appeared to be the town's main street. This was Maverick Junction?

A blue Cadillac, surely old enough to be in a museum, was parked nose-in to the curb. An incredibly ugly dog sat in the front seat.

Thank God, this, the final destination of her cross-country trip from Boston, was temporary. It looked like the kind of place you ran *away* from, not toward. If luck was on her side, she'd be out of here in a couple of weeks at the most.

And then a store door opened and her breath caught. *Go, Texas!* Look at that cowboy. So different from any of the men in her life. So... intriguing. She slowed to nearly a standstill and watched as he swiped an arm across his forehead, then dumped a grocery bag in the backseat of the old Caddy.

Cracking open a bottle of water, he turned his head in her

direction. Her breath hitched as his gaze ran lazily over her, her bike. Then he snagged a Styrofoam cup from inside his car and filled it before setting it on the blistering pavement for the dog waiting patiently beside him.

Leaning against the faded fender, he thumbed back his battered Stetson and chugged the rest of the water. Twisting the cap back on, he tossed the bottle into the recycling bin beside the grocer's door.

Annelise pulled her bike into a parking space across the street, deliberately turning her back on the stranger. While his clothes might have been stereotypical cowboy—worn jeans, a faded T-shirt, cowboy boots, and hat—he took everything from simmer to boiling point. The jeans hugged long legs, while the shirt stretched taut across his muscled chest. There was something very alluring about him and that surprised her. He wasn't the kind of man she was usually drawn to.

He shouldn't appeal to her.

He did.

Not so much as a breeze stirred. The flag on the post office hung limp, and the cheerful red, white, and blue balloons someone had hung outside a beauty salon drooped listlessly.

Unable to stop herself, she peeked in the bike's rearview mirror. Cowboy was bent over, talking to the dog. Quite a view, but she wasn't here to admire a fine jean-clad butt. She needed something cold to drink and something light to eat. Then she'd go in search of Dottie Willis and the apartment she'd rented over the Internet. Maverick Junction, Texas. Annelise wished she was driving through, wished she could view it as simply a spot on the map where she'd stopped for lunch one summer day.

Well, she'd just have to work fast.

But before she'd even taken two steps, her cell rang. She checked caller ID, blew out a huge sigh, and dutifully answered.

"Annelise, where are you? When are you coming home?" Her mother's voice sounded strained.

"Don't worry, Mom. Are you and Dad okay?"

"We're fine."

"Grandpa?"

"He's had a good day. A good week, actually." Her mother hesitated. "He misses you."

"I miss him, too."

"Then come home."

"I can't."

"You're being selfish."

"No, I'm not. I'm trying to help while the rest of you stand by and do nothing."

"We're respecting Vincent's wishes."

Her grandfather, her strong, always in control grandfather, had been diagnosed with acute myeloid leukemia. After aggressive treatment by the country's best doctors, Vincent Montjoy was in remission. But the prognosis wasn't good. Her grandfather needed a bone marrow transplant, and none of the family matched.

And then, Annelise's whole world had flipped upside down—again. There was hope. It turned out he might have a half sister. One who could carry the life-saving marrow match. One he'd adamantly forbidden anyone to track down.

Well, she would.

And that's why she was in Maverick Junction, Texas. Why she'd ridden her Harley here from Boston.

Her first stop had been at a sorority sister's whose husband was a whiz with both computers and genealogy. If anyone could ferret out the information she needed, it would be him. By the time she'd left the next morning, Ron had already been knee-deep in research for her.

But she hadn't taken into account the physical toll of riding the heavy motorcycle a couple thousand miles. By the time she'd been on the bike for an eight-hour stretch, her butt and legs ached. Sharing the highway with semis, hour after hour, alone, was no picnic.

"Annelise Elizabeth Katherine Montjoy, you *will* get on a plane today and come home. We'll arrange transport for that motorcycle of yours."

"Mom—"

"Not another word, honey. Tell me where you are, and I'll phone you back once your travel arrangements are made. Silas will pick you up at the airport."

"No."

Her mother sighed. "You're sure you're safe? Nobody—"

"I'm fine, Mother. Believe me. I'm right where I need to be." With that, she hung up.

Guilt nagged at her. When you had as much money as her family, the threat of kidnapping always hung over you. For as long as she could remember, she'd had her own bodyguards. Which equaled no privacy. Two muscle-bound men tagging along had turned more than one date into a fiasco.

But she couldn't let her parents or her grandfather worry. She'd call her cousin. Later. Right now, she was thirsty. She headed for the café.

*   *   *

Seated toward the back of Sally's Place, Annelise heard the door open and close. The bell overhead jingled as outside heat rushed in. Without even looking, she knew who'd blown in with it. Well, he was no concern of hers. In all fairness, she doubted there was anywhere else to eat lunch in this one-pony town.

Annelise went back to studying the menu. Chili, country-fried steak, burritos, enchiladas, and just about anything that could be deep-fried.

A pair of dusty boots stopped at her table. She lifted her head and looked straight into the greenest eyes she'd ever seen. For an instant, all sense left her; speech deserted her.

"Seems there're no tables left," Cowboy said. "Mind if I sit with you?" Without waiting for an answer, he pulled out a chair.

She blinked, sanity returning. Her gaze swept the wealth of unoccupied tables. "No empty tables?"

"Well—" He held out his hands, palms up.

Up close, Cowboy was wicked handsome. If she wasn't dead set on settling in today so she could head over to Lone Tree tomorrow— "Actually, I'm afraid I do mind."

He cocked his head, tipped back his cowboy hat. "Not very neighborly."

"Good thing I'm not your neighbor, then."

"Ouch." He grimaced. "I don't bite, and I've had all my shots."

Sadly, she shook her head. "I suppose someone told you that line was cute."

"Nope." He looked at the chair, then back at her.

"I don't mean to be rude, but I have a lot on my mind, and I really don't want company."

"Okay, let's head at it from a different direction. I do. Need company, that is. I've been out on the ranch with nothing but surly bulls and even meaner cowhands for way too long. Sure would be a pleasure to sit across from you for a few minutes. I won't hold you up. Honest. When you're ready to go, you go."

Her mouth dropped open. "Are all Texans this persistent?"

He narrowed his eyes in consideration. "We might be. Guess that's why we lost so many good men at the Alamo. Texans hate to throw in the towel. Never can tell when things might start going your way."

Despite herself, Annelise laughed. She hadn't expected such a rough-and-tumble-looking cowboy to be so optimistic.

The owner chose that moment to wander over. "Hey, Cash, ain't seen you in a while."

"Been busy breaking in a couple new horses and doing some branding. So, how's my favorite gal, Sally?"

"My feet hurt, and my cook's throwin' a tantrum. Other than that, all's good." Sally pushed at frizzy blond hair and snapped her gum. "How 'bout you?"

"Can't complain. Tell you what I'd love right now, though. A tall glass of your sweet tea. Lots of ice." He dropped into the chair beside her.

Annelise gaped at him. Cowboy was one smooth operator.

"Comin' right up. How 'bout you, sweetheart? You want some tea?"

"Yes. That would be wonderful. Unsweetened, please. And I'd prefer to drink it without company." She shot Cash a get-lost look. He simply smiled back.

Sally's gaze shifted between the two of them. When Cash made no move to change tables, she asked, "Need a minute to look at the menu?"

"No. I'd like your house salad with vinaigrette dressing on the side."

"That's gonna be your lunch?" Cash scowled. "That's all you're getting?"

Annelise sat up straighter. "I hate to be rude, but I have a lot to do today. I came in for lunch. Not company."

"Understood."

Still, he didn't move.

What was with him? So much for Texans being gentlemen. Anger, an emotion she rarely allowed herself, lapped at her. Mentally counting to ten, she turned her attention to Sally. "Just the salad, please."

"That's not enough," Cash said.

"Who are you? The lunch patrol?"

"You'd dang well be eating better if I was. I'd order a nice steak, some hand-cut fries, and a big old piece of Ms. Sally's apple pie à la mode for you."

"For lunch?"

"Darn tootin'."

"I'll stick with my salad, thanks."

When their waitress headed off, Cash said, "You're sure more hospitable with her than you are with me."

She shrugged. "Like I said, you can move to another table if you'd like."

His gaze traveled past her, and he stood suddenly. "Excuse me."

More than a little disappointed, she turned in her chair and watched him cross the room, his stride easy. Despite what she'd said, a traitorous part of her had actually hoped he'd stay.

He walked over to where an older woman struggled to slide her chair from the table. Giving her a quick kiss on the cheek, he reached out to her. "Can I help?"

With a sigh, the woman laid a shaky hand in his. "This getting old isn't for sissies." Standing, she said, "You're a good boy, Cash Hardeman. But that doesn't mean I've forgotten about the snake you and Brawley Odell put in my desk."

He picked up her purse and carried it with him as he

walked her slowly toward the door. "You've got a memory like an elephant, Mrs. Sandburg."

"And don't you forget it." At the door, she called out, "Sally, I left the check on the table. That pie of yours was as good as ever."

"See you next week," Sally answered.

"You bet." She patted Cash's cheek. "I can manage from here. Tell your mother hello for me when she and your dad get home."

"Will do." He waited till she started down the walk and then returned to Annelise's table.

Something about the easy candidness of this Texas cowboy tugged at her. His kindness touched her heart. But she needed to stay focused on the reason she'd come.

"So." He reached for the tea Sally slid him and took a long drink of the cool, soothing liquid. Setting it down, he asked, "Where were we?"

She raised her chin a notch. "I'd just told you that you could move if you didn't like my company."

"Right." He grinned. "I like it fine, thanks. You have a name?"

"Yes. I do."

"Ah." He nodded. "But you're not willing to share." He shot out a hand toward her. "I'm Cash. Cash Hardeman."

"I heard." She hesitated, then sighed and extended her own hand. "Hello, Cash. I'm Annelise."

"Nice to meet you, Annelise. You just get that bike?" He nodded toward the street. "Must've paid through the teeth for it."

"My guilty pleasure." She smiled. The bike represented her first rebellion—her first step toward independence. "I've had it for almost a year now. Some friends wanted to do the fall leaf tour on motorcycles. One of them took me to a Hanniford grocery store parking lot after hours and taught me how to ride. Then he helped me pick out a bike. My father about had a conniption."

Cash laughed. "I can imagine."

"Why?"

"Big bike for a wom—anybody to handle."

"Oh, good save." She laughed and shook her head. "You're fast."

"You'd better believe it." He studied her a minute. "The fall leaf tour? So you're from New England, Annelise?"

Her eyes shuttered. She'd screwed up. "No. I was there visiting." She almost choked on the lie, but she had no choice. His expression said he wasn't buying it. Well, too bad. Once she left this café, she'd never see Cash Hardeman again. A chance meeting. That's all this was. It made no difference whether or not he believed her.

"You ride a lot?" he asked.

"Unfortunately, no. I took the bike out for two weekends last fall and it's been parked ever since. Till this trip."

"Too bad." He swiped at the water ring on the table.

Her eyes widened. Through the front window, she watched the cowboy's mud-brown dog sail through the air and scramble into the old car.

"Cash?"

"Hmmm?"

She pointed toward the window. "That big, hairy dog of yours just executed the best impersonation of Superman I've ever witnessed."

"Huh?"

"The animal may or may not be able to leap tall buildings, but he sure managed to clear the door of that big old monstrosity you're driving. Right now, he's working his way through the groceries in the backseat."

"Oh, brother!" Cash jumped up and ran outside to salvage what he could.

She watched him go and stabbed a forkful of lettuce, wishing the salad would morph into that juicy steak he'd suggested. Oh, well, she sighed. Some things weren't meant to be.

* * *

Two steps out the door, the heat sucker-punched Cash. And instead of sitting inside drinking iced tea with Ms. Ride-into-town-on-a-Harley, he was heading out to deal with his scoundrel of a dog.

"Staubach! What in the hell am I supposed to tell Rosie about her groceries, huh? Shame on you!" he scolded.

And shame on me, he thought, *for leaving the dog alone*. Still…Annelise was some looker. All that black hair and those intense, ice-blue eyes. And the body. Whoa, boy!

Okay, she was about as friendly as a mama bear with week-old cubs. But if they'd been able to finish their lunch together, he might have been able to change that.

She hadn't given him a last name. What was that beautiful thing hiding? Or, maybe, she really, truly hadn't wanted to sit with him. Didn't want to exchange names.

Her voice held a hint of an accent. New England definitely, despite what she'd said. Maybe Boston? Well, whatever. The voice was hot. Silk. And though she had started off sounding totally teed off, he'd heard amusement and a sense of humor creep in.

He tossed the now nearly empty sack of groceries into the trunk. When he looked up, he saw Annelise at the counter, paying for her lunch. Might as well run the ad over to Mel in time for tomorrow's edition. Looked like he'd struck out with the tempting Ms. Cool Eyes. Time to pack up his bat and ball. Game over.

No doubt she planned to hop on that hog and ride out of Maverick Junction without a backward glance. Too bad. He'd have liked more time with her. Time to dig a little deeper. Unless he was mistaken, and he rarely was, there was more to Annelise than met the eye. She might ride a Harley and wear leather, but everything else about her screamed class and money, pampering and top-notch schooling.

Her hands were manicured to within an inch of their lives. The diamonds that winked at her ears could feed a small third-world country. Yeah, the lady had been indulged.

Maybe he had been, too, but to a far lesser degree.

His gaze landed on the Caddy, and he ran a hand over the hood. God, he loved this thing. He had a lot to thank the old man for. And one very good reason—no, make that two— for being royally irritated with his grandpa. But he wasn't about to travel that road right now.

Reaching under the front seat, he found the folder with the newspaper ad he'd put together last night. Time to hire some help. As much as the old guy would fight him about it, Hank, whom he'd more or less inherited from Gramps along with the Caddy, couldn't handle the responsibility of the barn area alone anymore.

"Come on, Staubach." The dog's ears perked up, and he came to heel. Cash took another look at the dusty black-and-chrome Harley, and his stomach knotted in lust. Both the bike and its rider were double-take worthy.

Black bike, black helmet, black shades, black leathers and shirt. One cool lady. One heck of an attitude.

And that mouth. Oh, yeah. He'd give up a Monday-night football game or two for a taste of that.

Chapter Two

Standing at the chipped and cracked counter, Annelise took her time paying Sally before carefully tucking her change in her wallet. Out of the corner of her eye, she watched Cash deal with his dog. She felt bad—for the dog. The poor creature looked crestfallen. The cowboy? He deserved what he got.

She chastised herself. That was uncalled for. She didn't know him, didn't have a clue what might be going on in his life. Her own was a disaster. Maybe his was, too. After all, why would anyone drive a vehicle like that unless he was really down and out? The thing was as old as Methuselah and practically as long as one of those semis she'd passed on the highway.

For all she knew, those groceries the dog had wolfed down were all the food Cash would have for the week. Maybe he'd go hungry.

No. She squinted through the tinted window. His boots, though battered and well-worn, had cost a pretty penny. His teeth, straight and white, had been well cared for, his haircut expensive.

He might pretend to be all down-home and simple, but she had a feeling this cowboy did all right for himself.

Pretense. She shook her head. She could certainly relate to that. How often did she hide her own emotions, her true feelings, behind a mask of sociability? For her, the question really boiled down to which Annelise was real—and which was a façade?

She swung open the restaurant's door and ran headlong into the wall of heat. The sun, almost directly overhead, beat down mercilessly. The wind whipped up and drove a small dust devil down the middle of the street.

She was a long way from home.

"'Bye now," Sally called out. "You come back."

Annelise stopped. If she planned on staying, she'd need to eat—and she certainly was no cook. Besides, Sally might turn out to be useful. She could be a good source of information. "I believe I will. Thank you."

As she stepped out onto the sidewalk, she took a minute to study the street and the shops that lined up shoulder-to-shoulder along its length. Mirage-like, the air shimmered in the heat.

Someone had made an effort to pretty up the town. Every ten feet or so, a pot of geraniums struggled to bloom in the oppressive Texas summer. Small American flags sprouted from each pot, no doubt in honor of the fast-approaching Fourth of July holiday.

A bakery three doors down had hung an awning of pastel pink and green stripes. Wind chimes hung from it and tinkled as a light breeze kicked up. A secondhand store with a huge banner in its window boasting twenty percent off everything sat across the street.

The town wasn't much to look at. Maverick Junction would never make a list of tourist destinations or be considered fashionable, but glancing up and down the street again, she decided the place had heart. The people who lived here, who called this town home, had tried to make it pretty. They cared.

And Sally had asked her to come back. Maybe it was something she said to all her customers, an off-hand comment. But to Annelise, it meant something. Sally didn't know who Annelise's father was or who her grandfather and great-grandfather were. Used to being fawned over because of her name, because of her family, Sally's casually given invitation felt genuine.

She hurried over to her Harley and pulled a map out of her saddlebag. An old wooden bench rested beneath the bakery's awning, and she sat down on it. Opening the map to Texas, she found Maverick Junction, traced her finger along the thin yellow line till she touched the tiny speck that marked her destination. She'd traced this path before, but needed to reassure herself.

Yes, this would work. She was about forty, fifty miles away. Not too far, not too close. If she simply showed up in Lone Tree, she risked someone recognizing her, realizing who she was, and putting two and two together before she had everything worked out. Her plan would blow up in her face.

It was one thing to sit at her desk in Boston making up an itinerary, plotting the course she'd take to uncover family secrets that would save Grandpa's life. Quite another now that she was actually here.

She'd wait to hear from Ron and do a little undercover work of her own before announcing herself. A week or two, maybe less, and she should know if her great-aunt still lived in the area. If she, indeed, *had* a great-aunt.

Once she tracked her down...Well, she'd play that part by ear.

The trip had been far more grueling than she'd imagined. Staying in Maverick Junction would let her get her feet under her and decide how to proceed. She assured herself that the decision, made in Boston, had nothing whatsoever to do with the green-eyed cowboy and his day-old stubble shadowing that strong, square jaw. Nothing to do with the deep dimples that winked when he smiled and made her fingers itch to touch them.

But this was a small town and strangers created curiosity. Since she seriously doubted she'd be met with open arms by her long-missing relative, she wanted to keep her mission quiet as long as possible.

If she intended to stay here, she'd need a reason. A reason the townsfolk would buy. She needed to think about that. Thank God, she had a place to stay. During her time on the road, she'd learned a few things about herself. And one of those truths was that she needed a nest, a place to come home to at the end of each day. If Maverick Junction was going to be home for a bit, she'd be glad to have a decent place. She'd checked the Internet on the off-chance Maverick Junction boasted a motel. They didn't. But she'd found an apartment listed that would do fine. Nothing fancy, but totally livable—if the ad could be trusted.

Problem was, she didn't have a clue how to find the place she'd rented. In a town this small, how hard could it be? Still...Her eyes came to rest on the storefront on the other side of the street. The *Maverick Junction Daily*. The local newspaper. Surely someone in there could give her directions.

Delighted excitement raced along her spine. Twenty-six years old, and she'd never had her own home. Even her bedroom had been decorated by her mother's designer without her input while she'd been away on a business trip, for heaven's sake. Very school-girlish, nothing about it said grown woman. Wouldn't it be fun to have a place of her own, if only for a short time?

And maybe, just maybe, she could pick up a temporary job to serve as a cover. A reason to stay put here in town for a bit. Wouldn't the paper have classifieds? A jobs wanted section?

As she passed her Harley, she ran a hand over it, caressed it. Buying the big machine had been the wildest thing she'd ever done. And this trip, despite the reason for it, was giving her no end of pleasure. The freedom of heading her motorcycle down the highway, the sun on her face. A few times she'd really thrown caution to the wind and left her helmet buckled to the sissy bar, had gloried in the sheer joy of the wind blowing through her hair.

Riding the Harley topped her list of sinful pleasures. She doubted even the best sex could trump it. And how long had it been since she'd even had a shot at that? She grimaced. The question didn't deserve an answer. It would only depress her.

Now, she planned to take an even bigger step.

She pushed open the door to the newspaper, and an overhead bell tinkled cheerfully. Cash Hardeman stood at the counter. The man sure did fill out a pair of jeans. She sucked in her breath and fought the impulse to head back out the door.

Cash looked over his shoulder and grinned. "Well, hello, darlin'. Miss me already?"

She rolled her eyes. "In your dreams...darlin'."

He laughed, and the sound swept over her, caused her stomach to do an erratic loop-de-loop. Her hand slid over it, rubbed.

Cash's eyes followed her movement. "You okay?"

"Yes." She licked suddenly dry lips. "Yes, I'm fine."

Behind the counter a seriously handsome blond about the same age as Cash said, "I'll be with you in a minute."

"I'm in no hurry," she assured him.

"Melvin, this here's Annelise," Cash drawled. "Rode into town on a hog so pretty it'd make you cry."

Mel's interest piqued. "Really?"

When she simply nodded, he turned his attention back to Cash. "This'll run tomorrow through the end of the week."

"Great. Hopefully, I'll find somebody to take the load off Hank. His seventieth birthday's coming up in a couple months, and the barn and horses are too much for him."

"He know you're hiring somebody to help?"

Cash shook his head. "Nope. I figure once it's a done deal, he'll have to suck it up and go with it."

"The old 'It's better to ask forgiveness than permission'?"

"Yeah, guess so. Damn it, the ranch is mine."

"For now," Mel muttered.

"Don't even go there," Cash warned. "Bottom line, I should be able to do whatever I want. I sure shouldn't have to ask the old codger if it's okay to hire a new ranch hand."

Annelise didn't even stop to think. "Don't bother with the ad. I'll take the job."

The instant the words left her mouth, she wondered who had taken over her body. *Me? A ranch hand?* She'd never, ever done any physical labor. She'd never worked anywhere but the family business. This was so far outside her comfort zone she couldn't even see the shadows of a boundary.

At the same time she berated herself, another part of her brain patted her on the back, saying, "Way to go." Wasn't this part of why she'd made the trip? Hadn't she hoped to find herself along with Grandfather's sister? Unhappy with her life, she wanted something more. Something with meaning. And to find that, she had to fight against the life she'd always known.

Both men looked at her as though she'd suddenly sprouted wings.

"You want to come work for me?" Cash asked.

"Yes." Her breath caught in her lungs. "Yes, I do."

"You have a résumé?"

She bit her lip. *Oh, boy.* She had no résumé. No experience—none that she could share with him. And she would not, absolutely would not give Cowboy her last name. But, shoot, now that she'd opened her mouth, she realized she really, really wanted to do this.

She *had* to do this. Maybe she could work around it.

"I know I don't look like your typical ranch hand applicant."

His lips turned up in a grin. "I'm so glad you pointed that out to me."

"No need to get all snotty about it."

He glanced from her to Mel, who gave him a you're-on-your-own-here look.

"I know horses. I've been around them all my life. I can and will do whatever the job requires." She almost added please, but stopped herself. She refused to beg.

"I didn't know you were planning to stay here in town."

She shrugged. "You didn't ask."

"Do you have a place to stay?"

It took all of her finishing-school lessons to keep from squirming. "Yes. That's why I stopped in here. I rented an apartment over the Internet and hoped Melvin could tell me how to get there."

Mel flushed. "I think I can help you with that."

"Forget it." Cash held up his hand. "Do you really think it's a good idea to stay with a stranger?"

"I won't be. I'll have my own apartment."

"In a stranger's house."

"You're a stranger," she reminded him.

"Nah. We broke bread together."

She opened her mouth, but he stopped her. "I know where you can bunk."

"I won't stay with you."

"Sugar, you make that sound like a challenge."

"I didn't mean—"

"We'll put that on the back burner for now. Actually, what I have in mind is Mrs. Willis's upstairs apartment. It's empty." He turned back to Mel. "We done here?"

"Yep."

"Okay. Come on then, Annelise, and I'll take you over to meet her. Mel, why don't you give Dottie a quick buzz and tell her we're coming?"

"Dorothy Willis?" Annelise asked.

"Yeah." Cash hesitated. "You know her?"

"I rented her apartment."

"Well, what do you know. Guess you won't be with a stranger after all. Dottie's a good woman." He took her arm and started for the door. "I'll run you over to her place. Mel, give her a call. Let her know we're on our way."

"Sure. Should I cancel your ad?" Mel asked.

Cash ran his gaze up and down Annelise. "Yeah. Position's filled."

Annelise resisted the urge to give in to a happy dance.

She insisted on following Cash on her bike. When he pulled his boat of a car into a long drive and parked behind a ten-year-old white Oldsmobile, she eased the Harley beside him. From this angle, the house looked presentable. Certainly not what she was used to, but if she was anxious to get back to what she already had, she should hit the road again and head back East. She wasn't. Trying out something different, living differently, and proving she could accomplish something on her own— that was all part of this whole odyssey.

A simple white two-story, its outside stairs led to a second-floor apartment. Cash's mutt jumped out of the car and whizzed past her, clipping the back of her leg and nearly taking her down.

Cash stuck two fingers in his mouth and emitted one shrill whistle. The cowboy pointed to a spot by his side, and the dog screeched to a stop, then sulked his way over to drop beside his master. Head on his front paws, he sent a pitiful look Cash's way.

"Ignore him," Cash told her. "He practices this. Give him an inch, you'll never, ever have any peace. He'll own you."

Still, Annelise's heart cracked, and she leaned down to rub the dog's head. In a flash he flipped to his back, legs in the air, belly exposed, whimpering to be fussed over.

Laughing, she dropped to her knees and made him one happy pooch.

Cash leaned in, whispered in her ear. "If I fall onto the ground, will you rub my belly?"

His breath brushed along her neck, sent tiny shivers over her skin. She turned her head, met his deep-green eyes, and arched a brow.

She could have sworn a bolt of lightning flashed between them.

Clearing her throat, she asked, "What's his name?"

"Staubach."

She frowned.

"You know. Like Roger Staubach, the Dallas quarterback." She shook her head.

"You gotta be kidding. Heisman Trophy winner? He took us to two Super Bowls."

"Nope, sorry."

"Roger could get out of any jam on the field. Served in 'Nam, too. A real stand-up guy. He had guts. He was loyal. Like my pal here." He reached down and scratched the dog's ears.

Dottie Willis pushed herself out of the porch swing and started down the walk toward them.

Cash removed his Stetson and held it at his side. "Mrs. Willis, this is Annie."

Annie? Annie? She grimaced. Nobody called her Annie—not even when she'd been in diapers. She'd been born Annelise.

"Glad to meet you, honey. Like I said in the ad, my place isn't much, but it's clean."

"That's all I'm looking for." Annelise realized she was actually nervous and wiped her palms on her pant legs. She really wanted this place. Wanted her first home.

"Should suit you well then."

"We sure do appreciate this, Dottie."

"No problem at all, sweetheart." She pinched his cheek, and Annelise watched the blush creep up Cash's neck to his face. Priceless.

Mrs. Willis nodded toward the Harley. "That's a mighty big bike."

Annelise grinned. "I like it. Lots of power, and I'm in control."

She caught Cash studying her and could have kicked herself. Far too much insight flashed in his eyes, almost as if he knew her secret.

Mrs. Willis, who'd moved ahead of them, was nearly at the top of the stairs.

He bumped her shoulder. "What are you running away from?"

She fought for cocky. "What makes you think I'm running away? The question might be what am I running to."

He considered that. "Well, if that's the case, I'm glad you came running in my direction."

"And my name is Annelise," she muttered.

Waiting for them on the landing, Mrs. Willis asked, "How are your mama and daddy doing, Cash?"

"They're great, Mrs. Willis. They decided to fly in from Paris tomorrow so they can be home in plenty of time for the big barbecue on the Fourth. You'll be there, won't you?"

"Couldn't beat me off with a stick." She dug a key from the pocket of her pink-flowered housedress.

The dress suited her perfectly, Annelise thought. This woman, the stereotypical grandma, could have played the role for any movie, any ad. Around five-three, she carried a few extra pounds and had the softest looking blue-gray curls. Pink-framed glasses dangled from a chain around Dottie's neck, and no-nonsense tie-up shoes along with bright pink ankle socks covered her feet.

She chatted a mile a minute as she showed them around the small one-bedroom rental. It looked even drearier in person than it had in the ad photos and was as homely as they came. But it had potential, and that was enough for Annelise.

"You still want it now that you've had a look around?" Dottie asked.

She nodded.

"Well, then, welcome to Maverick Junction and your new home." Mrs. Willis gave her a quick hug, then headed downstairs to bake chocolate chip cookies for the church bazaar, leaving her alone with her new boss.

A new home. A new boss. Oh, boy. She was really doing this. Annelise felt almost dizzy.

Cash ripped a paper towel from a roll he found in the kitchen and sketched a rough map to his ranch. He scrawled his phone number on the bottom. "See you in the morning— if you're still sure you want to give this a shot."

"I do."

Her stomach fluttering with nerves and excitement, Annelise walked him to the door, then stood at the window to watch as Cash and his ugly dog drove away.

Biting her bottom lip, she tabbed through her phone contacts. Time to call her cousin.

She answered on the first ring. "Annelise? Where in the world are you? Your mom and dad have been hounding me. They're sure I'm hiding you out here in Chicago. What's going on?"

Annelise sighed. "Long story, Sophie. One I really don't want to get into right now. Can I ask a huge favor?"

"Anything."

"Would you call my dad? Tell him not to worry. I'm safe, I left on my own, and I'll be back soon. No need to send the cavalry. I talked to Mom, but by the time she tells him what we said, it's going to be all screwed up. Ask Dad to pass the message on to Grandpa." She hesitated. "I'm sorry they've been giving you a hard time."

"I can deal with them."

"I know you can. I really don't want them worrying, any of them, though, or siccing the police or FBI on me, either."

"You know, cuz, to them, you're still their little girl. It doesn't matter that you're twenty-six."

"I know."

"So, really," her cousin persisted. "Where are you?"

"I can't tell you, Sophie. That way, when my parents' goons torture you, you won't be able to rat me out."

Sophie laughed. "Or save myself with the information."

"Wouldn't matter." Annelise chuckled. "You know they always kill the informant even if she talks."

"There's a cheerful thought," Sophie said. "Be careful."

"I will," Annelise agreed. "Love you." With that, she snapped her phone shut, removed its battery, and walked downstairs to drop both in the battered trash can on the curb ready for pickup. Then, resolute, she walked up the outside stairs to her new home. Drab and ugly.

Almost as ugly as Cash's dog. No pure breed there. Staubach had long, mud-brown hair, one white ear, one brown, a long muzzle, and slightly crossed eyes. She loved him.

And she loved this town.

Shocked, she dropped onto the top step and leaned against the railing. A couple of houses down, she heard the excited laugh of a young child mixed with the exuberant yapping of a small dog.

Who'd have guessed she'd fall in love with either Cash's clumsy mutt or this quirky town?

Not her.

The thing was, nobody recognized her. She was free to be herself, to be judged on who she was deep down inside. Money would have nothing to do with her relationships with the people of Maverick Junction. She was simply another person, not someone to make-nice to because of what she might be able to do for them. They'd either like her or they wouldn't. But there'd be no phony pretenses.

Traveling cross-country incognito in her motorcycle helmet, sunglasses, and leathers, no one had given her a second look. She grinned. Well, maybe a few guys, but not because she was a billionaire tycoon's granddaughter. Their looks had read 'hot chick' rather than 'dollar signs.'

She'd sat at an outside table and drank a McDonald's milk shake in Pennsylvania, rode a Ferris wheel at some little county fair in Tennessee, and the paparazzi hadn't captured a single moment of it. By taking this trip, she'd stumbled on a chance to find herself without a telephoto lens recording her, and she meant to make the most of it.

She walked into her new eight-by-ten living room and flopped onto the butt-ugly couch to stare up at the dingy, used-to-be-white ceiling. Cripes. Ugly dog, ugly apartment, ugly couch. Was everything in Maverick Junction ugly?

Cash popped into her head. Cash, with those emerald green eyes fringed with the longest, blackest lashes, that sun-kissed brown hair, a body honed by hard work, and she had her answer.

No.

That simple.

Some things in this blip on the map were flat-out gorgeous.

And wouldn't the macho Texas cowboy hate to have that adjective applied to him? She grinned.

Oh, yeah. But…if the proverbial shoe fit…

Chapter Three

Both the shoe and the horse were giving Cash fits. Sweating like a sinner in church under the heavy, protective leather apron, horseshoe nails clamped between his teeth, he bent at the waist. The misty-gray stallion's front leg braced between his own, he rested the gray's hoof on his knee. The two-year-old had been sorely neglected by a rancher north of Dallas, and Cash had rescued the rascal.

This was Shadow's first shoeing...and might very well be his last, damn it, at least here on Whispering Pines Ranch. He could go barefoot.

As bad-tempered as Shadow was, though, Cash doubted he'd ever seen a finer piece of horseflesh. He ran a calming hand over the horse's gleaming flank, then snarled and jerked back as the gray swiveled his head, teeth bared, intent on taking a chunk out of him.

"You're gonna be dog food, you do that again," he mumbled around the nails.

"Trouble?"

His stomach did a free fall clear to his toes. That voice, sexy as all get-out, made promises, conjured up thoughts of all sorts of naughty nighttime pastimes. He spit the nails into his hand and forced himself to take a steadying breath before he turned to face his new ranch hand.

Then he took another as he drank her in. Her dark cloud of hair had been pulled back and braided, highlighting that incredible face, those winter-blue eyes, and those X-rated lips. She wore faded blue jeans and a siren-red T-shirt that hugged the most incredible—

Whoa. Shut it down. Whispering Pines is her workplace, and you're her boss.

The thoughts ricocheting inside his brain had to be illegal—on so many levels. He needed to back off. Keep it professional.

She wore sneakers. Pristine white ones right out of the box. Not a speck of horse poo on them. Yet. A corner of his mouth tipped up. That was about to change in a hurry.

Didn't matter. She'd have to lose them after today, anyway. They wouldn't work here in the barn around the horses.

"You need boots." He nodded toward her feet.

"Excuse me?"

"Boots. And not those fancy little black ones with the stiletto heels you rode into town in." He raised his own foot and pointed. "Real boots. They'll protect you a little better if a horse accidentally steps on you." Then he shot a baleful glance at Shadow. "Or on purpose."

Annelise laughed. "I'll get a pair. Mrs. Willis gave me these this morning." She raised a sneakered foot. "Had them on a closet shelf. My size and all, so I figured what the heck. Otherwise, I would have shown up in those black ones."

Nodding toward the stallion, she said, "This one's giving you fits, huh?"

He sighed. "Yes, ma'am. Shadow can be a bit cantankerous. Once he's cut, that'll change. Maybe."

"Gelded?"

When he nodded, she winced. "If you say so."

"Believe me, once a male's—" He cleared his throat. "It'll help." Then he met her eyes, those beautiful, cool eyes. "Look, if you're gonna have to run out and buy boots...I mean, if you need it, I can give you an advance on your pay."

The expressions that crossed her face fascinated him. Pride, hurt, determination, anger, embarrassment, and, surprisingly, arrogance. She snuffed each out in rapid succession.

"No, but thanks. I can handle it." Her voice was tight.

"Fine. That's good." He turned his back. "Hank," he called, "the new ranch hand I hired is here."

From inside the tack room, a smoke-raspy voice said, "Told you. I don't need no help. I might be old, but I can still do my work. Can still take care of my barn and my horses. Don't need, don't want—"

Wispy gray hair stuck up in every direction on the head that peeked out around the doorway. The face was every bit as disordered. A bulbous red nose, watery blue eyes, and wrinkled, leathery skin.

"What's this?"

"Hank, meet Annie, our new hand."

"She's a girl."

"I noticed that." Cash ran his tongue over his teeth to keep from laughing.

"I'm a woman, actually."

"Same thing," Hank growled. "Ain't got no time to be hand-holdin'."

Cash opened his mouth, closed it again when Annelise's chin shot up.

"I don't want, nor do I need, my hand held."

"Sure you will. First time you need to lift a load that's too heavy or come up against a mouse in the hay, you're gonna come runnin' to me, pullin' me away from my work."

"Hank, I promise you I can and will pull my weight. I will not expect you to rescue me. I will not scream at the sight of a mouse." She held up a finger. "Give me one day. If I come running, screaming for help, or needing to be rescued, I'm history. If I do a satisfactory job and can stand on my own two feet"—she glanced at Cash—"my soon-to-be-cowboy-booted feet, I come back tomorrow. Fair enough?"

"I guess," the wizened ranch hand groused. "But I ain't gonna cut you any slack just 'cause you're female."

"I certainly hope not," Annelise answered. "It would really…" She hesitated. "It would really piss me off if you did."

Cash chewed a piece of straw. Well, what do you know? The lady was not only cover-model beautiful, but she had spunk. Be interesting to see how this played out. Taking off the leather apron, he hung it on a peg on the barn wall.

"Hank, Paco's out in the paddock. Call him in here. Have him shoe this damn horse." He threw the straw to the ground. "Then tell Annie what you want her to do."

"Already told you what I want her to do. I want her to go home."

"That's not going to happen, Hank." Annelise's face was set.

"Hmmph."

Cash left the two of them to their sparring match.

* * *

Eight long, grueling hours later, Annelise debated whether she should attempt the twenty-two steps to her apartment or simply lie down in the grass for the night. She'd mingled for hours with stuffed-shirts and prancing divas at receptions, smiled through hours of tedious conversation during business lunches, studied through the night at Harvard, but never, ever in her life had she been this bone-tired.

And she stank. Lifting her arm, she smelled her shirt. Horse, sweat, dung, and God only knew what else! Maybe she should build a fire and burn everything she had on, including the sneakers that needed to be replaced with boots. She couldn't imagine ever wanting to put any of it back on. And her hair. She didn't even want to think how it looked or smelled.

Unfortunately, a fire would take too much effort. She'd have to find wood, a match, something to strike the darn thing on. Her head dropped to her chest. She couldn't face all that.

So, she'd opt for a shower. About an hour-long one. Maybe she could leave her clothes on and wash everything all at once. But before she could do any of that, she had to tackle the stairs.

Hank had been mad at Cash, so he'd worked her extra hard. It didn't matter to him that it wasn't her fault she was there. Well, yeah, okay, maybe it had been her choice that put her there, but if it hadn't been her, it would have been someone else. The ad would have run in today's paper, and Cash fully intended to hire somebody. That somebody just happened to be her.

But the old man had taken it very personally and wreaked his revenge against Cash on her. She'd actually mucked out stalls! Annelise Elizabeth blah blah Montjoy scooping up horse manure! Oh, if her mother could see her now.

Strangely enough, even while she'd been bent over in the smelly stall with a pitchfork, she'd realized it beat sitting around with a bunch of elitist snobs discussing whose horse would run in the Derby, what a day's rain might mean for Wimbledon this year, or when Princess Kate would make her first serious faux pas. And it sure as heck beat a board meeting.

Annelise's stomach rumbled, and she sighed. She supposed she'd have to do something about feeding herself, too. Right now, she could be in Boston sitting down to champagne and fresh lobster. She shook her head. She'd take a pass. A nice perk, but one that came with a high price tag.

She'd survive. She'd learned to make a mean PB&J while at Harvard. As long as there was that and take-out, she wouldn't starve.

Only three steps into the climb, she stopped. Was there take-out in Maverick Junction? There had to be, didn't there? After all, this was the twenty-first century!

* * *

Inside her apartment, she headed for the bath, dropping clothes as she went. The lure of the shower called her. In the bathroom doorway, she came to an abrupt halt and drooped against the jamb.

How could she have forgotten? No shower. The plumbing on the second floor of the old house had not been updated.

Well, what the heck? Forlorn, she sat on the side of the old claw-foot tub and turned on the taps. When it filled, she submerged herself and scrubbed vigorously with a cheap, generic bar of soap she'd found still in its wrapper in the medicine chest. After she'd removed the worst of the day's grime, she pulled the plug and gave the tub a cleaning swish before refilling it, thankful there was still hot water.

Digging through her few belongings, she found the bottle

of expensive French perfume she'd squirreled away. Adding a couple of drops to the water, she sank into the fragrant warmth. She rested her head against the slanted back, closed her eyes, and sighed as the day floated away.

A bath might take more time than a shower, but it certainly wasn't half-bad, she decided.

When her chin hit the water, she startled out of her reverie. The bath had turned tepid. Climbing out, she enveloped herself in an old towel she'd dug out of the linen closet and headed toward the bedroom in search of something to put on.

*   *   *

A clean body, clean hair, and clean clothes gave Annelise a new outlook on life. She stood at the kitchen sink, admiring Mrs. Willis's small garden. Sipping an ice-cold Coke, she studied, with no little amazement, the tidy rows of lettuce and tomatoes, the rows of brown-eyed Susans and gladioluses. Pink and red roses bloomed in profusion along a short rock wall.

And then there was this. She spun to face the inside of the apartment. Could there be a more jarring aesthetic juxtaposition? Outside, a harmonious blend of color and form. Picture-postcard pretty. Inside, a hodgepodge of drab neglect. It had gone beyond mundane to offensive, with no saving graces that she could see.

Except, it did provide shelter, had given her a place to stay in Maverick Junction while she literally worked her fingers to the bone. She turned her hands palm-up, rubbed a finger lightly over the tender blisters. Hank had offered gloves, gloves she'd been too stubborn to accept. Tomorrow she'd eat that hardheadedness right along with her pride.

She set down the empty Coke can and settled her hands on her hips. If she truly intended to live here, even if only short-term, she had to do something, and what better than to work with horses. Problem was, she wasn't working with the right end of the horse.

Her laptop sat in the center of the wobbly table. She'd called Ron today on the barn phone. He hadn't found anything yet. Hating the need for a lie, she'd told him to e-mail her when he had something, that she had spotty reception on her cell. She couldn't bring herself to confess that was because she'd tossed her battery-less phone in the dump.

She had no doubt he'd find what she needed. Still, it wouldn't hurt to spend a couple of hours tonight doing a little digging of her own.

Dottie, who continued to surprise her, actually had wireless. Said it made it easier to keep in touch with her grandkids in Pennsylvania. What a bonus. Annelise could have kissed her!

As her stomach complained loudly, she acknowledged she needed to do something about food first. Last night, Dottie had taken mercy on her and fed her dinner. On top of that, she'd put together a care package of soft drinks, Pop-Tarts for breakfast, and some crackers for a snack. The woman was a veritable saint.

But it was time for her to pick up the reins.

"Okay, okay." She patted her belly and immediately thought about Cash asking her to rub his yesterday. Heat raced through her. No doubt his skin would be smooth, his body hard. Was he tan all over? Did he work without a shirt some days, exposing that long, lean body to the sun?

Her mother's scandalized face popped into her head. Had Georgia ever experienced this kind of sexual heat? Had the oh-so-proper Edmund and Georgia ever been in a mad rush to tear off each other's clothes, expose themselves body and soul to each other?

Not that she wanted to do that with Cash Hardeman. Heck, no! She hardly knew the man.

Food. Concentrate on food, something you can control. Yes, someone else had always taken care of the mundane, day-to-day concerns for her, but she could do this. She was an intelligent adult and certainly competent enough to make a trip to the grocers.

First, she needed to pay a quick visit to her new landlady. Hustling down the outside stairs, she winced when, without thought, she raised one abused hand to lightly skim the rail.

Her landlady's windows stood open, and Annelise could smell the right-out-of-the-oven cookies. Great. As hungry as she was, the scent of freshly baked cookies was the last thing she needed.

Before she could even raise a hand to knock, Dottie Willis called, "Come on in. My door's never locked."

A jolt of surprise ran through Annelise. Because of the constant threat of kidnappers and the like, she'd always been under lock and key. It seemed unfathomable that anyone would leave her house wide open. And all the time?

She poked her head inside. Pink. Everywhere. The kitchen walls, countertops, curtains. It was like being dropped inside a vat of cotton candy.

"Getting settled, sweetie?"

"Yes, ma'am. I had a couple of questions, though."

"Imagine you do." Dottie grinned. "Wouldn't involve a long-legged cowboy, would they?"

She fought the nervous twitch in her stomach and smiled back. "No, actually they don't."

"Want a cookie and a glass of milk?"

Cookies and milk. The memory brought a smile. Frannie,

their cook, offered her that for a treat after school. At least, on the days her mother hadn't scheduled French lessons or horseback riding lessons or ballet lessons. Whatever the class du jour, her mom had seen she took it.

"I'd love that, Mrs. Willis."

"Dottie, please. Have a seat." She bustled about the small room, pouring two glasses of cold milk and fussing with a delicate porcelain salver of cookies, the chips melted and gooey still.

When Annelise reached for one, Dottie stopped her by grasping her hand. She turned it over and studied the blisters. "You poor dear. What was Cash thinking? I'm gonna have to turn that boy over my knee. Give me a minute."

She left the room.

Annelise mourned the few seconds Dottie was gone because it meant postponing the cookie tasting. She couldn't ever remember a banquet as appealing as this simple snack. But then, she couldn't remember ever being quite this hungry. Manual labor certainly improved the appetite.

Down the hall, she heard something drop to the floor, followed by a muffled oath. Then Dottie hustled back into the room, scattering her first-aid paraphernalia over the center island.

"Okay, dear, let's see those palms again." She snagged her dangling glasses, set them on her nose, and went to work on Annelise's ill-used hands. She cleaned each one, then covered them with Neosporin.

The sting instantly disappeared. Annelise could have kissed her.

"There," she said. "That'll keep the blisters from getting infected and make them feel a bit better."

Annelise found herself fighting back unexpected—and

unwanted—tears. This woman, a virtual stranger, tended her without expecting anything in return.

"Thank you."

"You're more than welcome. Now eat your cookies and ask what you came to ask."

She blew out a breath, just like that having been put back on an even keel by Dottie. True, she'd found this place on the Internet, but, without being aware of that, Cash had known instinctively this was exactly where she needed to be right now when he'd thought of this as the place for her to stay.

Fighting to organize her thoughts, she chewed her lower lip, a habit her mother detested. *Never show nerves or weakness.* In the world according to Georgia, lip-chewing did both.

"Okay, Dottie, first things first, I guess. I didn't bring much with me."

"On that Harley of yours? I'd guess not," her landlady replied.

"Right. Anyway, the clothes I wore to the ranch today stink to high heaven. Where do I get them done?"

"Done?" She tipped her head. "You mean where do you do your laundry?"

Annelise swallowed. "Yes. I guess that's what I mean."

Oh, brother. Nobody in town did laundry? Another new experience coming up.

"'Fraid there's no washer or dryer upstairs. No room for them. Mabel's Suds and Dry is on the north corner of Main Street, though, and she runs a nice clean place." Her eyes narrowed on Annelise, who'd reached for a second cookie. "For tonight, why don't you bring them on down? I'll toss them in for you. You look plumb tuckered out."

Oh, she wanted to. It would be nice to let this grandmotherly soul pick up the slack for her. But, Annelise couldn't.

"That's okay. I appreciate it, but I have to get groceries any-way, so I'll do it all at the same time."

"Nonsense. It'll take you twice as long. You run upstairs now and get them."

"They're filthy."

"Imagine they are. From the looks of those hands of yours, you worked the business end of a pitchfork most of the day. Tossing manure tends to make your clothes want to get up and walk away. But believe me, my machine's seen worse."

"I seriously doubt that. Put those clothes of mine in your machine, and you may never be able to use it again."

She flicked a hand at Annelise. "Do as I say. Then you can ask the rest of your questions while I get them started."

Annelise gave in. Heading upstairs, she walked straight to the bedroom and scooped the offending articles off the floor. Not wanting to get too near them, she stuffed them in a plas-tic bag from a convenience store she'd stopped at for lunch the other day.

She shook her head, wondering when a cellophane-wrapped sandwich, a bag of chips, and a soda had come to constitute a meal. But when in Rome—

Back downstairs, Dottie opened the louvered doors to her antiquated laundry. She held the bag over the washer and dumped in the whole mess. Then her hand dipped into the tub and came back out with a lacey bra and thong.

"Whew! Pretty expensive-looking little thingamabobs. Don't know I've ever seen anything prettier. Can they be machine-washed?"

"I don't see why not," Annelise said.

"Okay." Dottie sounded skeptical, but she added deter-gent and softener, then closed the lid and turned the dial to start the machine.

Annelise watched carefully, tucking the procedure away for when she made her first trip to Mabel's. As much as it pained her to admit it, she'd never done a load of laundry. A silent, invisible army of household help ensured she had clean undies, pressed clothes, fresh linens on her bed, and on and on.

Even on the road, she hadn't needed to worry about it. Her sorority sister's housekeeper had washed some things for her before she'd left, and one of the hotels she'd stayed at had laundry service.

Embarrassed heat flushed her face. She'd taken so much for granted. Well, no more. She could and would take care of herself.

"Finish your milk and ask away, sweetie." Dottie sat back down at the table, snagging a cookie for herself.

"I think you've managed to answer all but one question already." She fidgeted in her chair. "I wondered if it would be all right if I painted the rooms upstairs."

"Honey, I flat out love you." Dottie grinned. "That place needs a fresh coat of paint worse than an orphaned puppy needs a home. If you don't mind doing the work, I'll be more than happy to buy the paint."

Annelise laughed. "That's okay. I can afford it." She caught the dubious look on her landlady's face. "Honest."

"If you're sure."

"I'm positive. Despite the fact that I went off to work today, money isn't a problem. I must be really looking down on my luck, though, because Cash tried to give me an advance this morning."

"You're a puzzle is what you are, dear. I know enough to realize that motorcycle you're riding cost some major money. I'm also honest enough to admit the place upstairs isn't the Ritz."

"No." One corner of Annelise's mouth turned up in a half smile. "I've stayed there, and you're right. My new home isn't the Ritz. That said, there are things here in Maverick Junction I can't find at the Ritz."

"Such as?"

It irritated her no end that Cash Hardeman and his dancing green eyes were the first things to pop into her head.

The irritation must have shown on her face. Dottie laughed and winked, too perceptive by half.

Annelise bit the inside of her cheek and answered, "The most important? Freedom to be me. When you're at a place like the Ritz, there are expectations. Here, no one expects anything from me, except maybe a hard day's work for my pay. And I like that. The people here are friendly and unassuming. And, the Ritz doesn't come with your cookies."

Dottie patted her hand. "Are you running from someone, dear, or from yourself?"

Annelise pulled her hand away. Cash had asked basically the same question. She had to be careful because, despite the fact she'd initially started this trip for her grandfather, she'd soon realized she was on a quest for herself, too. To discover if people liked her, Annelise Montjoy, for herself, or if it was simply her money and what she could do for them that attracted them to her. And wasn't that sad?

She couldn't screw it up by revealing her true identity—not even to Dottie. If she did, she'd never have a chance at an untainted relationship with the townspeople—their view of her would be colored by preconceived notions about her, about her life, and about her family. Her money.

Despite her sweet grandmotherly appearance, Dottie was one very intuitive lady, and Annelise didn't want her anywhere near the truth.

"I...I'm not running from anyone, Dottie. I just...I

wanted to get away from—" She broke off a piece of her cookie and crumbled it. "I was in a dead-end job."

That was true enough, she supposed. She was stuck in the family business. Like it or not, at some point in the future, she'd be expected to pick up the reins. No options. She felt almost claustrophobic at times.

She met Dottie's eyes. "I have something I need to do. And a nice bonus has been finding a place where I can try something totally different while I'm doing it."

Her landlady studied her a moment. "Well, if I'm not missing my mark, I'd say you succeeded."

"And then some," she said. Time to move this discussion away from her. "About the paint." She ran a hand up and down her milk glass. "I don't want white."

"Okay."

"I mean, I love color."

"Good for you." Dottie reached behind her for a small plate on the counter. "Try one of these."

The pale pink dish held more cookies, but they weren't the chocolate chip variety.

"Oh, but I already had—"

"One more won't hurt you. You're skinny as a rail. Besides, you're my guinea pig. This is a new recipe, and before I run them over to Vonda for the bazaar, I need a second opinion. Go ahead." She nudged the plate closer to her. "See if they taste okay."

Annelise reached for one, bit into it, and sighed. "Dottie, any time you need a guinea pig, I'm your girl." Cinnamon mixed with coconut and vanilla all wrapped up in a shortbread texture. Pure ambrosia.

She waved the half-eaten cookie. "If you don't like my color choices or if they'll make the apartment hard to rent when I leave, I can always redo them."

Dottie looked up from the sink where she'd started drawing dishwater. "Leave? Land sakes, I hope that won't be for a long time to come."

"Me, too." And Annelise realized how much she meant that. Right now, she was feeling slightly, okay, a lot, off-center, but she'd get her feet under her. She'd secretly check on the leads Ron found, then find a way to talk her great-aunt into being tested—if she was still alive or ever existed. Maybe after that, she could enjoy some time simply being Annelise. Steal a little time to live life her way, by her rules where money wasn't the be-all, end-all. And she'd do it privately, rather than under a microscope.

Dottie nodded. "If you look around, you'll see I don't cotton much for white."

Annelise smiled. "I noticed. But, ah, pink's not really my thing, either."

"That's okay. It'd be a pretty boring world if everybody wanted exactly the same, wouldn't it?"

"Yes, ma'am. It sure would be." She cleared her throat. "I'd like to pick up some different furniture, too."

Dottie chuckled. "What's up there's not your style, huh?"

Annelise pictured the broken-down couch, the lawn chair, the rickety kitchen table, and winced. "Not exactly."

"Can't tell you how glad I am to hear that. Roger Barry lived there before you. He filled the place with whatever he could find. His daughter came and got him 'bout two months ago. Took him to live with her and her husband. They left all that stuff behind, not that I blame them."

She put the leftover cookies on one platter and covered them with plastic wrap. "I had Stella come in and give the place a good cleaning, but that's about all. Hadn't really made up my mind what I was gonna do up there. Figured I'd advertise it, see if I had any takers before I decided. Anything you don't want, we'll have my neighbor Curtis and his son take care of. I reckon most of it probably needs to go to the dump. Anything worth keeping can be stored in the shed out back."

Dottie wiped a few stray crumbs off the counter. "Not that I want to get rid of you, but you'd better get going. Night's not getting any younger. I'll slip in and put your clothes on the table when they're done if that's okay."

"Absolutely. And thank you, Dottie."

"Don't mention it." She patted her arm.

Purse in hand, Annelise stepped outside just as Cash's big blue Caddy slid into the driveway. Country music pierced the nighttime quiet.

"Hey, Annie!"

She winced. *Annie?*

"For the umpteenth time, my name is Annelise." She hesitated. Didn't she want to escape her rigid, straitlaced, Annelise world behind for a bit?

Annie could be anybody she wanted. Annie could live in a second-story apartment with secondhand furniture and work on a ranch scooping poop. Annie could ride a Harley.

Annie. A good name. One that spoke of independence.

"What's going on in that head, Annie? You left me for a minute there."

She swallowed the quick laugh. Like she had anything to say about the name. Cash Hardeman would call her whatever he wanted. What the heck? She threw him a smile, one meant to dazzle. "Not a thing. What can I do for you?"

"Didn't get a chance to see you before you left the ranch today, so I thought I'd stop by to make sure you're okay. Hank said he pushed you pretty hard."

"He did, but I'm fine." She wavered a few seconds, then

decided there was no sense beating around the bush. "Do you pay house calls to all your new hires?"

He paused just long enough that she knew he was considering a lie.

"No. No, I don't."

Ah, an honest man.

"I only visit new ones who are female—"

She knew he saw the flash in her eyes because his hand shot up.

"Let me finish before you light into me. Only new hires who are female and new to town. I was worried about how you fared."

She wanted to hold on to a thread of anger but couldn't. Instead, she asked, "And how many of us are there in that club?"

"You'd be the first and founding member."

Then, as Mrs. Willis had done earlier, he turned her hands over, palms up, and studied them. "I'm sorry." His voice was gruff. "Hank shouldn't have—"

"Treated me differently from any of your other workers? I'm hired help, Cash." Her stomach dropped as she spoke the words, but she went on. "I don't expect any special treatment."

These blisters were, in a very real way, her badge of honor.

"Still," Cash argued. "He could have broken you in a little slower."

"Well, he didn't, and I survived. Besides, Hank did offer me a pair of gloves which I stupidly declined."

He grinned and chucked her on the chin. "Coming back for round two?"

"You bet. Wouldn't miss it for the world."

"Good. I figured you might be too tired to cook tonight. Thought maybe we could grab a pizza, a couple beers."

Pizza and beer. So normal. Even when she'd been attending Harvard, she'd had few invitations for casual dates. Of course, that might have had something to do with the ever-present bodyguards and the fact that, after her classes every day, she traveled back to the brick fortress her family called a home—in a chauffeured limousine.

"Is your interest personal or professional, Cash?"

"Truthfully? A little of both." He flashed his dimples. "So what do you say, Annie?"

"I say, why not." She moved with him to the car. As he opened the door for her, she saw the twitch of curtains at the kitchen window.

It seemed that Mrs. Willis, that gray-haired, cookie-baking dynamo, had taken on the role of her new bodyguard. Oddly enough, Annelise didn't mind at all.

Chapter Four

Even with the top down, Annie's scent wrapped around him. Warm, sexy, and expensive. The woman was an enigma.

Cash shot a sidelong glance at her. He didn't get it. Why was she in Maverick Junction? What was going on in her life that she'd chosen this detour over the status quo? Hank told him she'd worked her ass off today. She'd only gotten half as much done as an experienced hand, but it hadn't been for lack of trying. Her hands bore testament to that.

Hank had apologized half a dozen times. Said he'd only noticed them when he'd made her break for lunch with the guys, so he'd put her to cleaning out the tack room for the rest of the day.

Cash sighed. Nothing to do about it now except make sure it didn't happen again. But he knew in his bones she'd fight light duty if she caught on to what they were doing. And if they kept it too light, his reason for hiring her, to take some of the load off Hank, would be defeated. Talk about a rock and a hard spot.

Well, he'd find a way to deal with it. For tonight, he'd simply enjoy her company.

The lady cleaned up nicely. A subtle hint of color on her lids made those iceberg eyes as deep and inviting as his favorite swimming hole. When she was pissed, he swore they shot fire. What would they look like when she was turned on? What would desire and need do to them?

He bit down on that thought, tucked it away. *Best not to go there, cowboy.*

"Food first?" he asked.

"Oh, yes."

"You're not one of those vegetarians or vegans, are you?"

When she laughed, he felt it to the toes of his silver-tipped boots.

"No. I'm a carnivore."

"Good."

As they headed west, he said, "Lean your head back, Annie. Look up."

When she did, a soft sound escaped her, an almost-purr that arrowed straight to his gut. "Endless Texas sky over dry prairie as far as your eye can see."

"It's beautiful."

"Yeah." His voice came out gruff. "Yeah, it is."

A couple of miles later, he swerved into the dusty parking lot of Bubba's Roadhouse and hid a smile when she gripped the hand rest. The lady needed to learn to relax.

Annelise shook her head. Cash drove the same way he moved through life. He decided where he was headed and didn't stop till he got there, and yet the journey seemed unhurried. Relaxed. She envied him that.

Her eyes rounded as she took in the restaurant. Unpainted wood siding gave the place a rustic, slightly neglected aura. Neon lights in the windows advertised beer and good food.

Rough-hewn rockers and thirsty-looking potted plants littered the long porch.

"Best pizza in town," Cash said. "Course, they've also got steaks and prime-rib sandwiches that'll make you swoon if that's what you're hungry for."

"This is beef country, isn't it? I'd expect nothing less from Bubba's." She grinned. "Think I'll stick with the pizza, though. You put the thought in my head, and now that's what I want."

"Then that's what you'll have." He walked around and opened her door. Even though she was used to the small courtesy, it touched her. Cash Hardeman wasn't someone paid to fawn over her. No. He opened the door for her because his mother had taught him to do that when he was with a lady. It meant something.

She kept coming back to that. Gestures should mean something, not be performed by rote or because convention demanded them. She didn't want someone to take care of her because it was his job. She wanted someone to *want* to take care of her. To take care of Annelise, the person, not Annelise, the heiress.

And she wanted to earn that.

A thin rivulet of sweat trickled down her back. Part Texas heat, but also part nerves. And why was that? For Pete's sake, she'd eaten at some of the world's most prestigious restaurants, had dined with movie stars and heads of state.

Yet here she was, nervous about heading into a saloon with cow horns over the door. *Shake it off, Annelise. Breathe. In, out. In, out.*

Hand on her back, Cash showed her inside. Distracted by his heat and the quick stab of awareness at his touch, it took her a few seconds to appreciate her surroundings.

Bubba's Roadhouse could have been a Hollywood set,

the stereotypical Texas hangout. A huge Lone Star flag had been tacked on the left wall. White and brown cowhide stools crowded up to a huge slab of a bar. The walls, ceiling, and floor were all rough-hewn wood. Tables were scattered haphazardly throughout the small space, and the smell of barbecue blended with that of stale beer. Country music played on the chrome Wurlitzer jukebox in the corner.

Her stomach rumbled.

"Hungry, aren't you?" Cash leaned close and spoke directly into her ear. "'Cordin' to Hank, you did get some lunch today."

She tried to ignore the silly little dance her stomach did as his breath whispered across her cheek. "I did. But that, I swear, was another lifetime ago."

Cash nodded to a lone guy behind the bar. "Hey, Bubba, how's it going?"

"Roof's not leakin', and I've got food in my belly, so it's a good day." Bubba dried a glass with a bar towel, holding it up to the dim light to inspect it. "You two sit anywhere you want. Mitzy'll be right with ya."

"Thanks." Passing one of the blue and white oilcloth-covered tables, Cash tipped his hat to an elderly couple. "Evening, Harlan, Isabel."

"Howdy, Cash. D'ya get that parcel of land you were hankerin' for? The one that backs up to your place?"

"Yep, I sure did. Took some hard dickering, but old Nash finally gave in. Cost a few dollars more than I'd planned to wrestle it away from him, but"—he shrugged—"it was worth it."

Harlan's wife, dressed in jeans and a Western-style shirt, studied Annelise. "Aren't you going to introduce us, Cash?"

"Oh, sorry." He half-turned to Annelise. "Isabel, this beautiful lady is Annie."

"Well, welcome to Maverick Junction, honey. You staying long?"

Interesting, Annelise thought. No last names, and no one seemed to notice or care. "I'm not sure, but I'm hoping so. I rented an apartment yesterday and started work for Cash this morning."

"Oh?" Harlan looked at Cash. "You adding more hands?"

"Only the one right now. Thought Hank could use a little help in the stable."

Harlan nodded in approval. "Good for you, son. Good for you. Your grandpa would have been proud of you."

Grandpa. Her mind drifted to hers. What if Isabel was his long-lost sister? She could be. The age was about right. Her gaze drifted around the room. Was her great-aunt here tonight?

"You have a good evening, Harlan. Isabel," Cash said, drawing her out of her musings.

With a couple more head nods, they moved on toward a table tucked under one of the windows. Not many people were out tonight. Of course, Annelise thought, it was a weeknight. And if the rest of the people in Maverick Junction worked even a fraction as hard as she had today, they were probably already home in bed.

When Cash took her hand, she instinctively snatched it away. *No public displays of affection.* Her mother had pounded that into her head before she even realized what PDA meant. All it took was one hand held, one innocent kiss to make tabloid headlines.

His forehead creased in question. But instead of answering, she raised her hand to her mouth, hid a yawn behind it.

"Tired?" Cash bumped her shoulder with his, the casual gesture somehow more intimate than handholding.

"A little. I'm not used to doing a lot of physical work."

Several people's stares lingered on her, making her uneasy. Surely they wouldn't recognize her. She decided the best strategy was to smile and otherwise ignore them. After all, who'd expect to see the granddaughter of one of the country's wealthiest men dressed in jeans here at Bubba's Roadhouse? Very unlikely anybody would put two and two together. Still, jitters played tag in her stomach.

Once they sat down, though, she relaxed.

The waitress, dressed in jeans and a T-shirt like most of the customers, plopped two menus in front of them. "Hey, Cash." The redhead sent him a blinding smile. "Haven't seen you for a bit. Where ya been keeping yourself?"

"Busy at the ranch, Mitzy. How've you been?"

"Doin' okay. Same thing every day, you know?"

"Yeah, well, keep those big blue eyes of yours open." His gaze moved to Annelise. "You never know when something's gonna drop in that'll shake your world."

Annelise fought the heat rising in her face again. Had he meant her? Had she shaken his world? No. Maybe. A silly smile threatened.

"What d'ya want to drink?"

"I'll have a Lone Star. Ice-cold. How about you, Annie?"

"You know, I think I'll have one, too." Something inside her quivered in delight. Here she was, sitting in a small Texas barbecue, having a beer. And she intended to drink it right out of the bottle. Not a camera or paparazzo in sight.

She grinned.

Cash's brow rose, and he grinned back at her. "Something's rattling around in that pretty head of yours, 'cause the look on your face is pure mischief."

She laughed. "No. I'm just...just feeling good."

Now, both his brows shot up. "After the day you put in?"

"Yes, even after today, manure shoveling and all."

Mitzy returned with their beers and pulled an order pad from her blue apron's deep pocket. Annelise couldn't help herself. She checked for a wedding band. None there. Was their oh, so friendly waitress this free and easy with all the customers? Or did she pour it on a little thicker when Cash came in?

None of her business.

"So, what's it gonna be tonight?"

After some haggling, they decided to share a pizza—loaded.

"Cook's got a couple before you, so it'll be a few minutes."

"That's okay. We're in no hurry," Cash said. "We'll sit here and relax."

"Speak for yourself." Annelise patted her stomach. "I'm starving."

"How about I bring you a basket of rolls? That hold ya?"

"That would be great," she said. "Thanks."

When the bread basket arrived, Annelise all but pounced on it. The rolls were soft and warm and yeasty-smelling. Enjoying half of one, Cash stood and walked over to the jukebox. Her brows furrowed when he dropped in some quarters, then crooked a finger at her.

She pointed at herself and mouthed, "Me?"

He nodded.

"Cash."

"C'mon. Dance with me. It won't hurt. Promise. And it'll give us something to do while we wait for dinner. Take your mind off that empty belly."

The music started and she smiled, recognizing the George Strait song. It had played on the Caddy's radio on the way here. Not something she'd dance to at one of her parents' galas. Nicer. Better. Earthy and down-home.

Despite herself, she stood and strolled over to him. When he took her hand, electricity tingled clear to her toes. She pulled back.

"What is it?" His brow creased. "Your hands. I'm sorry." His own dropped to his sides.

"No! No, my hands are fine. Honest." She reached for his, prepared this time for the jolt. "I've never danced in Texas, so you're going to have to show me how to do this."

"It's a waltz."

"I don't think so."

"A Western waltz." He drew her into him, spun her around the floor. "Look. Everybody in here is trying to figure out exactly who you are. How we met. How deeply we're involved. And how a cowboy like me managed to get a looker like you out here on the dance floor."

She struggled to put distance between them, but he shook his head and tugged her closer still. "Huh-uh. Let's give them something to talk about."

"You're bad, Cash."

Annelise swore his eyes twinkled. "I'm gonna take that as a compliment."

She threw her head back and laughed. This was fun. And it melted her insides. He was remarkably light on his feet. One dance stretched into two, then three. As he held her close, she smiled. It was nice to be able to be herself. To not have to impress or pretend. To put away her worries.

In the next day or two, she'd have to see about getting to Lone Tree to start making inquiries. But for tonight, she could simply enjoy. Simply be Annie. For this little while, all her mother's rules faded away. No expectations, no bodyguards, no formalities. Just her and this beautiful cowboy.

The music stopped, and they walked back to the table, hand in hand. When she sat down, he leaned in close. She held her breath, sighed when he simply tucked a strand of hair behind her ear. Such a simple gesture, yet so intimate.

Before she could catch her breath to say anything, Mitzy showed up with their pizza. Too hungry to wait, Annelise took her first bite too soon, scalding the roof of her mouth.

"Youch." She fanned at her open mouth. "Hot."

Then, she let go and gave in to the moment, luxuriating in the meal, in the man beside her. Cash was right. Bubba's was home to the best pizza she'd ever eaten. But halfway through her second piece, a camera flash went off. She jerked upright, her gaze bouncing around the room.

Cash reached out to her. "Whoa, darlin'. You look like a skittish mare that's stumbled on a rattler." He tipped his head, indicating a table across the room. "Suzie, Farley Jamison's daughter over there, is celebrating her fifteenth birthday. Somebody took a picture for the family album. That's all."

Annelise smiled sheepishly. "Sorry. Don't know what got into me."

Mentally, she chastised herself. She needed to get a grip and quit acting like some spooked ninny. If she went around jumping at shadows, expecting the paparazzi to be hiding around every corner, it wouldn't take Cash long to get suspicious. The man might wear cowboy boots and jeans, but that mind of his was every bit as sharp as any Ivy Leaguer she'd ever debated.

And then that *man* reached across the table and snagged a piece of pepperoni from her pizza.

"Hey!" She slapped his fingers. "Hands off. This is mine, boss man."

He laughed and ordered another Lone Star.

A few minutes later, the birthday girl showed up at their table, holding out two plates. "I brought you a piece of my cake, Cash." She looked toward Annelise. "I brought one for you, too. It's really good. My grandma Bessie made it. Red velvet with cream-cheese frosting."

"Well, thank you, Suzie. Your grandma bakes the best cakes this side of the Mississippi." He winked. "Don't tell my mama I said that."

Cash took the plates from her, handing one to Annelise. As he made his way through the dessert, he talked amicably with the teenager, teasing her about her newest beau till her cheeks blushed. Annelise listened, envying him his casual, easy rapport. Cash Hardeman knew everyone in the restaurant, and they knew him. All laid-back and comfortable.

The young girl turned to Annelise. "You know, y'all really look familiar."

A nervous little prickle raced down Annelise's spine, but she simply smiled and shrugged. "You know what they say about all of us having a twin."

"I'm sorry, Suzie. This here's Annie," Cash introduced, pointing his cake fork at her.

Annie. Not Annelise. And she blessed the gods she'd not stuck to her guns about the nickname earlier.

"Happy birthday, Suzie," she said.

"Thanks." The teen twirled a dark brown curl around her finger. "Well, I'd better get back." With a wave, she was gone.

Lounging in his chair, long legs stretched out in front of him, Cash took a pull of his beer. "You know, if I'm gonna pay you, sugar, you need to fill out some forms for me."

"There's no hurry with that, is there?" she asked.

"Not if you're in no hurry for a payday."

She thought about her cash reserves, now stashed in the apartment's old refrigerator. She could use her mother's maiden name in a pinch, but it would still be risky. "Actually, I'm okay. For now."

He said nothing for a few seconds, then, "You want a coffee?"

"I'd love one."

"Mitzy's pretty busy. I'll mosey on up to the bar and get them. Save her a trip."

The second his back was turned, she snagged the paper from the table next to her. She'd spied the article on the lower left half of the front page when Suzie had brought their cake. It had been driving her nuts, and she'd prayed like never before that Cash wouldn't spot it.

Oil Baron in Remission. She skimmed the words, assuring herself that all was well with her grandfather, that his condition hadn't changed in the few days she'd been gone. Her mother had told her he was okay, but she sometimes sugarcoated things.

And then, there it was. At the very end of the article.

The entire Montjoy family attended the reopening of their newly renovated office branch in New York City. Montjoy's granddaughter Annelise, second in line to inherit the company, was conspicuously absent. When asked about her nonattendance, the family had no comment as to her whereabouts or the reason for her no-show. This is the second event Annelise has missed this week. What is the Montjoy heiress up to?

Shoot! She rubbed weary eyes, opening them in time to see a sexy blonde, dressed in a white, frilly see-through top, a red, barely-there skirt, and matching stilettos move up behind Cash at the bar and snake an arm around him, her hand caressing his shoulder.

Somebody obviously thought of Cash as her private property. Annelise wondered if maybe she should slip out unobserved. She didn't want his offer of dinner to cause trouble.

But she hesitated. That dance they'd shared. He hadn't felt committed to anyone else while they'd been on the dance floor. Had held her way too close for that. And she'd held him right back. And that was trouble enough for anyone—and a good enough reason to hit the road, to move on to Lone Tree.

She couldn't start anything with him. It would be totally unfair to both of them.

As she slid her chair away from the table, Cash turned. Met her eyes.

He gave a slight shake of his head, and she stilled.

Too far away to hear what he said, she saw his lips move, the tightening of the blonde's jaw. With a pat to her hand, he picked up the coffees and walked back to the table.

The blonde's gaze followed him, flicked to Annelise.

"Here you go, sugar. Should be strong enough to stand your hair on end."

She nodded toward the woman. "Who is she?"

"My grandma," he answered, deadpan.

She laughed, almost spurting her first sip of the ungodly strong coffee.

His eyes held steady. "I'm serious."

"Oh, God. You are, aren't you?"

"Yep."

She shook her head. "Your family might be more screwed up than mine."

Chapter Five

Annelise and Cash drank their coffee in silence. The fans whirled overhead, but they'd long since waved the white flag, admitting defeat. The room grew hotter, closer. A quick glance at the Howdy Doody bar clock showed a quarter till nine.

The only other time Annelise had been in Texas, she'd come with her grandfather. They'd flown in, been picked up at the Dallas airport by one of his friends, and had stayed in his sprawling condo, cocooned in air-conditioned comfort. When they'd ventured back outside, the interior of the limo waiting to deliver them to the fund-raiser was cool enough she'd needed a wrap around her shoulders. After the obligatory smiles, handshakes, and rubber chicken, they'd jetted home. Nary a drop of sweat had been shed.

Cash's world was far different and dominated by unfettered heat. Heat he seemed unaffected by.

She studied him. Whatever had gone on between him and his *grandmother* had sure put him in a sour mood. Gone was the laughing man who'd swung her around the dance floor. He played with his spoon, twirling it on the wooden table, his eyes avoiding hers, while his grandmother, legs crossed, skirt riding high, perched on a stool at the bar—watching them.

Grandma appeared to be very interested in her grandson and his dining companion and didn't try in the least to hide it.

Had to be a story here, and Annelise sure as heck wished she knew what it was.

"You ready?"

His deep voice jolted her, and she nearly spilled the coffee she'd only picked up.

"Yes, I am." She set down her cup. "Anything I should know?"

"Nope."

"Okay then." She placed her napkin on the table and started to rise.

He grabbed her wrist, stopping her. "Here's the deal." His voice sounded unlike him. Harsh. "My grandfather met and married Vivi on a weekend trip to Vegas. Eight months later, he died. I sure as hell wish he hadn't done either. But he did."

Cash shrugged. "Nothing for you to worry about, though. It won't impact your work on the ranch. Believe me, Vivi gives the barn a wide berth."

"Do you live with her?"

Instantly, she wished she could withdraw the question. Whatever was between Cash and his grandmother wasn't any of her business. After all, didn't she hate people prying into *her* private life? Cash deserved the same respect.

His laugh spilled out before she could tell him it didn't matter. "No, ma'am. She lives in the big house. The white one at the end of the drive. I've got my own place down by the lake."

"I see."

"I don't think you do, Annie. It's a mess. But it's *my* mess."

She frowned. *Back off, Annelise. You're out of line.*

"It's not important," he said. "Let's get out of here. Morning alarm's gonna be going off before we know it."

Annelise bit back a groan. So true. She'd been up before the sun this morning and would be again tomorrow. Ranchers kept grueling hours. Who'd have guessed? When she wanted milk, she went to the refrigerator. If she wanted a steak, she asked Cook for one or ordered it at her favorite restaurant. There'd been no thought about the men and women who raised that beef or crawled out of bed before dawn to milk those cows. It had never crossed her mind.

She smiled. "You're so right." When she stood, he put a hand under her elbow. *A gentleman through and through*, she thought. *Good old-fashioned manners. Refreshing.*

Despite the heat, the venomous look Vivi sent her as they passed could have induced hypothermia. Cash didn't seem to notice. He tipped his hat at the bartender. "Night, Bubba. Food was good as always."

The bartender swiped at the counter with his rag. "Night, Cash." He dipped his chin. "Ma'am."

They stepped outside. Crickets chirped, and some scary-sounding animal howled off in the distance. It reminded her of a movie set.

Annelise raised her eyes, and the breath caught in her throat. The Texas sky was huge and strewn with twinkling stars, so big and bright she fancied she could almost touch them. A sliver of a moon hung overhead as if it had been waiting for them to come admire it.

"Cash, it's...breathtaking."

He thumbed back his cowboy hat and stared up into the glitter-strewn night sky. "Yeah, it is."

They stood, shoulder to shoulder, in the middle of the parking lot. The night wrapped itself around them as intimately as a lover might.

Sighing, Annelise asked, "Are any stores still open?"

He checked his watch. "Sadler's stays open for about another hour."

"As much as I'd like to call it a night, I really need to shop for food. And I'd sure like to get some paint samples."

"Then let's do it."

They left the top down as they drove the couple of miles back into town. After parking the boat-of-a-car, he herded her into a large barnlike structure. Two steps inside the store's door, Annelise stopped. Cash bumped into her.

"Whoa, Annie. What are you doing?"

"I've never seen anything like this place."

"Not quite what you're used to?"

She shook her head.

Milk, vegetables, saddles, clothing, camping gear. Everything tossed haphazardly together inside four walls. Deer and antelope heads mounted on the walls stared at her from glassy eyes. Snake skins, tacked between them, slithered down the walls. A huge stuffed buffalo stood inside the door to her right. She almost laughed, thinking of the doorman at Tiffany's. Stuffed shirts, both of them.

The scent of overripe bananas and leather mixed. Somewhere toward the back, a baby cried. An old-fashioned cash register rang, and a country tune blared from wall-mounted speakers.

She didn't doubt for an instant the place had just about everything. From the worn, gray linoleum tiles to the wagon-wheel chandeliers overhead, the place spoke of age. Sadler's had been here a long time and was, no doubt, a Maverick Junction institution.

And here she was. By choice. Doing exactly what she wanted. A heady, foreign sensation rushed through her. *I'm free. Finally and truly free. Judged by what I do, not who I am.*

Cash ruffled her hair, then grabbed a cart and headed for the grocery section. Annelise tossed in a quart of milk, a loaf of bread, and some apples. Unsure what she needed, she walked up and down the aisles, adding random items: coffee, soap, and a couple of frozen meals.

"I want to look at the paint."

"Yes, ma'am. You're the CEO. You call the shots and run the show." He turned the cart and headed to the paint display.

She didn't follow.

He looked over his shoulder. "What?"

"What did you say?"

"I said…" His brow creased. "For Christ's sake, Annie, what's wrong? You look like somebody sucked out every drop of your blood. You're white as a sack of flour."

He left the cart and started toward her.

She put up a hand and started walking. "I'm okay. I just— I thought—" *Get a grip.* It was a figure of speech. She was the CEO in charge of the shopping trip. Period. Cash didn't have a clue who she was. But he would. Her heart skipped a beat. Would he hate her for deceiving him? What a mess. And *this* one was hers to clean up.

"I'm fine. Honest." Forcing a smile, she said, "Lead on."

Two aisles over, they found the paint. So many colors and brands. She put her hands on her hips and gawked at them all, trying to take them in. How many shades of red and blue could there be? Sheepishly, she faced Cash.

"I know this is going to sound, well, ungrateful, maybe

even unfriendly, but I really want to pick the colors by myself—without anyone else's input." She shook her head. "Don't tell me which ones you like or make comments about any of the samples I pick up. Okay?"

"I'm good with that." He grinned. "This is important to you, isn't it?"

"Yes." She nodded. "Yes, it is."

He pushed his hat back, giving her a better view of those fabulous eyes. "Is this your first home, Annie? Your first time on your own?"

"And how."

His smile disappeared, his eyes darkened. "Now don't go getting your back all up in the air, but it's pretty obvious something's going on with you. Something you think Maverick Junction can fix."

"I—"

He held up his hand. "None of my business. Unless I'm harboring a fugitive—or took a married woman out to dinner. Danced with her."

Fugitive? The word echoed in her mind. God, was she a fugitive? No. She was twenty-six years old. Nothing illegal about her leaving home without checking in with her parents first. Most women her age had moved out on their own years ago, were married with children or career women.

But her parents might have the police searching for her, despite her assurances she was fine. Despite Sophie's call.

Her forehead creased as her anxiety grew.

"You *are* married."

She almost laughed. How typically male to head there first.

"No. I'm not married nor have I ever been married." She raised her hand in pledge. "So help me God."

Douglas DeWitt's face flashed across her mind, but she stomped on it and squashed it as quickly as she had that huge black spider that scuttled across the stable floor today. She shivered. Douglas was her parents' choice for her, never hers.

Determined to put away those thoughts, she concentrated on the rainbow of colors. She pulled one sample, then another, replacing some, adding others to her stack.

"Hate to spoil your fun, darlin', but the store's gonna close in about fifteen minutes."

"Oh, no!" She thrust the samples at him. "Why don't you take these out to the car, and I'll finish up here?" She still needed undies and a few other things, and she'd rather he wasn't hanging over her shoulder while she made her choices. What she'd brought with her really wasn't appropriate for ranch work.

He chuckled. "You want to get rid of me."

Her cheeks warmed. "For a bit, yes."

"I'll take these and go on over to talk to Vern while you finish up." He tucked the paint chips into his shirt pocket. "I'll keep an eye open, and once you're checked out, I'll drive you home."

"I didn't mean—"

"Hey." He took her chin between his thumb and forefinger. "Sugar, you need to stop worrying so much about what other people think. You're stocking up. You'd like a little privacy. Want to sneak in some Twinkies or some Ben and Jerry's. Got that. No skin off my nose, Annie."

She nodded.

"I offered to bring you." He leaned a little closer. "And I enjoyed dinner. Enjoyed dancing. Enjoyed watching you shop." He turned her loose. "Now finish up. You don't have much time left."

Whistling some silly song, one thumb hooked in his jeans pocket, he strolled toward the butcher.

Hurrying up and down the aisles, she tossed a package of Hanes Her Way panties into the cart. Added an ugly, utilitarian cotton bra. Some socks. A muumuu-style cover-up that could serve as a robe. And all the while, her mind was in disbelief mode. What would her mother think? Buying her unmentionables in a store with dead animals on the wall and bins of potatoes and fragrant onions.

Oh, boy. Best not to go there.

Thing was, she hadn't come prepared to work. Hadn't really thought this whole thing out very well. She'd brought along the essentials, but her Harley's saddlebags weren't stocked for this new life. Having never done anything like this before, she'd seriously misjudged.

And now, she'd rectify that.

One thing for sure, though. If she intended to spend her days in the barn, she needed boots. No doubt they were lurking around here somewhere. Scanning the aisles, she figured if they made it, Sadler's carried it.

Sure enough, she found a display of beautiful leather cowboy boots. Or, in her case, cowgirl boots. Not at all what she'd worn on her feet at the fancy equestrian school her mother had insisted she attend.

Now, she needed to thank her for that. She loved horses, loved riding—and she was good at it.

Annelise ran her fingers over the tooled leather, marveling at the intricacy. Then she remembered what she'd be doing when they were on her feet and decided the boots really didn't need to be pretty. They needed to fit well and protect her feet.

As she tried on several pairs, guilt again seeped into her head. Strangely enough, she didn't feel guilty for hightailing it halfway across the country without telling her family. In this case, the end did justify the means. She'd come to

Texas to try to save her grandfather's life. Let everyone else sit on their butts. She didn't intend to. She didn't worry, either, about any of the obligations she'd walked away from. None of them had been of her choosing.

But deceiving Cash? That gnawed at her. Being dishonest with him didn't sit well. So open and honest himself, when he found out who she was, how would he react?

Badly. Without a doubt. He'd feel duped, taken advantage of. And she couldn't blame him.

She thought of the paint chips in his pocket. Lovely jewel colors. But would she be here long enough to get them up on her walls?

Hard to tell.

First and foremost, she had to track down her grandfather's half sister, a woman who would probably hate her on sight—if the rumors she existed were true. Then would come the persuading, convincing this stranger whom the family had turned its back on that she should help them.

This trip, though, had provided an unexpected bonus, something Annelise hadn't even considered. She realized, now, how important this undertaking was for her. How vital to have an identity divorced of her family name and money, even if only for a short while.

Picking up another boot, she sighed. She wanted to stay here for a while. She had such wonderful plans for Dottie's upstairs apartment.

Tomorrow, she'd stop at LeRoy's Used Furniture and buy the comfortable, stretch-out-on-me couch she'd spotted in the display window. Maybe she'd even check out the Sew and Save for some splashy fun fabric for cushions. Of course, then, she'd have to find someone who could sew. Maybe Dottie knew someone who could help her.

Yes, she was being hypocritical. She accepted that. While

she cursed the responsibility of her money, she admitted to being shallow enough to enjoy the comfort it could provide. But it had been a long time since she'd been so excited about anything. Her chest tightened, and her fingers crushed the boots she held. She couldn't give up on this chance for a little freedom. This was her opportunity to find herself. It was *her* life. Why shouldn't she decide how she'd live it?

Maybe she could do both herself and her grandfather a favor here in the Lone Star State.

* * *

Half an hour later, Cash pulled up in front of her new home. Grabbing bags, he headed up the steps, taking them two at a time. The man had energy to burn, Annelise thought.

She scooped up the last two bags from the backseat and trudged behind him. Her muscles ached, reminding her she'd shoveled barn stalls all day. She didn't know what Cash had done today, but he hadn't mucked stalls.

As the cashier'd rung up her purchases, she'd been appalled at the total. She hadn't bought that much. Hadn't bought anything that was really fun. Again, the reality of how sheltered her life had been hit home. She'd never grocery-shopped. Never had to be concerned with the basics. Someone—one of the staff—simply made certain those things were always there, always available.

And these basics had taken a healthy nip out of her piggy bank tonight. Well, she was a working girl now. Eventually, she'd recoup her expenses.

Except she really wouldn't be here that long, would she?

At the top of the outside steps, Cash moved to one side while she unlocked her door, then moved into the small kitchen area and dumped everything on the counter. Her laundry, neatly folded, lay on her table beside a small plate of Dottie's wonderful homemade cookies. Smack on top of the pile were her bra and panties.

Cash's gaze traveled over her lingerie, and he grinned. With one finger, he hooked her bra strap, dangled it. "Very nice."

She snatched it from him and picked up the pile of clothes, hugging it to her chest. Heat radiated from her face, and she gave him her boardroom stare. "I like it."

"Bet you do." Unfazed, he snitched a cookie and took a huge bite. "Mmmmm, mmmm. Can't beat these, can you?" Then, scanning the cramped space, he asked, "You good to go now?"

"Yes. I think I have everything I need. Thank you."

"Lock up behind me."

Her brows rose. "Is there much crime here?"

"In Maverick Junction?" He laughed. "Nah. But just the same, when you're here alone, it wouldn't hurt to throw the lock."

She nodded. *Throw the lock. If he only knew.* Her everyday life revolved around elaborate security systems, video cams, and ever-present bodyguards.

Not anymore. She was on her own now. For the short-term. But she would take his advice. No sense being stupid.

"Dottie doesn't."

"I know. She should. I've told her that."

After setting her laundry back onto the table, lingerie-side down, she followed him to the door. He opened it and paused to give her a quick, friendly peck on the cheek.

She turned her head at that instant, and his lips missed their mark, landing squarely on her mouth.

Both pulled away as if burned, and she stepped back. Their eyes met and locked. Heat swept through Annelise; her breasts felt heavy. The man was potent!

His voice gravelly, Cash said, "Night, Annie." Without another word or a second's hesitation, he hurried down the stairs and into the night.

Annelise laid her fingers over her lips. Her tingling lips. Innocent. Accidental. The kiss had meant nothing. So why was her heart racing?

His car door opened, closed. The Caddy's big engine roared to life, drowning out the cicadas' incessant chirping.

Leaning against the stair railing, she watched his red taillights disappear into the darkness. He'd given her a job, helped her find a place to live, then spent his entire evening taking her to dinner and grocery shopping. Who was this man?

Used to people doing for her, she understood this was innately different. This was personal—and Cash Hardeman was very good at it. Good at making her feel welcome. Special.

With those skills, he'd do well in the boardroom—far better than she. He'd have everyone eating out of his hand. And at stuffy, formal dinner parties? Closing her eyes, Annelise breathed in the heavy night air. Oh, yeah. She could see him. A tailor-made tux that fit his muscular build to perfection, his black Stetson, and his cowboy boots. And a smile with dimples sure to dazzle every woman within a sixty-mile radius. Her most of all.

The killer Texas heat spiked another twenty degrees.

Chapter Six

Hot enough under the collar to ignite a brush fire, Cash stalked toward the big house. Damn Vivi all to hell. This latest fiasco was her way of getting back at him for last night. He knew it as surely as he knew his own name.

So now he had to take time out of the middle of the workday to smooth things out with Rosie. The Fourth of July was coming up fast, and the little league ball team he coached, along with their families and half the rest of the county, would be here expecting to eat and celebrate their country's independence. It took a lot of planning and organization to pull off the annual event. If Rosie, his housekeeper and cook, wasn't happy, that wasn't gonna happen.

One thing about Vivi, her timing was spot-on. She knew exactly when to throw her little snit fits to cause the most damage.

His boots thudded loudly on the wooden porch steps. Without stopping to knock, he barged through the door, the screen banging shut behind him.

"Vivi!"

"What?" His grandfather's widow poked her head out of the living room. Every hair in place, her makeup applied perfectly, she'd no doubt expected him. The short white shorts showed off miles of tanned legs, and the neon-pink tank top hugged a perfect pair of breasts.

Cash guessed he could see what had tempted his grandfather. But at seventy-two, the old codger should have had the sense not to buy the cow—especially with a forty-four-year age difference between himself and that cow. Unfortunately, Gramps hadn't been using the head on his shoulders and had rushed headlong into matrimony, creating one hell of a mess.

If he'd waited, even a little while, he'd have seen through the façade to the wicked witch inside that showgirl's body.

Maybe. He hadn't really been himself the last year or so. He got confused easily, forgot things. They'd never have let him go to Vegas alone if they'd known that's what he'd planned to do.

They'd been frantic when he disappeared, then reassured when he'd called to tell them he was fine. Too damn bad one of them hadn't hopped in the plane and flown to Vegas after his call because, while he'd claimed he simply needed to get away for a couple of days, he hadn't run nearly fast enough. Vivi, damn her hide, caught him.

Gramps had been an easy target. Lonely and disoriented.

They'd buried him three months ago. A fist of pain squeezed Cash's heart. God, he missed the old man.

"I see your girlfriend's here again."

"Annie's not my girlfriend."

Vivi rolled her eyes. "Um-hmm. Could've fooled me."

"Don't start, Vivi."

"Where'd you find her?"

"She's new to town."

His *grandmother* curled a strand of highlighted blond hair around a finger. "She looks awfully familiar. I could swear I know her from somewhere."

"I seriously doubt that. Don't think you two run in the same social circle. Besides, it doesn't matter. As long as Annie does her job, there's no problem."

"Exactly which job are you talkin' about, Cash? Her nine-to-five one here at the ranch or her nighttime job takin' care of you?" She tipped her head to one side. "Doesn't it strike you strange she just happened to show up needin' a job when you're countin' down to the big three-oh? When you're runnin' out of time to—"

"Stop. Right now." Anger flared.

"Ah," Vivi purred. "You've already wondered about it. I can see it in your eyes."

"What? You worried about your inheritance, Vivi? Think Annie knew exactly when I'd be in town so she could lure me in?"

"Maybe. Maybe that part was luck. But I'm telling you, Cash, the lady has her line in the water, and she's trollin' for you."

"Well, you'd certainly be the expert on that, wouldn't you?"

Vivi simply smiled at him.

"What in the hell was Gramps thinking when he got mixed up with you?"

"Oh, come on, Cash. You know the answer to that. It's the same thing you're thinkin' every time you look at Annie."

"Go to hell."

"I already have. It's called Maverick Junction, Texas."

Cash kneaded his forehead and took a long, slow breath. "What's going on between you and Rosie?"

"She's lazy."

"Lazy?" He rocked back on his heels. "The woman's sixty-eight and can work rings around you. And does."

"She won't take direction."

"Excuse me?"

"She's stubborn. She won't do as she's told. I made a couple itsy-bitsy changes in the menu, and the way she took on, you'd think I committed the crime of the century."

He kept his eyes on hers. "Itsy-bitsy changes?"

Vivi stomped her sandaled foot. "I don't see why, just because something's been done a certain way in the past, it has to be sacrosanct."

"Ooh, big word, Ms. Vegas. You been studying up at night?"

"Damn you to hell and back, Cash Hardeman."

"Thank you."

"'Sides, what else have I got to do at night, hmmm? All alone in that big old king-size bed." She pulled a pout.

A muscle twitched in Cash's jaw. "I'm going back to the kitchen to talk to Rosie. See if I can settle her down." He pointed a finger at Vivi. "And you stay the hell away from her."

Vivi threw him an icy smile. "She's *my* cook."

"Thank you for reminding me." Frustration seeped into him. His hands fisted. "You don't want to be here on this ranch any more than I want you here. What'll it take, Vivi, to buy your half out?"

"We've already been through this, darlin'. The ranch isn't for sale." She stepped to him, laid a hand on his cheek. "Marry me, Cash, and the ranch is all yours."

"I'd rather eat glass." He removed her hand from his face.

"Well, if that's the case, I'm sure Rosie will be only too happy to fix it for you." Vivi turned and flounced up the highly polished oak staircase, her hips swiveling in her tight shorts.

Cash blew out a breath and headed to the kitchen, his boots loud on the shiny hardwood floors. He avoided the thick accent rugs in blues and orange that Vivi'd added. Too fancy by far, for his taste.

The minute he stepped into the bright, cheerful room, Rosie hustled to him, shaking the wooden spoon in her hand. As wide as Hank was thin, she looked practically apoplectic in her tomato-red housedress. "Cash, you've gotta do somethin' about her." Dark eyes snapping with anger, she nodded her head in the direction of the front of the house. "It's her or me. One of us has to go."

He scrubbed his hands over his face. "You know I'd send her packing if I could."

"You can. You know what you gotta do."

"Rosie—"

"Never mind. Have you had lunch?"

"Not yet."

"Then wash up and let me feed you. Like I used to do before *she* moved in." Again, she jerked her graying head toward the front of the house.

Cash went to the sink to lather up, scrubbing away the morning's dust and letting Rosie vent before turning the conversation to the upcoming barbecue.

"That's the problem. Look at this." She dug a list out of her mammoth apron pocket and slapped it on the table.

He turned it around so he could read it. The menu. The one they'd used for as many years as he could remember. Whispering Pines' Fourth of July barbecue was legendary. Angry red lines slashed through most of the items on the list. New dishes had been scrawled beside them. His eyes widened.

"Ah, Vivi told me she'd made a few small changes."

"A few small changes?" Her stubby finger came down on the scratched-out barbecue pork. "We're supposed to have prime rib instead. And see here? No apple pies. Instead, I've been told to make Baked Alaska."

"Well—"

"Ain't gonna happen. Baked Alaska," she grumbled. She rested both hands on her hips. "Not in this lifetime. And potatoes au gratin instead of corn on the cob? At a Whispering Pines' barbecue? Humph! The menu stays as it's always been. Ms. Fancy Pants will have to make do."

"That's more than fine with me," Cash said.

"Yeah, well, that's real easy for you to say. You're not cooped up with her here, day after day after day. She can get nasty. *Real* nasty."

"I know she can, and I'm sorry, Rosie."

"I know you didn't make this mess. Mr. Leo's responsible for it, bless his soul. But one more thing you've got to know. I've already talked to Hank, and he's agreed. If that woman fires me because of all this, he's gonna retire a little earlier than he'd planned. We'll both be done."

Hank retire? Rosie leave? Cash's stomach burned, and it wasn't from the extra coffee he'd had with breakfast.

"She won't do that, Rosie. You and I both know she'd starve to death if you left."

"We'll see. The woman's crazy. Like this here new floor. White tile in a ranch house kitchen? What's wrong with her brain? Can't keep it clean, but then she doesn't much care about that. Ain't her down on her hands and knees scrubbin' it."

"You shouldn't be, either, Rosie. That's what we hire the cleaning girls to do."

"Uh-huh." With that Rosie changed the subject. "Your mama and daddy will be here?"

She set a mammoth sandwich down in front of him, a pile of thinly sliced roast beef cradled between two thick slabs of homemade bread with juicy tomato slices nestled amongst the meat. His stomach rumbled.

"Yes, they will. I'm making an airport run to pick them up later today." He lifted one slice of bread, saw the horse-radish sauce she'd slathered on it, smiled, and took a bite. "Mmmmm. Good stuff, Rosie."

"'Course it is. Made it, didn't I? Here's a glass of cold milk to go with it. Drink it like a good boy." She plunked it down on the table in front of him, poured a cup of coffee for herself from the old percolator on the stove, and sat down across from him. "It'll be good to see your folks. It's past time for them to come home."

She sneaked a sidelong glance at him. "Maybe *they* can talk some sense into you."

"Rosie," he warned. "We've already covered this ground. I'm not gonna do it."

"Yeah, yeah. I know."

"You've got a lot to take care of in the next couple days. Anything I can do?"

"Yeah. You can gag and bind that woman upstairs and lock her in a closet."

He grinned. "Anything else?"

"Nope. I've got the rest under control. Estelle and Mary are coming in the next couple days to help. They'll be back early on the Fourth to finish things up. I'm making the apple pies myself, though. Can't be trusting anybody else with those. Baked Alaska," she muttered. "In a pig's eye."

He smiled and wiped his face with the napkin Rosie handed him. Leaning across the table, he kissed her cheek. "Thank you."

"Ain't no need to thank me. I'm just doin' my job."

"We both know you do more than that." He hesitated. "Has Hank said anything about the new help I hired?"

"The old coot was madder than a banty rooster when she showed up. Thought I was gonna have to double up on his blood pressure meds. But after that first day, he settled down. Said even though the girl looked like some pampered princess, she wasn't afraid to get her hands dirty or too good to put her back into what needs doing."

"That's pretty high praise, coming from your husband."

"Yeah, it is. So I figure this Annie of yours must be okay."

"She's not my Annie," he said quickly.

"Hmph." She arched her brow. "Maybe she should be. Now get out of here and let me do my work." She swatted him with a dish towel.

"Yes, ma'am." As he let himself out the back door, he thought about what Rosie had said. His Annie. Somehow, the idea of that didn't put him off nearly as much as it should.

And Vivi's accusations about Annie? Absolute rubbish. Good move on her part, though, he admitted reluctantly. Make him doubt Annie, her intentions. Drive a wedge between them. The woman would do whatever it took to protect her interests.

Well, he wouldn't think about it anymore. She was wrong.

Barbecue crisis averted, for now anyway, he meandered over to the barn. He'd check on Hank, make sure he was indeed taking things easier. He refused to admit his trip had anything to do with catching a glimpse of Annie.

Sticky hot and feeling more than a little grouchy, he stepped into the barn. Annie was nowhere in sight. Bathed in shadows, the building was a good ten degrees cooler than outside. It smelled of horse and fresh hay, familiar and comforting.

Crouched in a stall, Hank wrapped one of the mare's legs. Cash leaned against the wood railings. "Annie around?"

"She's out in the paddock."

"Okay."

He straightened to leave, but Hank, madder than a hornet, said, "You gotta do something about this mess."

"There's nothing I can do, Hank. You know I would if—"

"Don't go givin' me that, boy. You gonna stand back and watch everything your grandfather worked for go down the drain?"

"He did that himself."

"No, by damn. You and I both know the old man wasn't in his right mind."

Cash sighed, took off his hat, and raked his fingers through his hair. "This whole thing is beyond ludicrous. I don't think any of us understood how jumbled Gramps's mind had become."

"Rosie tried to tell me," Hank said. "Even before Vivi. I didn't want to hear it. Didn't want to believe Leo's mind was going."

"None of us did."

"You know," Hank said, "in some twisted way that must have made sense to him, he was only givin' you a nudge."

"Well, I don't want to be nudged." Cash jammed his hands in his pants pockets. "And this is a hell of a lot more than a nudge. A hard shove off a rocky cliff is more like it."

"Your grandpa was right about one thing. Time you settle down. Start a family."

"Did you put this stupid idea in his head?"

"No, sir, I did not. Wouldn't do anything to give the new missus a bit of ground. Your grandpa might have been willin' to bet with the ranch, but not me. No siree."

"I won't get married, Hank, not even to keep the ranch. Marriage shouldn't be a bargaining chip."

"I understand that, but I sure as hell don't want to work for Vivi. That gal wouldn't know a stallion from a heifer! And you. What're you going to do?"

Cash rubbed his chest. "She'll have half interest. That's it. You'll still be working for me."

Hank muttered something under his breath.

Cash ignored it. "I'm gonna tell it to you straight, Hank. Stipulating I had to be married by the time I'm thirty or I share the ranch with Vivi? Big mistake. I'm not gonna be manipulated. I'm not getting married. End of discussion."

"So you're gonna turn your back and let that gold digger steal the homestead?"

"No." Cash shook his head. "I'm gonna let my grand-father's widow inherit the house she's living in. If she leaves, according to the will, she walks with two hundred thousand. She knows her half interest is worth way more. So I offered her three times that, but still no dice."

"Over half a million. Not bad for eight months with one of the nicest men God ever put on Earth. Too bad about all of it. You, your Gramps," Hank groused.

"I'd have to agree. On all counts."

Hank let loose with enough curses to turn the air blue. "She hates it here. Why doesn't she take the money and run?"

Cash shrugged.

"It ain't right!" Hank spit tobacco juice into a can, then shot a glance at Cash. "Don't tell Rosie I'm chewin' out here."

"What happens in the barn—" Cash spread his hands.

"Yeah, yeah." Not done yet, Hank said, "It ain't only the house, and you know that. If that was all she'd get, maybe I could stomach it. But you've worked your ass off on this ranch. Ever since you finished that degree of yours, you've devoted yourself to Whispering Pines. Hell, even before that, you spent every weekend your daddy didn't need you over here helping Leo."

"Yes, I did. And it seems that was a mistake."

"You could contest the will."

"We've been through this, Hank. I'm not going there."

"Whispering Pines is your birthright."

"Gramps owned it. He could do what he wanted with it."

"Yeah, and if he'd been in his right mind, he'd have left it to you. Wouldn't have married Vegas in the first place."

"But he did."

"What about that new house you built for yourself down by the lake?"

"I'm gonna dicker with Vivi a little. See if maybe she'll sell me the piece of land it's on free and clear. Separate it from the rest of the package."

"Yeah, like that's gonna happen."

"There's nothing else I can do." His voice rose in frustration, and several of the horses shifted uneasily, including the one Hank worked with.

Hank ran a hand over the mare's flank. "Easy, girl." His face tightened. "Never took you for a quitter."

Cash's own face darkened. "Careful."

"You got options."

"I'm not marrying Vivi, not taking my grandpa's leavings."

"No. Don't expect you to do that. She does, though."

"Yeah, I know. She's made that crystal clear."

"Still, I'll repeat, you got options." The old hand spit another stream of tobacco.

"Sometimes, the fight's simply bigger than a fellow should take on."

"Yeah, and sometimes a fella flat-assed doesn't know

what's good for him." Hank tossed the end of the leg wrap into the corner and stormed out of the barn.

"Shit." Cash kicked a wooden stool beside him and sent it skittering. It hit the wall, and the mare snickered.

"That's what I say." Cash strode out into the bright sunshine, but the shadows followed.

* * *

Annelise, in the paddock, saw Hank stalk from the barn.

"You okay?" she asked.

"Yes. I am. And if you know what's good for you, you'll stay out of Cash's way for a bit."

"Why?"

"'Cause he's stupider than a jackass today."

"Okay."

Some of the guys were hauling tables from an outbuilding, and she went to help with that. Because they'd been stored there after the last big to-do, they needed to be scrubbed before the barbecue. She pitched in, glad to have something to keep her busy.

Her mind drifted to her grandfather. She'd been too tired last night to do anything more than drop into bed after Cash left. Tonight she had to get busy digging on her laptop.

Grandpa was in remission. It could be months or even years before he came out of it. There was no way of knowing. But without the bone marrow transplant, the threat would always be there, hanging over his head like a loaded gun.

The chemo treatments had given them precious time, had done their job. Now she had to do hers.

Cash found her while she was taking a water break, sitting with her back against a tall oak.

"Hey, darlin', I've been looking for you."

"Are you okay?"

"Sure. Why wouldn't I be?"

"No reason." Whatever he and Hank had argued about had apparently blown over. Cash looked, right now, like he didn't have a care in the world.

He sprawled beside her, his long legs stretched out in front of him. Staubach plopped down in the grass beside him and fell instantly asleep, his nose twitching as he dreamed. No doubt he chased a long-eared jackrabbit through the meadows behind the barns.

Head propped on one hand, Cash reached up and casually took a lock of her hair between his fingers, playing with it. Annelise willed herself to sit still, though her stomach started tumbling around itself at his touch, at his presence. This man made her heart stumble. And that was bad. But if Cash could play it cool, so could she.

"Gonna share?" He nodded at her water bottle.

"Oh. Sure." Their fingers touched as he took it from her, and the same electricity as before flooded her. Did he feel it?

If he did, he didn't let on. He took a huge swallow and passed it back.

She took a smaller drink, placing her lips where his had been, remembering the accidental kiss on her stairs last night.

"Cash, would you mind if I worked with Shadow? I—"

"No. Stay away from him."

"But—"

"No buts, Annie. Shadow's not ready for you or anybody else yet. He's got history. His last owner abused him."

"I understand that."

"Then you understand he might hurt you."

"Cash, I'm a big girl. I've worked with and around horses

all my life. I love them. I think I can make a difference with your beautiful gray horse."

"I appreciate that, but the answer's still no."

She said nothing and took another sip of water.

"Now you're pouting."

"I'm not pouting," she groused.

"Sure you are. Look at you."

"Without a mirror, that's kind of difficult. I simply choose not to argue with you about it."

"Good. Listen, I gotta go pick up my parents at the airport." He took her hand in his, ran a thumb over the back of it. "Want to come with me?"

Oh, yes, she certainly did. But that would be foolhardy. And whatever else Georgia and Edmund Montjoy had or had not done, they'd not raised a fool for a daughter.

"No, thanks, Cash. I've still got a lot to do here."

"I'm the boss." He leaned in closer. He smelled good. Clean, healthy male. "I can get you excused from some of those duties."

She pulled her hand from his and laid it on his cheek. "And as much as I'd like that, I don't want anyone accusing me of not pulling my weight or of being boss's pet."

He pulled back. "Has someone insinuated—"

"No." She shook her head. "They haven't. And I want to keep it that way. Besides, I'm filthy. I don't want your parents' first impression of me to be the way I look—and smell—right now."

Grinning, he put his nose in the crook of her neck and inhaled. "You smell good, Annie. Good enough to eat."

Her hands were halfway to his head, to cradle him, pull him closer, when she caught herself. With a strangled laugh, she pushed him away. "Right. You'd better be careful. Someone's going to lock you up in the loony bin."

"Long as they lock you up with me, I don't care."

Laughing, Annelise stood. She'd come a long way in these two short days. Working, flirting, and feeling good about it. She'd never experienced this instant chemistry. This link. This intense magnetism. She liked it.

"My break's over, boss. Gotta get back to work." She met his eyes. "I'll be looking forward to meeting your parents. They have to be great people."

And she walked away without once glancing back. Self-preservation. Cash Hardeman spoke to her like no other man ever had.

Even with Doug, with whom she'd spent so much time, her response had been tepid at best.

With Cash? Steaming hot. She felt him in every cell of her being.

Yes, he was nice to look at—and wasn't that the under-statement of the century? But it was more than that. He was...he was good. He was honest. He was caring.

He was also trouble. In capital letters.

Chapter Seven

Headed for the airport, Cash sped down the interstate. Cool air blasting from the vents, the radio at full volume in his parents' cherry-red Cadillac Escalade, he followed the flow of the crush of traffic around him. He sang along with Garth, his thumb drumming on the steering wheel.

He might be dusty boots and even dustier dashboard as a rule, but today he was picking up his mom. So he'd shined the Escalade from bumper to bumper. His mother was, after all, his favorite lady.

Staubach had carried on something awful at being left at home. If the car moved, he expected to be in it. The old mutt had stubbornly followed him clear to the end of the drive before sitting on his haunches to howl pathetically as Cash turned onto the main road. He'd have to give him double doggie treats when he got back.

In truth, the dog wasn't the only creature feeling pathetic. His mind refused to clear. Normally, he loved time like this. Short stints away from everything. Away from the demands and responsibilities of the ranch, away from petty squabbling among the hands. From the bickering between Vivi and Rosie. Time alone to think.

Today, though, he didn't much like being alone with his thoughts. He didn't like the direction they kept taking. Didn't like that he and Hank had argued.

A passing truck honked. What was his problem? Cash glared at the semi as it roared past and, though it was small of him, hoped a trooper waited around the next corner to pull his butt over.

Vivi.

Annie.

Neither woman gave him a moment's peace. By themselves, either would be enough to drive a man to drink. But together? The two of them running around in his head was definitely cause for a six-pack or two.

Toss in that damnable codicil in Gramps's will, and it was a wonder he wasn't bonkers. He'd known the old man hoped he'd settle down and make him some grandbabies. What he hadn't understood, he guessed, was how badly Gramps had wanted that. Maybe. And maybe it was simply the senility talking.

Cash couldn't believe Gramps had wanted it enough to risk it all. Enough to throw away everything he and Grandma Edith had worked for. 'Cause that's the way it was gonna turn out. Damned if Cash intended to get hitched in the next six months in order to keep the ranch. No piece of land was worth that. He was footloose and fancy-free, and that was exactly the way he wanted it.

If and when he got married, it would be his decision, his choice. The time, the place, and the bride.

Yet the thought of walking away from Whispering Pines, of turning over the reins to Showgirl, really pissed him off.

Despite what he'd told Hank, he wasn't at all sure he could work with Vivi. When it came right down to it, would he walk rather than spend day after day after day butting heads with her? If he did relinquish his rights, he'd lay odds on Vivi selling the ranch immediately to a third party and heading back to Vegas in search of her next victim. If she stayed put, she'd run the Pines into the ground in under a year.

Either way, the ranch would be lost to him, his grandfather's legacy kaput.

Cash knew with a bone-deep certainty that any amount of money he proposed wouldn't be enough. Vivi had turned down every offer he'd made. Nope, she would sell the place to someone else and for less money—simply to spite him.

So many had made the Pines their home. Rosie and Hank, the wranglers and ranch hands. A lot of good people would suffer if he couldn't reach some sort of compromise. His jaw tightened as the weight settled more heavily on his shoulders.

And the pretty little house he'd built with his own hands, his own sweat. He'd situated it down by the lake on the far corner of Gramps's land, figuring it would be home forever. He liked the solitude. Loved the land.

A dull ache settled behind Cash's eyes and refused to budge.

He missed his grandfather. Missed their morning talks over coffee, their walks by the old fishing hole. He missed the smell of Gramps's cherry pipe tobacco and the mints he carried in his pocket. He missed his voice, his quick wit. Even with the fog slowly taking over his mind, he'd still been able to hold up his end of any conversation.

Cash had never begrudged his grandfather anything, but if Leo—in a moment of irrationalness—had needed a sexy, young thing, why couldn't he simply have bought one a big old pair of diamond earrings or a bracelet or something, bedded her, then come on home? Why'd he have to put a ring on it and bring her home as his wife?

And why had this man who'd never been sick a day in his life suddenly keeled over from a heart attack and died, leaving Cash to deal with the devious, scheming bride turned widow? Vivi managed to ruffle everyone's feathers. Running interference between her and the ranch hands, his sister, and his parents had practically turned into a full-time job.

The funeral barely behind them, the grieving widow had wasted no time putting her stamp on things. She'd hired a crew of designers from Dallas to redo the old farm house. The place had great bones. But Gramps hadn't changed a thing since Grandma Edith had passed away eight years ago. The same cabbage-rose wallpaper had hung in the living and dining rooms. The linoleum in the kitchen had been worn and faded and the furniture comfortable but well-worn. Grandma's collection of tea kettles had filled the breakfast nook's hutch.

Not anymore. The house had been done over from top to bottom in slick, bright colors and fussy furniture. Cash felt like a stranger in the house he'd practically grown up in. More than once, Vivi had offered to share it with him. All he had to do was marry her.

Hell would freeze over first.

Then there was Annie. He'd known her two days now, but it seemed like forever. Felt as though he'd waited for her always.

And wasn't that gibberish? Beneath his dark glasses, he rubbed at the tic in his eye. If he said something like that to any of the guys, they'd lock him in a rubber room. And rightly so.

Annie was intelligent, fun, unexpected, and damned easy on the eyes. He sighed and swerved the Escalade around some slower-moving traffic. His exit was coming up, so he slid back into the right-hand lane.

He'd like to say she was comfortable to be with because she was. But at the same time, he felt worked up when he was with her. Agitated. Yeah, a sexual thing. The woman gave off heat without even trying. Simply looking at her made him want to turn caveman and drag her off to his bed. Hardly a good thing since she worked for him. Maybe he should just fire her, cart her off to bed, and be done with it.

Something was fishy, though. She shut down when the conversation turned to her. Hell, she wouldn't even fill out the paperwork so he could cut her a paycheck. Every time he brought up anything personal, she talked her way around the barn and back without really telling him a thing. She was close-mouthed. Hardly the basis for a good relationship.

But then, he didn't really want a relationship with her, did he?

She hadn't bought much at Sadler's, had brought less than nothing with her. Exactly what he'd expect from someone on the run. He figured one morning she wouldn't show up for work, and he'd head on over to Dottie's place to find her gone without so much as a note. Not a clue as to why or where she'd gone.

Wasn't that essentially what his pal Brawley had done to Maggie? Led her on, then cut and run? Cash had been the one left behind to help her pick up the pieces. Not pretty.

He and Annie really didn't have a "thing," though, did they? Might be best if she did take off before whatever was going on between them developed into more.

His mind worried the situation like a tongue on a sore

tooth. Annie's manners, her jewelry, the new Harley. Had to be some money someplace.

He'd been born and raised here. This was home. But Annie? What was she doing in Maverick Junction, Texas? Cash reached for the mug of iced tea he'd brought along and took a swig. What brought her here, and why did he care? It was none of his business. None whatsoever. And he'd do well to remember that.

Still, as he exited the main highway and took the ramp to the airport, his mind drifted to last night. That simple, accidental kiss had burned him. But when they'd both pulled away, she looked surprised but unaffected.

Annie was a hard nut to crack. If he was smart, he wouldn't even try.

* * *

Annelise finished the last of her chores, then scurried into the little bathroom at the back of the barn. She washed up as best she could and slipped into the fresh top she'd tucked into her saddlebag that morning.

She sighed, relishing the feel of silk against her skin. She loved this blouse. She'd bought it in Paris at one of the last runway shows she'd attended. It was a world apart from the cotton tanks she'd picked up at Sadler's.

Giving Hank a shouted good-bye, she escaped into the sunlight. She had plans.

When she straddled her Harley and slid on her helmet, she accepted she'd willingly give up silk forever for this. She dropped her dark glasses into place and with the wind in her face, headed to town.

Staying busy was her key to maintaining her sanity, because she would go nuts if she didn't do something while waiting to hear from Ron. Grandpa was all right—for now. He was back home, living life. True, he was a ticking bomb, but it wouldn't go off today or tomorrow.

The treatments had bought them some time. But she couldn't just sit and twiddle her thumbs. Better that she get her hands dirty, spruce up Dottie's apartment, and make it her own—even if only for a short while. Dottie had taken her in and given her a place to live. A home. Her very first on her own. The least she could do was leave it a somewhat better place than she'd found it.

First order of business—some different furniture, and she knew exactly what she wanted. She wanted the broken-in, chocolate-brown couch she'd spotted in the store window the night before. It was perfect.

She parked in the same spot she had two mornings ago when she'd first ridden into Maverick Junction. BC. Before Cash. It blew her mind how so much had happened in such a short time.

Cash. That cowboy could matter to her—a lot—if she let him. But the foundation of their relationship had been built on dishonesty.

Now that she knew him better, she didn't doubt for a heartbeat he'd boot her out of his life when he discovered the truth, that she'd been less than straightforward with him. And he would find her out. Eventually. Somehow. It was simply a matter of time.

Best-case scenario would be her coming clean and telling him who she really was and what she was doing here. But that would change everything. Would ruin the easygoing give and take between them, between herself and the other ranch hands, the people in town. Money always changed things—whether you had it or didn't have it. It got in the way.

Before she told anyone, she wanted a chance for them

to get to know her. *Annie.* Not Annelise, the heiress to the Montjoy Oil fortune.

It made her stomach jittery to think of the house of cards she'd built. It made her stomach even more jittery to think of Cash. And that couldn't be good.

The bell over the door jangled happily as she stepped inside LeRoy's Used Furniture.

"Howdy." A man appeared from the backroom. "Name's LeRoy. What can I do for you?"

She didn't bother to check the price, didn't even think of bargaining with him. "Hello, LeRoy. I'm Annie, and I want the couch in the window."

"It's a good one."

"I agree."

"That do it for ya?" He picked up a pad and pen and an old pair of reading glasses.

"No, I'm going to take that mirror. The one in the corner." She moved closer, saw several others leaning behind it. "Actually, LeRoy, I'd like all four of those mirrors."

They'd be great in the apartment and would give the room the appearance of more space. She almost laughed. Could anything make those rooms look bigger? Well, she'd give it a go.

Surprised, LeRoy nodded and gathered them up.

She waded through the jumble of tables, lamps, and knickknacks, pointing at things as she went. "And I want this. And this." An off-white wingback chair caught her eye, and she added it to her list.

She wandered around the crowded store, making her selections, mentally placing them in her small apartment, imagining what they'd look like with her paint choices. She'd spray-paint the metal mirror and the lamp to match the chair.

Standing in the center of the jumble, she raised her arms and pulled her hair up in a ponytail. "If I buy all this, is there any chance I can get it delivered? The only vehicle I have is my Harley." She tilted her head toward the street.

"Oh, she's a beauty," he said. "Saw it the other day when you were in to Sally's. Yes, ma'am, I surely can deliver this for you."

"Tonight?"

He checked his watch and nodded slowly. "I've got a truck out back and a son and his friend with strong, young backs. I'm figurin' you must be the gal rented Dottie's place."

Her body stiffened in surprise. Small towns and their gossip mills. People here seemed to know what she was going to do before she did. But at least it wasn't splashed in full-color in the tabloids for the entire world's viewing. And most of all, no one judged her or told her what she could and couldn't do.

"Yes, LeRoy, I am." She forced herself to relax. "You know, then, where all this has to go?"

"Yep, sure do."

"One more thing. If I buy some paint, would you throw that on your truck, too, and deliver it with the furniture and things?"

"Be more than happy to."

She paid him and then walked down the street to Sadler's, color chips in hand. Once inside the eclectic store, she arranged for the paint to be mixed and delivered to LeRoy's. Maybe she'd eat at Sally's Place as long as she was here. Tomorrow would be soon enough to tackle the kitchen.

Besides, once she got back to Dottie's, she had homework to do. It was way past time to get back to her search for her long-lost relative. No doubt Ron would turn up something, but in the meantime, she intended to do some cyberspace snooping of her own.

And while she was at Sally's, she could ask around a bit. She'd tried with LeRoy, but he'd been a dead end. It was like walking a tightrope. If she was too subtle, she couldn't unearth anything. Too specific, and she'd have the paparazzi swarming the town.

They were almost an inevitability at some point. But not yet.

She swung through Sally's door. Who knew? She might get lucky.

* * *

Two hours later, Annelise stood in the center of her living room, a huge grin on her face. Dottie, bless her heart, had been true to her word. When Annelise arrived with the furniture truck, her apartment had been emptied of all the old pieces. Curtis, Dottie's neighbor, had stored everything in the shed.

Now, the new-to-her pieces were scattered around the rooms, bringing some much needed color and pizzazz to the space. Her mother would have a fit that she'd bought secondhand furniture, but, really, when you thought about it, what were antiques except really, really old used furniture?

She'd chosen Tiffany-blue for her walls and wanted to start painting in the worst way, but her body simply refused. She'd used muscles today she hadn't known existed.

Instead, dressed in a pair of soft, white cotton shorts and a pale yellow ribbed tank top, she grabbed a cold soda from the fridge, popped the top, and plopped down on her new sofa with one of Dottie's cookies and her laptop. She'd opened the windows when she came home, and a breeze

wafted in, fluttering the white gauze drapes she'd found at
Sadler's. LeRoy'd hung them for her before he and the boys
left. The scent of roses drifted up from Dottie's garden.

And all was well with the world.

Well, almost. She hadn't turned up any clues about her
aunt, but she would.

She deleted four unread e-mails from Doug and lost herself in her research.

A knock sounded at the door.

Startled, she jerked upright, nearly spilling the last of her
drink. It was dark. Who in the world would be visiting this
late? Had she locked up when the guys left?

Setting the can on the kitchen counter, pulse racing, she
moved to the door and flicked on the porch light.

Cash.

Her heart started its own Texas two-step.

She threw open the door. "Is everything okay?"

"Yep." His gaze traveled over her. "It is now."

"Did your parents have a good flight?"

He nodded. "They did."

She grinned. "Would you like to come in?"

"I would." He stepped inside, then hesitated. "Something
I've got to get out of the way first, though. And I want it perfectly clear that neither of us is on the clock, right?"

"Right."

"Good." He thumbed back his cowboy hat. Then his arms
snaked around her, drawing her close. Very slowly, green
eyes intent, he lowered his head, sniffed her neck, and sent a
shiver to her core.

"Nice," he murmured.

Her hands fisted in his shirt.

His lips met hers for the briefest of moments, lightly,
softly. He started to pull away, stopped, slanted his lips

across hers again. This time the kiss was that of a starving man, demanding, taking, his tongue tasting hers, dancing with it. Hot and wet.

She trembled. She wanted more. Oh, so much more.

When he lifted his head this time, she ran her tongue over her swollen lips, stared into his desire-darkened eyes, and realized he looked as shaken as she felt.

As he released her, she reached out to steady herself. "Whew."

"I'll second that." Cash's voice was husky. "I had to know if that kiss last night, as brief as it was, was really as potent as I remembered."

"Cash—"

He laid a finger over her lips. "No, don't say anything. Let's leave it alone for now. I actually came by to see if you wanted to go for a ride. It's a beautiful evening."

"A ride? Now?"

"Yeah. You ever take your Harley out at night?"

She shook her head.

"Then, darlin', you don't know what you're missing. The cool wind in your face, the single beam of light slashing through the dark, lighting a narrow path. Everything else hidden. Just you and your machine." He showed his dimples. "I brought my own helmet."

"That was presumptuous."

"Huh-uh. That was being prepared."

She shouldn't. She knew she shouldn't. She had work to do. But, oh, she wanted to give in to the temptation. She played tug-of-war with herself and lost. Her grandpa's sister had been lost for over half a century. One more night wouldn't hurt.

"Let's do it." She reached for the key she'd laid on the small table by the door.

"You got some new furniture." Then he let out a long laugh and crossed to the sofa. "I don't believe it."

"What?"

He ran a hand over the back of the soft, brown sofa. "This was my grandpa's. It's one of the things Vivi dumped when she redid the place. I love this couch." He dropped onto it.

"So do I."

"I'm glad it's here with you. Gramps would be happy, too. He'd have liked you."

In some small pocket of Cash's brain, a warning bell sounded. His grandpa *would* have liked Annie. The same grandpa that wanted him married. Now his sofa had ended up here. If Cash was a superstitious kind of a guy, he'd be worried.

Luckily, he wasn't.

"So change into some jeans and let's go." He sprang up from the couch. "You're gonna let me drive, right?"

"Wrong."

Chapter Eight

Annie, I'm the guy. The guy drives."

"Not always."

"In Texas he does."

She rolled her eyes. "That is so male!"

"There you go. I'm a male."

"It's about control. You're used to being in control."

Hands on his hips, he thought about that. "Yeah, guess I am."

"Well, so am I. And it's my bike." She dangled the keys in front of him. "My keys mean I drive."

"But you don't know where we're going," he argued.

"So you'll be my co-pilot. Direct me. How else am I going to learn my way around?"

He scowled, not at all comfortable with the way this was going down. "Tell you what. Why don't we take the Caddy? Top's down, and it's an amazing night. It'll be nice."

She laughed, the sound curling itself in his belly. "Nice try, but uh-uh. No way. You talked me into a night bike ride, Cash, and that's what I intend to have."

"You might want to think about this."

"Oh, I have." A quick grin lit her face. Then, mimicking *his* stance, she rested her hands on those curvy hips and tilted her head. "You're not afraid to ride with me, are you?"

His eyes narrowed. "Afraid? Me? Not in this lifetime."

"Good."

After he stepped onto the stair landing, she closed and locked the door behind her. Then she headed down the stairs and hopped on her Harley. In the driver's seat. He felt unbelievably silly as he slowly swung his leg and slid behind her. He sure as hell hoped nobody saw him sitting in the sissy seat. "Annie—"

"Hold on, big boy." The bike rumbled to life. She spurted out of the drive so fast he barely had time to wrap his arms around her slender waist.

He held himself stiffly as she navigated her way through the side streets, fuming that she didn't trust him to drive her motorcycle. But then, as they headed out of town along the dark road, the night air wrapped around him, and he began to relax.

Not half-bad. Rather than hands on the controls, his arms were free to slide around Annie. His palms rested on her taut stomach, imagined the soft, warm skin beneath that butter-colored tank. He leaned into her, breathed in her purely feminine scent. Nuzzled her neck just below her helmet.

The bike wobbled and he pulled back, laughing.

Throwing caution to the wind, they wound through narrow back roads as he directed her across his grandfather's land to his little place by the lake. His sanctuary. He didn't often take anyone there.

As it came into view, she slowed. "Oh, Cash. This is incredible."

It was, he thought. The moon hung low, glimmered in the lake. The stately pines that rimmed the far side reflected in the smooth-as-glass dark water. And his house, with its cedar siding and high-pitched cedar-shingled roof, looked like every man's dream. He'd worried when his mother had insisted on planting those daisies flanking the porch and walk. But their white heads glistened in the moonlight and actually added to the place's charm.

He cleared his throat. "I like it."

She turned off her bike, and the two of them sat listening to the bullfrogs, the cicadas, the hoot of an owl off in the distance.

His fingers itched to run along her moon-gilded arms and shoulders, and he found himself wishing he hadn't suggested she change out of those little white shorts before hopping on the bike. His hands itched to tangle themselves in the mass of curls that tumbled free when she removed her helmet.

Instead, he said, "Come on. Let me show you around."

They left the helmets on the bike and walked across the yard to stand by the lake. Before they reached the water's edge, Staubach came barreling toward them, whimpering and shaking with delight.

"I thought you were locked in the house, pal." Cash snagged his collar, and the dog dropped to the ground.

Annie crouched beside him, and the dog wriggled loose from Cash and rolled onto his back. With a laugh, she gave in. "You like this, don't you, you silly thing."

"Nothing silly 'bout having a woman's hands on you."

Their eyes met in the pale light, and he had to remind himself to go slow. To resist the urge to join her on the grass. To fight the almost overwhelming need to put his own hands all over her.

"Up for another ride?" he asked impulsively, spotting the canoe he'd left tethered to his dock.

"Now?"

"Sure, why not?"

She grinned. "Why not?"

"You're staying here, Staubach."

The dog, happy to have his person home, sat on his haunches, tail wagging.

Cash helped her in, then settled himself on the center bench. This time he was driving, by God. His paddle dipped almost silently into the water as they glided toward the middle of the lake.

Overhead, stars winked, and the moon scattered soft light. Not a single cloud drifted by to mar the sky's obsidian perfection.

Totally relaxed, she leaned back, dipping her hand in the cool water, letting her fingers trail as they slipped smoothly along.

"Look," she whispered. Fireflies winked and darted across the water.

Cash angled the paddle back into the canoe and leaned forward. His arm slid around Annie and drew her close. She yipped when the boat rocked.

"Shhh. It's okay. You're safe."

Still, she held on to the sides.

He pried her fingers loose and put her hands on his arms. "Here. Hold on to me."

Before she could protest, he lowered his mouth to hers.

Annie's grip tightened on his biceps. With a sigh, she

leaned closer still, seeming unconcerned when the canoe listed, then righted itself. Her mouth opened, and she gave him everything. He changed the angle and deepened the kiss.

Heart hammering in his chest, Cash finally broke the mind-staggering connection. "Annie—"

She shook her head, laid a finger over his lips. "Don't say anything, Cash. Kiss me again."

With a groan, he did just that. One kiss led to another and another. His hand worked beneath her shirt, ran over skin as soft as dandelion down. The woman smelled like sin and tasted twice as good.

A gust of wind created a small wave, and their canoe rode up and over it.

"Maybe we should take this onshore," he managed.

"Yes." Annie ran a hand through those long, black curls, tucking them behind her ears.

He smiled, noticing her voice wasn't steady. Good thing, 'cause his sure wasn't.

He paddled toward the house, his strokes not nearly as clean now, the ride less smooth as he chopped through the water. He wanted this woman. In his arms. In his bed. Now.

Then what?

Damned if he knew, but he'd worry about that come sunup.

He hopped onto the dock, slipped the knotted rope around the piling, and reached down to help Annie up. Those big, beautiful eyes of hers looked sleepy, heavy-lidded, and sexy as hell. He wondered if they'd make it past the hammock on the porch.

They did. Barely. Staubach whined as Cash closed the door, barring him entry.

Once inside, he drew Annie to him again, his lips hungry to taste her, his hands ravenous to touch. He craved every delicious inch of her. Together, they fell onto the sofa. It wasn't long, though, till they rolled off the cushions onto the soft rug he'd thrown in front of the stone fireplace.

He pulled off his shirt, desperate to feel her hands on him. He hesitated, looked at her for permission. She smiled slowly and, with one quick tug, pulled her own shirt over her head.

God, she was more beautiful than he could have imagined. Her skin glowed in the silver light. Her breasts spilled over the cups of the tiny scrap of lace she wore. On some level, his brain registered that no way in hell had she bought that bra at Sadler's.

His body thrummed. He wanted to bury himself in her and let go. Wanted to make love to her all night long.

Breath ragged, he whispered against her lips. "Annie, I need to get protection. I hadn't planned, hadn't thought— It's upstairs in my nightstand."

He pulled away, leaned back in to drop kisses along her midriff, up her neck. His lips met hers for one last smoldering kiss before he drew away, taking his body heat with him, leaving her chilled despite the sweltering Texas night.

"I'll be one minute." His eyes met hers. "Don't go anywhere."

*   *   *

Annelise lay where she was, watched him take the stairs two at a time, heard his footsteps overhead. Then a drawer opened, but didn't close.

She ran her fingers through already mussed hair. Hair Cash had mussed. She closed her eyes. What had she done? She'd never gone this far. Caught up in the moment, in those killer kisses, she'd forgotten who she was. What was at stake. Why she'd come.

He raced down the stairs and dropped onto the rug beside her. Then he tipped his head, eyeing her warily. "You've changed your mind."

"It's not—"

"You've changed your mind," he repeated.

She reached out and laid her hand on his leg. "We need to talk."

He gave a half laugh and drew away from her touch. "Right now?"

"Right now."

He rolled away from her, onto his back, and threw an arm over his eyes. "All this time, I've been asking questions and you've been avoiding them." Slowly, he pulled his arm away and looked at her. "Now you want to talk?"

She swallowed. What little courage she had began to slip away. "I can't do this, Cash. I have reasons, but—"

He threw her a sharp look. "You said you weren't married."

"No. I most certainly am not." She wrung her hands. "That's definitely not the reason. I'm…I'm sorry. So sorry. And I'm not a tease. Please, believe me. That's not what's going on here."

He said nothing, simply kept those dark green eyes steady on hers.

"I can't do this." She rubbed her temples. "I thought I could, but I can't. And I can't explain. Not now."

"Give me one reason." He held up a finger. "Just one."

"We have to work together." She was grasping at straws and knew it.

"We're not working tonight. We're simply two people who want each other."

"But tomorrow…and the next day…" She averted her eyes.

"That's an excuse. What's the real reason, Annie?" His

voice sounded tired. Deflated. "I've asked you before. What are you running away from?"

She stiffened.

"Shit, Annie. Don't do that. Don't pull away from me. Don't shut down."

He reached for her, but she twisted, avoiding his hands. This was the time. The time to come clean. To tell him everything. It would never be more perfect.

She couldn't. Couldn't admit she was a fraud, an imposter. Couldn't face the betrayal, the disillusionment that would cloud his eyes.

"I'm sorry. I want to go home, Cash. I bought my paint and stuff today, and I really need to pull my apartment together. I have tomorrow off, and I want to get an early start."

Annelise Montjoy, you are a coward.

"We'll go over in the morning, Annie. Together. I'll help you, and that'll make up for me taking you away tonight."

Her resolve splintered around the edges, and she nearly gave in. She craved his kisses, his caresses. His body. Wanted all of this Texas cowboy.

He nestled into her, tucked a stray strand of hair behind her ear. Ran the palm of his hand along her cheek and neckline. "Tomorrow's plenty of time, darlin'," he whispered in her ear. "Tonight is for us. Here."

Oh, God, the man tempted her. But if there was one absolute...She would not give in. Could not. It would be bad enough for him to find out she'd deceived him. How much worse if she took him as a lover tonight? How much deeper the cut?

She straightened. "I'm sorry, Cash. No."

"Fine." A muscle ticced in his jaw. "No big deal."

"Your expression says differently."

"Yeah, well, I'm a big boy." He grabbed his shirt, stuffed

his arms in it. "I can control myself. If a woman says no, I don't go there. I've never forced a woman, and I'm sure not gonna start now. Let's get you home."

He scooped up her shirt, tossed it to her. "You know, Hank told me that, despite your faded jeans, you reminded him of a pampered little rich girl when he first saw you. Damned if he wasn't right."

All the blood drained from her. She licked dry lips. "What?"

"I said—"

"I know what you said," she bit back. "Why?"

"Why? That look you shot me just now was pure ice princess, and believe me, honey, you've got it down pat. Apparently I, your humble servant, have displeased you."

"Don't be ridiculous."

She'd been right, Annelise thought. She should have come clean. But the moment had passed, and instead of doing the right thing, she'd dug herself in deeper, made her lies—albeit by omission—greater. Slipping on her shirt, she stood and tugged it down over the waistband of her jeans.

* * *

Cash could have kicked himself. He'd come close to begging, and the sad truth was that he didn't care. If he hadn't stopped, hadn't run upstairs, this ache in him would be eased. He and Annie would be cuddled up together, enjoying the aftermath of great sex. Instead, he watched her move to the door, her hips swaying enticingly.

"Wait a minute, Annie."

"No. I'm going home."

"I have to go with you," he growled. "My car's at your place, and I'm gonna need it come morning."

"Oh."

The ride back to her apartment was silent and swift. The night no longer held any magic. Even the cicadas seemed to realize there was no reason to sing. Cash held on to the seat and sat ramrod straight.

When she pulled into her driveway, he hopped off, strode over to his car. Hand on the door, he turned. "Hey."

At the base of the stairs, she stopped.

"I almost forgot." He pulled a cell phone out of his back pocket. "For you." He tossed it to her.

Startled, she caught it. "What's this?"

"In case I need to get in touch. Besides, it's a long drive out to the ranch. There's always the possibility of bike trouble, and I don't want you stranded along the road."

She gave him a you've-got-to-be-kidding look. "How do you know I don't already have one?"

He shrugged. "I don't care if you have one or not. It makes no difference. I figure if you won't even tell me your full name, you're sure as hell not going to give me your phone number."

He pointed to the phone in her hand. "I know that one."

He turned his back on her and slipped behind the Caddy's wheel. Forced himself to drive away from the temptation that was Annie.

She wouldn't give an inch. Well, neither would he. For every wall she erected, he'd find a way over. And now, he could call her at midnight if he wanted to. He wouldn't, but knowing he could, while she lay in bed, all warm and tousled from sleep, made him smile.

Cash smacked the steering wheel, fighting off the wish they were home in his bed right now. What a disaster. And the blame lay right in his own never-thought-to-carry-a-condom pocket.

Chapter Nine

A quick call to Ron, using her new cell, had netted no information. She'd learned nothing from the locals. Cash was beyond angry, and she'd gotten next to no sleep. Good morning! Hah!

Annelise took out her mad on the wall, slapping paint on it fast and furiously. But the roller fought back, and in no time, she had blue splatters on her face, in her hair, all over her clothes. She gritted her teeth and glared at the roller. "Go ahead. Cover me in paint. Doesn't matter. I *will* see this job through to the end. I'm not going to be here long, but I refuse to live in a drab box." The roller zigzagged across the wall. "More importantly, I will not give up and go home. I'll finish both this and the job I came to do."

Verdi's *La Traviata* spilled out of her new, very cheap sound system. Stepping back, she studied the partially painted wall and smiled. Yes, she would get it done. Not yet eight o'clock, and already the morning sun poured through her windows, washed over the walls.

What a difference. The color transformed the space. A happy, bright blue, so different from the dingy white, so different from the staid colors in her parents' Boston home. New life zinged through the apartment. She sniffed. It even smelled fresh and clean. She loved it!

Her thoughts wandered to Cash. What would he think of it? Her smile slipped. Damn him, anyway. She'd really looked forward to today. But thinking about last night could really put a damper on her mood if she let it.

Well, not all of last night. Some of it had been pretty fantastic. Her first nighttime motorcycle ride, with the stars above and Cash's arms around her. A cowboy whose kisses topped out the Richter scale.

The end of the evening sucked, though. Big time.

Stooping to cover her roller with more paint, she squealed when someone rapped on the door. Her left hand flew to her chest. Oh, no! Had her parents tracked her down and sent someone to collect her? Whisk her back to Boston?

Well, she wouldn't go.

Cautiously, she swiped at the paint on her face. The slick smear spread farther along her cheek. Why hadn't she picked up some rags for cleanup? Well, too late now, so what the heck.

Her heart thundered as she marched through the kitchen, prepared to do battle. Instead, when she opened the door her mouth simply dropped open. Dressed in jeans and a faded green T-shirt that had, no doubt, once been the color of his beautiful eyes, Cash stood on the landing, two cups of go-coffee and a bag of donuts in his hands. Not Starbucks, but she'd take what she got.

He held them up. "Peace offering?"

Her eyes moved to the bag of donuts. To those long-fingered hands. Remembered what they'd done to her last night. Where they'd been.

He didn't have his cowboy hat on this morning, and his hair curled at his nape. Delicious.

Embarrassed heat crawled up her neck.

He shifted uneasily. "I'm sorry about last night, Annie. I was out-of-line."

"No, you weren't. I—" She pushed at her hair, remembered too late the paint on her hands.

He caught a strand between his fingers. "Nice color."

She gave a strangled half laugh. She felt awkward, didn't know what to do with her hands. This man was her boss. Had come within a hair's-breadth of becoming her lover last night. Her chest tightened. It was hard to breathe.

"I figured if we intended to work together, it might go better if we were actually speaking to each other."

"Cash, I'm the one who needs to apologize." She waved her hand, only then realizing she still held the paint-filled roller. "I overreacted." Stepping to the side, she opened the door wider. "Come in."

Walking back to her paint tray, she bent and laid the roller in it.

"We're okay, then?" He stepped inside, shrinking the already small space.

Annelise nodded.

"Okay, so it's water under the bridge. Nice look, by the way." He nodded at her paint-splattered face.

"Argh, pretend you can't see me. That I'm invisible. I'm a mess! There's more blue on me than on the wall. How anybody paints for a living is beyond me. And why would they wear white to do this?"

Sniffing appreciatively at the coffee, she said, "Mmm, heaven."

"Thought I could give you a hand with the painting."

Casually, he leaned toward her, made a big to-do out of searching for a paint-free spot, then gave her a friendly peck on the cheek. "Sleep well?"

"No." Her pulse sped up in response to his closeness, the brief touch of his lips. The crisp, masculine smell of him. "You?"

"Nope. And I woke with the roosters this morning." He stared down at the toes of his scuffed boots. "I really am sorry I got so short-tempered last night."

"It wasn't your fault, Cash. It was mine." She stumbled. *Now. Tell him now.* "I need to—"

"No, Annie. No explanations necessary." He hesitated. "On second thought, maybe you're right. We do need to deal with the elephant in the room."

She frowned and rested her hand on the counter. "What?"

"Sex."

Her brows shot up.

"Or, rather, the lack of it."

Her mouth opened, closed.

"C'mon, Annie. We're both thinking about it. I sure the hell am. That's what kept me up most of the night. I shouldn't have come onto you like I did. I—"

"Don't you dare apologize." She shook her head.

"But—"

"No. Last night was—consensual—as far as it went. When I said stop, you stopped." She eyed him. "Don't tell me you're sorry about what we did."

"Sorry?" He laughed. "Hell, no. Believe me, I enjoyed every second of it. The thing is, Annie—" He swiped his toe across the ugly, cracked linoleum. "I'm as single as a one-dollar bill, and I like it like that. I'm not interested in a relationship."

"Whew!" Annie sighed and rolled her eyes. "Thank God! I was afraid that, well, one kiss and you'd be thinking engagement rings, orange blossoms, and wedding bells. What a relief."

One corner of his lip threatened to tip in a grin. "Anybody ever tell you you've got a smart mouth?"

"I think it's been hinted at once or twice." She swiped her hands on her shorts, leaving new smudges. "Now that we have that sorted out, what do you say we eat? Those donuts are calling my name."

"You're a strange one, Annie."

She grinned. "Thank you."

He jiggled the bag in his hand. "Okay, let's sugar-up for breakfast, then slap some color on the rest of these walls."

Setting the bakery bag on the end of the counter, he squinted at her current work zone. "Looks like you got a good start already."

She gave a muffled grunt as she opened a cupboard door and took down mismatched plates and bright yellow napkins while he literally ripped open the bag of donuts. Mentally, she shook her head. So male.

"I think I'll buy a few throw rugs to cover this horrible green linoleum."

"Good idea. It really needs to be replaced."

"Not today," she said.

Sitting at her kitchen table, they ate and talked about the horses and Hank, about Cash's sister and her kids. It was easy and comfortable. The sun played on his hair, kissing it with golden warmth.

The conversation turned to his parents' trip.

"They brought back all kinds of nonsense. More souvenirs to gather dust. My mother's a collector—of everything." He smiled. "She's all excited about some framed document certifying the biggest oil field find ever in Texas."

Annelise's scalp tingled.

"It's hard to imagine something like that rattling around in a French antique shop, but there you go. It probably ought to be in a museum somewhere. However, if my mom is set on it decorating Dad's office, then that's exactly what it'll do. She generally gets what she wants."

The bite of donut stuck in her throat.

"I think you'll like her, Annie. The two of you are both pigheaded."

"Resolute and strong-minded," she corrected.

Cash snorted. "Whatever." Then he nodded at the last half of the donut she'd laid on her plate. "You gonna finish that?"

She shook her head, and he picked it up, wolfed it down in two bites. Then he stood, crushing the bag, and winged it into the wastebasket across the room. "Okay, let's hit it, sugar. Get this show on the road. First, though, that music's gotta go."

"The music?" Her brow creased. "What's wrong with the music?"

He cupped her chin and tipped her face upward. "Annie, darlin', this is important now, so pay attention. You're in Texas." He wagged a finger in front of her face. "No high-brow classical music allowed in Maverick Junction."

Annelise exhaled a slow breath as he moved away. It was as if his warm fingers still touched her.

He fiddled with the dial till he located a country station.

Tapping the top of the radio, he said, "Now, this is music, Annie. Tim McGraw, Josh Turner, Miranda Lambert, Reba. When we're done with the walls, there's gonna be a quiz. You gotta know who these people are if you're gonna live here."

Again, she shook her head.

"Hey, God's truth." He raised his hand as if taking an oath and then went to work unwrapping a second pan and roller. With his height, he didn't have to climb up and down the stepladder to reach the ceiling and top of the walls, so he did those while she concentrated on the lower half.

He knelt to refill his tray, and a blob of blue dripped from her roller onto his nose.

"Oh, oh." She stood motionless. "It's your own fault," she said quickly. "You should have moved away from where I'm painting."

"Oh, yeah?" Still crouched, he looked up at her. "Maybe I like sharing spaces—and paint."

He moved quickly, burying his head into the curve of her neck. Then he twisted his head back and forth, streaking the paint onto her.

She laughed and pushed away, trying to ignore the heat that flashed through her when his breath skittered along her neck. "I feel so sorry for your mother. You had to have been an awful child, Cash Hardeman." She took several steps back and wiped at the paint with the shoulder of her already-ruined shirt.

"Want help?" He inched toward her, reminding her of an animal bearing down on its prey.

Her heart raced. The man was impossible, too tempting by far. "No. Go paint your wall."

"You sure?"

She nodded, almost sorry when he picked up his roller again.

But four hours later, the walls glistened. Stepping back to admire their handiwork, they high-fived each other.

"I can't believe we're done." Annelise grinned. "This is awesome."

"To say nothing of colorful," Cash said.

"Yes, it is, isn't it?" Her grin grew. "Thank you." She threw her arms around him. "I'm not sure I could have done it alone."

"You would have." He hugged her back, then stepped away. "Somehow, some way. You're one determined lady, Annie. Like I said, pigheaded."

"I'll take that as a compliment. Particularly since you've compared me to your mother."

His green eyes darkened. "It was meant as one."

"Then thank you again."

With the Tiffany blue in the living room/kitchen area, she'd done one accent wall in a softer hue. She'd painted two bedroom walls the quieter blue and two in cream. A nice combination, she thought. The bath was solid Tiffany.

"You planning on wearing sunglasses when you're here?" Hands stuffed into his back pockets, Cash stood in the center of the living room and turned in a circle, taking in the change.

"They're not that bright."

He shrugged. "Guess not."

"Come on." She bumped him with her shoulder. "Admit it. You love them."

His lips drew together. "Honest? The colors aren't what I'd have picked, but they suit you. And that's what's important."

"What colors did you use in your house, Cash?" She blushed and cleared her throat. "I mean...well...I really didn't notice last night."

He laughed. "And I'll take *that* as a compliment. But, no, I guess you wouldn't have. We were otherwise engaged." He wound a piece of hair that had come free of her ponytail around his finger. "Tell you what. How 'bout I have you over for dinner one night? You can see for yourself."

"You cook?"

"I can grill a steak with the best of 'em. And I'll sweet-talk Rosie into throwing together a salad for us."

"That sounds good."

"It's a date, then."

Her pulse skittered. "Yes. Yes, it is." Her eyes drifted to the Felix-the-Cat wall clock she'd found at LeRoy's. "Are you hungry? I've got a frozen pizza."

"I wouldn't say no."

"All right." She retrieved the pizza from the freezer, removed all the wrappings, and slid it onto a plate. Standing in front of the microwave, she chewed at her lip.

"What's wrong? You gonna nuke that thing or what?" He nodded at the pizza.

"Nuke it?" She frowned.

"Yeah. Cook it."

"Yes, I will, but I need to figure out how this works."

"You can't use a microwave? Where'd you grow up? Mars?"

"Almost. A different world, for sure."

He frowned.

"Kidding," she said. "Just kidding. Every microwave's a little different, you know?"

Cash contemplated that, not sure he believed her. What exactly was going on here? One minute Annie seemed so worldly, the next so naïve and inexperienced.

Riding into Maverick Junction on that Harley of hers, dressed in black leather with those mile-long legs, she'd quite simply been the sexiest woman he'd ever seen. She'd also been cocky and full of attitude. Last night, she'd more than given back everything he gave. Kiss for kiss. Heat for heat. And yet, there'd been something about her that shouted innocence.

A mystery here, and he generally loved a good mystery.

But darned if he could unravel the clues. Not yet, anyway. But he would.

"Need some help with that?"

She set the pizza inside the microwave, closed the door, and cocked her hands on her hips. "Yes, actually, I do."

He crossed the room, pushed a couple of buttons, and watched as the pizza circled inside the microwave. "Not rocket science."

"Guess not, but, well, let's say I wasn't ever expected to do much around my house. Heck, the truth is I was actually discouraged from doing anything."

"Not even zap a pizza in the microwave?"

She shook her head. "No. The microwave was in the kitchen, and the kitchen fell under the cook's domain. I sneaked in once in a while, and she'd feed me cookies or let me lick the beaters, but not often."

"Sounds to me like you had a pretty screwed-up childhood," he said. "The kitchen at the ranch is Rosie's turf, and when I was still living at home, my mom's. But that doesn't mean I didn't learn how to cook."

He wondered again about Annie. Maybe she came from way more money than he'd originally thought because this sounded like some stiff upper crust way of living. That or she had parents with sticks up their butts. Either way, it didn't sound like much fun.

"Didn't you at least make midnight raids on the fridge?"

"No way."

He shook his head. "Downright sacrilegious."

She laughed.

As she set the table with her quirky, mismatched china, he walked over to the TV. "Mind if I turn it on while we wait for the pizza? I didn't catch the stock reports this morning."

"No. Go ahead."

Cash turned to a news station. In the solemn tone reserved for bad news, the anchorman reported, "Annelise Montjoy, absent at the opening of the company's New York branch, was missing yet again today when the family flew to Camp David to meet with the president concerning world oil prices. As the newest board member, she'd been expected to attend."

A full-screen picture of Annie popped up. Behind him, Cash heard Annie's gasp, and a plate thudded onto the table. A buzz started in his mind and blocked the rest of the announcer's words. A caption beneath the photo announced it had been taken while Annie—Annelise—attended a dinner at one of Dubai's extravagant resorts.

Cash swore all the air had been sucked out of the room.

"What the—" He dropped onto the saggy sofa. His head swiveled, and he pointed first at the TV, then at her. "That's you."

She said nothing but nodded as she moved beside him.

"Well, shit. I've had an heiress scooping manure in my stables?"

She made a sound, halfway between a laugh and a sob.

"I don't get it. Why in the hell are you shoveling manure when you could buy my ranch ten times over?"

"Partly because I want to prove myself."

He reached for her hand, and she jerked it away. Without a word, he took it in his again and turned it palm up. He studied the calluses on it.

"Well, darlin', I'd have to say you're doing one rip-roaring job of it." He dropped her hand. "Guess that explains the microwave and all the rest of everyday living you're so clueless about."

His brows knit as he rose and faced her, legs braced. "You've always had a bevy of servants at your beck and call, haven't you? Always had someone right there to take care of your every need."

Temper flared in her eyes. "It's not my fault. Not something I chose. And I've never once played the poor little rich girl card."

No. As much as he hated to admit anything that would earn her points right now, Cash had to give her kudos for wading right into the deep end. For working her butt off. For working till her hands blistered and her back ached.

He knew when to back off. "I didn't really mean that."

"Yes. You did."

He blew out a loud breath. He wouldn't win this one. Still...Incredulous, he stared from her to the TV, back to her, to the TV. "You're really Vincent Montjoy's granddaughter? *The* Vincent Montjoy?"

"Yes."

"Why didn't you tell me who you are?"

"I did."

"No, you didn't. Annelise. Just Annelise."

"That's my name."

"Even when I told you about the document my mom bought? You knew it was the Montjoy oilfields I was talking about. You didn't think that maybe you should say, 'Oh, by the way, Cash, that would have been my great-grandfather's company'?"

Annie's jaw tightened. "I tried to tell you earlier. This morning. You said no explanations were needed."

"I think this comes under a slightly different heading."

"Only because you want it to."

Cash shook his head. "No wonder you hemmed and hawed when I wanted your work info."

"You never came right out and asked me what kind of work I'd done before."

"Would you have told me?"

She didn't hesitate. "No."

A stream of curses poured out of him and smoked the air.

"Nice mouth," she said.

He simply stared at her for a full minute. Then his gaze dropped to her lips. "Speaking of nice mouths, you've been using that one to tell some real tall tales, haven't you? Or should we call a spade a spade? You've been lying to me."

She straightened. "I have not!"

"Oh, yeah? You suffering from selective amnesia, maybe?"

Her cheeks flushed, and he swore again.

"You don't have, like, an entourage or something that travels with you?"

"Usually, yes." Her voice had gone prim. "I'm never alone...or rarely. Because kidnapping has always been a real threat, I don't go anywhere without bodyguards. Or I didn't. Until now. I escaped."

"You escaped. And came to Maverick Junction." He shook his head. "So does this mean when Daddy tracks you down here with me—"

"First, I'm not actually *with* you. Second, I called my cousin, Sophie. She called my dad. He knows I'm safe."

Cash tried to put himself in her dad's shoes. He seriously doubted a single phone call via third person would be enough to satisfy Edmund Montjoy.

"Is some kind of bodyguard SWAT team going to surround my ranch and start shooting at us when they find you?"

Now, laughter did bubble out of her.

He fumed. "Hey, I'm not kidding, Annie. Damn it, I've got a lot of people at the ranch, people I'm responsible for."

She quieted, but the humor remained in her eyes. "No. No gunfights or standoffs."

His finger jabbed the air. "I specifically asked you if you were in trouble—"

"You asked if I was wanted by the law."

"Same thing," he shot back.

"No." She shook her head. "It isn't. I didn't break any laws. I didn't do anything wrong. I'm twenty-six years old and can do as I please."

"Yeah, sounds like it to me."

"You're being mean."

He was feeling mean. He hit Cancel on the microwave and leaned against the fridge. Annie sat across from him in a wicker chair she'd bought, hands folded in her lap. White showed on her knuckles.

"How can I fix this? What would you like to know?" she asked quietly.

He rubbed at his temple. "For God's sake, Annie, your grandfather is Vincent Montjoy."

"Yes."

He dropped into one of the kitchen chairs, and his leg jiggled impatiently. "There isn't a person in these parts who doesn't know that name. His father, your great-grandfather, discovered one of the biggest oil fields this side of the pond."

"He did, yes. But that doesn't change anything. I'm still the same person I was fifteen minutes ago. Before you knew my last name. My family background."

"So what are you doing here, Annie? The truth."

For a few seconds he didn't think she'd answer. Then, very quietly, she said, "My grandfather is sick."

"I remember hearing that, thinking that money couldn't fix every problem." He glanced at her. "Sorry. That sounded cold. I didn't mean it that way. He's your grandpa. I know how hard this is for you. But that still doesn't answer the question. In fact, it makes things even more of a puzzle. If he's sick, I'd think you'd want to be with him. Instead, you ran away."

"It's a long story." She looked out the window, then turned her big blue eyes back to him. "But I didn't run away. Not from him or the situation. I'm trying to help."

"By leaving home? Making him and your parents worry?"

She loosened her ponytail and ran her fingers through her hair. "It probably seems that way. On the surface, anyway."

"Take my word for it. It does." He rubbed his chin.

"I told you I called Sophie."

He shrugged.

"Grandpa has leukemia. All the time he's spent around oil refineries and petroleum, the exposure to benzene..." She sighed. "He needs a bone marrow transplant, and none of us are a match. I'm here to find his half sister. To talk her into being tested."

"Okay." He blew out a breath and settled back on the couch. "You couldn't call her?"

"No one knows exactly where she is."

"So why not hire a private investigator to track her down?"

"I'm not sure she actually exists."

Cash put a hand to his forehead. "Annie, this is beginning to feel like 'Who's on first?'"

"I know, I know, but it's really complicated."

"Ahhh."

"Ah is right. And for reasons only he knows, my grandfather has expressly forbidden anyone to search for this long-lost half sister of his."

"So you're disobeying him."

"Yes. I have to. Grandpa says when his time is up, he'll go—even if this half sister might be a match." Her voice broke. "Might be able to save his life."

Her mouth twisted in distress. "In my book, he's almost

the lucky one. He'll be done with it. We'll be left here with regrets and what-ifs. We'll be left to miss him."

Cash's heart lurched. He understood only too well the pain of being left behind, of losing a grandfather. Didn't he wish every day for a few more hours with his?

Annie tucked her feet up under her. "So, anyway, that's my big secret. And here I am in Maverick Junction, Texas. Hiding out from my family, and trying, against my grandfather's wishes, to save his life. My father and mother, for reasons beyond me, have agreed to go along with his fatalistic stance."

She made a face. "I can't do that. I can't just throw up my hands and let him die. If there's anything I can do, any possibility of help, I have to give it a shot. I'll be the first to admit I have a lot of faults, but being a quitter isn't one of them."

"No, you're not." He'd watched her work in the barn, with the horses. Watched her keep going way past exhaustion. She'd never once cried uncle.

"Why doesn't this half sister fly to Boston to help on her own? Surely she watches the news. She has to know what's going on."

"She might not realize she's his relative."

His brows drew together.

"She was, as they used to say, born on the wrong side of the blanket."

"Okay. Got it." Cash tapped his fingertips together. "Geez, Annie. This is like a recap of one of the soaps Rosie watches."

"I know, but, believe me, it's real. And it's my life."

"I gotta tell you, darlin', for what it's worth, if it was me, I'd do anything possible to find that old gal."

"Thanks." Her eyes misted. "But Vincent Montjoy isn't like anybody else I know."

"So what happens now?"

"I have a friend, a researcher, doing some digging. I've been scouring the Internet, trying to find a lead since I caught whiff of her. I've made some inquiries around town. If she's real, I'll find her."

"You think she lives here in Maverick Junction?"

"No."

"Close to here?"

"Maybe."

"You're not going to tell me any more, are you?"

"Not yet. I'm sorry, Cash."

"It's okay." He got up and walked to the sink, braced his hands on it, and stared out the window. He didn't know what to think. Annie obviously didn't trust him enough—yet—to share. He turned back to her.

"So, you're not a down-and-out lady in distress." It wasn't a question.

Annie shook her head, studied her fingernails.

"You're actually a billionaire oil tycoon's heir." Despite his good intentions, anger bubbled up inside him. If there was anything he despised, it was deceit. Look at Vivi. A prime example of the mess a person could land in with a single bad decision.

He'd been played, and he didn't like it. "When I offered you an advance on your salary, you must have laughed your head off at my gullibility." He couldn't keep the temper from his voice, didn't even try.

"No, I didn't." She flicked a glance at him, then looked away again. She didn't defend her actions any further.

"You didn't figure I had the right to know who you were. Didn't need to know what was going on in your life. After all, I'm just the country-bumpkin cowboy who gave you a job. Tried to help you out because I thought you needed a hand."

"A country bumpkin?" Annelise's stomach churned and her own temper flared. "I *never* felt you were less than me. Never treated you that way."

"Don't give me that bull." His jaw tightened. "Pretty hard to write down heiress for your last position held, isn't it? What lie did you intend to tell me next, Annie?"

She set her mouth in a tight line. She refused to fight with him—which only seemed to make him madder.

"You used me."

That did it. Anger boiled to the surface and spilled over. "I did not!"

"Oh, yeah, you did."

She jumped up from the chair and poked him in the chest. "You have no idea."

"Then tell me." He stepped so close their toes bumped, then poked *her* in the chest.

She gasped.

"Oh, excuse me," he snarled. "The little rich girl's body is off-limits? I don't think so." His arm snaked out, grasped her, and pulled her in. His mouth covered hers, hot and ready. His tongue invaded, plundered.

And, God help her, she loved it. Here was real. Cash wasn't kissing the Montjoy heiress. He was kissing Annie, the ranch hand. He was kissing the *real* her.

And wasn't it glorious?

Her fingers snaked through his hair. Her mouth gave back as good as it got.

Abruptly, he pulled away. Setting her away from him, his face closed and shuttered. "Apparently, I'm good for something, huh? A quick roll in the hay, maybe, but not good enough for the Montjoy family."

"That's not fair!"

"None of this is."

"Well, you won't need to worry about it anymore because I quit."

"You can't quit. You're fired."

"I quit first."

"Enjoy your life, Annie."

"Go to hell, Cash."

"Can't. Too much to do. I just lost a ranch hand."

He turned on the heels of his cowboy boots and stalked out, leaving her alone in the middle of her beautiful, cheerful room. She stamped her foot and hit Power-Off on the TV remote, then took the cold pizza from the microwave and dumped it in the trash.

She was unemployed. Damn.

Chapter Ten

She'd sooner pass up a new pair of Christian Louboutin shoes than sit here in her apartment and feel sorry for herself. Wallowing was *not* Annelise Montjoy's style.

But then, neither was that fight she'd had with Cash. She'd been trained in the arts of diplomacy and negotiations straight out of the womb. So what had happened?

She'd been herself. That's what had happened. She'd dared to show him the real her—warts and all. She'd never, ever allowed herself to do that. But Cash, simply by being Cash, allowed her that freedom. She didn't need to hide behind social niceties with him. Didn't need to be anyone but herself.

It felt so good not to have to hold back, to think before she spoke. Before she acted.

And she'd screwed it up.

Well, no way would she sulk about it.

Nothing cured the funks like a long soak. Drawing a bath, she jumped when her cell phone rang. Smiling, she grabbed for it. She knew once Cash had time to really think it over, he'd understand.

But it wasn't Cash. It was Ron. He'd hit a brick wall. His research had dead-ended. She wanted to cry, wanted to scream at the unfairness of it all. Instead, she thanked him politely and hung up.

Carefully, she laid the phone on the edge of the sink. Misery seeped into her heart, her bones, and the tears fell. Sinking into the frothy water, she cried as she washed away both the paint streaks and Cash's scent. Half an hour later, wrapped in a towel, she opened her closet door and studied her choices through tear-reddened eyes.

A week ago, she'd stood in a closet almost the size of this whole apartment, surrounded by a veritable warehouse of designer outfits. No more. Her choice. Shoving aside a faint wistfulness, she plucked one of her two clean T-shirts off the hanger and slid into it and a pair of jeans, then walked barefoot into the kitchen. Time to get to work.

Twenty minutes later, she sat in front of her computer. Back in Boston, she'd already Googled, searched Wikipedia and Yahoo!, and run a gazillion AOL searches. She'd rummaged through the Mormon Church genealogy records, dug through ancestry and family search websites. What could she do that she or Ron hadn't already done?

There had to be someone left, someone in Lone Tree who would have an answer for her. So, even though she'd gone over and over them, she had to believe something would turn up. No matter how long she dug, though, she couldn't find anything on family members still living in Lone Tree.

Knowing the futility of it, she typed in another search and her heart beat a little faster. Unbelieving, she stared at her screen. She'd found a casual mention of wildcatter Davis

"Driller" Montjoy in an article about Lone Tree's history. A cross-reference at the end directed her to another site.

The page popped up on her screen, and she couldn't hold back the smile. The text contained a brief narrative about a housekeeper who'd saved Driller's life. Her great-grandfather, at the age of thirty-five, had suffered an attack of appendicitis. No big deal now, but Annelise understood the nearly hundred intervening years made a huge difference in medical care—and its availability.

Driller's timing couldn't have been worse. According to the article, a tropical storm had blown through the area several days before, and the then dirt road had become impassable, literally cutting them off from town and the only doctor.

Lucky for old Driller, his housekeeper had nursed at a Dallas hospital before coming to work for him. She'd performed a crude appendectomy right there at the house. Annelise cringed at the thought, then saved the information on her computer.

She stood, stretched, then walked to the fridge and pulled out a soda. After rubbing the ice-cold can over her cheeks and neck, she popped the top and took a long drink. Blowing a strand of hair from her eyes, she went back to the computer. If she and Ron had missed this article, maybe they'd overlooked something else.

After giving it another hour, she signed off. No amount of crawling around on websites had unearthed anything more.

But…she had something. Finally, an avenue to explore. Excitement crept through her again as she played with this new information. While she still didn't have a concrete lead and no actual name or address to visit, this was a start, wasn't it?

Antsy, unable to stay in her apartment, she grabbed her

helmet and motorcycle keys and headed out of town. Time to get off her duff and go Montjoy hunting.

Every day since she'd hit Maverick Junction's city limits, she'd promised herself she'd drive over to Lone Tree. Yet something always got in the way. She'd had no idea simply taking care of the basics of life could be so time consuming. And the job at Whispering Pines took up a lot of her hours. Maybe that had been a mistake.

Way down deep inside, though, she knew she wouldn't do it any differently given another chance.

She headed south, the vista unchanging except for random patches of bluebonnets and Indian paintbrush. Geez, Louise, could it get any hotter? Dust devils swirled along the side of the road, and a sense of urgency and expectation whipped through her.

When the Lone Tree city-limits sign came into view almost an hour later, she gave a whoop of joy. That died fairly quickly, though. Looking around, she had a pretty good idea why they'd named it Lone Tree. Hardly more than a wide spot in the road, the town's starkness intimidated her.

She drove slowly down Main Street on her Harley. None of Maverick Junction's charm overflowed into Lone Tree. No awnings welcomed shoppers respite from the sun. No pretty flowers smiled from barrels along the sidewalk.

One thing for sure, though. She didn't need to fight for a parking spot. Pulling alongside the curb, Annelise released the kickstand and stared up and down the street, trying to decide where to start now that she'd arrived. Amazing to think Grandpa had actually been born here, started school here. She'd never known her great-grandfather, but from the stories told about his almost obsessive-compulsive need for perfection, he had to have been more than happy to see the backside of this town.

A sleek black cat slunk in and out of doorways, wrapping itself around a light pole. Did it have a home, she wondered, or was it a stray? The cat made its way to her, and Annelise threw a leg over her bike and knelt beside it to rub its chin. No, this feline definitely wasn't homeless. Up close, it appeared well fed and way too well taken care of to be living on the streets.

Speaking of well fed, after she'd tossed the pizza she had made for her and Cash, she never had eaten lunch. She frowned, thinking about her first few minutes in Maverick Junction. She'd headed into Sally's Place, and that's where she'd met Cash.

Her stomach plummeted. Cash was so angry with her, and she could blame no one but herself. She should have been up-front with him—or at least confessed at his cabin who she was. She couldn't have handled things any worse if she'd tried.

Cash wasn't the reason she'd come here, though. She'd driven to Lone Tree for her grandfather. His life depended on her finding his sister. Why not start with the local café? She could squash her building hunger while, hopefully, ferreting out information.

She hung her helmet on the sissy bar and removed her small purse from the saddlebag. Two doors down, the Cowboy Grill appeared to be the only choice for Lone Tree restaurants. Without giving herself more time to think, she walked inside. She saw no one. Not another soul. Not sure what that said about the food, fearing the worst, she reminded herself it didn't matter. She hadn't expected a five-star restaurant. She almost laughed. Good thing, that.

But somebody had to be here. A waitress or a cook? A busboy? Somebody. This felt creepy, like being the sole survivor after a nuclear attack. Or falling into the pages of a Stephen King novel.

Forcing herself to move farther inside, she headed for the counter, a place she always avoided. If she really wanted to chat, though, she needed to step outside her comfort zone—as if she hadn't already. Taking a seat at the bar, she plunked her purse down on the stool beside her.

"Hello?" she called. "Anyone here?"

A gruff-looking guy with a day's heavy stubble and a food-smeared apron swung out from a side room. He grabbed a plastic-coated menu from a stack and plopped it down in front of her.

"Sorry. Didn't hear you come in." He nodded at her. "What'll you have to drink?"

"A huge glass of ice water, please."

"Got that. Though if we don't get rain soon, that might change."

Within seconds he returned with a gigantic red pebbled-plastic glass, condensation trailing down its sides. He set it in front of her. "Don't guess I've seen you before, so welcome to Lone Tree. Name's Oliver." His voice sounded like a garbage can rolling across a gravel pit.

"Thanks, Oliver. I'm...Annie." Annelise smiled, unaccountably comfortable with this rough-edged, burly man. Hope sprouted inside her. Maybe she'd get lucky with Oliver, and he'd have some information that would help her. Since she seemed to be his only customer, they should have plenty of time to chat.

"Well, Annie, looks like you're stuck with me." He waved his counter cloth toward the window. "You hit smack-dab in the middle of our downtime. I sent Judy out to run a few errands, so I'll be the one takin' your order *and* doin' the cookin'."

"I'm good with that." She took a long drink of water, then turned her attention to the menu.

Very similar to Sally's, it had a few Lone Tree twists. Ollie's half-pounder took center stage. Annelise decided to forgo that and ordered a turkey sandwich with a side salad.

Waiting for her meal, she focused on the song coming over the small radio on the back counter. Reba. One of the songs she'd listened to earlier with Cash. Score one for her quiz.

Tranquility settled over her. The hurt from her argument with Cash, the niggling doubts she'd not find her relative, the anger her parents and grandfather undoubtedly sent her way—all of it scurried off to a dark corner of her mind. She hadn't a doubt that this diner, with Oliver at the griddle, was exactly where she was supposed to be right at this moment. It felt safe, a place a person would want to spend time.

Leaning her elbows on the counter, she watched Oliver. Efficient and competent. He'd obviously been doing this a long time. No wasted effort. Every move purposeful.

And maybe, just maybe, he knew her lost aunt—or knew something about her. If not, well, she'd enjoy herself and the summer afternoon.

She'd call Sophie later for an update on her grandfather.

Oliver set a plate in front of her, and she was embarrassed when her stomach rumbled.

"Sorry." She laughed. "I had half a donut for breakfast and skipped lunch. This looks great."

It did. Two slabs of homemade-looking bread piled high with shaved turkey, tomatoes, and lettuce. Yum.

"You passin' through?" Oliver asked, hands on hips, watching as she took her first bite.

Nodding, she chewed and swallowed. "Yes, I am. Actually, I'm working as a ranch hand at Whispering Pines over in Maverick Junction."

"Boy, you're a long way from there. You drive all those miles for a late lunch?"

She shrugged, chewed another bite, and calculated how best to broach her subject. "I had the day off. After I took care of some things this morning, I thought I'd take a ride."

He glanced out the window and whistled. "That's some sweet bike. Nothin' better than a hog." He swiped at the already clean counter. "What brings you to Texas? Obviously, you're not from these parts."

She grinned. "What was your first clue?"

He grinned back. "You don't exactly sound like a native. I'd say you've got a little Boston in you."

"You'd be right." Oliver had handed her the opening, and Annelise ran with it. "Actually, though, my family used to live here in Lone Tree. So in a roundabout way, I am from here."

She hesitated. Here was the root of her problem. If she gave him her last name, it wouldn't be long till he told someone who told someone, and quicker than a Tom Brady smile at a cocktail party, the press would be breathing down her neck. If she *didn't* give her name, how could she get help tracking down her relative?

"Any of your people still around?"

Her mouth went dry, and she took another, much-needed drink of water. "I'm not sure."

"Well, if you're interested in findin' out, I know an old gal who might be able to help you. I'm no good with names, but I can tell you who is. Miss Thelma Hanson. She lives a couple miles outside of town on the old family homestead. Miss Thelma and her family have been here since before Texas was a state. If your kin lived here, she'd know about it."

Hope stirred in Annelise. "Oh, I'd love to visit her."

"Miss Thelma's gettin' on, so it might be better if you called instead of surprisin' her."

She nodded.

"Let me give you her phone number." He scrawled it on his order pad and tore off the page, handing it to her. "Here you go. Tell her Ollie down at the Cowboy Grill told you to give her a call."

"I'll do that. Thanks." Surprised, she looked down at her plate—her empty plate. She'd eaten every crumb.

"Want some dessert? My wife made a lemon meringue pie today. Ain't nobody makes them better."

"Oh, I'd love a piece, Oliver, but I'm too full. Maybe next time."

"Good enough. Look forward to seein' you again and hearin' what you find out from Miss Thelma."

"Why don't I give you my phone number, too, just in case you think of anything else that might help?"

"Sure thing. I'll stick it in the register here."

She grabbed a napkin and jotted down the number for the cell Cash had given her. "Here you go."

Annelise paid for her meal and thanked the owner again. Tucking the slip of paper in her purse, she stepped out into the Texas heat. Eyeing the sky, she figured Miss Thelma would have to wait. As much as she wanted to head over there right now, it was too late to visit her today. It would take a good hour to get home. Considering the wild game, the livestock, and armadillos that made a habit of wandering onto the roads, she didn't want to tackle the trip in the dark.

Did Thelma Hanson hold the key to her family's history?

No Texas waltz here. Anticipation did a lively Irish jig in her stomach.

How would she stand the wait? It was like being handed a beautifully wrapped gift and then told you had to hold it for a day or two before opening it.

Whatever gem lay inside would still be there, though, wouldn't it?

Chapter Eleven

The morning sun barely skimmed the treetops when Annelise turned off the highway and onto Hardeman Lane. Cinders crunched beneath the wheels of her Harley. Pausing on the side of the drive, she breathed deeply and revved her bike. Not yet seven o'clock and she was already tired. Between her fight with Cash and the new lead from Oliver, she'd barely slept. Her mind refused to leave either alone.

How would she make it through the workday ahead? But then, maybe she wouldn't have to. Cash might send her packing the minute he laid eyes on her. No going back. One more breath, then she drove through the massive wrought-iron archway announcing Whispering Pines Ranch.

How had things gotten so messed up?

Well, at least she had a backup plan for the day in her hip pocket. If Cash refused to listen to reason, she'd drive to Lone Tree this morning. To Ms. Thelma's.

And be sorrier than she could say.

Heading down the long driveway, dust boiled up behind

her. She slowed to a crawl and studied the huge red barn, the weathered sheds, the paddocks with horses already grazing.

The big white house sat at the end of the lane, pots of geraniums marching up its wide steps. Roses trailed over a trellis and added another splash of red. The old house looked like it wanted to wrap you in a warm hug. The same sure couldn't be said for the woman who lived inside. Vivi wasn't likely to be putting out the welcome mat for her anytime soon.

Yesterday, she'd been all fired up, excited about making her new home truly hers. The fact that Cash had shown up, stayed to help, and share the day had been, well, the absolute icing on the cake. Until their fight.

After they'd finished slinging hurtful words at each other and he'd left, she'd switched the radio from his country-and-western station back to her classical music. Even though her heart hadn't been in it, she'd knuckled down and plodded on, putting the apartment together.

What a shame. The makeover deserved more than a half-hearted effort. She'd wanted it to be perfect, the paint along with every single piece of furniture, every doodad, every piece of fabric.

She'd agonized over the color, then given into whimsy. Tiffany's in New York was one of her favorite places in the world. The amount of time she'd spent there, the money she'd left there, the number of little blue bags she'd carried out—embarrassing.

This morning, though, the sun barely peeking over the horizon, she woke up feeling as though she was inside one of Tiffany's jewel boxes. Trimmed in cream and oh, so fresh smelling. It made her smile. Sunlight crept through the gauzy ivory curtains and reflected off the secondhand crystal lamp she'd placed on the now cream-colored night-stand.

Dottie, dressed in a more subdued than usual pink and white housedress, had wandered upstairs last night, her arms filled with flowers from her garden. Texas bluebonnets, daisies, foxglove, and some baby's breath. Arranged in a thrift-store vase, they looked better than any florist's bouquet.

Annelise had held her breath while Dottie moved from room to room, her hand trailing over surfaces, her eyes moving constantly from one area to the next. Finally, unable to wait any longer, she'd blurted, "Do you like it?"

"Like it?" Her landlady laughed. "Honey, this place hasn't ever been this pretty." She'd patted Annelise's cheek. "You did good. Real good."

High praise.

Lying in bed, she'd hugged herself. She'd done it. With lots of elbow grease and a hodgepodge of new-to-her treasures from LeRoy's, she'd transformed the dingy place. Expunged Roger Barry's presence.

Annelise Montjoy lived here now. Maybe.

She'd originally come to Maverick Junction because she thought it would be a good jumping-off spot for her search. Close enough for access, but far enough away to hide her true agenda. After she met with Ms. Thelma, there'd be no need for subterfuge. Come to that, there'd be no need to remain in Maverick Junction—except, if she was totally honest with herself, for Cash.

If he wouldn't speak to her, wanted nothing more to do with her, or worse, insisted she leave—Well, that was too painful to think about. And she refused to examine too deeply the reason for that.

She hoped he hadn't really meant it when he fired her

yesterday. Besides, how could he fire her? He wasn't even paying her. So, in reality, she was volunteering. A volunteer couldn't be fired. Could she? But he could accuse her of trespassing. Maybe even have her arrested.

But he wouldn't. Would he?

She had to talk to Thelma Hanson. And the less anyone knew about her, the closer she could get to the truth. So much was riding on this. Another couple of days and she'd know.

They needed rain. Everything was as dry as a two-day-old croissant. Morning and night, she practically bathed in the cheap moisturizer she'd picked up at Sadler's. If she stayed here much longer—and, God, she prayed she could—she'd have to start buying the stuff by the vat.

Since, in this case, discretion seemed the better part of valor, she pulled up behind the barn and parked her bike. She went in through the back door and refused to think of it as sneaking in.

Bent over a saddle, Hank rubbed oil into the heavy leather. He glanced up when she walked in. Then he took a good hard look and straightened. "What's ailin' you?"

She jammed her hands into her jeans pockets. "Nothing. Why?"

"'Cause you look like forty miles of bad road, that's why."

Her mouth fell open.

"Yeah, yeah, I know. Hell of a thing to say to a pretty gal like you. But, Annie, if you so much as looked in a mirror before headin' out here today, you gotta know I'm tellin' the truth."

She blew out a breath and scuffed the toe of her boot over some loose straw. "I didn't get much sleep." Taking her hands out of her pockets, she ran them over her hair. "Do I really look that bad?"

Hank nodded toward the small bathroom. "Mirror's in there."

"Well, I—"

Cash strode through the front door, Staubach at his heels. "Hey, Hank, do you know where—" His gaze landed on Annelise and turned hard. "What are you doing here?"

"Working."

"No, you're not. I told you, you're fired."

Staubach danced around her legs, and she leaned down to rub his head, his chin. She swore the dog grinned.

"Staubach, get over here." Cash snapped his fingers and pointed at a spot beside him.

The dog dropped heavily onto the floor at Annelise's feet. Cash glared at him as Staubach's tail wagged happily.

"Traitor," he muttered.

"I love working here, Cash."

"Oh? So just like that, I should keep you on? Consider everything okay?"

She shrugged.

"You held back a few cards, Annie. Some trumps. You played me for a fool."

Out of the corner of her eye, she saw Hank pick up the rag he'd been using on the saddle and disappear into a backroom. Coward.

Cash swore. Nothing even remotely hospitable or sympathetic showed in the eyes that met hers. "I came to you yesterday morning, Annie, hat in hand, and apologized for making unwanted advances."

"They weren't unwanted." Her voice sounded small and tentative, even to herself.

"Come on, Annie. Get real."

"Oh!" Frustrated, she slapped her thigh. "You get real, Cash. You know darn well that both of us actively partici-

pated the other night at your place. We're equally account-
able for what went down there. Cliché or no, it does take two
to tango, and I was every bit as caught up in that dance, in
the moment, as you."

"I can't deny that, no." He wrapped a hand around a stall
post and leaned a shoulder against it. "But you're the one
who hit the brakes. Why? Pretty simple, really, now that I've
got the facts. You're out of my league, Annie…and we both
know that. Me, I'm comfortable in cowboy boots and jeans.
Beer in a bottle. You're used to designer clothes and diamonds. Champagne in fancy crystal flutes."

He shook his head, the muscles of his jaw working. "I
have to wonder what you're doing here. Besides the grandpa
thing. Are you looking for a good time? Bored and hunting
for a new experience? Admit it, darlin'. You don't care one
whit about me. I read the tabloids. Your highfalutin friends
chew up men like me and spit them out. Maybe you figured
it'd be fun to have a romp with an honest-to-God cowboy."

"Romp?" Heat flared in her cheeks. She glanced around,
wishing she could lay her hands on something to throw
at him. "I thought, I truly thought, you saw the real me.
The real Annelise Montjoy." She swallowed hard. "But you
don't. You're no different than anyone else."

"Annie—"

"Don't you dare Annie me. You can cheapen what happened between us, but I won't. You honestly think I'm
laughing at you?" She closed her eyes, pinched the bridge of
her nose. Making herself meet his eyes again, she said, "If I
laughed, it was *with* you because I was having fun. Enjoying
your company. I never, ever laughed *at* you."

She opened her mouth to say more, but in one swift
move, he pushed away from the post. "Bullshit! You're
good, Annie. Very good. You're quite the little actress, and

you've taken on a lot of roles the last few days. So the question is—how do I know which one is the real you? Or, for that matter, if any of them are."

He tipped his head, and his eyes roamed over her. "I like the woman I met in the diner. The woman who slings muck in my barn and smears paint on her cheeks. But is that you?"

Her chest hurt. She could barely breathe. "You're right, Cash. You *don't* know me. Not if you have to ask that question."

"Thanks for the newsflash, darlin'." His fists clenched at his sides. "What a sucker I am. I watched you ride into town and thought you were the prettiest thing I'd ever laid eyes on. But you looked so lost. Right away, I jumped to the conclusion you needed help. So what did I do? Made sure you got settled somewhere safe, even helped you paint the damn apartment. And all the while, you don't bother to tell me you're Davis Driller Montjoy's great-granddaughter. That you could buy and sell the state of Texas without coming up for air." He kicked the nearest stall and had several of the horses whinnying. "Christ, Annie, that's more than a small oversight. I feel stupid, and I gotta tell you, I don't like the feeling."

Annelise took several steps toward him.

"Stop." He held up one hand. "Stay right where you are. I'm not in an especially friendly mood right now."

"I'm not afraid of you, Cash. Not even the tiniest bit." She walked closer. "I know you."

He removed his cowboy hat, raked his fingers through his hair, then settled the Stetson back in place. "You probably do know me a whole heck of a lot better than I know you."

He leaned forward and crawled right into her face. "And why is that?" He paused. "Oh, yeah. That would be because I was honest with you. Truthful."

Her heart thumped like a flat tire on macadam. But she couldn't back down. Not now. If she did, she'd have to leave, and she really, really didn't want to do that.

Drawing in a deep breath, she closed the distance between them. Now, they were nose to nose and toe to toe. "I *couldn't* tell you the truth. Not the first day we met. I didn't know you, Cash. The paparazzi are beating the bushes for me. There's a big price tag on my head. A lot of money to be made for a photo of the missing heiress." She looked toward the rafters and blew out a huge sigh. "I simply couldn't take the chance they'd find me. Not till I'd located my great-aunt."

Rubbing the back of her neck, she said, "Then, when I started to get to know you, when I realized you would never betray me..." She shrugged.

"Damn you, Annie."

So quickly she didn't see it coming, he dipped his head and covered her mouth with his.

The kiss burned, it punished, it made her curl her fingers into the fabric of his shirt and hold on for dear life. When he finally pulled away, she was breathless. Brainless.

"Why is all this so important to you?"

She blinked. "What?"

"I said, why is all this so important?"

"The ranch?"

"No." Impatient, he gripped the pommel of the saddle Hank had been oiling and almost ripped it from the stand. Then he slashed the air with his hand. "The whole running away thing. I understand the grandfather part, but there's more to it than that."

His comment caught her off guard. He was right. She leaned against Shadow's stall and, without thought, rubbed his muzzle when he bumped his head against her. Her hand trembled. She hadn't dared admit it even to herself, but, yes, there was more.

Her eyes found his, shaded by the brim of his hat. "Have you always wanted to run a ranch? This ranch?"

"Careful there." He nodded toward Shadow. "That no-good hunk of horseflesh would as soon nip you as look at you. He's a sneaky SOB."

"He won't hurt me." She scratched the horse between his ears. "We're friends, aren't we?"

Cash made a sound low in his throat, somewhere between a growl and a humph as the horse nickered. Even Staubach kept a wary eye on the horse.

"And you"—she pointed a finger at Cash—"you didn't answer my question. Have you always wanted to run Whispering Pines?"

"Yeah. I have."

"Have you ever left here? Been free of the ranch?"

He squinted at her. "Free of it? Strange way to put it, but, yeah, I guess so. When I was away at college."

"Where'd you go?"

"Texas A&M. That's where all Hardemans go."

"Is it the school you wanted to attend?"

"Hell, yes. Go, Aggies." His eyes clouded. "Too bad you won't be around come football season. I'd take you to a game. But then, you have better things to do."

The man was seriously trying her patience. Bracing for another dig, she asked, "Like what?"

He didn't disappoint her.

"Oh, I don't know. Spending Daddy's money, flying off to movie premieres, having brunch with the girls. Some women like to spend other people's money."

"You're comparing me to Vivi."

He said nothing.

"That's unfair. And untrue."

He shrugged his shoulders.

"It is, and you know it. Admit it."

He said nothing.

"You're wrong, because I'd take you up on that football game invitation. Too bad I won't be here, though. Why won't I, you ask?" She waited a beat. "Because I don't have a job. I got fired, and the boss is being a real bozo about hiring me back."

"That right?"

"Yes."

"Why should he?"

"Hire me back?"

"Uh-huh."

"Because I give him a hundred percent. Because I know horses. Because he's a good man."

He drew in a breath. "You're hitting below the belt on that last one."

"Stating the facts." She rubbed her temple. "I know I...didn't tell the whole truth about a few things."

His brows shot up.

"Okay, okay." She rolled her eyes. "So I misled you. On purpose—at first. Guilty as charged. But I had a legitimate reason." She paused, laid a hand on his chest. "My response to you the other night, though, was real. I didn't fake that. I couldn't."

Cash pinched the bridge of his nose and swore again. "*Really* low blow."

She met his eyes, didn't waver.

The silence stretched. "Maybe I can put in a good word for you with the boss."

"I wish you would. This job's important to me."

"Why?" He hesitated. "I still don't get it. You could do

what you came to do and get the hell out of Dodge. Why would you want to bust your back working here at Whispering Pines? It defies logic, Annie."

"Because..." She hesitated, considered. "How did you feel when you were away at university, Cash?"

"I missed the ranch, the horses. I missed the smell of the barn, the smell of the air after a good rain. My family. Not that I didn't like college. Don't get me wrong. I had a good time. Got a first-rate education. Learned skills I've since put to use here."

"But while you were at school, you did pretty much what you wanted?"

He shrugged. "As long as I kept up my grades."

"See, that's the thing." She reached into her pocket and pulled out a couple of sugar cubes. Absently, she held up her palm, let Shadow lip them, heard Cash's nervous intake of air.

"I've never had that freedom, Cash. Never been free to be me. Never been free of family responsibilities and expectations. Until now." She wiped her hand on her jeans. "I'm not ready to give it up. Not yet."

She pulled at her ponytail. "Actually, when it comes right down to it, I'm still not entirely free. But this thing with Grandpa is because I love him, not because of duty. I'm working a couple of angles there."

He looked at her questioningly.

"I can't say anything else yet. Trust me. Please, Cash."

He scowled. "You're playing me like a fiddle."

"No, I'm not."

"Yeah, you are." He huffed. "Still, Hank needs the help. I suppose you can stay till I find your replacement." With that he turned and stalked out of the barn. "Staubach," he called. "Let's go."

The dog slowly rose to his feet and started to the door. He threw one last pathetic look over his shoulder as he trotted out of the barn.

Annelise stood where she was, tears stinging her eyes. "Need You Now," a country song she recognized from yesterday, drifted from Hank's radio. Dropping to the straw-littered floor, head cradled in her arms, she listened while Lady Antebellum put voice to *her* feelings.

Under different circumstances, she and Cash could have been so right for each other. If only their paths weren't so disparate—he a down-to-the-bone cowboy, and she a filthy-rich city girl.

* * *

Cash went over the figures a third time, then rested his elbows on the big cherry desk in his grandpa's office and scrubbed his hands over his face. The coarse stubble on his jaw reminded him he hadn't bothered to shave this morning. He supposed he could run the electric razor he kept in the top desk drawer over his face, but what the hell. It didn't make two cents worth of difference.

He looked back at the computerized list on his monitor and swore. The supply order had to go in by tomorrow, but he couldn't concentrate on muscle liniments, horseshoe nails, or oats and barley. The price of a new currycomb and the number of vitamin pills needed for the stock didn't seem relevant. He couldn't focus on anything except Annie. Make that Annelise Montjoy.

In a few short days, she'd gotten under his skin. Crawled right in and taken up residence. Enough so that he hadn't been able to stay away yesterday. He'd woken up wanting to see those eyes, that hair. Needing to taste those lips. Hear her laugh. He was enough of a realist to understand the lady was totally out of his league. Whatever fantasies he'd been dreaming up about him and Annie needed to be swept up and dumped in the trash can. Any involvement between them was over, finished, and done. Hell, it had never started. Not really.

He couldn't get the picture of her out of his mind. Annie in the canoe, moonlight bathing her features, highlighting her high cheekbones, that aristocratic nose. Annie in his living room all but naked. The smell of her. The touch and taste of her. Those soft little sighs way down low in her throat.

Shit!

He leaned back in the chair.

Well, Miss Annelise Montjoy could stay till he figured out what to do about help for Hank, but from now on, Cash Hardeman intended to draw the line between personal and professional and stretch it tight. As tight as any barbed-wire fence on the ranch.

Good luck with that, cowboy.

The thing was, Annie was so damned unpredictable. He'd left her place yesterday fully expecting never to see her again. Then, he'd walked into the barn this morning and there she stood, bold as brass, even after he'd sacked her. She and Hank had been in the middle of some serious discussion from the looks of it.

Sweat glistened on Cash's forehead simply remembering the picture she'd made. That tiny red tank top hugged her breasts, molded her waist. Toned, tanned arms all but begged a man to touch. She'd looked tired, though. Walking away from her had been tough. Then, when he'd made it to the barn door, "Need You Now" came over Hank's old radio, and he'd nearly turned around.

But he hadn't. He'd somehow managed to escape. Now if

he could only manage to scrub all traces of Annie from his mind.

She'd infiltrated too deeply. Way too deep.

He drained the coffee mug Rosie'd filled for him and saved the mess he'd made of the ordering sheet. Maybe he'd take a ride. That would help clear his head. But that meant heading back to the barn, to Annie. Well, nothing said he had to stop and visit with her, now did it? She was one of his hired hands. Period. Nothing more, nothing less.

And if that wasn't the biggest bunch of BS he'd ever heard, he didn't know what was. Feeling surly and more than a little mean, he stormed out of the house.

The screen door slammed shut. He was halfway down the stairs when Rosie hurried out. Standing on the porch, drying her hands on a worn dish towel, she asked, "Where are you going, Cash? Lunch is ready. I'm minutes from putting it on the table."

"I'm heading out for a ride. I'm not hungry."

"Let me pack you a lunch."

He rounded on her. "I'm not five years old, Rosie. I can take care of myself."

"Yeah, I can see that." She lifted a brow. "So which of the barn cats do you intend to kick?"

He closed his eyes and took a deep breath. When his eyes met hers again, he saw concern. "Look. I'm in a rotten mood. I know it. I need to get away. Be by myself for a bit."

Vivi sauntered onto the porch. "I'd be more than happy to keep you company, Cash." Dressed in Daisy Dukes and a white halter top, she pursed Marilyn-Monroe-red lips.

"Oh, lordy," Rosie muttered.

"I appreciate the offer, Vivi. I truly do." He rubbed at the headache skewering his brain behind his left eye. "But like I told Rosie, I'm after some alone time right now. Be best for everybody."

Pouting, Vivi wrapped her arms around the porch banister. "You don't do anything with me anymore."

"Honey, you and I never have done anything together. You're my grandpa's widow, so you're part of this family. I owe *him* that. But, you and me? Ain't gonna happen. We have less than nothing in common."

"I'm gonna go get that lunch together for you," Rosie interrupted. "I'll have it ready by the time you've got that rascal Moonshine saddled up."

When he opened his mouth to object, she shook her head. "Huh-uh. You'll thank me for it later."

He tipped his hat to her. "All right. Thanks, Rosie. I'll stop by the house and pick it up." He swiveled on his boot heel and headed across the yard, leaving one steaming mad woman behind and anticipating another in the barn. He mentally girded his loins, gearing up for the next face-off with Ms. Hogwash Montjoy.

Damn it. Try as he might to think of her that way, he couldn't. She wasn't Ms. Montjoy. She was Annie, pure and simple. Shit!

The barn, after the bright outdoor heat, was dim and ten degrees cooler. Several large overhead fans stirred the air. He stood motionless in the doorway, waiting for his eyes to adjust.

He heard her first. Annie's clear, true voice whispered in song to Shadow—in his stall. Cash's heart nearly stopped, but he fought back his initial reaction, didn't run to yank her to safety.

Instead, he stood at the ready and watched and listened. While she sang, Annie brushed the currycomb over the horse's flanks.

Sensitive animals, horses didn't suffer fools gladly. Often used in rehab situations, they picked up on a person's inner feelings and needs, intuiting the sincere from the disingenuous.

His eyes widened when Shadow, this monster horse, turned his head and actually nuzzled Annie, bumping her shoulder with his muzzle. While he watched, she laughed and slid one of those long-fingered hands over Shadow's forelock.

Cash hardened with need. Cursing every god he'd ever heard mentioned, he lamented that, of several billion women in the world, it was this one who held such power over him.

She went back to grooming the horse. Steady, long strokes. Her voice, soft and sensuous, curled in his belly.

"J'espère, j'espère, oh oui, j'espère."

Unable to fight it, he added his baritone to her quiet voice. "Oh, yes, I hope."

Startled, she swung around. The comb slid from her fingers. "I didn't hear you come in."

"No. I don't guess you did." He nodded toward the comb. "Careful. Your boss doesn't like his things damaged."

"Oh? He tell you that?"

"Damn tootin'. You speak French well."

"I spent some time in Paris."

"Of course you did."

Her blue eyes iced. "We have an office there. But I don't seem to be the only one who speaks French. Apparently you do, too."

He lifted a shoulder. "Not really. You picked one of the few songs I know."

She smiled slowly. "I love the melody."

"Me, too." And he was glad, since he figured he'd hear it in that sweet voice of hers over and over tonight while he fought for sleep. "I never did ask. Where'd you learn your way around horses?"

She laughed at his abrupt change of subject. "My mother, never easy around them, insisted I take riding lessons. She had me in a saddle by the time I turned three. Despite the enormous amount of money Dad paid for my lessons, Duncan, my instructor, insisted I groom my own animal when we came back from a ride. He said that was a huge part of being a horse person. So, I learned at an early age how to brush down my horse and clean his hooves. How to saddle my own mount. Duncan did a good job. I owe him a lot. He taught me responsibility along with the love of riding."

"Guess so." Grabbing his saddle, he moved across the barn to Moonshine's stall. "Have you ridden Shadow?" He turned and locked eyes with her. "The truth."

Chin rising defiantly, she said, "Yes. I have."

"I figured as much watching the two of you together." He shook his head. "He ready to ride with another horse?"

She nodded.

"Okay. Saddle up. Show me."

She gaped at him. "You're serious?"

"As a heart attack."

"Yes, sir, boss."

"Don't get cheeky on me." He opened Moonshine's stall. "Rosie's putting together a basket lunch. We'll stop by the house on our way and pick it up." And he knew exactly where they'd share it. He had the perfect spot.

"That sounds wonderful." Annie threw a heavy wool, red-and-black plaid blanket over Shadow's back, then lifted the saddle in place. She reached beneath his belly, attached the girth strap, tightening and then rechecking to make sure it was secure.

Cash watched her work. Watched the way her efficient

fingers ran over Shadow. She talked to the horse the entire time. Cash figured she'd forgotten he could hear as she rubbed and cooed to him.

"You had a rough start, hmmm, pretty boy? That's okay. You're safe now. You're okay. You can trust Cash. He'll take good care of you."

Chapter Twelve

W here are we going?"

Standing in his stirrups, Cash pointed to a group of trees on a rise in front of them. "Right on the other side of that cedar break."

"Are you going to dock my pay, boss?"

He laughed. "Nope. We're exercising the horses. It's part of your duties."

"Okay, then." She reached back and removed the band from her hair, loosening it. Shaking her head, she laughed. "It's beautiful here, Cash. I can see why you love it so much."

And it was. Rolling hills, green meadows filled with brilliant red and blue and yellow wildflowers, and thick groves of trees. A feeling of belonging. He had it all right here.

He kneed his mount and took the lead. For the hundredth time, she wondered why no woman had claimed him. Cash Hardeman was every bit as beautiful as his land. On the back of a horse, reins held easily in those big, strong hands, he made her want things. Things she'd never considered important.

This man rang bells and set off feelings she'd never experienced. He made her want to pull him from the saddle and tumble on the ground with him.

Her mind flitted to Douglas DeWitt, her parents' last attempt to set her up. Around them, he played the perfect suitor. In truth, he was cold and self-absorbed. The very antithesis of Cash. She wouldn't think about him today. Not with the sun on her face and Cash beside her.

When they made the top of the hill and rounded the trees, she gasped. A pond, as still and cool-looking as glass, lay in front of them in the middle of a lush field of green, green grass. Texas bluebonnets and yellow and white daisies bobbed their heads in the slight breeze. A stand of cattails clustered near the far bank. The outstretched branches of a huge lone oak shaded one side.

"Cash, this is incredible."

"It is, isn't it?" With his thumb, he nudged back his hat brim. "When I was a kid, I spent a lot of summer days splashing around in this water. Now, well, I rarely make it here. Always seems to be too much to do."

He dismounted and reached up to help her down. Pulling her close, her body slid down the length of his till her booted feet touched the ground. Heat built in her. And, she noticed, in him. He held her close for several seconds, then stepped back.

Her heart hammered so loudly she figured he couldn't help but hear it.

Removing his Stetson, he swiped the back of one arm across his forehead. "Wish this heat would break. It's so damned hot, Paco said the hens are laying hard-boiled eggs today."

She swatted at him. "I have my doubts about those chickens of yours, but I sure can't argue the heat. It's brutal." She looked longingly at the water and wondered if she dared go wading.

"Ever been skinny-dipping?"

Her eyes widened. "No."

He undid his first button.

She stared at it. "You can't be serious."

"Sugar, it's a hundred in the shade. There's cool, spring-fed water in that pond."

"I can't—"

"Sure you can. Come on." He reached for the hem of her tank top. When his fingers curled beneath and touched her bare midriff, a shiver went through her.

She shook her head and backed up a step.

"Let your hair down, Annie," he whispered. "Come swimming with me. You know you want to."

"It's the middle of the day, Cash. Somebody will see us."

He made a face. "Annie, we're smack-dab in the middle of nowhere. Not another soul for miles and miles. It's just you and me." His voice had grown husky.

"I can't." Her gaze moved to the trees, the surrounding fields.

"Okay." He released his hold on the hem of her shirt and yanked his own over his head.

She almost swallowed her tongue. The sun turned washboard abs golden. He undid the button on his jeans.

"Change your mind? I'll tell you again. There's no one else anywhere around, Annie."

A delicious thrill ran along her backbone. He was right. They were alone. No one to spy on them, to sell their secret moment. She and Cash, all alone beneath this gorgeous Texas sky. Did she dare grab this gift and enjoy?

"Annie?"

Her glance landed on his hands as he reached for the zipper on his jeans. A trail of dark hair led from his chest and disappeared into his jeans. The male. What a phenomenal animal, so different in all the best possible ways.

Flustered, she bit her bottom lip.

"Okay, darlin'. But I've gotta be honest. I'm not gonna turn my back on this." He nodded toward the pond. "You can stay right here on dry ground and watch me enjoy it."

Her hand snaked out, touched his, then jerked back as she realized where his hand rested. Where hers had gone. She wet her lips with her tongue. "Can I leave my underclothes on?"

"Technically, that's not skinny-dipping."

"Cash—"

"Okay, go ahead. It'll make for a soggy ride home, but sure, if that's what you want to do."

"Will you leave yours on?"

"What makes you think I wear any?"

Her mouth dropped open.

He laughed and chucked her chin. "Kidding, Annie. Yeah, I'll leave my boxers on if it'll make you feel better." He stepped out of his jeans and kicked them off to the side. "Last one in's a rotten egg," he yelled over his shoulder.

She watched as he splashed his way into the water. Taking a deep breath, she shed her jeans and tank and joined him.

The water was warmer than she'd expected. The soft, slimy bottom gushed between her toes. Flopping onto her back, she let go of the day and floated. Overhead, huge fluffy clouds drifted across a brilliantly blue sky.

Could it get any better than this?

From the oak, a bird serenaded her, made her think of

Cash in the barn earlier. The man had a beautiful singing voice. Husky. Sexy. A bedroom voice that made her think of rumpled sheets and candlelight.

She heard a splash behind her a second before Cash's hands caught her around the waist and pulled her to him, her back against his front. His callused hands, so different from Douglas's soft ones, sent tingles through her. Goose bumps danced over her skin. Here was the spark, the sizzle that had never been there before, not with Douglas or any other man.

One of those oh-so-male hands moved from her waist up her torso, skimming the side of her breast with a feather-light whisper. Annelise didn't even try to stop the small sound that forced its way out of her.

Moving his hand to her neck, Cash brushed her hair aside and dropped soft kisses on the back of her neck, trailed heat around the side to her ear and nibbled the lobe. She sank into him, fitted herself to his rock-hard body. Every inch of it. His male hardness pressed against her backside. This man was killing her slowly.

The water rose and fell against them, warm, soft velvet.

When his hand moved from her neck to her front, the thin camisole provided no protection, no barrier. Her nipples stood at full attention, aching for his touch. His other arm encircled her, his big hand resting on her stomach.

He curled his fingers over the edge of her camisole. "This is wet. You should get out of it before you catch your death of cold."

"You're probably right."

She lifted her arms in invitation, and Cash, inch by inch, removed it, tossing it to the grassy edge. His boxers landed beside it.

When he reached for her panties, though, nerves got the better of her, and she splashed away from him.

"You okay?"

She pushed the hair from her face and looked over her shoulder to where he stood. The water lapped at his waist; the sun bronzed his skin. And she realized she was okay. Very okay.

Suddenly feeling very light-hearted, she laughed. "I am. I think, though, that maybe you should have to work a little harder for this last little bit. If you can catch me..."

A lazy smile on his face, he watched as she played in the lake. Feeling like a kid, she sent a spray of water in his direction. He disappeared beneath the surface and swept her off her feet. In seconds, her panties joined her camisole in the grass.

"Annie, you're perfection. You take my breath away." He caught her hand in his and entwined their fingers, turning her till they faced one another. With his lips a breath away from hers, he asked, "You gonna kiss me?"

Her gaze moved to his eyes, back to those sensual lips, then returned to those green eyes, gone dark now with need. She answered, not with words, but with lips that ached for the touch of his, hungered for everything he offered.

His hands slid down her body, touched the spot between her legs, and she bowed back. He fed on her breasts, tasted her body. Her hands roamed the length of him, touching everywhere.

Annelise decided it was a good thing they were in the water. Otherwise, they'd have certainly set off a brushfire with the heat they created.

When she thought she couldn't stand it any longer, Cash swooped her up, hand behind her knees, and headed for the bank. Wrapping her arms around his neck, she kissed him hungrily.

Reaching the grassy bank, he slowly lowered her to her

feet, never taking his mouth from hers. Then, drawing back, he ran a tanned finger over one ivory breast. "Hot-damn but you're beautiful, Annie."

He left her for a moment to remove a quilt from his saddlebag. With one fluid motion, he spread it on the ground, then crooked a finger at her. He lay down on the cool cotton, and she joined him.

Within minutes, she was smoldering again. The man had magic hands. And his mouth—oh!

When he reached in his jeans and pulled out protection, Annelise stiffened. The moment of truth.

Oh, God.

She pushed on his chest. "Wait."

He groaned and dropped his forehead to hers. "Not again. Please." The words were hardly loud enough for her to hear.

"No, not again." She kissed the side of his neck where his pulse throbbed. "I want to do this." She gave a shaky laugh. "Believe me, I'm more than ready. But before we do, we need to talk."

"Talk? Now?" He groaned again, then took her hand in his, trailed it down his body. "I need you. Feel me, Annie. Feel what you do to me."

Her sigh was ragged. "There's something you need to know."

"Later." He pulled her back to him.

"No." She shook her head. "Now."

"Annie, you're killing me." He rolled off, scrubbing his hands over his face. Then he turned his head on the blanket to look at her. "What? What's so darned important it can't wait?"

"I've…" She swallowed. "I've never done this before."

She swore all the blood drained from him. His suntanned face paled. But he didn't move a muscle.

"What are you saying?"

She licked Sahara-dry lips. "I've never been with a man, Cash. Not like this."

He jerked to a sitting position and stared down at her. "You're a virgin?"

Tears pricked her eyes, but she blinked them away. "Don't make it sound…dirty…or like I've got some sickness or a disease. There are reasons. Valid reasons."

He shook his head. "I'm sure there are, but for the life of me, I can't imagine what they might be. You're twenty-six years old."

"I know that. But you need to understand that for me, sex isn't simple."

"Don't guess it should be."

Surprised, she tilted her head. "You're right." She brushed back the hair that had fallen over his forehead. "School has kept me busy, then the business."

He shook his head. "Uh-uh. Not buying that. You can always find time for…this."

She frowned. "Okay. The biggest reason? It comes down to simple logistics. I could never figure out how to manage it."

His brows shot up, then he sent her a slow smile that had her already racing pulse rocketing to the stratosphere. "I believe I can help you with that, darlin'. Come here. I'll show you. I'll be your personal tutor. One-on-one instruction." He reached for her.

She rolled her eyes. "I don't mean the logistics of the actual physical act. I might not ever have…you know, but I have a pretty good idea about what goes where." Her face flamed, and she covered it with her hand.

He drew it away and laced their fingers together. "Honey, this isn't something to be ashamed or embarrassed about. Sex is a natural act."

"Spoken like a man. Okay. It's—well, I'm never alone, Cash. Until now, here in Maverick Junction. Everywhere I go, my bodyguards, my driver, the paparazzi are right there. And it's amazing how many people recognize me. I can't check into a hotel or go home with a man. I sure can't take them to my place, since I still live with my parents. And how pathetic is that?"

"Yeah, guess all that would present a problem." His mouth quirked.

She nudged him in the side. "I'm serious."

"Honey, believe me, so am I."

She started to move away, but he reached out and grasped her wrist. "No you don't. Come back here." He bent over her until his lips met hers. His kisses were soft and tender.

Then he deepened the kiss till she was certain her soul was being consumed. Heat erupted, and her hand skimmed his bare thigh.

"You honor me, Annie, allowing me to be your first."

Her first. But, even now, he didn't want to be her last. She understood that. This wasn't forever. She closed her eyes, determined to enjoy the moment. To live in the here and now.

"I want to make this good for you. Special." He nibbled his way down to her belly button. "I can't believe this, but I'm nervous."

"Isn't that supposed to be my line?" she whispered.

"Should be."

"Well, I'm not." She curled her fingers into his hair and arched her back. His arm moved beneath her, pulled her closer still.

Her thoughts fragmented when he entered her. A tiny burning sensation, then her entire world shifted on its axis. Whatever she'd imagined paled as waves of intoxicating pleasure swept through her.

* * *

They lay side by side, snuggled into each other, holding hands. The sun beat down on them, warming their skin. Cash stroked a hand over the curve of her waist, along the smooth skin, and felt the shiver run through her.

He'd practically sweat bullets. Even at fourteen, he'd dated older girls. He'd never been somebody's first. At that initial resistance, he'd nearly pulled out. Nearly given in to his panic. But she'd moved her hips, urging him to take more. And he had. God, he had.

How could she look so fragile, yet possess such strength? He'd been afraid at first, afraid he'd snap her in two. But the lady took no prisoners, gave no quarter. Her toned body matched his, need for need. Fiercely, she'd drained him dry.

Nobody had ever touched him the way Annie did.

"Are you okay?" He kissed the top of her head.

"Okay?" She shook her head. "No. Okay is such an anemic word. It doesn't begin to do justice to what just happened. The way I'm feeling right now..." She sighed. "It far surpasses anything I could ever have expected."

She nuzzled her face into his chest. "And I'm thinking how much time I've wasted by waiting so long."

Her words, her voice, tickled against him, and he grinned. "Personally, I'm glad you did."

She tipped her head to look at him. "You know what? So am I."

"Sing to me, Annie," he whispered. "Like you did to Shadow."

And she did. She moved her lips to his ear, sang softly, and totally devastated him. He hadn't come so close to losing it since he'd been a randy, wet-behind-the-ears teenager.

Rolling over quickly, one hand on her lower back, he

gathered her to him. Then, he plunged into her. Nothing slow or easy this time. Both took from the other, gave to the other.

If he'd thought the first the best he'd ever had, he couldn't even begin to describe the second.

Staring into the sky, trying to catch his breath, he heard Annie say, "Boy, was I wrong. I thought riding a motorcycle down the highway was the ultimate experience. Not even close. Sex is, by far, better than any motorcycle ride."

When her hand trailed over his stomach, he caught it in his. "Have I created a monster?"

"I think so. If my mother could see us now, she'd be appalled."

"Honey, if your mother could see us now, *I'd* be appalled." He flashed a quick grin.

Annie smiled. "You know what I mean. For years, she's drilled into me that sex isn't to be taken lightly. Because of who I am, I have to be careful—my reputation, my family's reputation, blah, blah, blah. She forgot to tell me how much fun it is!"

"Thank you." He shot her a sideways glance. "You know, your great-grandfather apparently didn't play by the same rules your mother fed you."

Her brows furrowed. "What do you mean?"

"Well, if he had, you wouldn't be here hunting for his illegitimate child now, would you?"

"Guess not."

"I owe your great-granddaddy a big, old thanks." He kissed her, then sat up. "You hungry?"

"Famished."

"What do you say we take a quick rinse in the pond, then break out the picnic lunch Rosie packed?"

"Sounds great." She ran ahead of him, straight into the water, splashing as she went.

His phone vibrated, and he picked it up, glanced at the caller.

Annie stopped and looked back. Water streaked down her body and glistened in the sunlight. She looked pretty as a picture. She quite literally stole his breath.

"What are you doing?"

"I had a message."

"Here?"

"Yeah, we had a tower installed so the guys could stay in touch when they're out on the range." He tossed the phone onto his crumpled jeans. "I turned it off. Nothing I need to take care of now."

He raced into the water, needing to be with her.

Ten minutes later, cooled off and dressed, sitting cross-legged under the big oak, they shared the best fried chicken Cash had ever tasted. Rosie had outdone herself today. Potato salad and homemade bread-and-butter pickles had been tucked in his lunch, too. And to top it all off, she'd added two huge slices of chocolate cake. He swore the woman had some supernatural ability. She knew Annie'd be sharing his lunch and had packed enough for both of them.

He took the last bite and licked the thick frosting from his fingers.

Annie put her hands to her stomach. "I'm so full I don't think I can move."

"Lay your head right here." Cash patted his damp jeans. Annie slid close and laid her head in his lap. Two birds in the tree overhead sang to each other. A butterfly flitted from daisy to daisy, and a frog croaked from a lily pad in the center of the pond.

It had been ages since he'd taken off in the middle of a workday. He thanked God he had today. What a magnificent gift these last couple of hours had been.

He ran his fingers through her damp hair. She smelled of the fresh spring water. Yet beneath was the scent of her, of Annie. Pure female.

"So, Annie, what did you study in college?"

"Business. How boring is that?"

"Not. A lot of my classes were in business. That's what the ranch is, after all."

"True. And because my mother insisted, I carried dual enrollment and got a degree in fine arts, too. The perfect accessory for every well-dressed woman."

He grinned. "Yeah, there's that."

"Since Daddy and Grandpa weren't in any huge hurry to turn over the reins," Annie said, "I finished up my college career with a doctorate in economics."

"You're a Ph.D.?"

"What? You don't think I'm smart enough? Capable enough?"

He kissed the tip of her nose. "You're all of that, Dr. Montjoy. It just doesn't fit the bad-girl, Harley-riding woman I first met. You may have to give me a couple minutes to merge the two."

She laughed. "That's because, essentially, the doctorate and the escapee are two completely different people."

"I'm not so sure of that," Cash said easily. He drew her hair back from her face and nibbled on the side of her neck. "They're simply two sides of one coin."

"I never thought of it that way."

The sun dipped lower in the sky. He rolled to his side and tickled her nose with a piece of grass. As much as he hated to, it was time to head home. Chores waited. With a last kiss from Annie's now-swollen lips, he pulled her to her feet.

Stashing everything back into the picnic bag, they folded the blanket and tied it to Moonshine's saddle.

"Thanks for a lovely day, Cash."

"Believe me, Annie, when I say the pleasure was mine."

With a sly smile, she said, "Oh, I'm not so sure it was all yours."

"Down, girl, or we'll never make it back to civilization." As he handed her up on the horse, he realized not a single soul who saw Annie would have the slightest doubt about what they'd been doing on this fine sunny afternoon. With her stubble-burned cheeks and neck, her red, swollen lips, and wet, tousled hair, she looked like pure, unadulterated sex. Everyone would know they'd shared a little afternoon delight.

Well, they'd take a slow ride and maybe head back the long way. That was only fair to Annie.

On the way back, as they ambled through a field of wildflowers, Annie drew up, pointing to a jackrabbit. The animal, on alert, sat on its haunches eating a blade of grass and watching them watch him.

"Maybe it's Thumper, from *Bambi*."

Cash's heart lurched in his chest. She looked so amazing, so awestruck. Exactly the way he felt—amazed and awestruck. Riding up beside her, he hooked an arm around her neck, drew her close, and kissed her. Beneath him, his horse shifted. Shadow stood still. She'd done a good job with him.

"I can't get enough of you, Annie."

She smiled, and a twinge of conscience pricked Cash. He flashed to the terms of his grandpa's will. Thought about Vivi. Reminded himself what a huge mistake a man could make if he let himself act on impulse.

Still, Annie wasn't Vivi. The two were as far apart as they came. If he ever did get married... but no. That wasn't in his plans. What about Annie? She'd just given herself to him.

Her first. Did she expect more because of that? Surely she understood he didn't have any plans for their future.

And yet who knew what went on in a woman's head.

A trickle of cold sweat ran down his back. Before he could stop himself, he asked, "You ever get really serious about anyone, Annie? You know, like, thought about getting married?"

"Married?" Her eyes widened. "No, I haven't. I've never met anyone I'd want to spend the rest of my life with. Have you?"

"No." Cash thought about his folks. They had a good marriage. But this wasn't a "like father, like son" thing. Vivi and his grandfather had been a disaster. And the woman continued to be a royal pain in his side.

Annie was a good person. She had a lot of heart. A trusting heart. He couldn't risk hurting her. He'd made it a rule to be totally upfront with any of the women he'd been involved with. Before things reached the point they had with Annie.

The thinking part of his brain had deserted him, though. Now it was working again—in a limited fashion.

Calling himself all kinds of a fool, he knew he had to deal with it. Had to be totally honest. After all, hadn't he been livid when she'd been less than that with him? Wasn't that what yesterday's fight had been about?

"Annie, this afternoon was, well, pretty damn wonderful."

She grinned at him, and he nearly swallowed his tongue.

But he untangled it and went on. "This—what happened this afternoon—doesn't change anything between us, you know? I mean, you're here for a short time. Until you find your great-aunt and get a few things settled in your head. And me, I'm not interested in anything long-term. I'm not ready to settle down, not looking for anything permanent."

He heard the sharp intake of breath. Saw the raw pain on

her face, in her eyes. And then he watched the lights simply go out in those magnificent eyes. They turned from warm pools of blue to shards of ice in seconds.

"Good. Then we're on the same page." She nudged Shadow, and the two tore off across the meadow, her back ramrod straight.

Chapter Thirteen

Cash cursed himself. He'd *so* screwed up. He'd taken what had been beautiful and transformed it into the bad and the ugly. This afternoon had been Annie's first time.

She'd handed him the gift of her virginity, and he'd hurt her. Not physically. No. She'd been right with him there. He'd been careful. But afterward, he'd been a bastard.

He'd told himself he was watching out for her. That he was simply being honest with her.

What a crock! Truth was, he'd been so afraid of the feelings building inside him, so afraid of where they might lead, that he'd cut her to the quick by intentionally making light of what had happened between them. Of what had been the most incredible experience of his life.

He'd basically told her she'd been a one-night stand. Had turned her special day to shit. What an arrogant, callous bastard. If anybody else had treated her that way, he'd beat his ass. He deserved a thorough trouncing, and if he could figure out how to go about it, he'd give himself one.

He couldn't remember ever making such a monumental mess of things.

Giving Moonshine his head, he urged him on faster. Inside a couple minutes, he rode alongside Shadow and Annie.

The lady sat a horse well.

When she turned those cold eyes on him, he found himself relieved she had no riding crop in her hand, certain she'd have used it on him. And rightfully so.

"Annie, pull up. Listen to me for a second."

"I think you've said everything there is to say. I need to be getting back to work. Boss."

"Stop it. I—" He hesitated. "I didn't want you to—"

"I got the memo."

He swore again.

She drew up her horse and simply sat looking at him, one brow arched imperiously.

"Oh, you do that well."

"What?"

"That haughty lady-of-the-manor thing. Can't believe I didn't figure things out sooner."

"Shifting the blame?"

"No," he answered. "I'm not. But we're wet. Disheveled. If we ride back looking like this, every hand on the ranch is going to know exactly what we've been doing."

Her face flamed.

"Let's ride over to my house. Dry our clothes and clean up a bit."

When she looked at him suspiciously, he held up his hands, palms facing out. "Nothing more."

"You've got that right."

* * *

An uneasy truce stretched between them.

When they rode up to his house, she pulled gently on her horse's reins. Leaning down, she patted him. "Good job, boy."

Then, she simply sat there, drinking in the scene. Even through her anger, she had to admire Cash's home. At night, it had been magical. In the daytime—absolute perfection. Rather than clashing, it blended with its surroundings. The wood and stone structure welcomed. The lake stretched out, reflecting both the house and the trees around it.

Under normal circumstances it would no doubt be peaceful. Tranquil. But these were far from normal circumstances, and Annelise ached from the tension in her shoulders.

Unlike the other night, no Staubach ran out to greet them. They'd left him in the barn with Hank when they'd rode out.

She dismounted and followed a silent Cash inside. This time, when she walked into his home, her brain wasn't clouded with passion. She stood in the center of the two-story foyer.

"You built this yourself?" She kept her tone cool.

"Most of it. I had some help." He shoved his hands in his pockets. "The bath's upstairs to the right. If you want to shimmy out of those wet clothes, toss them out the door and I'll throw them in the dryer. There should be a robe hanging on the back of the door. Take a shower if you'd like. Shampoo, soap, everything's there."

When he took her elbow to guide her to the stairs, she pulled away.

"Sorry." He dropped his hand.

"You should be."

"Annie, I know you're pissed at me, but—"

She held up a hand. "Don't."

Conflicting emotions buffeted her and made her angrier

still. Fighting the urge to turn into him, to bury her face in his shirt and cry, she took a step away instead. She wanted to throttle him, and still his touch created a need in her. Heat boiled in her stomach at the thought of his hands moving over her, touching her, of his mouth tasting her. Him inside her.

After everything that had happened between them, the thought of using his shower, his soap made her stomach flutter. Without another word, she walked up the stairs and into the bathroom, locking the door behind her,

Leaning against the wall, she closed her eyes. Maybe he'd been right to draw the line. To set the rules. Because something major was going on inside her. Yes, physically she found Cash thrilling. But it went deeper than physical. And that scared her.

He'd been right when he'd said she was here short-term. She'd come to Maverick Junction to find her great-aunt, then she'd return to her life in Boston with her boardroom and her power suits. Back to a world she understood.

Nothing about what was happening here made sense.

How had the search for her aunt turned into a mission to find herself?

How had a chance encounter with this cowboy turned into so much? They came from two totally different worlds, and she'd known that from the start. Still, she'd let herself get caught up in something that frightened her with its intensity.

Apparently it scared Cash, too. Did that mean he felt the same way? Was this more for him, too?

Chilled, she peeled off her wet jeans and tank. Hesitated at her bra and panties. Should she give them to him? Have him put them in the dryer for her? It seemed so intimate.

It *was* so intimate.

What they'd shared at the pond—the ultimate intimacy.

Since her only option would be to crawl back into wet panties after her shower, an extremely unappealing prospect, she slid out of them and into the robe. Pulling the collar close, she held it to her nose and breathed in his scent.

Oh, boy. Big, big trouble.

Unlocking the door, she opened it a crack and piled her clothes on the floor outside. "Here're my things, Cash."

"Okay. I'll be right up for them." After a second, he asked, "Want an iced tea?"

"That sounds wonderful."

"It'll be down here on the kitchen table waiting for you."

"Thanks." She closed the door. After a few seconds, she flipped the lock again and guilt rushed over her. Still...she'd enjoy her shower more knowing for absolute certain she wouldn't have a guest.

Finished, wearing only his robe, she headed downstairs. Today, she had time to take in his house, and, in spite of the situation and her mood, she loved it. Very masculine in browns and creams, sunlight showered in from large windows. Along the back of the house, floor to ceiling windows opened onto a magnificent view of the lake.

Rough timbers spanned the two-story ceiling in the living room, and hand-carved stone formed the columns that separated it from the kitchen.

Cash sat on a bar stool at the island. While she'd cleaned up, he'd showered, too, and changed into fresh clothes. From another room, Annelise heard the sound of her things tumbling in the dryer.

He handed her a glass of tea. "Here you go. Mind if I turn on the TV? I'd like to catch the stock report."

"Not at all." But her mind flew to another time the two of them had shared kitchen time, another time he'd flipped on the TV—and the ensuing disaster.

She sat on a stool next to Cash as he clicked on the remote, flipped through the channels for the local news, and stopped at the stock report.

Despite herself, a bubble of laughter burst from Annelise. When he turned to her, quizzical, she said, "I'm sorry. I'm so used to listening to the stock report—from Wall Street. This..." She waved a hand at the television. "This really is a stock report. They're talking about cows."

"Honey, beef is big business here in Texas. Hard money on the hoof."

"I guess so." She sipped her drink, relishing the cold blast of caffeine. The news correspondent's next words, though, sent her into a tailspin. Déjà vu.

"Speculation is running rampant with the impending annual fund-raiser for Now and Then only two days away. No one has seen or heard from Annelise Montjoy, founder and sponsor of this charity, in nearly three weeks. Tickets for the event sell for a thousand dollars a plate. When we spoke to those in charge this morning, they insisted all is well."

Annelise slapped her forehead and ran to a wall calendar that sported a buxom cowgirl in a black, almost-there bikini. Oh, my gosh. How could that be? How had she so lost track of the days?

"The question remains," the announcer continued, "will oil heiress Annelise Montjoy show, or will she disappoint the hundreds of children who depend on the money raised yearly by this event?"

She met Cash's eyes. "I have to go."

"I know."

She'd expected to be back home in Boston, her grandpa's sister in tow, in time for the fund-raiser. But then everything had taken longer than she'd planned. The trek to Texas, the search for her aunt. And she'd gotten sidetracked by a man she thought she'd come to know. A man she'd allowed to mean something to her. Her mistake.

As if reading her mind, Cash said, "Annie, my mouth moved faster than my brain awhile ago. I handled this whole thing badly."

"I can't argue with that."

"Boy, you're a tough nut to crack, aren't you?"

Her chin trembled. "I can be."

He moved to her, wrapped his arms around her, and pulled her close. "I'm sorry." He kissed her forehead.

She wanted to stay mad, but so much was going on. Inside her. Around her. Now this. It was all too much.

She let him hold her.

"Once I resurface, show my face in Dallas, they'll follow me. The press. They'll come to Maverick Junction if I return here. This"—she waved a hand—"will all be gone." She swiped at a rogue tear. "And I haven't found Grandpa's sister. I haven't found his miracle. Grandpa will die because I failed."

"Darlin', we'll find some way—"

She shook her head. "No. Too many kids depend on this, Cash. I can't let them down. I need to contact the organizers right away." She sniffed. "And I'm being a baby. It's just, I'm not ready to quit my search. I'm not ready for any of this to end. Not yet. But Grandpa will be so disappointed in me if I miss the fund-raiser."

Now the tears started in earnest.

He scooped her up and carried her to the leather sofa, sat down and held her close, rocking and soothing her.

Somehow, in the midst of her misery, she realized this man comforting her was the same one who'd nearly destroyed her earlier. How did she meld these two sides of him?

The soft kisses he dropped on the top of her head, her forehead, the side of her neck changed subtly. The atmosphere shifted from compassion to sexually charged. His fingers moved to the tie on her robe, undid the knot. Beneath it, she was naked.

She moaned when his palm flattened on her belly, arched her back when his mouth took her breast. Her hand snaked up to curl around the back of his head.

When his lips trailed lower, dropping kisses along her stomach, she could have cried with pleasure. Instead, straining for some small vestige of willpower, she slid away from him.

His eyes, dark with passion, lifted to hers. "Annie? What's wrong?"

What's wrong? she wanted to shout. *You broke my heart.* Instead, she said, "This isn't a good idea."

She pulled the robe together and knotted the belt, his eyes watching every movement.

"It's...well." She fiddled with her small pinky ring, twirling it around her finger. "You said you're not looking for anything permanent—"

"That's what this is about? I apologized already. I admitted to being an ass. I don't know what more I can do or say."

"It's not entirely about that. Hear me out. You're not interested in a long-term relationship, and neither am I." She looked away. "So I think it's better that we don't, you know, do this again."

"Guess I deserved that."

She narrowed her eyes, tried to read the expression in his but wasn't quite sure what she saw there. Hurt? Maybe. Maybe it was simply disappointment that he hadn't scored. That he'd struck out.

Instantly, she rebuffed that idea, ashamed of herself. This was Cash. He'd understood at the pond and taken only what she'd offered.

But her heart ached. She tried to convince herself it was simply hurt feelings and wished like heck she could believe that.

"It's getting late, Cash. I have a ton of things to take care of. Do you mind if I take the rest of the day off?"

"Nope. Do what you need to do." Without another word, he moved to the laundry room and returned with her clothes, now dry. He tossed them onto the sofa beside her, then went back into the kitchen.

Ten minutes later, they were on horseback. Neither spoke during the ride.

When they walked their horses into the barn, Annelise saw an older man and woman beside one of the stalls, talking to Hank.

"Hey, there, son. Riding the fences today?"

Beside her, Cash tensed. "Might say that. Annie, my mom and dad. Pauline and Quentin Hardeman."

Annelise slid from her horse. Keeping a firm grip on Shadow's rein, she led him to where Cash's parents stood. Extending her hand, she said, "It's so nice to meet you, Mr. and Mrs. Hardeman."

Cash's father swallowed her hand in his huge one. "Nice to meet you, Annie. Quentin, please, and Pauline. We're not big on formality here."

"Thank you, Quentin." She took Pauline's hand, surprised at how strong it was. "I've heard a lot about you, Pauline, from your son."

"I'll bet you have." Cash's mom shot her a smile. "Don't believe half of it, and I won't believe everything he tells me about you." Then she moved to give her son a hug.

Annelise studied Cash's parents. His father, a good half-foot shorter than Cash, fell a couple of inches shorter than his wife, too. He stood somewhere around five-feet-eight and carried an extra twenty to twenty-five pounds, all of it in his midsection. A handsome man, his face was tanned and lined, no doubt from time spent outdoors. Slightly bow-legged, he'd probably spent a lot of that time on the back of a horse.

Pauline Hardeman wore her thick, chestnut hair in a short, no-nonsense style. Cash took after her slender build but had his dad's dark hair, tanned skin, and miss-nothing, emerald-green eyes.

"What are you guys doing here?" Cash asked. "I figured after being gone all this time, you'd have enough catch-up at your place to keep you busy for a week."

"We do," his dad groused. "I made the mistake of taking your mom into town for breakfast. To Sally's."

Cash grimaced.

His dad laughed. "Yep, she told us all about your new ranch hand." He nodded toward Annelise. "Couldn't keep your mom away."

Annelise wanted to squirm beneath his parents' scrutiny but called on her years of training. She smiled at them, praying they wouldn't read on her face how she and their son had spent the afternoon. One glance at Cash, and she knew his mind had taken the same route.

But if either of his parents guessed their son and the new ranch hand had been rolling around naked on a quilt at lunchtime, neither let on.

"Where are you from, Annie?" Pauline asked.

Grateful the truth was out, Annelise answered honestly. "Boston."

"Whoa, that's a long way from here," Quentin said.

"Don't guess you wandered into Maverick Junction by mistake then."

The man was nobody's dummy. "No, I didn't. I used to have family in Texas and thought I'd visit. I decided to stay for a while, and Cash was good enough to offer me a job."

She doubted he'd buy that as the whole explanation, but, to her relief, he let it go.

"If you'll excuse me, I need to give Shadow a good rub-down after our ride." She threw his parents a smile, totally aware Pauline had a thousand questions. Not today. They'd have to wait till she had her feet under her.

Annelise turned to Cash. "If you don't need me, I think I'll head home after I finish here to make those other arrangements."

Cryptic, but she didn't want to go into any more detail.

"That'll be great."

The phone Cash had given her rang, and she dug it out of her hip pocket. She answered it as she led Shadow away. She didn't look back, didn't want to see the questions in Pauline's and Quentin's eyes. Didn't want to catch Cash's gaze.

The phone call captured her attention immediately, blocking everything else.

"Yes, yes, I can make it. Thanks so much, Oliver. I appreciate this more than I can say."

Hank entered the stall and lifted the saddle off Shadow for her.

"You didn't need to do that, Hank."

"I know it. Maybe I wanted to."

"Well, thanks."

"No problem." With that, the unpredictable old hand turned and walked into the office in the back. Pauline and Quentin followed him in, having been promised a cold drink.

By the time she'd finished grooming Shadow, the tension

in her neck and shoulders was almost palpable. It had been an extraordinary day. One every girl dreamed about. One that usually involved romance, candles, and flowers.

She didn't mind one bit the candles had been missing. As for flowers, she'd had those. The meadow had been filled with wildflowers, the ultimate in fantasies. And romance? Oh, yeah, her cowboy provided that and then some. He'd quite literally swept her off her feet.

If it had ended right there on that blanket by the pond, she'd be seeing stars and singing operettas. But it hadn't. It ended with him telling her it had been nothing more than an afternoon's fling.

Not exactly what a girl hoped to hear after giving a guy her virginity.

She hadn't expected a declaration of love. Hadn't *wanted* a declaration of love. But she would have preferred he wait a bit to spell things out. She could have wished for a little less reality so soon.

"Hey, Annie." Cash came up behind her, startling her. Shadow nickered.

Hand on her heart, Annelise turned to Cash. "You need something?"

"Thought maybe you'd like to grab some dinner together tonight."

Oh, yes. She'd love that. Her heart whipped into fifth gear. But she couldn't. This man was dangerous to her equilibrium, and she needed to remember that. It might be best for everyone if she made the trip to Dallas for the fundraiser, then kept right on going, back to Boston and her life there.

The thought made her unbelievably sad.

"I'm sorry, Cash, but I can't."

"Can't or won't?"

"Both, actually."

He cleared his throat. "Look, I know you're mad at me." He kicked at the bottom of one of the stalls. "And you have every right to be."

"This isn't about you. Not everything is."

"Ouch." He shook his fingers as if burned.

"What? I hurt those delicate feelings?" She shrugged. "So sorry."

"Yeah, you look like it."

"That phone call? It was from Oliver. He arranged a meeting with Ms. Hanson for this afternoon. I need to drive over to Lone Tree."

"You want to borrow my truck?"

She shook her head. "I'll take the bike. It's not that far." She met his eyes. "It'll give me some time to clear my head."

From the look on his face, he understood. He'd taken a magical moment this afternoon and destroyed it with his careless words, his poor timing. She'd given him something precious, something she'd held on to for so long. And he'd taken that gift and smashed it.

But she'd learned a valuable lesson. She certainly understood the power of sex now. Why people, sensible people, did stupid, stupid things for it. And she'd no doubt learned that lesson at the hands of a master.

Today hadn't only been about sex for her. She'd waited a long time for the right person. She'd believed Cash was that person. She'd been wrong.

Oh, she wouldn't fool herself into believing he wouldn't be up for another romp or two with her. But from now on, it had to be strictly business between them.

His gaze searched hers. Finally, he said, "All right. If there's anything I can do, let me know. I understand how important this is to you."

He turned and started to walk away, then swung back around to her. "Annie, about today—"

"It's okay, Cash. We're two consenting adults. Nothing happened today that either of us didn't want. We both participated. It's okay," she repeated.

With a nod, he stuffed his hands in the back pockets of his jeans and walked away. His phone buzzed, and he pulled it out of his shirt pocket as he stepped into the Texas sunshine.

She put away her grooming tools, gave Shadow and Moonshine some water and a handful of oats each, then went into the tiny bathroom in the back to freshen up. No sense going home. She'd leave from here.

Cash and her feelings for him, whatever they were, had to be put on the back burner. She had something more important to focus on.

Thelma Hanson.

Did she hold the key to their futures? To her grandfather's health? She'd soon find out.

* * *

Reaching for her helmet, Annelise turned when Vivi's little red sports car pulled up behind her. She watched as Vivi hopped out, her dress more suitable for a Vegas casino than a stable.

"Hey, Annie, I was hoping to catch you before you left for the day. I've come to do you a favor."

Knowing how Cash felt about his *grandmother* and having witnessed her hands-on approach to him at Bubba's, Annelise went instantly on guard. She hooked the helmet back over the sissy bar. "Really?"

"Really." Her short skirt riding up her thighs, Vivi tiptoed across the dirt patch. "I don't expect you and me's ever gonna be BFFs or anything like that, but still..." She shrugged. "I hate to see you hurt."

"Who's going to hurt me?"

"Cash. I saw you two ride in this afternoon. He took you to the pond, didn't he?"

Annelise felt as if she'd been slapped.

"He's playin' you like a fine fiddle, honey. And while he's doin' that, he's playin' with me, too. In bed. And I gotta tell you, he's makin' me sing."

Annelise's heart stuttered, stopped, kicked into overdrive. She said nothing. Couldn't.

Vivi rubbed her shiny red nails over the skirt of her dress. "You thought the pond was special to you and him, didn't you? That you were the first he'd taken there?"

When she remained quiet, Vivi laughed. "You did. What a shame. You should have known better. I mean, do you honestly believe an uptight, straitlaced girl like you could keep a man like Cash happy?"

Vivi stared at her, unblinking. "You can't compete with me, Annie. I'm a showgirl, through and through. I know how to give one hell of a performance, earn a standing ovation, if you get my drift."

Her eyes turned hard. "You can't give him what he needs. Cash is mine. Don't let me catch you poaching on my territory again."

With that, she scooted into her little red car, backed out onto the drive, and roared away.

Annelise watched her go, her mind reeling. By the pond, what she and Cash shared had seemed so right. She'd never, ever expected to come close to what she'd felt this afternoon.

Cash had told her he'd never taken another woman there. She wanted to believe him. But Vivi knew about the lake. She sounded credible.

One of them was lying to her. Which one?

Self-doubt reared its ugly head. She was a novice.

Cash wasn't.

Maybe she *had* left him wanting. She chewed her lip and watched the dust cloud grow behind Vivi. He *had* warned her not to harbor expectations. Business, she reminded herself. She had to keep it business with him. Nothing more.

Hank stepped out of the barn, and she jumped. "Hank. I didn't see you."

"Nope, don't imagine you did." He spat a stream of tobacco juice onto the ground. "Probably ain't none of my business, and I'll apologize right up front for eavesdroppin', but that woman Leo got mixed up with upset you, and I'm not gonna stand back and let her get away with it. No, sirree."

"I have to go." She blinked quickly, praying she could hold back the tears. "I have to meet someone in Lone Tree."

"Understood," he said gruffly. "But you'll take a minute first." His tone broached no argument.

"I didn't catch everything she said, but whatever it was, you'd do best not to believe her. I don't especially like to speak ill of anyone, but that woman is plain evil. She's hurt a lot of people with her lies and deceit."

Annelise wanted to believe him, but truth? What Cash did with Vivi wasn't likely to be something he'd broadcast. Hank really had no way of knowing what went on between Vivi and Cash behind closed doors.

Or at the pond.

"Thanks, Hank. I appreciate it."

"You think on what I've said." He turned and disappeared back into the shadows of the barn.

She rode off, remembering a short story she'd read in high school. "The Lady or The Tiger?" The accused had to decide between two doors to determine his guilt or innocence. If he chose the tiger's door, he'd be torn to bits. If the lady stood behind the door, he lived but had to marry her even if his heart was elsewhere.

It all came down to trusting your instincts.

More and more, she was coming to understand that. She had to make her own choices. Had to trust herself and her own instincts about people.

She could make business decisions all day long without the slightest hesitation. But when it came to personal? She lacked confidence. And it was lowering to admit that. Barely able to decide on a paint color, how could she decide what to do about Cash?

She wanted to trust. Wanted Hank to be telling the truth.

But after today, could she?

Chapter Fourteen

The drive to Lone Tree had seemed endless the first time Annelise made it. Today, it was endless times ten. Between the possibility of finding her aunt and the hurtful words Vivi'd tossed out, she was on overload. Excitement, nerves, uncertainty, and dread—all raced through her like a dog trying to catch his tail, playing havoc with her emotions.

First things first, though. She mentally shoved Vivi and Cash into a dark, dusty corner of her mind. Rethinking that, she stuck them in opposite corners. Now she'd concentrate on her grandfather.

She felt like kicking herself. This was the reason she'd come to Texas, this quest for her grandfather's sister. His life depended on it. Yet now that she had an actual lead, she found herself reluctant to open that proverbial can of worms. Who knew what she might uncover at the bottom?

Fate, though, stepped in. As luck would have it, Thelma had decided to stop into the Cowboy Grill for lunch today. Oliver, acting as Annelise's patron saint, explained as much as he knew to the town's longtime resident and had actually set up a meet.

No going back. The die had been cast.

Annelise swung her Harley into the passing lane and around a slow-moving cattle truck out of self-defense. Following it on her bike in a hundred degrees made for quite the odiferous ride. One she could happily live without.

As she slid in front of the truck, her mind veered back to her grandfather. His remission was temporary; his only hope rested in a bone marrow transplant. A half sister could very well carry the cure for Grandpa's leukemia. A permanent cure.

So, the big question. The one that haunted her and kept her awake at night. Why didn't her grandfather want this woman found? Annelise couldn't begin to count the times she'd asked herself—and him—that question. He'd told her it didn't concern her. And that, to his way of thinking, ended the discussion.

Well, as far as she was concerned, it was far from over. The reason didn't matter. Nothing mattered except restoring his health. If there was even the smallest chance this mystery woman was a match, Annelise was determined to find her.

Once she did, well, she'd tackle that problem when she got to it. One step at a time.

Annelise prayed her meeting with Ms. Hanson would bring results. She didn't know how much longer she could stay on at Whispering Pines. She could simply walk away from the job. It had been a cover, a reason to stay in town. She didn't need that anymore, did she?

Pulling into a parking space, she rubbed at a spot on her chest. The idea of saying good-bye to Cash hurt. In a short time, he'd wormed his way into her life.

Too bad she hadn't done the same with him.

She drew up short. Long-term between herself and Cash? It couldn't happen. He was so right. Neither could live permanently in the other's world.

Yanking off her helmet, she swung her leg over the bike. Putting three quarters into the parking meter, she set out across the street.

Since she had time to burn, she'd check out the dress store she'd spotted on her last trip. The hand-painted, flamboyant calligraphy script on the front window read *Maggie's*. Annelise didn't hesitate. Lone Tree wasn't Fifth Avenue, but who knew?

The instant she walked through the door, she fell in love. Somebody with a real eye for fashion and design had pulled this place together. The store didn't shout small town. It didn't even whisper it.

White lace curtains hung at the windows. Sunlight poured through them and formed sugar-frost patterns on the deep brown carpet underfoot. Soft, pale pink walls, their crown moldings the same chocolate brown as the floor, welcomed her.

Clothing, shoes, and accessories spilled over the interior in what Annelise realized was a very well-planned, but totally random-looking design. Lingerie tumbled from the open drawers of an antique dresser. Jewel-toned perfume bottles scattered across the surface of the beautiful oak piece.

A drop-dead gorgeous redhead stepped from a backroom. A magnificent scarlet and purple swingy top and pencil-thin black pants set off a model-perfect figure and face. Not what Annelise thought to find in Lone Tree, Texas. She'd have put down money the owner would turn out to be Dottie's look-alike cousin.

The redhead sent Annelise a wide, open smile. "Hi. Welcome to Maggie's."

"Thank you. Your store is wonderful. Not at all what I expected." She cringed inwardly. "I didn't mean—"

"It's okay." The redhead laughed. "Lone Tree doesn't exactly lend itself to a Madison Avenue mood, does it?"

"No. I'm afraid those weren't the vibes I picked up when I drove down Main Street."

Walking to her, hand extended, the redhead said, "I'm Maggie."

"Hi, Maggie. I'm Annie. This shop is adorable. I saw it when I was in town yesterday. Since I couldn't get in then, and I'm here for an appointment and have some extra time, I thought I'd stop by."

"Glad you did." Maggie looked around her, out the front window. "Is that your Harley?"

Annelise nodded.

"Oh, wow. I saw it parked there yesterday. Must be fun to ride, huh?"

"It is that."

"Scary?"

"Only at first. Once you get the hang of it, there's nothing like it. Maybe I can take you for a ride someday."

"That would be great!"

"Speaking of great." Annelise turned back to the clothes. She fingered a dress in a rich red, black slashes streaking almost haphazardly across the bodice. "This is fantastic. I've never seen anything quite like it."

"I hope not." Maggie's soft laughter accompanied her words. "It's one of my designs."

Annelise looked away from the dress, met the other woman's gaze. "Seriously?"

"Yep. I designed it, then ran it up on my sewing machine in the back." She nodded to the room she'd come from. "My studio." She grimaced. "Someday, if I'm very,

very lucky, I'll be able to afford something bigger. More workable."

A dreamy smile lit her face. "In New York City, the center of the universe."

Annelise grinned, then studied the dress closer. The work was impeccable, the design clever. "Are all the ones on this wall yours?"

Maggie nodded.

Annelise moved from one to another, then another, amazed at what she'd stumbled upon. Maggie's work could put any of the big name designers to shame.

And wouldn't you know it? Her smile grew. She needed a dress, didn't she? Something to wear to the fund-raiser. Maybe, just maybe...

Her mind working a mile a minute, she turned back to Maggie. "It so happens I'm in need of something to wear to a rather important get-together. It's formal, though, so I need an outfit that's a little more, I don't know, elegant, for lack of a better word." She waved toward the wall.

"When do you need it?"

"Ah." Annelise arched her brows. "And there's the rub. I need it day after tomorrow."

"Well, Ms. Annie, why don't you come on in the back with me. I've got a couple more elaborate designs I've been toying with. Problem is, nobody around here wears dresses like them." She took a few seconds, let her eyes run the length of Annie, taking in her jeans, T-shirt, and scuffed cowboy boots.

"I know. I don't look the part of some fancy socialite. I'm—" She hesitated, not sure how to explain what she was doing here in Texas. "I'm only here for a little while. While I am, I'm doing some work at Whispering Pines."

"Really? For Cash Hardeman?"

"Yes." Surprised, Annelise asked, "Do you know him?"

"Know him? I practically grew up with him. I used to live in Maverick Junction, and I graduated from high school there. Pops, my grandpa, lives here in Lone Tree. Now that he's getting on and Granny passed away, we didn't want him living alone. So, I moved here to be with him. I get free rent, which lets me spend more on fabrics, and he gets company and somebody to cook and clean for him." She held out her hands. "So far, so good."

It really was a small world, Annelise thought.

"Cash is a good man," Maggie said.

"Yes. Yes, he is." Annelise's throat tightened at the thought of that good man. Of his kisses. A good man and an honest one. He didn't intend to lead her on—even if she might want him to.

The thing at his house after? Well, they'd both gotten carried away. Again. The chemistry between them was explosive.

She followed Maggie through the doorway into the backroom, and Annelise felt as though she'd stepped into another world. Oh, yes, this was definitely where Maggie created. Where the magic happened. A huge table, strewn with fabrics, zippers, and sketches, backed against a brick wall. On the end wall, a sewing machine sat, the unrestored wood floor littered with pieces of fabric and thread clippings.

"Sorry for the mess. Didn't expect company back here today."

"Don't worry. I find this fascinating."

Maggie plucked a drawing from a bulletin board that hung over the large table. "This is the one. It's perfect for your build. It would look great on you."

"Oh!" Annelise traced a finger over the dress's silhouette. It was a study in contrast. The gown, diaphanous and flowing, bared one shoulder. Maggie had combined it with a very tailored short-sleeve jacket. It should have been an impossible pairing. It shouldn't work. Yet it did.

"What did you use for the fabric?"

"Nothing. Yet." Maggie grinned. "This one hasn't come out of the drawing stage. It's still incubating."

"Oh." Disappointment shot through Annelise. Maggie was right-on. The dress would have been perfect for the fund-raiser.

"I thought I'd use an ivory-colored organza with an under layer of silk in the same color. For the jacket, I'd keep it entirely sheer. Maybe a single crystal-covered button." She rummaged in a bright pink plastic bin. "Like this one." She held out the fastener.

"I love it." Annelise leaned a hip on the table. "If only I'd found you sooner."

"I can make it tonight."

"What?"

"If you really do want it, and you're not just being polite, I can put it together for you tonight—after I close up."

"Honest?" Delight danced in Annelise.

"Honest."

"But, can you get the material?"

Maggie stepped to another door, made a come-here gesture. Annelise followed her into a smaller room that looked like an old pantry. Its wooden shelves overflowed with bolts of fabric.

Maggie walked straight to one and drew it out, laying it on an old drop-leaf. "This is the one I thought I'd use for the jacket and overlayment." She rooted around till she found what she wanted and pulled another bolt loose. "This would go underneath for the dress itself."

"Perfect."

"You're sure?" Maggie asked.

"The real question is yours. Do you really think you can do this so quickly?"

"One-hundred percent positive." She started to say something, stopped. Then, eyes on Annie's, she said, "You haven't asked the cost."

"It doesn't matter."

"What?" A startled giggle escaped her. "Of course it matters."

"Okay. So it matters. Give me your price."

Maggie debated, pulled a pencil from her mass of red curls, and began figuring on a scrap of paper she dug from her pocket. She winced. "I don't know. This might be too high. What do you think?" She turned the paper so Annie could read it.

Annelise skimmed the figures. "I think it's highway robbery."

Maggie paled. "You do?"

"Unquestionably. If I took this dress for that amount of money, I'd be stealing it from you. Maggie, it's worth four times this."

The redhead said nothing, simply stared at her, lips parted.

"Maggie?"

"Yeah. It's... well, I don't ever remember a customer telling me I wasn't charging enough."

"Well, you're not. How about I pay you three times this number?" She tapped a nail on the paper. "Then we'll both feel we've done right by each other."

"Did Cash take you in from a rest home or an insane asylum?"

Annelise laughed. "Neither. But the simple truth is that I know fashion. I also recognize genius and great work when

I see it. You've got both in your clothes, and you deserve more from them. If you want, you can call the extra money a bonus for the rush I've put on the job."

Maggie still hesitated.

"I won't buy the dress unless you meet my price," Annelise said.

"This is nuts." Maggie chuckled. "Okay, if you insist."

"I do."

"Then I need some measurements."

Annelise checked her watch. She had enough time to do this and still be on time for Ms. Hanson.

They'd barely finished when the bell over the front door tinkled.

Buttoning her blouse, Annelise said, "Go ahead. Take care of your customer. I'll be right out."

Maggie opened the door. "Pops, what a great surprise. I didn't know you were coming into town today."

"Oh, I needed a couple things from the hardware store. Thought I'd fix that sticky faucet in the hall bath."

Annelise stepped out and smiled at the tall, slightly stooped white-haired gentleman wrapped in Maggie's hug. His weathered face smiled back at her. She noticed he had the same moss-green eyes as Maggie.

"Pops, this is Annie. Annie, my grandpa, Fletcher Sullivan. Annie's ordered one of my evening gown designs."

"That right?" He walked to her and extended his hand. "Good for you, young lady. You got good taste."

"Your granddaughter is extremely talented. I haven't seen anything better during fashion week in Paris." She could have bitten her tongue off the instant the words were out.

"You've been to fashion week? In Paris?" Maggie practically squealed. "Oh, my gosh, tell me all about it."

Annelise shrugged. "Not that big a deal."

"Easy for you to say."

"Tell you what. When I come back for my dress, I'll share some gossip. Right now, though, I've got to run. I cannot be late."

"Where you rushing off to?" her grandfather asked.

"I have an appointment, Mr. Sullivan."

"Call me Fletch."

She nodded.

"An appointment? Here in Lone Tree?"

"Yes." She debated how much to say, then realized it didn't really matter. By morning the entire town would know she and Thelma Hanson had talked. These small communities were a breed unto themselves.

"I'm meeting Thelma Hanson, sir."

"Fletch," he growled. "You make me feel like an old codger when you call me mister or sir. What in the world are you doing with Thelma?"

"Pops, that's her business." Maggie laid a hand on the old man's arm.

"No. It's okay. My family used to live here, Fletch. I'm trying to track down a relative."

"Thelma?"

She shook her head. "I think she might be able to help me, though."

"Humph. What's your family's name?"

Oh, boy. Annelise took a deep breath. Once she threw her name out there, there truly would be no going back. "Montjoy."

Silence settled over the shop, stretched out for what seemed an eternity.

"You Driller's kin?"

"Yes. He was my great-grandfather."

"Well. I'll be damned! Oh, sorry. Pardon my French, but

I'll be..." He threw back his head and laughed. "I knew your granddaddy. Vinnie and I were buddies all through elementary school. BFFs, I think you gals would say today."

Maggie grinned. "Way to go, Pops."

Annie, trying to digest this latest bit of information, realized Maggie had turned back to her, was staring at her.

"What?"

"I kept thinking I should know you. God, you're Annelise Montjoy, the missing oil heiress."

"Guilty as charged."

Maggie's green eyes widened. "The dress. It's for that big fund-raiser in Dallas, isn't it?"

"Yes. And there's bound to be press there. If anyone's interested, or if I can find a way to work it in, I'll be sure to give Maggie's in Lone Tree a pitch. I'll tell everyone I can about Maggie Sullivan, the latest fashion genius."

"Oh, my gosh." Maggie clapped her hands. "I should be paying you, Annie, for wearing one of my designs."

"No way. Think of all the basking I can do, taking credit for having discovered you."

"From your lips to God's ear," Maggie whispered.

"So, how's Vinnie doing?"

Despite herself, tears welled in Annelise's eyes. "Not so well. He has leukemia."

Fletch's face deflated. "Oh, honey, I'm real sorry to hear that. Anything the docs can do?"

"Not unless we can find a bone marrow match for him."

"And that's why you're here," Maggie said.

Annelise nodded.

"Boy, sure wish I could help." Fletch rubbed the back of his neck. "I don't know what to tell you. One day, old Driller just up and moved the family to the East Coast somewhere. Seemed there'd been some kind of family trouble or something, but I was a ten-year-old kid. Whatever went on wasn't discussed in front of me if anyone even knew, and I didn't care. All I knew was my best friend left, and I missed him like hell.

"I might have a picture or two of us from back then. I'll look around. If I find one, Maggie can make you a copy, give it to you when you come 'round to pick up that new dress she's gonna whip up for you."

"I'd like that very much." Annelise walked toward the door. "I'd better get going. I don't want to keep Ms. Hanson waiting."

At the door, though, she stopped. "You know, Cash is throwing what I assume is his annual Fourth of July picnic at Whispering Pines. I'd love it if you two would come as my guests."

Maggie threaded her arm through her grandfather's. "Oh, I'd love that. How about you, Pops? Want to be my date?"

"I'd be honored."

"Can you get away for a fitting tomorrow, Annie?"

Annelise rested a hand at her waist. "Is a bluebird blue?"

Maggie laughed. "I'll take that as a yes."

"About two o'clock?"

"Two will work fine."

* * *

Running across the street, Annelise noticed a few parked cars and trucks. People like Fletch coming into town to do their business. And they'd all know each other, their family history. Everyone would smile and wish each other a good day. Not a bad way to live.

Her grandfather had that for the first nine years of his life. Had best buddies. Then had all the security torn away.

Fletch might not know why, but Annelise figured she did. A threatened scandal over infidelity had chased Davis "Driller" Montjoy out of Lone Tree. What a shame. And, yet, the very act that had torn her grandpa's life from him was now the only thing that could save it. Or so she hoped. What a convoluted jumble.

She stepped into Ollie's and waved at him behind the counter.

"Hey, good-lookin'." Ollie wiped his hands on his apron. "How are you today? Saw that bike of yours out there and wondered where you'd gotten off to."

She grinned. "I ran into Maggie's."

"Ahh. Find anything?"

"As a matter of fact, I hit pay dirt." She looked at him, blew out a nervous breath. "Now, if I can only be as lucky with Ms. Hanson."

"I'll keep my fingers crossed for you, honey." He slid a piece of paper toward her. "Here're the directions to her place." He trailed a stubby finger over the drawing. "Be sure you turn when you get to this sign. You do that, you can't go wrong."

He glanced up. "You got your cell phone?"

"Yes."

"Good. There's a big tower outside of town, so you'll have decent reception. You get lost, you call me, and I'll come find you."

Again, she felt the sting of tears. "Thank you, Ollie." She leaned over the counter and kissed his cheek. "I can't tell you how much I appreciate this."

"Ah, get out of here. Go." A big grin split his jowly face. "Good luck."

She threw him another kiss as she rushed out the door.

At her bike, she studied the crudely drawn map. It seemed

simple enough. The problem was, a lot of territory rambled out there. Well, she had her phone and didn't doubt for a minute Ollie really would come rescue her if she needed him.

Turning the key, the bike rumbled to life beneath her. She backed out of her spot and turned south. Maggie waved at her from the window of her shop, and Annelise waved back.

In a matter of a week, she had more friends here than she had in Boston. Regardless of the outcome with Thelma Hanson, regardless of whether or not she found her great-aunt, she would never regret this trip.

*　*　*

Thelma Hanson lived at the end of a rutted dirt road. Annelise imagined every filling in her head would have to be replaced as she bumped along.

When she reached the end of the lane, the door of a weathered two-story white house opened, and a rail-thin woman stepped out. "You must be Annie."

"Yes, ma'am." Annelise removed her helmet and shook out her hair.

"Oliver tells me you're looking for family and that they came from here at one time."

"Yes."

"Why don't you come inside out of this miserable heat? We can talk in there as well as out here and won't suffer heat stroke while we do." With that, Thelma Hanson opened her door wide and welcomed her in. "Where are you from?"

"Boston. But my great-grandfather was from here. My grandfather lived here for a while, too."

"Well, then, Annie, I probably knew them. The Hansons have lived on this homestead since before history."

Annelise smiled. "That's what Oliver told me."

"What was your great-granddaddy's name?"

And here's where the fat met the frying pan. "Davis Montjoy."

"Driller?"

Annelise nodded.

"Oh, for heaven's sake. Why didn't Ollie tell me that?"

"He didn't know." Annelise took a deep breath. "I didn't tell him."

"Why ever not?"

She shrugged, uneasy.

"Hmmm." Thelma switched subjects. "Bet you'd like something cold to drink, huh? Wash down that road trip. Surprised me to see you pull up on that big motorcycle. Not the usual mode of transportation for a girl like you."

"No, it's not, but I love it. And I'd really appreciate a glass of iced tea if you have any. If not, even water will do. I think I've swallowed enough dust to fill a sinkhole."

Ms. Hanson made a cackling sound. "That'd be about right for Texas mid-summer. Need to get us some rain. And soon. Or the whole state's going to blow away to Nebraska."

"Yes, ma'am."

Annelise trailed after her and stood in the arched doorway as Thelma moved on into the kitchen, as old-fashioned as any she'd ever seen. A chipped, white porcelain-topped table sat in front of the chintz-covered window. A white cupboard that she knew would have a flour bin and sifter inside sat against the far wall. The whole house had been freeze-framed sometime in the forties—or earlier. An antique dealer would go nuts in here. Off to the left in the dining room, she recognized a beautiful oak icebox, now serving as a side table.

Thelma Hanson, though unbelievably thin, stood tall and

straight. Annelise guessed her for somewhere around eighty. Her face had obviously seen its share of the Texas sun and had the wrinkles to prove it. She wore a navy and white cotton shirtdress and had obviously fixed her hair in anticipation of Annelise's visit.

She wondered how many visitors Thelma had. Not many, she guessed. Not anymore. Living out here must be a lonely life, filled with memories of what once had been a bustling ranch, a family home.

When Thelma moved back to the living room, Annelise took the tray of tea and shortbread cookies. Placing it on the coffee table, she sat. Thelma handed her a napkin, then set one of the teas close to her on a coaster and passed her the plate of cookies.

Taking one, she said, "Thank you, Ms. Hanson. I can't tell you how much I appreciate you meeting with me."

"Like I told Ollie, I don't know if I can help you. Call me Thelma, please."

"All right. Thelma." She sipped her sweet tea and tasted the slight tang of orange. "This is great."

"Family recipe."

"Did you know *my* family?" She gripped the glass tightly, more nervous than she'd have thought possible.

"I didn't know Driller well. I was too young. He became kind of a legend here, you know. A man from Lone Tree falling into all that money. Now your granddaddy, I knew him better. He was a couple years younger than me. Vinnie was a sweet boy. Even after his daddy came into all that money, he never changed a whit. Never got all uppity like so many nouveau riche do."

Thelma set the last of her cookie on a napkin. Standing, she beckoned to Annelise. "I think I might have a picture for you."

In the dining room, she moved to an old steamer trunk. Lifting the top, she sifted through the contents till she found the box she wanted. Placing it on the dining table, she said, "Have a seat, Annie, and let's see what I have here."

As they went through photo after photo, Thelma reminisced, telling Annelise about the people in the photos. Finally, she found the picture she'd been searching for.

"Here you go." She laid the sepia-toned photo in front of Annelise. "There's Driller and Vinnie, your great-grandfather and your granddaddy. He was so young, then, wasn't he?"

"I've never seen a picture of him as a child." She stared at the boy and his stern-faced father, both dressed formally in white-collared shirts, ties, and suit coats. Her great-grandfather sat in an upholstered chair, while her grandpa stood behind him, a hand on his shoulder. Neither smiled.

"You can keep that." Thelma shook her head. "Darn shame about all the fuss. Such a nice family. After the scandal, they moved away. Never heard from them again. Except once in a while on the news, of course. And you must be the one who's gone missing."

"Yes, I needed some time away." But Annie's mind wasn't on that. Her ears had pricked up at Thelma's comment about the scandal. Exactly what she'd come for.

The story of Driller's illegitimate child.

Her mouth cotton-dry, she wished she'd carried her tea to the dining room with her. "Ms. Hanson, Thelma, the scandal. Did it involve a child?"

"Indirectly, I suppose. You sure you want to hear all this?"

"Yes. It's the reason I'm here." She picked up the photo and studied it. "I came for my grandfather."

"How is Vinnie? I heard he was sick."

"He has leukemia and needs a bone marrow transplant. Relatives are generally the best matches. None of us are, though. I'm thinking that—"

"A sister might be."

"Exactly." Goose bumps raced over Annelise's skin. "I've heard rumors he might have had one here. A half sister."

"He did."

"Is she still alive?"

Chapter Fifteen

Vivi wants to do what?" Cash sprang from his chair. He'd been worried when Gideon had asked him to stop by his law office. But this beat all.

"She's filing papers to legally change the name of the ranch, and I'm not violating any client privileges by telling you this. She specifically asked me to. She wants you to know."

"She's gonna rename the ranch Vivi's Valley?"

"Now settle down."

Cash rested his hands on Gideon Crain's cluttered mahogany desk. The gray-haired, bespectacled man had been his grandfather's lawyer from the time he'd graduated law school. Leo Hardeman had been his first client.

"Settle down? Settle down? I don't think so. Tell me she can't do this."

"I'm afraid she might be able to. Since the ranch will be split fifty-fifty, she'll have as much say as you. This arrangement's pretty dicey."

Cash sputtered and paced the small room.

"You're the only one who can stop this nonsense."

Cash halted mid-step and glared at the elderly lawyer. "Don't lay this on me. Grandpa created this fiasco." He pointed a finger at the lawyer's chest. "How could you let him do this?"

Gideon shook his head. "Believe me, I tried like hell to talk him out of it. He wouldn't listen. Your grandpa could be a stubborn old cuss."

"Don't I know it."

"Because of lawyer-client privacy laws, I couldn't tell you what he planned to do," Gideon said. "I figured, given time, he'd come to his senses and change it."

"But he ran out of time."

"Yes, he did."

A deep sadness settled over Cash. "You know, as hard as it's been, as hard as it is not having Gramps here, maybe that heart attack was the kindest thing that could have happened. The way his mind was going—hell!" He stuffed his hands in his jean pockets and wandered over to the window. "What am I gonna do?"

"I can't answer that for you, Cash." Gideon peered over the bridge of his glasses. "Tell you what, though. I sure am glad I'm not in your boots. Hell of a pickle Leo put you in."

Cash rested his fists on the windowsill and looked out over Main Street. Henry Foster and Walt Johnson headed into Sally's Place. They were running late today. They generally met for lunch. In fact, they'd been there the first time he'd laid eyes on Annie.

Annie. His chest tightened.

Life went on.

Not for Leo Hardeman, though. Why had the old man felt the need to orchestrate things after his death? If he'd simply left the ranch to his widow, it would have been easier to swallow. But dangling Whispering Pines in front of him— well, it didn't go down well. And it was totally out of character for his grandfather.

"Never could figure out what Leo saw in that woman."

Cash raised a brow. "Sure you did."

Gideon laughed. "Okay, okay. Guess I did. But why didn't he settle for playing sugar daddy?"

"Wish I knew the answer to that question. My take on it is Gramps was too much the gentleman for that."

"Damned shame." Gideon carried his mug over to the coffeepot and poured a fresh cup. He held it up to Cash. "Sure you don't want some?" He looked increasingly uneasy.

"Nope. Lay it on me, pal. There's something else, isn't there? You're about as nervous as a June bug in a henhouse."

The lawyer cleared his throat. "Yes, I'm afraid there is more. Another reason I called you in today."

Cash let out a loud sigh. "Oh, boy. I can hardly wait. It must be a real doozy." He ran his fingers through his hair. "Another of Grandpa's stipulations?"

"I don't know. He left a letter for you. I was only supposed to deliver it if you were nearing the six-month mark unmarried."

"And in six months and three days, I turn thirty. Grandpa's deadline for me to march down the aisle." He dropped back into the chair and scrubbed his hands down his face. "Okay. Hand it over."

Gideon went to a safe and withdrew the letter. Without another word, he passed it to Cash. "I'll mosey out and keep Staubach company. I'm assuming you left him in the outer office like always."

"Yep."

"Okay, then. I'll leave you alone with this, but I'll be right outside if you need to talk."

With a sinking feeling, Cash took the envelope. His name was scrawled on the front in his grandfather's chicken-scratching. The office door closed.

He tapped the envelope on his forehead. What would happen if he simply threw it away without reading it? What was the penalty for that? Might be a hell of a lot easier.

Then he looked at it again, at his grandfather's familiar handwriting. A band of pressure wrapped itself around his chest and made it hard to breathe. God, he missed the man. Tears blurred his vision.

He slid the envelope back and forth between his fingers. Wasn't the letter really like an unexpected gift in some ways?

Maybe.

Maybe not.

Blowing out a huge breath, he slipped a finger in the corner of the seal and slit it open. After another deep breath, he withdrew the paper and unfolded the single sheet.

Then he simply sat there and gave himself a full minute to compose himself before moving his eyes to the paper. The familiar handwriting alone was enough to bring a lump to his throat.

I've got a feeling, Cash, that you're probably none too happy with your old grandpap right about now, because if Gideon's given this letter to you, I'm dead and you're not married and have no prospects. Hell of a note.

I loved your grandma Edith more than the air I breathe. Breathed, I guess, since you're reading this.

Edie and I want you to have someone special to share your life, too.

And damn it all, seems neither of us are there to nudge you along, boy. I'm almost glad Edie didn't live to see what a durned old fool I turned into. Of course if she'd lived, none of that—and by that, I mean Vivi— would have happened. I'd still have been sitting out on the porch of a summer evening, holding hands with my best girl.

Cash smiled. Every evening when it was warm enough, his grandparents had sat in their red rockers and enjoyed dessert and iced tea. He hadn't thought about that in too long. It was a good memory.

He returned his attention to the letter.

Vivi—well, I don't know. Guess I got lonely. She made me feel young again. Then, she made me feel like the old fool I am.

Your grandma chewed me out well and good for that one, don't you worry. She came sometimes at night to visit, you know. We had a humdinger of an argument over that other woman, as your grandma called her.

Cash laid the note down in his lap and stared out the window. More than once in the last year or so, he'd seen his grandfather confused. Heard him talk about his Edie as though she was still alive. Reality had obviously become blurred for him. Cash forced himself to read on.

Anyway, getting back to the reason for this letter. The thing is, your grandma says you're gonna get your back up and not marry because of the will. I don't want that. Don't want you getting all stubborn and defying me on principle.

Cash snorted. "Me get stubborn, Gramps? Oh, that's rich," he muttered.

If you do, Cash, you'll break both your grandma's heart and mine. Love can't be rushed or forced. We know that. But my guess is you're not even looking. If this backfires, I'm damn sorry. That wasn't our intention.

You're too hard on yourself. Loosen up. Open those eyes of yours and start looking around. My guess is that love is staring you straight in the face, and you're too cussed ornery to latch on to it.

Annie's blue eyes, full of hurt, swam into his mind. Damn! He blinked, rid himself of the image.

Let go, Cash. It's time to move on to the next stage of your life. Give your mama and daddy a new daughter. Give them some grandbabies.

Make us all proud.

> *With much love and affection,*
> *Grandpa*
> *Leo Hardeman (I'm only adding this to get Gideon off my back. He insists it's not legal without my signature. I told the old goat you knew who Grandpa was, but he says the courts might not. What difference that makes is beyond me. I wrote this letter to you, not the courts.)*

God, that was his grandfather. He could hear him and Gideon arguing over the proper signature. He missed the old man.

The clock on the wall ticked off the minutes and still Cash sat, hands in his lap, the letter gripped tightly. His jaw ached with unshed tears. An overwhelming sense of loss nearly suffocated him. He couldn't imagine a lifetime without Gramps.

And Grandma Edith. It had been over eight years now, but he could still see her in the kitchen making oatmeal and raisin cookies, standing by the corral while they broke a new horse, carrying gallons of ice water to the hands. She'd worked hard, but she'd always had time to kiss a scratched knee all better or to read a book with him.

He stood, folded the letter into its envelope, and tucked it in his back pocket. Time to let Gideon go home.

He opened the door and stepped into the outer office. His dog scrambled to his feet and came over to meet him. "Hey, Staubach." He rubbed his head.

"We're gonna get out of here so you can finish up. I appreciate your time."

His grandfather's friend studied him. "You okay?"

"Yeah," Cash answered, even though he had a headache starting behind his right eye. "I'm gonna take a little time to digest all this, then I'll get back to you if I need anything."

"Sounds good." He hesitated. "You think you might want to contest the will?"

He shook his head. "You and Hank. You're singing the same tune."

"I think we've got grounds," Gideon said.

"Maybe so, but I don't want to do that. And before you ask, Mom, Dad, Babs, and I have already discussed this. They agree with me."

"Would the letter help us?"

"Oh, yeah. But the answer's still no. Why drag Grandpa's good name through the courts. Hell, Vivi's his widow. Maybe it's only fair she gets half."

"If she was a different person, I might agree."

"Yeah, well, what are you gonna do? She is what she is."

Gideon walked with them to the door. "Your grandfather loved you, Cash."

"I know." With that, he and his dog loped down the stairs and stepped onto the non-bustling street. When he went no farther, Staubach looked up at him and whined.

"I'm okay, boy, I'm okay. Got way too much running around in my head, though. Not sure which side is up anymore."

His grandfather's letter hadn't told him anything he didn't already know. It had, though, reminded him of a few things he'd forgotten.

His grandfather had been a good man. A decent, hard-working man.

Cash had been a good, decent man, too. He wasn't so sure that was true anymore.

He wanted it to be.

He thought about Annie. He'd done her wrong. Not because they'd made love. Not even because he'd taken her virginity. He'd done her wrong because he'd been a certifiable ass afterward. He couldn't understand why she hadn't clocked him, right there and then. If the shoe had been on the other foot, he was pretty sure he would have.

"Staubach, we've got some shopping to do." He wagged a finger at the dog sitting so patiently at his feet. "And you will not get in the bags and eat any of it. Understood?"

Staubach barked and wagged his tail.

"Okay, then. Let's go." Digging the car key from his

pocket, he headed to his old blue Caddy, his dog following behind. Staubach waited till Cash opened the door, then hopped into the front seat, tongue hanging out, ready to go.

They drove to Sadler's store. "You stay right here. I'll only be a minute."

He ran into the store, pulling his phone from his shirt pocket. "Hey, Barbara Jean, it's your baby brother. Listen, I need a no-brainer recipe. Something that will impress, but is easy, fast, and can't fail." He listened while his sister listed a few possibilities.

"They all sound good, but she's in an upstairs apartment, and it's hotter than Hades. I don't want to heat it up with the oven."

"She? This would be Dottie's upstairs apartment? Cash, are you fixing dinner for Annie? Lots of gossip about the two of you going around town."

Argh. He'd said too much. With her blabbermouth, everybody in the county would have the latest scoop by sunup, including his mother. *Shoot me now.*

Well, nothing to do but man up. "Yeah, I am. So?"

"So, nothing."

But he heard the glee in her voice and knew she was deciding who to tell first and whether it should be by smoke signal, phone, or e-mail.

They finally decided on their aunt Eileen's fruit salad, French bread, and grilled kielbasa. Dottie had a small barbecue in the backyard, and he figured she wouldn't mind him using it, especially if he fixed her a plate.

Via phone, Barbara Jean walked him through the aisles, telling him exactly what he needed. For something so simple, he sure seemed to be tossing an awful lot of stuff in his basket.

After paying, he wheeled his cart to the car, took one look at a smiling Staubach, and loaded his bags into the trunk.

Annie wasn't home. He hadn't factored that possibility into the equation. He knew she'd driven over to Lone Tree, but figured she'd be done and back by now.

Dottie spotted him on the steps. "Hey, Cash, looking for Annie?"

"Yeah, I thought I'd stop by and—" Oh, what the hell. "I figured I'd fix dinner for her. I've got stuff in my car."

"Well, don't let it spoil. Bring it in, then you can take it up when she comes. I'm in the middle of cleaning out my kitchen cabinets and decided to take a break. I made a fresh pitcher of lemonade this morning. You and I can sit out back with our feet up and a cold drink and wait for her."

"Sounds good to me."

Half an hour later, they'd solved the majority of the world's problems and started on their second glasses of lemonade. They'd also polished off a plate of sugar cookies.

The rumble of the Harley broke the stillness.

"Still surprises me to see the girl riding that bike everywhere."

He chuckled. "I know. But, that's Annie."

"Yes, it is." She pinched his cheek. "Give me that glass, and I'll take these things and disappear inside."

"Don't forget. I'm fixing dinner."

"I haven't forgotten. Not every day a handsome man offers to cook for me."

"Flattery will get you everywhere, Dottie."

"I certainly hope so." She studied him. "Is my girl gonna be happy to see you?"

"I messed up today, Dottie."

"Thought so." She gave him a quick hug. "Not like you

to botch things, Cash Hardeman. But if you have, you need to fix it. Annie deserves it."

"I did. And I'm gonna try my best to set it right."

"Good enough. Staubach can stay down here with me. That doghouse might get a little crowded with both of you in it."

Chapter Sixteen

Annelise spotted Staubach sprawled on the sidewalk, his head resting on his paws, those big brown eyes on her. Her stomach clenched. If he was here, so was Cash. She wasn't sure she could face him yet. No, actually it might be better if she did.

"Hey, pooch, what are you doing here?" She knelt down and petted him. "My guess is you didn't drive that old Caddy yourself, so where's your master, huh?"

"That mutt has no master, believe me." Cash peeked around the side of the house. "He only keeps me around to feed him."

"Cash." She ran a hand through her wind-tousled hair. "I didn't expect you tonight."

"I know, and I probably should have called, but, well, Staubach and I missed you."

"Missed me?" Her heart lurched. Had she heard him right? After he'd warned her not to expect anything? After what Vivi had said? How was she supposed to be able to recognize the truth?

"I thought I'd stop by and see if you'd let me make dinner for you."

"Make dinner for me?" She felt like a parrot. "I'm not sure that's a good idea."

"It's an apology, Annie." His voice was husky. "You deserve it after the way I treated you."

"Why would you want to make dinner for me when you're sleeping with Vivi?"

"What?"

"Your ears quit working?"

"No! Damn it, what the hell are you talking about?"

She tried to sidestep around him, but he moved in closer, cupped her chin.

She jerked away. "*Are* you sleeping with her?"

A look of absolute horror crossed his face. "Annie, as God is my witness, I've never touched that woman. Nor will I ever."

"That's pretty much what Hank told me."

"Hank?"

"Long story."

"Annie." He reached for her hand, but she drew away. "You have to believe me."

She closed her eyes, blew out a huge breath, and met his gaze once more. "No, I don't have to."

"What's going on here?"

She tried to turn away, but he wouldn't let her.

"Who upset you?"

"Besides you?"

He flinched.

"Cash, because of who I am there're not a lot of people in my life I can trust. I thought you were one of those few. Now"—she shrugged—"I don't know."

"Annie, I'd give anything if I could take back those words."

"Why would you? It's how you feel, isn't it?"

"I'd take them back because they hurt you. Because—" He removed his hat, raked his fingers through his hair. "Because I never should have said them. They were a mistake."

"But they summed up how you feel." She refused to back off.

"Yes. No! God, Annie, I don't know." He closed his eyes. "I'm confused. The one thing I do know is that I hurt you, and I've never been sorrier. I miss you. There's a gulf between us, and I want it gone."

She wasn't ready to forgive him or let him off the hook for his less-than-tactful words on the ride to his house. But she couldn't send him away, either.

"About dinner," she said. "I'm still not sure that's a good idea."

"Give it a try. I'll leave whenever you say."

"My cupboard's pretty bare."

"We've got that covered. Staubach and I stopped at Sadler's on the way."

She glanced at the dog, who sat up now, smiling at her. "Did anything survive the trip?"

He laughed. "I locked it in the trunk. It's in Dottie's refrigerator now. I wasn't sure when you'd get home." He tugged at her hand. "Come on. I'll show you how to make my aunt's fruit salad. You'll like it."

"This doesn't mean I've forgiven you."

"Understood."

* * *

"Did you find any clues to your lost relative?"

Annelise nodded. "I'll tell you about it while we fix dinner. I'm starved. I thought about stopping at Oliver's, but now I'm glad I didn't."

They walked up the outside stairs together after collecting the groceries from Dottie, who'd added two beautiful, ripe tomatoes from her garden.

"These tomatoes." Annelise palmed one. "I've never tasted anything like them. I stood at the sink yesterday and ate one like an apple, juice running down my chin and grinning like a loon."

"I've been guilty of doing that a few times. Maybe not the grinning, but—" He stood in the doorway when she unlocked it, and Staubach squeezed in. Cash frowned at him. "You were supposed to stay downstairs."

He sat in the middle of the kitchen, his brown and white tail thumping happily on the floor.

"Let him stay." Kneeling by him, she shook hands with the dog. "You're welcome anytime, boy."

The dog shot Cash a hah-hah look.

He shook his head, then swept a hand toward her space. "This is great, Annie. I haven't seen it all finished."

"It is wonderful, isn't it?" She hugged herself.

"You amaze me." He set the bags on the counter and took her face in his hands. "You have so much, yet it takes so little to make you happy." He brought his lips close.

She felt his breath against her face and started to draw back.

"Don't pull away from me. Please." His lips met hers, and she melted into him.

Though his words still haunted her, she forced them to the back of her mind. Wrapping her arms around him, she fought to get closer still. He did something incredible to her.

He didn't want forever. Well, then, she'd make the most of today.

His lips, feather-light, roamed to her eyes, her chin, nuzzled her neck and sent shivers through her. Would she ever get enough of this man? She seriously doubted it.

His fingers tugged her tank from her jeans and lifted it up and over her head. His hands cupped her breasts, slid down to her waist, and unsnapped her jeans.

Breathless, she pulled away. "Cash, I need a bath. The dust—"

His lips silenced her. One arm beneath her knees, the other at her back, he carried her into the bathroom. Setting her on the edge of the tub, he began drawing water.

Staubach started in. "No way, big guy. You stay out there." He pointed toward the living room, and the dog left. With his foot, Cash nudged the door shut.

He cocked his head. "You think that thing's big enough for both of us?"

"You're kidding."

He unbuttoned, then unzipped his jeans and let them slide to the floor. "Nope."

Within minutes, she was nestled between his legs in the tub, bubbles practically up to her chin. He lathered her, used a cup to wash and rinse her hair, and did things to her body she swore were impossible.

Water sloshed over the rim of the old claw-foot tub. She giggled. "If it starts flooding downstairs, Dottie's going to be up here. What will you tell her?"

"The truth." He nipped at her ear. "That you seduced me into your bath and had your way with me."

"And she'd believe you."

"She would."

Annelise twisted, caught his mouth in hers.

In one smooth move, he rose, taking her with him. More water splashed onto the floor. They ignored it. Dripping wet, he carried her into her bedroom, flipped back the spread and top sheet, and laid her down.

She stretched her arms up to him. "Come here."

Their wet, slick bodies all but steamed.

* * *

Make-up sex definitely lived up to its reputation—and then some, she decided.

The sun was setting by the time they made it into the kitchen, him in unsnapped jeans and bare feet, her in her cheap cotton robe from Sadler's. Her mother would have a coronary if she saw them now, ready to make and eat dinner like this. Having grown up with very little, her mom had made it her life's work to perfect the airs of aristocracy. She seldom wavered. Dinner was always a dress-up affair.

Annelise smothered the giggle that threatened. This— with Cash—was an affair, too, plain and simple. And as long as she remembered that, she could have the time of her life, away from all the madness that cluttered her days and nights.

"I'm famished." Cash dug into the grocery bags. "Babs said the fruit salad was supposed to chill. Don't think we'll have time for that, but it should be okay anyway."

"Babs?"

"Barbara Jean. My sister. She promised I couldn't screw this up. We'll see. Jury's still out."

Opening a can of chunked pineapple, he drained the juice into a small pan. "Why don't you slice up the fruit?" He nodded toward the bags. "I'll fix the sauce." He added a packet of vanilla pudding to the juice, heated and stirred till the combination turned into a thick orange goo.

He eyed it skeptically. "This is it, I guess. Put the fruit and walnuts in a big bowl, then I'll pour this over it."

That done, he set it in the fridge and slipped into his shirt. Grabbing the sausage, he said, "Set the table, woman, and I'll be back with the meat."

Halfway out the door, he stopped. "Oh, there's French bread in one of the bags if you want to slice that. The wine was chilled when I left the store, but..." He shrugged.

"I'll take care of it." She grinned. When she heard his footsteps on the stairs, she did a little happy dance through the kitchen.

Turning on the old radio, she found his country station, lit a couple of candles, and set her mismatched table. The flowers from Dottie's garden made a perfect centerpiece.

Finding the bread, she unwrapped it and got out her cutting board. She'd slice one of the fresh tomatoes Dottie'd given them and drizzle a little olive oil over top. Then she took out a third plate to make up for her landlady.

A breeze came through her open window. Life was suddenly a whole lot better than it had been a few short hours ago. She still needed to call her mother, but that could wait. They'd eat first. No sense ruining her appetite worrying about it.

When Cash returned with the grilled meat, Staubach came to attention. Cash put a piece of the sausage on a paper plate and set it in front of the grateful dog.

Annelise watched him. "Can I ask one more question?"

He groaned.

"One more. Then I'm done. Promise."

"If I say no, will that stop you?"

She shook her head.

"I didn't think so. Shoot."

"It's Vivi."

He set the platter on the table. "Annie, I swear to God—"

She shook her head. "The look on your face when I asked about that told me everything I needed to know. You're not sleeping with her."

He grimaced. "I can't imagine why you'd ever think I was."

"She told me you were."

"When?"

"This afternoon."

He swore a blue streak, then apologized again.

"Here's the thing, Cash. Why is she so antagonistic? I don't get it. I haven't done anything to her, but it's like she's holding a grudge."

"It's not really you. It's, well, complicated."

"Anything I should know?" Annelise asked.

Slowly, he shook his head. "Not really."

"Why don't I believe you?"

"You're competition, all right?"

"For what?"

"For..." He waved his hand in the air. "For being the most beautiful woman on the ranch."

"That is such BS."

He laughed, then breathed deeply. "Smell this sausage. You as hungry as I am?"

She put her hands on her hips, studied him. "Okay. And we're changing the subject."

"Yep."

The meal, despite, or maybe because of, its simplicity, was one of the best she'd ever eaten.

"Cash, you can cook for me anytime."

He took her hand, ran his thumb over the back of it. "I mean to have you over to my place for more meals like this."

She didn't know whether to laugh or cry, her emotions on a dizzying roller coaster ride. It had been quite the day.

"I have a hot tub." His eyes went smoldery.

She almost choked on the grape she'd just popped into her mouth.

He laughed.

"If I go to your house, can we have the make-up sex without the fight?"

"You bet, darlin'. In fact, why don't we consider it a prerequisite?"

They cleared the table together. "I really do need to call my mom. It's late on the East Coast, but fortunately she's a night owl, so it won't matter."

She sat down, picked up a tablet, and added to her list. "I almost forgot. I'm going to need an escort."

"An escort?" Cash's forehead creased. "Like from one of the services in the phone book? Is that even legal?"

She reached out and punched him on the arm. "You're being deliberately obtuse."

"Yeah, I am." He sat down on the arm of her chair and played with a strand of her hair. Staubach wandered over and flopped on the floor beside them.

"So who usually accompanies you to these things, Ms. Montjoy? Some obnoxiously rich heir apparent?"

"Don't be like that." She punched him on the arm again.

"Sorry."

"No, you're not."

"Okay, you're right. I'm not sorry. And you're dodging the question. Who takes you to things like this?"

"Friends of the family. Acquaintances." She shrugged. "Douglas."

"Does Douglas have a last name?"

"DeWitt."

"Well, sugar, Douglas DeWitt won't be taking you this time. I'm gonna be the guy on your arm. And I promise on Rosie's chili, the best this side of the Rockies, and that's saying something, that I'll behave myself."

"You'll hate it."

"Maybe."

"It's a simple enough thing for Douglas to meet me there."

"Nope. Not gonna happen. See, I've got this hang-up, I guess you could call it. When I'm sleeping with someone, I want to be the only person in her bed."

Annelise felt her cheeks burn and knew she must be red as a beet. "It's not like that."

"Does Douglas know?"

"We've never—you know."

"Yeah, I know. And I'd like to keep it that way."

"You're an interesting study in contrasts, Cash. You warned me not to expect anything beyond the moment. Now, you're talking exclusivity if I'm understanding you correctly."

"Yeah, well, exclusivity doesn't mean, you know, forever. It doesn't have to mean that."

She studied him more closely. He looked as flustered as she felt. "You'll need a tux."

"Okay."

Just like that. Okay. The man could drive her to distraction. "When I call Mom, I can ask her to arrange one for you. But I'll need your measurements."

"Not necessary."

"Are you sure?"

"Positive."

Doubt settled in her stomach like a fist, but she'd have to trust him. Trust wasn't always her strong suit when it came to something like this. She liked to be in control, liked to know for absolute certain everything was taken care of. Things like this forced her to pop Tums.

"One more thing before I call Mom. Two, actually. The first, I'd like to take Dottie along."

"A chaperone?"

She was too slow in answering.

He laughed. "Darlin', I understand there's gonna be a lot of press there. I got that. And I'm sure there'll be a ton of expensive photography gear with most of it aimed at you. Since I've already promised on Rosie's chili to behave, I have to assume it's you you're worried about."

She snorted. But he was way too close to the truth.

And it was all his fault. He *had* created a monster. He'd given her a taste, well more than a taste, more like a heaping plateful of what it could be between a man and a woman. And she wanted more.

With him.

Even if he intended to let her walk away when her job here in Maverick Junction was done.

"You said two things."

"What?" She brought herself back to the conversation.

"You said there were two things you needed to settle."

"Oh, the second Mom will handle. You really don't mind if Dottie goes, do you? I thought she might get a kick out of it all. She's been so good to me, and I thought it might be a way to repay her a little."

"You're a good person, Annie. I think Dottie will have the time of her life there. It'll be a real treat for her."

"Thanks."

"So what's this second thing your mom will handle?"

"Transportation. We have to get from here to Dallas."

"Not a problem. I've got it covered."

"Are you sure?"

"Annie, you're starting to sound like a broken record. Trust me. I'll get you there. Are you always this nervous before an event?"

She sighed and fell back against the chair. "Yes. I hate making public appearances. And I can't simply show up and mingle. They'll make me get up on stage and say something, something that should be profound."

He said nothing, simply sat there on the chair arm and grinned at her.

"What?"

"Nothing."

"Then stop laughing at me."

"I'm not laughing at you. I'm marveling at you. So brave."

"No, I'm not. Didn't you hear what I said? I hate public appearances, public speaking. They scare me to death. I'm always afraid I'll screw up and, I don't know, besmirch the family name."

"Yet you do it, despite all that. Like I said, you're brave."

"Stupid is more like it."

Now he laughed. "Annie, Annie, Annie." He tousled her hair. "Call your mom."

*   *   *

Letting out a huge sigh, Annelise turned off her phone. "And that's that," she said.

Staubach, stretched out beside Cash's chair, snored quietly, his tail thumping slowly on the rug.

"Grandpa's doing fine. Mom will call the charity to let them know I'll be there, and her secretary will issue a press release tomorrow."

"Go, Mom."

Annelise grinned. "Georgia Montjoy is never happier than when she's busy taking care of the world." She curled up in his lap. "Mmmm."

He tightened an arm around her, and she laid her head on his chest. His heartbeat was steady and strong. Like him. As awful as it had been, today's storm had cleared the air between them. Had given them both a better understanding of each other.

"She also chewed me out for being so irresponsible. She's been afraid that any day now the rags in the supermarket check-out lines would have my picture splashed all over them with some made-up story about me being in rehab or worse."

"What will her reaction be to pictures of you and a Texas cowboy?"

"Once she sees you?" Annelise pulled back a little to look up at him. "Catches a glimpse of this beautiful face?" She lifted a hand to his cheek.

Cash caught it in his. He kissed her palm, then trailed those lips to her fingertips. Sucking gently on her pinkie, he drew it into his mouth.

Her heart thumped, and her lashes fluttered against her cheeks.

He bent his head and kissed her. Slowly. Carefully. Thoroughly.

She was breathless when he lifted his head.

"What else did your mother have to say?" His mouth was a mere whisper from hers.

"What?" She couldn't think.

"She okay about Maggie?"

"Oh. Not quite, but she will be. Maggie's crazy good. Her name will be on everybody's lips by this time next year. People will be clamoring for a Maggie original."

"It's good of you to wear one of her designs."

"I'm the lucky one. I can't believe she's willing to do this on such short notice."

"No, the lucky one would be me, Annie. I'll be there with you when you wear it."

Annelise bit her lip. The thought of a night with Cash practically had her hyperventilating. They'd have to be careful, on guard. The press would be there. One slip and there'd be hell to pay.

"You miss them."

"My family? Yes, I do."

"This is a courageous thing you've done. Coming here to Texas."

"Not really. I can't stand to lose my grandpa. I have to try to save him." She placed her hands on either side of his face. "I'm so, so sorry you lost yours." She kissed him, tenderly. Felt the sorrow in him. Tasted the grief.

He drew back. "Tomorrow's going to be a long day. We'd better get some sleep." He arched a brow. "Want me to tuck you in before I go?"

A slow smile curved her lips. "I think I can manage. But thanks for the offer."

She walked with him to the door. "Maybe I can take a rain check?"

"You sure can."

She fingered the no-frills disposable phone Cash had given her earlier. With so much riding on this dinner, she couldn't toss it like she had her other one. Without a doubt, her parents would use it to pinpoint her location.

Or they'd track her through Cash after the fund-raiser.

Any way she cut it, her time in Maverick Junction was fast running out, and she'd yet to find the missing aunt. And then there was the fact that she flat-out didn't want to leave yet. Maybe in another thirty or forty years, but not now.

"Cash, does your phone have a camera?"

"Yeah, sure."

"Could I borrow it for tonight? Promise I'll return it in the morning. And I won't call any sex lines."

"You want to call a sex line, give me a ring." He winked at her. "My rates are cheap."

"I appreciate that."

"Can I ask why you need it?"

"To take a picture of Dottie. Mom's personal shopper will arrange for an outfit for her, but if I send a picture, she'll have a better idea what to choose. Dottie needs to look totally smashing."

"You're a good woman." He dropped a kiss on the tip of her nose. "Come on, Staubach." He and his dog disappeared into the summer night.

She stood on the landing, listened to the hearty roar of the Caddy's engine. Waited till it faded to nothingness.

Checking the time on the kitchen clock, she debated whether to invite Dottie to Dallas in the morning or do it now.

She was keyed-up.

Last night, a long hot bath might have provided a cure for that. Somehow she seriously doubted going anywhere near that tub tonight would calm her jangled nerves.

So she headed downstairs in search of a chaperone, someone to hold Cash at bay.

She pictured him, jeans unsnapped, chest bare versus Dottie in her pink housedress and sensible shoes. All in all, a fairly even match.

Chapter Seventeen

The next day passed in a blur. Working the barn, Annelise arranged tack on the wall, her mind buzzing. So much still needed to be done.

Dottie had been over the moon last evening at the idea of a big night out in Dallas. Immediately, she started to fret over clothes. When Annelise explained that was taken care of, that a new outfit would be waiting for her at the hotel, the woman had teared up.

However, when Annelise explained she needed a photo to send to her mother's personal shopper, the tears stopped immediately. Even though it was after midnight, Dottie insisted on putting on makeup and fixing her hair before she'd allow Annelise to snap her photo.

Footsteps sounded behind her, but she didn't need to turn around to see who'd come into the barn. She felt him.

"Did you get some sleep?" His deep voice practically vibrated the air around her.

"I did. You?"

"Yep. Slept like Staubach in a shady patch on a hot summer afternoon."

She couldn't help but smile, thinking of the dog asleep at their feet last night. "So you snore, do you?"

He shrugged. "Never had any complaints."

"Guess you wouldn't—when you sleep with dogs."

"Oh, ho! Low blow."

She tried to swallow her laugh. "Yeah, and probably not smart since I need to ask a favor. Can I borrow your truck this afternoon?"

"Sure."

"Just like that?"

"Just like that."

"Boy, aren't you easy?"

"Again, no complaints."

She tossed a rag she'd been using at him. "You're going to have some pretty soon, you keep that up."

He came to her, slipped an arm around her waist.

She gave him a halfhearted push. "Not here, boss man."

"Not even a good morning kiss?"

She shook her head.

"You're tough enough for both of us, huh?"

"I've learned to be...discreet."

He laughed. "Oh, yeah. Last night in that old claw-foot, you were the epitome of discreet, all right! And I, for one, loved that discretion." He leaned close and whispered in her ear. "Maybe we can do it again tonight."

She swatted at him as heat roared through her, flashed across her chest and face. "Be good."

"Oh, darlin', I'm trying."

A flat-out heat wave scorched her body. She turned her head, their lips inches apart. "There's a lot of the bad boy in you, isn't there, for all those cowboy manners?"

"I sure as heck hope so."

She backed up, licked her lips, and had him groaning. "About this afternoon. I need to run over to Lone Tree. My dress will be done except for a few final touches after a fitting. I can't get it home on my bike. I don't want to scrunch it up in my saddlebag."

He nodded. "Want me to come along?"

She thought about it for a minute. "No. I don't think so. I'd like to keep the big reveal for the night of the gala."

"Okay. Why don't you break off after lunch and take care of that."

"You sure?"

"Yeah." He traced a finger down her arm. "That way, you'll be home in time for our date."

"Our date?"

"Come out with me tonight, Annie."

Come out with me tonight. His words held such an old-fashioned, romantic flavor.

"Let's go to the drive-in. We can eat dinner at the snack bar," he said. "Greasy, salty food that'll clog our arteries but have our taste buds dancing."

"Really?" Her heart did a little pirouette of its own. "I've never been to a drive-in."

"Go on."

"Seriously."

A devilish grin transformed his face. "Another first. I'll show you why it's the number one make-out choice. What do you say I pick you up about six thirty?" He gave her a quick swat on the butt. "Now get back to work before the boss chews us out."

* * *

Instead of eating lunch with the boys, she opted to wait till she reached Lone Tree. She wanted to thank Oliver for all his help. Whether or not it ferreted out her aunt, he'd gone out of his way for her.

By now, the road was familiar. Because of that, she relaxed into the drive. It was nice to be at the wheel of Cash's pickup. It smelled like him. She'd had to pull the seat up a couple of inches to make up for their difference in height.

When he'd handed her the keys, he'd apologized for the condition of the interior. It was a ranch truck and had a lot of hard use. She'd tossed a couple of soda cans in the recycle bin before she'd left. As long as Maggie had plastic to wrap her dress in, no harm, no foul.

The fact there was a gun rack in the farm truck, complete with rifle, astounded her. Who carried guns out in the open like this? She answered her own question. Cowboys. Cash.

She turned the air-conditioning to high and rolled down both windows. It was, she supposed, an odd habit, but, while she didn't like to sweat, she enjoyed the play of the wind against her face, in her hair.

Speaking of playing. She reached over to the sound system and pushed Power. What CD did Cash have in his work vehicle's deck?

She wasn't surprised when a country song poured out of the speakers. Not her style, but the song was catchy. When it finished, she ejected it to look at the artist's name, Keith Urban. "Somebody Like You."

She played it again and sang with it this time. Boy, the lyrics said it all. One step forward and two back. Wasn't that the truth? When Keith sang about his arms around her, she could practically feel Cash's from last night, holding her tight.

Somebody like you. Who'd have ever thought he'd be a long, tall Texan on horseback?

By the time she hit Lone Tree, she had the song memorized.

Parking the truck, she locked up and went straight into the Cowboy Grill. Starving, she swore there must be something about the Texas air because she'd never eaten so much in her life. Or maybe it was the manual labor. Whatever, she was enjoying the good food.

Oliver was working the grill, his back to her. An older woman, in a red dress and white apron, pointed at a table by the door. "Have a seat. Be with ya in a minute."

"Okay. Thanks."

"Hey, I recognize that voice." Oliver, spatula in hand, turned. "Annie. How ya doin'?"

"I'm doing well. You?"

"Can't complain." He pointed the spatula at the waitress, who set drinks at a table in the back. "Specially not with the wife by my side. Hey, Judy, this here's Annie. Remember I told you about her. She's lookin' for her relative."

Annie winced at her personal laundry being made public. Though she should be used to it.

"Yeah, sure." Judy wiped her hands on her apron. "You talk to Thelma? She able to help ya?"

"I did meet with her, yes. Ms. Hanson is a jewel. She's working on some things for me. I really appreciate your husband's help."

"Yeah, he's a pretty good guy." She elbowed Annelise. "Guess I should keep him, huh?"

Resisting the urge to rub her bruised shoulder, Annelise nodded. "I think so."

"You're a real pretty lady. Got anybody special in your life?"

Not sure how to answer, she hesitated long enough to give Judy the go-ahead. "Reason I'm askin' is 'cause my nephew's out of rehab—third time—and I'm thinkin' a good woman might be exactly what he needs to straighten him out."

"Oh. Well. I, ah, I actually do have someone." Temporary counted, didn't it? She crossed the fingers of the hand hidden by the plastic tablecloth, just in case.

"Darn shame. He's not ugly."

Annelise swallowed her laugh. "Sounds like it's my bad luck, huh?"

"Judy, stop jackin' your jaws and take the lady's order. Annie came in to eat, not to get set up by no matchmaker."

"All right, all right. What'cha gonna have?"

She went with fried green tomatoes, ribs, and a salad to ease her guilty conscience. Then, throwing caution to the wind, she ordered sweet tea.

She chatted with Oliver and Judy till her meal came. Then they actually got busy, and she concentrated on her food. Between this and the meal Cash promised tonight, she'd have a month's ration of fat calories today.

"You meetin' with Thelma again?" Ollie asked while she was paying.

"No. She's going to call me later. Right now, I'm running over to Maggie's to pick up a dress."

"Aren't her things fabulous?" one of the women at a table of four asked.

"They sure are. With her talent, I'm amazed she's not in New York."

"New York City?"

One look at the appalled expressions on everyone's face and Annelise realized her gaffe. Time to leave.

"'Bye, Ollie. Nice to meet you, Judy." She nodded toward the other customers.

Several women were milling around Maggie's when she walked in. As she listened to them, she realized they'd driven in from Austin, and it wasn't their first trip to the shop. She didn't blame them in the least.

"Your dress is finished," Maggie said. "I'll be just a few minutes."

"Absolutely. That'll give me some time to look around a little bit more." It had dawned on her on the ride to Lone Tree that she had black leather pants, a couple of pairs of jeans, and a handful of T-shirts. Period.

While Maggie helped the three with their selections, Annelise found a pair of white slacks and an incredible gauzy top for the trip tomorrow. She'd need something to wear the morning after the fund-raiser, too. On the Maggie originals wall, she spotted a short skirt in a fresh geometric print. A short-sleeve blouse in the same coral as in the skirt caught her eye.

"Okay if I try these on?"

"Sure. The dressing room's in the back corner."

On her way to the changing room, she spotted a pair of pale pink shorts. She picked them up and, rummaging through the racks, found a white top with a sweetheart neck-line. The outfit would be perfect for a drive-in date, wouldn't it? With a Cheshire cat grin, she added it to her finds.

Everything fit as though they'd been custom-made for her. She hung them by the counter. "I'm going to take these, too."

"Oh, there's a great necklace on the mannequin over there that would match that top perfectly," one of the women from Austin said.

She was right. Annelise added it to her growing pile.

When the women left, bags in tow, Maggie sighed. "They're good customers. About once a month, they make the trip to check out my new stock. Okay. Let's go to the back and try on this dress of yours."

She flipped the door sign to read CLOSED. "We don't need any interruptions. It shouldn't take too long."

Once in the sewing room, Maggie removed the dress from a cover bag.

"Oh, Maggie."

"I know." She grinned ear to ear. "I want you to turn your back to the mirror." She slid the dress over Annelise's head. She sighed as the silk whispered along her body.

Typical designer, Maggie wouldn't let her take even the tiniest peek till she fussed with it a bit, then slipped on the sheer short-sleeve jacket. "Okay." Maggie turned her toward the mirror.

The dress was everything Annelise could have hoped for and more. This should, pretty please, knock the boots right off Cash's feet.

"Maggie Sullivan, you've got magic in those fingers of yours."

The young woman laughed. "I don't know about magic, but I have a few thousand pin pricks."

"Did you get any sleep last night?" Annelise couldn't help running her fingers over the dress's skirt. It made a wonderful little shushing sound.

"Enough," Maggie said. "It's energizing to see a creation come to life."

"It must be wonderful to be so talented." She turned and peered over her shoulder to see the back. "I promise I'll mention your name every chance I get. We'll see if we can plaster you all over the news."

Maggie hugged her. "That would truly be a dream come true." She studied Annelise's reflection. "What are you going to do for shoes? Accessories?"

"My mom's taking care of that."

She frowned. "Okay."

Annelise laughed. "I called her last night. Believe me, there's nothing she likes better than to get her fingers in the details. I'll have everything I need."

Maggie helped her out of the dress and, while Annelise slipped back into her jeans, she zipped it up in a protective bag.

They went into the front where she paid for the rest of her purchases. "Not bad for an hour of shopping. Thanks again, Maggie. I'll see you soon."

"Great. Have fun tomorrow night."

Once she had her things safely stored, she decided to give Thelma Hanson a call before she left town.

On the third ring, Thelma answered.

"Ms. Hanson? This is Annelise Montjoy."

"I know who you are. 'Spose you're wondering if I've had any luck so far."

"Well, yes. I'm in Lone Tree this afternoon, so..."

"I'm having lunch with your aunt tomorrow."

"You are?" Her breath hitched. Her aunt! For the first time, it seemed real. Before, she'd been a vague idea. "Does she know about me?"

"No, ma'am, she don't. Didn't figure I'd tell her about your visit till I was sitting face to face with her. Give her less chance to pretend she doesn't know what I'm talking about. You know, she might not be too happy to see you."

"I understand."

"You've waited a long time, honey. Give me a little more. I'll call when I know something or can get her to agree to talk with you."

"Thank you. I appreciate this so much, Ms. Hanson."

"Didn't we agree to Thelma?"

"Yes, ma'am, we did. I appreciate your help, Thelma. I have to go to Dallas tomorrow to attend a fund-raiser for a charity I sponsor."

"Now and Then. I know all about it. Been reading about you through that Google thing on the Internet."

Of course. Wasn't her life an open book? "I'll be staying overnight and coming back the next day. I'll have my phone with me, though, so you can leave a message if I don't answer."

"Fine."

Annelise found herself with a dead phone held up to her ear. Well. Brevity could be a good thing, she supposed.

Chapter Eighteen

Annelise's phone rang. Giving her new dress one last pat where it hung in the tiny closet, she bolted for the kitchen and her cell.

"You home?" Cash asked.

"Yes. I got here a few minutes ago."

"Did your dress turn out okay?"

"It did. Better than I dared imagine."

"So, my guess is you're in a pretty good mood, then."

"I am."

"Up for a movie? Maybe a hot dog and some popcorn?"

"You bet. In fact, I'm counting on it."

"Thought we'd take the Caddy. Put the top down and sit under the stars."

Annelise smiled clear to the tips of her toes. It sounded heavenly.

"Do you mind if Staubach tags along? He's promised me he'll hang out in the backseat and not bother us."

She laughed. "That would be more than wonderful. Thanks, Cash. This sounds like fun."

"I still can't believe you've never been before."

"See? Goes to prove little rich girls don't have all the fun."

There was silence for a few seconds, then she chuckled. "It's okay, Cash. I can poke fun at myself."

"You're too much."

She wrapped an arm at her waist and hugged herself, hearing the laughter in his voice.

"Can you be ready in half an hour? I need to run a couple things over to my parents' place first."

His parents. Her heart dropped to her toes. Memories of them in the barn—right after she and Cash...Well, it was inevitable she'd have to face them again at some point. Might as well get it over.

Then she thought of the new shorts and top waiting in the bedroom. Her new *drive-in* outfit. Before she'd run over to Lone Tree, she'd taken a quick shower at the ranch. Still, a bath sure would feel great. "Give me forty."

"Deal."

She drew a tub and added some bubbles. The sultry scent of bergamot, vanilla, and orchid rose from the hot water. She slid into the tub, leaning back and closing her eyes. Had she ever felt as alive as she did right now, here in this tiny town, working with horses and sharing kisses with Cash?

Tomorrow, once she attended the fund-raiser, this ideal would undoubtedly come to an end. So she'd better make the most of tonight, hadn't she?

He rapped on the door as she gave her lashes one last flick of mascara. She took a moment to check herself out in the mirror. The top fit like a glove, the shorts were fun and flirty. And she was as nervous as a kid at her first piano recital. She took one last calming breath and went to answer the door.

He leaned against the jamb and let his gaze slide over her. Then he let out a long, wolf whistle. "Well, round them doggies up and bring 'em home. You look like dessert served up on fancy Sunday china, darlin'."

She mock-curtsied and batted her lashes. "Why, thank you, sir."

When she righted, she met his eyes, eyes dark with desire. Before she could say anything, he pulled her to him and kissed her. And he took no prisoners!

"We don't have to go to the drive-in. We could stay right here," he whispered.

"Not on your life." She pushed away. "You promised me a movie and popcorn, and I'm holding you to it."

"Grab your purse, then, and let's go."

Staubach waited in the backseat. She rubbed his head, and he gave her a sloppy kiss. "Argh." She wiped her face.

Once they were headed down the road, she looked in the side mirror. The dog held his head high, ears flapping in the wind and, she swore, grinning.

She grinned with him.

Cash turned off the highway onto a gravel road. The sign read BIG SANDY RANCH.

"Your folks live here?"

"Yep. It belonged to my mom's parents."

"Did your grandpa leave his ranch to Vivi or your dad?" She turned to face him. "Or to you? You're the one keeping it together."

Cash's face showed no emotion. "Kind of a long story there." He gave her a half smile. "Nothing for you to worry about."

Hmm. She begged to differ. She suspected that long story wasn't totally to Cash's liking. She saw it in the way he held himself, in the short answer, in his unwillingness to quite meet her eyes. Obviously, though, it wasn't something he wanted to discuss.

He pointed to his left. "There's the old homestead. Mom and Dad decided to leave it as it was. Outside. Inside, that's a different story. Mom's gone through every inch of the place, redoing and redecorating—almost on a daily basis."

As they drove closer, Annelise couldn't take her eyes off the house and grounds. A rambling two-story sprawled across a well-manicured green lawn. Bushes and flowers lapped at the foundation. A wrap-around porch boasted a swing and comfy looking lounge chairs. Pots of bright flowers and trailing ivy lined the front steps.

A big red barn, doors open, sat at a distance from the house. Another smaller structure appeared off to the right. A huge garage sat across the drive from the house.

A few horses cropped grass in a paddock, and she heard cows lowing in the distance.

It looked like home. Looked like a Norman Rockwell version of a Texas ranch.

Pulling up to the sidewalk, Cash got out and went to the back of the car. Opening the trunk, she heard him grunt as he lifted something out.

She opened her door and watched as he swung the saddle over his shoulder and slammed the trunk.

Holding out a hand to her, he said, "Come on. I'll only be a minute."

At the front door, he knocked, wiped his feet on the welcome mat, and stuck his head in the door. "Anybody home?"

"We're in the kitchen, honey. Come on in," his mother called.

"I've got the saddle Dad wanted. I'll put it down in the hallway here." He dropped the saddle onto the burnished oak floor. To Annelise, it looked incongruous beside the antique side table with its stained glass lamp and fancy little doo-dads.

"That's fine. Are you hungry?" She peeked her head around the doorway. "Oh, hi, Annie. I didn't realize Cash had brought you with him." She wiped her hands on a tea towel. "Excuse my manners."

"I'm the one who dropped in uninvited."

"Dad's in the barn finishing up a couple last-minute chores. Would you two like to stay for dinner? It's pick and lose tonight, so..." She spread her hands. "We'd love to have you." Mrs. Hardeman included Annelise in her welcoming smile.

"Thanks, Mom, but we can't. I promised Annie I'd take her to the drive-in." He winked. "She's never been if you can believe that. We'll grab something at the snack bar for dinner."

"You sure?" She walked to them and rubbed her son's back. "I don't feel like we've seen much of you since we've been home. Maybe tomorrow night?"

"Actually, Annie and I have to fly to Dallas tomorrow afternoon. She's got a thing there. We'll be staying overnight."

"Oh?"

Annelise grew warm with embarrassment. "Dottie's going with us," she said quickly.

"Really? That's wonderful. Dottie's a good person."

"Yes, she is."

"Gotta go, Mom. I left Staubach out in the car. If I leave him there too long, he'll eat the upholstery."

"That dog is liable to eat more than that. Never saw anything like him." She kissed Cash's cheek, then surprised Annelise by hugging her and giving her a quick kiss. Laying a hand on Annelise's face, Mrs. Hardeman said, "You come back."

"Thank you. I will."

"And have a good time tonight." She pointed a finger at Cash. "And you. Remember where you are. No fogging the windows. Let this poor girl watch the movie."

"That what you and Dad did when you went? Watched the show?"

She gave him another loud kiss. "Do as I say."

"Not as you did?"

"Go on." She laughed. "Get out of here."

Halfway down the walk, Annelise stopped, her mind replaying something he'd said to his mother. "Flying? You didn't tell me we were flying to Dallas. I assumed we'd drive."

"Flying's faster."

"Is there an airport nearby?"

"There's one at Whispering Pines."

"Whispering—" Her forehead creased.

"I'm flying us, Annie. I keep a little plane at the ranch. And you don't need to worry. It's big enough for the three of us and all the luggage you two gals will have."

Her mouth opened, closed. Finally she asked, "You fly?"

"I do. It's a handy skill to have when you live this far from everything."

She'd slipped on her sunglasses, but she pushed them down her nose to look at him. "This won't be your first solo?"

He laughed and opened her door for her. "No."

"You own your own plane?"

"Yes, I do."

Oh, for someone who prided herself on her ability to quickly size up the competition, she'd pegged this man so wrong. She remembered their first meeting. How she'd judged him on the old Caddy, his run-down boots. Worried he wouldn't eat because Staubach had raided the bag of groceries. She hadn't only missed the bull's-eye, she hadn't landed anywhere near the target.

She slid into the front seat. He waited while she tied her hair back, then off they went, Kenny Chesney singing about sunsets and tequila.

"What in the world is pick and lose? Some Texas dish you've hidden from the rest of the world?"

He laughed. "It's my mom's name for leftover night. She cleans out the fridge, and you pick from whatever's on the table. A little bit of this, a little bit of that. Since it's all a day or two old and has been warmed up once or twice, a lot of times you lose on the quality. Pick and lose. But then you probably didn't eat leftovers, did you?"

She turned on the seat to look at him. "Does it bother you that I might not have? Leftovers have no bearing on who I am."

"Oh, honey. Yeah, they do."

"You're wrong, Cash. And you know what? You're the one being the snob here. Not me."

He swung out onto the main road. "I didn't say you were a snob."

"Yes, you did."

"When?"

"Right now. You insinuated it. You do that a lot. Little digs."

He glanced at her. "They're not intentional."

"Doesn't matter. A dig is a dig."

"Staubach?"

The dog's ears perked up, then flattened again in the wind.

"Stay away from girls. They're touchy creatures."

Annelise swatted him.

When they got to the drive-in, he pulled up to what looked like a toll booth and paid. Then they drove on through.

"How close to the screen do you want to be?"

"I don't know. Where do you usually park?"

"I like to go to the back. That way nobody bothers you on their way to the concession stand. And no one interrupts when things get hot and heavy."

She laughed. "Right. I should have known. So how many lucky ladies have come here with you, Cash?"

He shook his head. "Huh-uh. Not going there." When she started to open her mouth, he said, "A gentleman doesn't kiss and tell."

"I'm not asking for names, just numbers."

"Nope. That's like asking if an outfit makes your butt look wide. No good answer."

"Oh, my gosh. Do I look fat in this outfit?"

"See what I mean? But that answer is an unequivocal no, ma'am, you do not. In fact, when you answered the door, I about swallowed my tongue. You've got some legs, Annie. Miles and miles of beautiful, tanned legs. You ought to show them off more."

"So you like the shorts?"

"Oh, yeah. You're prettier than a speckled pup in a new red wagon at Christmastime."

She rolled her eyes. "You've got a real way with words, Cash Hardeman."

"That's what all the ladies say."

"Well, this lady bought these shorts at Maggie's today— especially for you."

"And I gotta say I appreciate them. Nice gift, darlin', on one spectacular package."

"Me and the speckled pup."

He grinned. "You and the speckled pup."

Pulling into a space toward the back, he edged forward. "Can you see okay from here?"

"Yes." She leaned over the car door. "They've mounded the parking spots."

"That's to give a little elevation. Kind of like stadium seating in a movie theater."

"I love it."

He reached for the speaker and, raising his car window slightly, hooked it over the glass.

"What's that?"

"Our sound system. A lot of drive-ins have gone to radio, but not Smittie. He still uses the old speakers. Claims playing the radio runs folks' batteries down, and he'd end up having to spend an hour after the movies finish with a set of jumper cables."

"He's probably right." Annelise marveled at the activity around them. The place looked like a giant ant farm. People jumped in and out of cars, some headed off to the concession stand, others walked back to their cars carrying giant popcorns and sodas. "This is great. I love watching people."

"You notice they're all looking back at us. Wondering how I ended up with the prettiest girl here." He draped his arm over the back of the seat.

"You are so full of it."

"Come here." With one quick tug, he pulled her close. "Let me show you the real reason everybody loves the drive-in." He drew her close, bussed her neck, her ear. He ran a hand down her back, down her side, lightly brushing the undersides of her breasts.

"I've been waiting all day to do this." His lips moved to hers in a hot, wet kiss.

She groaned, then remembered where they were. This

was what his mother had warned him about. Or had she actually been warning her? With the top down, Annelise assumed they wouldn't be fogging any windows, but it sure wouldn't be for lack of trying. And they were putting on quite a show. From no PDA to this. The man moved fast.

Heart skittering, she drew back. In the dimming light, his green eyes looked nearly black.

He rested his forehead against hers. "You make me crazy, Annie. How about we put the top up? Make it a little more private."

"How about we don't?" She shook her head. "You've created a voracious appetite in me, Cash." Her voice sounded husky to her ears. "One touch, one kiss, and I want more."

"Want to go home?"

"No way!"

She started to slide to her side, but he stopped her. "Don't. Stay here by me. That's one of the beauties of this old car. It's made for sitting close to your baby. If I had a new car, we'd have bucket seats and wouldn't be able to cuddle."

She curled into his side, tucked in close, his arm wrapped around her. She rested her head on his chest, and he took her hand in his.

A funny feeling rolled through her. She'd never been called anybody's baby. Cash stirred emotions in her on so many levels. And it felt so, so good.

The movie came on, the newest James Bond film. Holding hands, they watched as 007 saved the world from the latest villain. Cash took full advantage of the dark. His hands and lips kept coming back to her as though he, too, couldn't get enough. When the gearshift practically skewered his ribs, he swore a blue streak.

"And that's the problem with necking in a car," he muttered.

"Necking." She sighed. "It's taken me twenty-six years to get to this. I like it." She ran her hands beneath his shirt, trailed her fingers over the six-pack she found there. Sighed again.

From the backseat came another big sigh, this one from Staubach. He sounded pleased, too. However, when a huge, on-screen explosion ripped through the speaker, the dog whimpered and buried his head in the upholstery.

"What a wuss," Cash muttered. "You hungry?"

"Ravenous."

"Let's go get something then." Pointing a finger at his dog, Cash ordered him to stay put. "If you're good, I'll bring you back something."

Staubach wagged his tail.

Ten minutes later, they were back loaded down with hot dogs, popcorn, and sodas. Cash unwrapped Staubach's sandwich and laid it on the floor. Two bites, and it was history.

He turned big brown dog eyes on Cash. "That's it, guy. You're all done." But he took pity and tossed his pet some popcorn. The dog caught it mid-air.

The first film ended, and Cash turned down their speaker.

He wrapped a strand of her hair around his finger. "I wish... Ah, hell. Wishing's for little girls."

"What did you say?"

"Wishing's for little girls."

"Bull!" She smacked him on the shoulder. "Little girls my eye. Everybody needs to wish. Everybody needs to dream and hope."

"Yeah, maybe so, but by the time you're a big boy, you've learned that no matter how hard you wish on the first star of the night, your wishes don't always come true."

"Oh, Cash." She laid her hands on the sides of his face.

"What is it you want? What do you wish for that seems so unreachable?"

"You, Annie." He dropped a light kiss on the tip of her nose. His lips inches from hers, he said, "And you're so not what I expected. So not what I wanted to want."

He sat up straight and met her eyes under the star-studded sky. "Hell, I didn't want anything or anybody. But, now, well, you make me crazy. You make me plumb crazy."

"I'm glad," she whispered, "because I'd hate to go crazy alone."

Their speaker crackled and a disembodied voice came over it, telling the moviegoers the snack bar would close in ten minutes.

"Want anything else?" Cash asked.

She shook her head and snuggled into the crook of his arm.

Half an hour into a really bad film about a family's vacation that had gone terribly wrong, they decided to call it a night.

The drive home was quiet. Staubach snored in the back, worn out by all the evening's excitement. Annelise rested her head against the seat and stared up at the stars. She liked the old Cadillac. As strange as it seemed, it fit Cash to a T.

Luke Bryan sang a catchy tune on the radio, and Annelise was shocked to realize how fast she'd recognized him and the song. She'd fallen waist-deep into life here—and found it quite pleasant.

* * *

When they pulled into her drive, Cash insisted on walking her to the door. A small light shone from Dottie's kitchen window. No doubt she was watching her late-night talk shows. Well, she didn't have to get up while it was still dark to feed horses.

Rather than go in right away, though, Annelise sat down on the top step. Cash wiggled in beside her.

He took her hand, played with her fingers. "Tell me more about your family, Annie."

"Oh, what is there to tell?" She laid her head on his shoulder. "My mom didn't come from money. Her dad worked in a factory, and her mom was a cook. I think that's why she pushes so hard to be—perfect. And why she wants so much for me. She's trying to prove herself worthy of being a Montjoy."

Cash raised her hand to his lips, kissed the tips of her fingers. "How about your father?"

"My dad pretty much runs the company now that Grandpa is sick. The two of them still see me as their little girl." She pulled the band from her ponytail and ran a hand through her hair. "Which means I sit on the board and attend functions, but I really have no voice, no responsibilities."

"That sucks. Any aunts? Uncles?"

"One aunt and uncle. And my cousin, Sophie. She's the one I called when I first got here."

"You two are close?"

"Yes. None of my family will be at this dinner tomorrow night, Cash," she assured him. "You won't have to meet any of them. There'll be no expectations and no grilling."

"Good to know." He sighed. "I'm sorry to say, I can't give you the same reassurance about the barbecue. My whole crew will be there."

"What should I expect?"

"You've met my mom and dad. Both of them grew up right here in Maverick Junction. They went to school together. Neither of them felt any need to stray. The Big Sandy

Ranch belonged to my mom's parents. They gave it up in favor of moving into town about twenty years ago. Grandma and Grandpa Parker are both still alive and well."

"Will they be at the barbecue?"

"No, afraid not. They're up in Canada. They have a travel trailer and spend most of the summer traipsing around the continent."

"Good for them."

"Yeah." He folded her hand in his. "You pretty well know about my grandpa Hardeman. Grandma Edith died eight years ago." He sighed. "Grandpa got lonely. Thus, Vivi, the Las Vegas showgirl."

"He must have loved her, Cash."

Frowning into the night, he said, "I think he got caught up in the moment. He'd been having some trouble with... Well, I think dementia was becoming a problem. None of us realized where he'd gone till he called. Kind of like you." He glanced at her.

Annelise raised the hand holding hers and kissed the back of it.

Cash cleared his throat. "Anyway, by the time he brought her home, he realized he'd made a mistake. But, he was a gentleman and stuck by his agreement with her."

He scratched his jaw. "Barbara Jean, or Babs, is my only sibling. She married Matt Taylor right after college, and they have two great kids, Austin and Abilene. Austin's eight. He's a great little football player. Abbie's six and a real sweetheart."

He slid his hand up and down her arm. "That's about it. I have an assortment of aunts and uncles, cousins—all on my mom's side. Dad was an only child. My summer camp was working on Grandpa's ranch, and I loved it."

"I'll bet you did. He was really special, wasn't he?"

"Yeah, he was. That's why it makes no sense—" Cash broke off, squeezed her knee. "But that's another story. Right now, I'd better let you get to bed. We've got a big day tomorrow."

"I'm a good listener," she whispered. "Whatever is bothering you might be better shared."

"I'm fine, darlin'. And it's getting late. That old sun's gonna be sneaking up over the horizon before we get to bed if we don't watch out." He kissed her lightly on the lips, then took her key and unlocked her door. "Night, Annie."

She touched her fingers to her lips, felt his touch long after his taillights disappeared. What was she going to do about that cowboy?

Chapter Nineteen

They'd agreed to work a short day. Annelise packed before she left that morning and trudged down the stairs with her newly purchased suitcase, dropping it off at her landlady's.

"Remember, Dottie, we have to be in Dallas by four to make sure everything's been taken care of and that there aren't any last-minute emergencies. Sure you don't need to be picked up?"

"Nope. I'm fine."

"Okay. But you need to be out to the ranch by one."

"I'll be there. Don't you worry about me."

"And you'll remember my suitcase?"

"I will."

Dottie hugged herself. "I haven't been this excited since my baby girl walked down the aisle on her wedding day."

"We'll have fun." Annelise kissed her cheek, then headed off to work, enough of Dottie's homemade cookies tucked in her saddlebags to feed every ranch hand for a week.

The morning flew. They had so much to do before they

left. The big Fourth of July barbecue was day after tomorrow, so in addition to all the regular chores, there was a lot to do to get ready for it. Before she could come up for breath, Cash moved behind her, taking hold of her elbow.

"Did you want to catch a quick shower before we head out? Or were you planning on doing that at your place?"

"I'm not going home first, so I think I'll take one here. It'll be faster. I won't mess with my hair till we hit Dallas."

He checked the barn clock. "You'd best get that shower now, then. About time to take off. I've already had mine."

"I see that." She tousled his still-damp hair. "Are you sure you don't want to fly back tonight? We could leave the minute it's over and not be too late."

"No. Let's stay overnight like we planned. We could make this even more special, though." He winked. "Change the sleeping arrangements."

"No way."

"Let Dottie stay in the single room. We can share the other one, the suite."

"I can't."

"Sure, you can."

She shook her head. "Dottie would be horrified."

"No, she wouldn't." He brushed his fingers along her cheek. "I asked her about it earlier, and she told me to go for it."

Annelise's mouth dropped open. "She did not."

"She did. She was married, Annie. She knows what it's like to want somebody so bad you hurt."

"Oh, Cowboy, you really know how to stir up a girl. But we can't. There'll be too many eyes on me tonight. We have to go with the arrangements as planned. Dottie and I share. You bach it."

"You're a hard woman, Annelise Montjoy."

"And in a few minutes, I'll be ready to go." She left him standing there and hit the shower. Cash had almost had her. He had no idea how badly she wanted to share that room with him. A couple kisses and she might have caved.

By the time she'd cleaned up, Dottie'd arrived.

Cash threw their bags in the back of his pickup and they drove to the airstrip. She and Dottie stood beside the truck, watching as Cash and one of his employees went through the pre-flight checklist.

Before she knew it, they were on the plane and airborne. Annelise watched Cash, as quietly competent navigating a plane as riding on the back of a horse.

Once all the mundane tasks were accomplished, Cash said, "So, Annie. I probably should have asked this question before now. What exactly is this fund-raiser of yours raising funds for?"

She grinned. "It's my Now and Then Foundation."

"You mentioned the name last night, but I really don't know much about it. Give me some details. What are you planning to do with all this money you'll raise?"

"Half of it will go to help feed hungry kids. The other half goes to college scholarships or vo-tech training for those same kids when they're ready. That way, we help them now in the present and then in the future. Now and Then. Hopefully, they'll not only be self-sufficient after graduation, but they can help by giving back to the program. I kicked it off when I was nineteen." She smiled, looking for all the world like a proud mama. "Our first kids headed off to college this past year."

"Oh, Annie," Dottie said from the backseat of the aircraft. "That's a wonderful thing."

"Thank you. It makes me feel good. And the foundation is growing quickly, which means we can help more kids. We hold one of these annual dinners in ten different states now."

It was a short flight, and they landed a little before three. Annelise's mom, as promised, had a car and driver waiting for them at the small private airport.

Dottie slid into the limo, eyes as big as her chocolate chip cookies. "Look at this. Look at me. My kids will never believe it."

Annelise took a camera from her bag and snapped a photo. "You can send them a copy."

She laid a hand on Cash's. "I hate being put on exhibit, even when it's for a good cause. I love that, in this case, it does some good, but I wish I could work behind the scenes. Do the organizing from the sidelines and have someone else be the public face of it. But, though Dad and Grandpa won't give me any real responsibilities, they still expect me to go out, look glamorous, and sell the company goods." She spread her hands. "Welcome to my life."

"Sorry about that, darlin'. It's sure not for me."

"It's not for me, either," she complained.

When they reached the hotel, their baggage was unloaded for them and taken to their rooms. The three walked through the revolving doors. In the opulent lobby, with its crystal chandeliers and dark wood, Cash stuffed a hand in the pocket of his dress slacks, frowning.

"So do I call you Annelise tonight? Ms. Montjoy? Am I supposed to bow to you as the savior of young children when we walk into the dinner? What's the protocol here?"

Hurt tore through her. "What are you doing, Cash? I said you didn't have to come. This was your choice. Don't start sulking now."

He studied the lobby ceiling. "It's just—I don't know. You pull up in your limo, and people practically fall over themselves to do for you."

She tipped her head and met his gaze dead-on. "You don't have to stay, Cash. Hop in your plane and fly home to Whispering Pines. Take care of your horses and your upcoming party. Dottie and I will be fine."

A muscle in his jaw tightened. "That's not what I meant."

"Oh, really? It sure sounded like it to me."

By now, they were facing each other, hands on their hips, chins jutting out, and looking for all the world like they were ready to start punching.

Dottie, who'd wandered off to look at some of the artwork, came over to them. "Children, if you're going to fight, take it outside. Or better yet, upstairs. I suggest, though, that you hang up your gloves and make nice. If one of those photographers with the cannon-sized cameras hanging around his neck wanders across the two of you right now, the picture he takes will be splashed all over the news."

Exasperated, Annelise turned on her heels. Every time she started to think she and Cash might be able to mesh their worlds, something happened to prove her wrong. To prove that this thing between her and Cash, however good it seemed, could only be temporary.

"You're right, Dottie. Thank you. Let's check in."

She took two steps and stopped. "Hello, Rufus."

The giant standing straight and tall beside a huge potted fern smiled. "Hello, Ms. Montjoy."

Crossing to him, she asked, "Did Dad send you?"

He nodded, his bald ebony head shiny with reflected light. "Yes, ma'am."

She sighed. "I suppose you had to take a red-eye to get here early enough to suit him."

"Suppose I did, ma'am."

"I'm sorry."

"I'm sorry you took off the way you did. Your daddy about chewed our heads off."

"Yes, he probably did. I had no choice. Honestly."

"Figured you'd say that." He hesitated, then said, "Tell me you didn't really ride that Harley of yours cross-country."

"I can't do that, Rufus." She grinned. "But it was incredible. You should try it sometime."

"Might do that. In fact, next time you take off, I'll have plenty of time to do just that. Because I'll be unemployed."

She laid a hand on his arm. "I am sorry."

He studied her face, then grinned back at her. "No, ma'am, I respectfully disagree. I don't think you're a bit sorry."

She laughed. "Is Silas here with you?"

"He's upstairs, outside your room."

She nodded. "Oh. My manners. Rufus, this is Dottie Willis and Cash Hardeman."

Handshakes were exchanged all around. Annelise realized Cash had gone on full alert. "Rufus and Silas are my...my bodyguards."

Cash's jaw tightened. "I think I can do an okay job taking care of you."

"I know, and you can. But my father is somewhat over-protective."

"Another of those differences between us, Annie."

At the use of the nickname, Rufus's brow shot up. A slow smile spread over his face.

Cash and Dottie, who kept looking back over her shoulder at the bodyguard, moved to the check-in desk.

"No need to do that," Rufus said. "Here're your keys." He handed one to Annelise and one to Cash. "You're good to go."

As they headed to the elevator, Annelise leaned toward Rufus and whispered, "Do you approve of my cowboy?"

"I believe I do," he rumbled. "I believe I do."

* * *

Halfway down their hallway, Dottie spotted the large, blond man, dressed in a suit and tie. "Is that Silas?"

"Yes, it is." A few steps closer, she said, "Hi, Silas. I saw Rufus downstairs. Sorry you had to fly out here."

"Hello, Ms. Montjoy. It was no problem."

"Rufus said Dad was pretty hard on you two. I'll apologize for taking off like I did, but it was something I had to do."

He nodded and opened her door. "I'll be out here if you need me." He stared fixedly at Cash. "You'll be in that room." He pointed to one two doors down.

"Thanks. Don't know if I could have found it on my own." Cash bounced the bag he'd insisted on carrying higher on his shoulder. "Later, Annie. Dottie."

When he walked away, Silas said, "A little touchy, huh?"

"Yes, I think you and Rufus being here have hit a nerve."

Once in their suite, Dottie ran from one thing to another, touching and oohing and ahhing. She tried out the sofa, flicked on the TV and sound system. Sticking her head in both of the bedrooms, she asked which was hers.

"Whichever you want."

She chose the blue room, then spying the fruit basket, she unwrapped it and munched on grapes even as she stuck her nose in the beautiful bouquet of fresh flowers to smell them.

Staring out the window at the Dallas skyline, she asked, "Annie, this is how you live?"

"Well, every day isn't quite like this."

"But it's close."

"I have a very nice life, yes. I've been fortunate."

"And you're living in my rental apartment?"

"And loving it," Annelise said.

"I know." The older woman patted Annelise's cheek. "I guess that's part of what makes you so special."

Annelise's throat constricted. "Go look in your closet, Dottie. I think there's another surprise for you in there."

With a little squeal, Dottie headed into the bedroom on the left.

Annelise crossed her fingers, praying her mom had come through big time on this one and that Dottie liked her dress. She heard nothing. She listened for another minute, then peeked into Dottie's room.

She sat on the edge of her bed, a stunning pink creation cradled in her arms, with tears streaming down her face.

"Dottie?"

"Yes, dear?"

"Is everything all right?"

Dottie lifted her tear-streaked face. "All right? All right? Have you seen this?"

She held up the dress for Annelise's inspection.

Annelise reached out to finger the silk and lace gown. "It's beautiful."

"It's the most beautiful thing I've ever seen. I can actually wear this tonight?"

"Yes. And then you can zip it back in its bag and take it home with you. It's yours."

"Oh, Annie, I can't take this. It's so expensive."

"My mother bought it for you. There should be shoes and some jewelry to go with it."

Dottie hurried back to the closet. From the happy sounds inside, Annelise figured she'd found them.

There was a discreet rap at the hall door. "Let me get that."

When she opened the door, Silas wheeled in a table from room service complete with tea, coffee, and finger foods. Dottie stood in her bedroom doorway, looking like a kid in a candy store.

Annelise smiled. She was glad she'd brought her. Dottie had been so good to her. It was nice to be able to repay her, even a little bit.

"In fifteen minutes, the masseuse will be up, Ms. Montjoy. Then your mother has arranged for a team to help you and Ms. Willis with your hair and nails and anything else you might require."

A masseuse. Annelise nearly wept with joy. She'd worked her butt off this past week, and there were nights she'd have given anything, anything at all for a massage. Bless her mother.

Then she glanced down at her nails. They'd worked hard, too. And they looked it. She doubted even the best nail technician would be able to help her with these nubs. Well, she'd let them do what they could, then keep her hands hidden from sight as much as possible.

Throughout the next couple of hours, Annelise couldn't keep the silly smile off her face. She had to admit that as much as she'd enjoyed her stay in Maverick Junction and as much as she enjoyed working at the ranch, it was nice to be pampered, buffed, and shined.

And watching Dottie! No kid on Christmas morning could be happier. The older woman giggled when the woman doing her pedicure ran the pumice over the bottom of her feet. She turned scarlet when the masseuse had her disrobe to her panties. She beamed at the makeup artist as he added the finishing touches. She begged Annelise to take a picture of her new hairdo.

All in all, Annelise couldn't remember when she'd enjoyed herself so much. The memory of Cash's hands on her, his mouth on her, at the pond returned. Oh, yes. That surpassed even today. But in a totally different kind of way.

What was Cash doing? Reading, watching TV, napping? She missed him. Did he miss her—even a little bit? She hoped so.

He'd been a little rough since they'd landed and he'd spotted the limo and driver. The deferential treatment when they'd arrived. Rufus and Silas. All this didn't sit well with him. He was used to being in charge and calling the shots. She'd given him a good hard yank out of his comfort zone, and guilt pricked her conscience. He hadn't signed on for any of this when he'd agreed to hire her.

But then, she'd become more than an employee, he far more than her boss. How would this trip with all the fuss and the press affect their relationship? She seriously doubted anything could be the same and regretted that.

Responsibility weighed heavy on her shoulders.

She considered sending the masseuse to his room. Considered snitching a bottle of her oil and paying him a visit herself. Then, she got real and decided against both. He needed to work off the snit by himself. He was a big boy and would deal with it.

In the meantime, Annelise remembered she had a speech to give tonight. While she prepared her remarks, Dottie took a nap—sitting up in a comfy upholstered chair so she didn't mess her hair or makeup.

*　*　*

Right at seven, Silas and Cash came to collect her and Dottie. Cash walked in behind them. Her cowboy was gone. In his place stood as urbane a man as she'd ever seen. The man, so at home in jeans and boots, looked positively yummy in his black tux and crisp white shirt. He filled the tux out oh, so, well. He about knocked her off her stilettos.

He was busy doing his own perusal. "Darlin', you looking like that, I could just sop you up with a biscuit."

She grinned. "Cash, that might be the best, and most honest, compliment I've ever received. Thank you."

He took her hand, spun her in a slow turn. "Let me get a good look at you."

She obliged. The gown Maggie had created was stunning and fit her impeccably. The pale, sheer fabric set off her dark hair. The jewelry Neiman Marcus sent over for her was perfection. Nancy, her mother's personal shopper, had chosen dangly diamond and onyx earrings and a diamond-studded cuff bracelet. She'd decided against a necklace, and she'd been right. The dress didn't need it.

"Dottie? Are you ready?" she called.

"Am I ever." Her bedroom door opened, and Dottie stepped out. She spread her arms wide. "What do you think?"

"Oh, Dottie. You're beautiful," Annelise said.

"Darlin'," Cash said, taking Dottie's hands in his, "if I wasn't so hung up on this filly beside me, I'd get down on one knee right here and now and beg you to run off with me."

Rising to her tiptoes, Dottie kissed his cheek, then wiped off the lipstick smudge. "And if I was a few years younger, I might consider giving Annie a run for her money, Cash Hardeman. Who knew you'd clean up so well? Mmm, mmm."

Then she turned her attention to Annelise. "You look like

a storybook princess in that dress." She reached out to touch the earrings. "Real?"

"Yes."

"Did you see mine?" Dottie turned her head, pushed her hair back. Emerald-cut tourmalines in a soft pink winked at her ears. A matching pendant hung at her neck. Silver bracelets circled her wrists.

"They suit you."

"I feel like a princess myself. And you're my fairy godmother." Tears welled in Dottie's eyes. "Today has been magical."

"Don't cry," Annelise admonished. "You'll ruin your makeup."

Dottie blew out a big breath. "I know." She waved a hand in front of her face. "I had a massage, Cash. I've never had one before. It was totally decadent, and I loved it. And someone did my hair—and my nails."

She held out her hands, then stuck one foot in the air to show off the pink toenails peeping out of her new shoes. "I've been royally pampered this afternoon."

Annelise caught the look Cash sent her way, thanking her with his eyes. She smiled back at him, turning her attention his way. "And you. I can't believe the change. From rancher to debonair escort. I have to say, you look unbelievably handsome."

She told herself to shut up, but her mouth refused to obey. "You are model-perfect. The ultimate man in a tuxedo."

His dimples deepened. "Oh, yeah?"

"Every woman in that room tonight, from nine to ninety, is going to wonder where I found you and what they have to do to steal you away from me."

"She's right," Dottie said. "Told you, I'd be mighty tempted if I could figure out how to shave a few years off my age."

"Maybe I like older women," he teased.

"And maybe they like you." Her eyes twinkled. "I've got to believe, though, that right now, a younger woman's got your eye."

"And you'd be right." He ran a hand down Annelise's arm.

"Before we go downstairs and get caught up in the mad rush, I have to ask, Cash," Annelise said. "Where did you manage to find a tux so fast? And one that fits so well."

"That's an easy one to answer. I found it in my closet. Right where I hung it after the last time I wore it."

"You— Oh! It's yours, not a rental. I'm sorry. I shouldn't have assumed—"

He *tsked* at her. "Those assumptions, Annie. They'll bite you in the butt every time."

"Oh, and there's the pot calling the kettle black!"

Ignoring her comment, he reached out and looped his arms through both women's. "A stunner on both arms. What more could any man want? We ready to do this?"

"You bet."

At the elevator, Silas reached into his inside pocket. "Your mother sent this."

The ring her grandfather had given her on her sixteenth birthday.

"She thought you might want it."

"She was right." Emotion thickened her voice. "Thank you."

"You're more than welcome." Silas rode the elevator down with them, then followed at a discreet distance.

"Is he going to do this all night?" Cash asked out of the corner of his mouth.

"Yes. He is. Every time I turn around, either Silas or Rufus will be watching me. I warned you. I tried to explain the cons of my life. Everyone tends to see only the benefits. All in all, though, I guess it's a small price to pay for the opportunities I've been given."

"But you have no privacy, no freedom," Cash said.

"There is that."

Chapter Twenty

Cash couldn't believe this woman was the same one who'd ridden into Maverick Junction on a Harley. Who'd cleaned his stalls, spoiled his horses, and gone skinny-dipping with him at the old pond.

He'd stood in the doorway amazed and more than a little shaken. She'd knocked his socks off.

But he warned himself to be careful. Annelise had the ability to break his heart if he let her. When he'd seen her standing there, he'd fully accepted for the first time that she truly was the Montjoy heiress.

Not his. She'd never be his. Their lives were poles apart. They could never mesh them—not long-term.

Silas at their heels, they walked into the hotel's ballroom. While Cash had thought the lobby over the top, this room put it to shame. The press milled around the door, waiting like vultures for their money shot. The instant they spotted Annelise, an entire bank of photographers started snapping pictures, the flashes nearly blinding.

Cash liked to think of himself as pretty self-assured. He knew who he was and liked that man. Still, he found himself slightly overwhelmed by the crush and all the attention. Annie dealt with this on a daily basis. And even though she had a serious reason for setting out cross-country, he understood why she'd enjoyed the interlude in Maverick Junction. It must have been a breath of fresh air.

No wonder she'd fought so hard to keep her true identity a secret. From everyone. It gave her freedom for the first time ever. That she'd lied by omission to him suddenly became understandable. Didn't mean he had to like it, but he could sure see where she was coming from.

She smiled and turned slowly, giving each photographer in the sea of cameras a chance to capture her on film. And yet Cash realized the smile didn't reach her eyes. This was her polite smile. But even this semblance of the real thing lit up the room.

On his other arm, Dottie was like a teenager, grinning and waving at the press. He smiled. The paparazzi had no clue who she was. Not ready to take any chances, they snapped shot after shot of her. She'd wished her kids could see her. No doubt they would.

The way she looked tonight, no one would ever figure her for a grandma who was at her happiest baking cookies in her kitchen. She looked amazing in her new outfit and preened and posed like an Oscar-winning star walking the red carpet.

Annie had given Dottie an incredible gift, one she'd never forget. For that alone, he loved her.

Loved her? He almost stumbled over his own feet. Whoa. No sense getting carried away. He liked Annie, sure. He lusted after her and couldn't wait to get her back in his bed. But love? He wasn't going there, Whispering Pines and Grandpa be damned.

Annie threw him a quick are-you-okay glance, and he sent her a shaky smile.

"I'm good."

They moved past the photographers. Annie shook hands and made introductions and small talk with the flair of a well-seasoned pro. So did Dottie. To Cash's amazement, now that they'd arrived, the older woman's nerves had fled. She handled the fanfare with all the aplomb of someone long used to being the center of attention. He loved it.

Waiters circulated with trays of fancy hors d'oeuvres. Dottie nibbled her way through the crowd, tasting everything and drinking champagne delivered on silver trays by black-tuxed waiters.

"I feel like Cinderella." She giggled. "My new tenant. Who'd have believed all this?" She beamed at Annie.

Her new tenant indeed, Cash thought. Annie, at home in evening gown and diamonds, drinking champagne from crystal flutes, while he'd give anything to have a beer in his hand right about now and be wearing his faded blue jeans and an old tee.

But, this wasn't about him. Tonight belonged to Annie. She'd sacrificed a lot to show up at this shindig, much more than he'd originally realized. The least he could do was smile and pretend to enjoy himself.

In the morning, he'd fly her home. After that—well, who knew? They'd cross that stream when they came to it, wouldn't they?

Not every man wore a tux, he noted. The ones who didn't, though, were outfitted in perfectly cut black suits with tailored shirts and big, silver belt buckles. Turquoise and silver bolos took the place of the bow tie currently strangling him. Raising his chin, he tugged at it.

He glanced at Annie again. That dress was sexy as hell,

yet somehow demure at the same time. He wasn't quite sure how Maggie had pulled it off. He'd have to give her a call, though, and thank her. She'd outdone herself and had made Annie...and him...very happy.

"I'm gonna sidle over to the bar. Think I'd prefer a Scotch to this bubbly. Unless they've got a cold Lone Star in a long-necked bottle, and I don't guess the chance of getting that lucky is very good."

"All right. You know where our table is?"

"Yeah. I spotted it when I came in."

Annie slid her hand in Dottie's, and the two melted into the throng of benefactors.

He made his way to the bar and grabbed an empty stool. "I'll have a Scotch neat," he said when the bartender approached him.

"Cash?"

The man beside him turned.

"Brawley? Brawley Odell? What the heck are you doing here?" He wrapped an arm around his best friend and clapped him on the back.

"I might ask the same. You're lost, bro. Last time I checked, Maverick Junction was due south of the Big D."

Cash chuckled. "To be really honest, I'm not sure what I'm doing here. This is so not my thing." The bartender placed his drink in front of him. Cash tipped him, took a sip, then set the glass on the counter. "You here alone?"

"No, my date's the brunette over there in the red dress." He pointed at a well-endowed woman a few tables away. Brawley nudged Cash in the side. "Rachel's a Dallas cheerleader. Flexible. Very, very flexible, if you know what I mean."

"Yeah, I think I get the picture." Cash laughed. "Well, having you here, the night just got a whole lot better."

"Who'd you come with?"

"I came with Annie. Actually, I flew her and Dottie Willis up from Maverick Junction today. We'll stay overnight, then fly back to the ranch tomorrow."

"Dottie's here?"

"Yep."

"Did she bring any cookies?"

"It wouldn't surprise me to find a stash of them hidden in her suitcase."

"So who's Annie?"

"Annelise Montjoy. She's—"

He started to point, but Brawley stopped him.

"I know who Annelise Montjoy is. The entire world knows Annelise. She's tonight's star attraction. Stepping up in the world, huh?"

"Hardly." A dark cloud flitted over Cash's head. Everybody except him. How had he not known her? But then neither had the people of Maverick Junction. Guess it was a case of what you expected. No one expected to see the Montjoy heiress dressed in jeans and tees, working on a ranch, so they didn't. She'd been out of her bubble.

The town had seen only a hardworking, down-to-earth woman. She'd been hiding in plain sight.

"You're really here with Annelise Montjoy?"

"Yeah, she's actually working for me. On the ranch."

"Come on, you're pulling my leg."

"No, I'm not."

"No shit." Brawley slapped him on the back. "Her Now and Then Foundation does good work."

"Have you met her?"

"Nope."

Cash dragged Brawley across the room to meet Annie, who finessed a place for him and his date at their table.

It was like homecoming. Cash, Brawley, and Dottie chatted about friends and neighbors. They talked all through dinner, catching up with one another's lives.

Cash noticed that Annie, though she'd carried champagne while schmoozing, stuck to soft drinks. He probably would, too, if he had to speak in front of this group. On second thought, if it was him taking center stage, he'd need more than a few stiff drinks to make it through the ordeal.

Dinner cleared away, Annie took her place on stage and waited for an introduction. At some point, Rufus had joined Silas. He noticed both men now flanked the stage. They took their job seriously, and he was glad.

Cash welcomed the chance to sit back and watch Annie. To enjoy her cool, elegant beauty. He marveled at how calm she looked in front of this group of movers and shakers. As she stepped to the podium, no one would have guessed she hadn't spent hours preparing. She looked totally confident and self-assured.

She made light of the introducer's remarks about her having dropped out of sight. Smiling, she said, "I didn't really. I knew right where I was."

The audience laughed, and Annie continued. "I've been incredibly busy, keeping my head low and getting work done. There's a lot that happens behind the scenes to keep a business going, as I'm sure everyone here is all too well aware of."

Cash studied the audience, the nodding heads, and knew she'd be okay.

Then she placed both hands on the lectern, leaned into it, and became one with the audience. Her voice, clear and impassioned, rang out over the room.

"Tonight, you and I shared a wonderful meal. We ate

more than we should have and will, no doubt, hit the gym a little harder tomorrow as a result. Yet right now, children are going to bed without dinner. Their bellies hurt, not from overindulging, but from lack of sufficient food, day after day after day."

Those spectacular blue eyes moved through the crowd, connecting and making it personal. "No child deserves that. In this land where we're so blessed and have so much, there's no excuse for hunger."

She paused for effect. "Equally important is seeing to it that when that child reaches adulthood, he can feed himself, can then pass it on and help another hungry child. That's why our foundation focuses not only on today, but tomorrow. Now and then."

His chest swelled as he listened to her.

"Children will be fed because you attended tonight. Children will be educated and become productive members of our society, and I thank you for that. My thanks, too, to the hotel and the wait staff for all their hard work. Without them, tonight wouldn't have been possible."

As she received a standing ovation, Cash realized all over again that although she'd been brought up with everything, she never forgot the ones behind the scenes, the ones who did the grunt work. And didn't that make her all that much more attractive? His Annie was beautiful through and through.

Make that Annie. Just Annie. Not *his*.

But oh, how he wished she could be. She'd become important to him. Very important. He didn't want her to leave.

He realized she had to. This was a train stop for her. Him, his ranch—they weren't her life. Annie belonged here amidst this glitter. Here, tonight, this was her world.

It wasn't his.

She wove through the tables, shaking hands and exchanging pleasantries. When she reached their table, Cash stood and pulled out her chair, then dropped a light kiss on her cheek.

"You did well, Annie. Really well. You've raised a lot of money tonight for one heck of a worthy cause. I'm proud of you."

Surprised, her eyes widened. "Thank you." Turning her head, she brushed her lips over his. "If that picture makes the morning news"—she shrugged—"I can live with it."

Chapter Twenty-One

Cash and Brawley returned from a bathroom break to find the star-struck Dottie twisting and turning in her seat, taking it all in.

"Dottie, am I gonna have to track down a chiropractor for you before the night's over?" Cash asked.

Surprised, she swiveled toward him. "Why would you have to do that?"

He chuckled. "The way you're craning your neck, it's bound to be sore."

"You're bad, Cash."

When the talk turned to Maverick Junction, Cash noted Rachel's polite yawns behind her hand. Yet he couldn't help notice she was somewhat in awe of actually sharing a table with Annelise, the belle of the ball. Whenever one of the bigwigs came by, Rachel's interest spiked, and she turned on the charm.

Annie, in contrast, chatted happily—with or without a rich or famous audience. She charmed him. Such an old-fashioned term. How many times had his grandfather used it in regards to Grandma Edith? Cash understood now a whole lot better exactly what Grandpa had been talking about.

People stopped at the table, most to meet Annie or have their picture taken with her. Some, though, were friends of his. When the senator walked away, Annie looked at Cash.

"You're pretty shrewd, aren't you?"

"Me?" he asked.

"Yes, you. You come off as the aw-shucks rancher. That's not you at all."

"Yes, it is."

"Part of you, maybe. But there's a whole lot more to you than that." When she reached over and straightened his tie, he caught the twinkle in Dottie's eyes. "You're a man of many facets, Cash Hardeman."

"Aren't we all?"

She thought about that a minute, her full lips pursed. "I suppose so."

"Well, then, there you go."

The talk turned to Doc Gibson, Maverick Junction's vet for the last forty years or so.

"I had him out a few days ago to look at one of my fillies."

"He's one of the best," Brawley said. "I was lucky to train under him."

Cash took a sip of his Scotch. "He's making noises about retiring. I told him he can't do that. We wouldn't have a vet within a hundred-mile radius. But I think he's serious this time."

"Yeah, he's called me a couple times."

"Why are you even discussing this, Brawley? I mean, why in the world would he call you?" Rachel asked, twining her arm through his. "It's not as if you're thinking about ever going back to that—"

She cleared her throat. "Back to your hometown." She ran her other hand along the length of his arm.

"No, we were talking, that's all. Doc Gibson wanted my take on it. He wondered if I knew anyone who might be interested in something more rural."

"Something more rural? That's kind of an understatement, isn't it?"

And there you go, Cash thought. The reason why, when he'd reminded Odell of the annual barbecue, he hadn't wanted to include his Dallas cheerleader. She'd be as out of her element as a newborn colt in a herd of mule deer, nothing in common but the most basic factors. And somehow, he didn't see Rachel as being a basics kind of gal.

But, then, he'd been wrong about Brawley, hadn't he? When his best pal had moved to the city, Cash had been certain he'd hate living in Dallas. Instead, he'd thrived here.

The band began to play, and Cash looked at Annie, nodded toward the dance floor. With a slow smile, she stood and took his hand.

She smelled so good. Relieved to finally have a chance to hold her close, Cash released the breath he swore he'd been holding all evening. With her in his arms, he didn't care about the fancy, schmantzy room, the people who'd sucked up to Annie all night, the tie that still threatened to strangle him.

It was incredible. It was like making love while standing up. He kissed her ear, the top of her head.

He swore she purred.

He spotted Brawley and Rachel on the dance floor and knew he'd pegged the situation correctly. Their body language said it all. As far as Brawley was concerned, they were over, but Rachel still had a ways to go before she crossed the finish line. Tough spot to be in.

When the song ended, Cash walked Annie back to the table and stepped behind Dottie's chair. "Hey, sweetheart, do me a favor? Come dance with me. Let's show these people how it's done."

Brawley seated Rachel, then turned to Annie. He held out a hand, and the two men led their partners onto the floor.

It was a jitterbug. Cash twirled Dottie and delighted in her laughter. All the while, he watched Annie and Brawley. In addition to having a good seat when it came to horses, Annie moved well on her feet. She'd removed the sheer jacket, and her pale skin sparkled in the chandelier's dimmed light. Had she dusted her shoulders with something? Or was the shimmer simply Annie?

Exhausted and smiling, they collapsed in their seats at the end of the dance.

"I'm giving up the ghost," Dottie said. "You young people enjoy. It's been a long day, and I'm tired. I'm going to turn in. Have fun. You certainly don't need me here to do that." She winked at Annie. "I won't stay up waiting for you, honey—if you get my drift."

Annie blushed.

Cash threw back his head and laughed. Standing, he pulled Dottie's chair out for her. "Night, Dottie. Sleep well." He gave her a quick buss on the cheek.

Brawley stood, too, and gave the woman a hug. "Night, sweetheart. It was so good to see you."

"Oh." Dottie clasped her hands in front of her. "This has been the best day. I can't wait to tell my kids. Annie, honey, I can't thank you enough."

"It was nothing."

"Bull. Don't you even try feeding me that line." She pirouetted. "All this." Her hand trailed over her earrings, down the length of her dress. "You thought of everything."

Giving Cash a hug, she whispered, "Don't screw this up and don't hurt her, or you'll answer to me."

* * *

The band played their last song of the night. Annie again thanked everyone involved, and they said their good nights.

"See you soon, Brawley?"

"You bet."

As Cash walked out, hand in hand with Annie, he said, "You didn't eat much tonight."

"I never do at these things. About the time I eat something with spinach in it, someone will pop a picture of me with green between my teeth. The tabloids would love it."

He laughed. "I suspected as much. Let's go grab something."

"At midnight?"

"You bet. My carriage hasn't turned back into a pumpkin yet."

"You don't have a carriage here in Dallas. You left it back in Maverick Junction."

"True." He nodded toward Rufus. "Think it'll be safe to take a short walk with the hulk there guarding us?"

She grinned and nodded.

"Good. I know a great dive not far from here."

And that's exactly what it was. He and Annie shared a greasy burger and even greasier fries. Heads turned at their formal wear, but no questions were asked.

Cash invited Rufus to sit with them, but he declined, taking a booth across from them. As if that provided them privacy, Cash thought. Still, he'd take what he could get.

"How did you know about this place?"

"I have my ways." He grinned. "There's more to me than just a pretty face."

"You have such beautiful dimples. Hey, Rufus," she called across the aisle. Several heads turned toward them. "He's pretty, isn't he? He likes to joke about it, but isn't this man drop-dead gorgeous?"

Rufus grunted in response.

"I didn't hear you," she teased.

"Whatever you say, Ms. Montjoy."

Cash shook his head. "You sure do know how to embarrass a guy, Annie. Pretty?" He sat back, a smug smile on his face. "I'm handsome. *Ruggedly* handsome."

The elegant heiress snorted.

They took a slow walk back to the hotel. Even with the city lights, stars winked at them from the heavens. The temperature had dropped slightly. It was one of those nights when you had to be happy to be alive. Rufus kept a respectable distance behind them.

The doorman welcomed them back, and the three rode up to their floor in the elevator. Rufus stayed at his post at the end of the hall, giving them the appearance of privacy.

Cash walked Annie to her room.

"Thanks for the burger," she said. "And thanks so much for this evening. You've been wonderful, Cash. It was my lucky day when I walked into Sally's and found you." She reached up to kiss him lightly on the cheek.

"No way," he growled. "Rufus, close your eyes because I'm gonna kiss the girl."

At the end of the hallway, Rufus covered his laugh with a fake cough.

Annie rolled her eyes. "That wasn't very convincing, Rufus."

"See if this is." Catching her face in his hands, Cash

turned slightly so his lips met hers. He deepened the kiss, lingered over it. Their tongues danced and mated. He needed her.

He broke the kiss, buried his face in her hair. "God, Annie, you smell so good. You're incredibly beautiful. Come back to my room with me. Take pity on a starving man."

"I can't. Dottie—"

"Is asleep. You have separate bedrooms. She won't know. She won't care."

"Cash, I can't. You don't understand."

"I do understand."

"No, you don't. The photographers—"

"Screw the photographers."

"No. No way. They'll have us splashed over every page of every magazine, every newspaper, every tabloid, every TV show. You can't imagine."

"Annie, who cares? We're two consenting adults. What we do doesn't affect anyone else. It's between you and me."

"I care, Cash." She thumped her chest, then lowered her voice. "I care. And it isn't only us who would be affected. I have a company whose shareholders care. Perception can be everything. I make the front page of the tabloids and our shares drop. That's money out of someone's pocket. Someone who very well might not be able to afford it."

He laid a hand on her shoulder. "You're carrying a hell of a lot on these shoulders, aren't you?"

"Yes, I am." Her expression intense, she said, "And remember, I came here to find my great-aunt. I came hoping to find a cure for my grandfather. That's the reason I'm here, not to have a fling."

Smarting, he stepped away. "I'm a fling?"

"No. I—bad word choice." Her face softened. "Now I've hurt you." She laid a hand on his arm, ran it up and down.

"You're more than that, so much more. You're—I honestly don't know what you and I are to each other. You said yourself this is temporary. I've never—this is all new to me, Cash."

Her fingers played with the button on her jacket. "But first and foremost, I came to Texas to save Grandpa's life. That has to be my priority. I can't have some tabloid story get in the way of that."

Her eyes misted with tears, and he felt like the world's biggest jerk.

"Annie, I'm sorry. I know you love your grandfather as much as I loved mine. Losing him—well, it was devastating. I would have done anything to save him, absolutely anything. I really do understand."

He kissed the top of her head. "Guess I let my testosterone get away from me. Started talking from the wrong part of my body. It's just...I want you so damn badly." He rested his forehead against hers.

Pulling away, he said, "You know, though, there's no way in hell that anybody, photographer or not, is getting off that elevator on this floor tonight. Not with that guy standing there. Rufus isn't about to let anybody get close to you." He cocked his thumb at the bodyguard who, though fully alert, had judiciously turned his back.

His voice fell to a whisper. "At least tell me what you have on under this." He fingered the sheer material of her dress.

"I—"

Without warning, he hooked a finger in the neckline and took a peek. "Very nice!"

"Cash!" Her head jerked up, and she looked quickly up and down the hallway, her gaze stopping on Rufus, then coming back to him.

A grin kicked up the corner of Cash's mouth. "Darlin', you look guilty as hell."

"That's embarrassment, not guilt. Shame on you. You're so bad!" She smacked his fingers. "If anybody should look guilty, it's you."

"I'm not, though. That short glimpse of heaven was well worth the little love tap." He laughed at her outraged expression. "I'm a man, Annie. A man who's fraying at the edges. What can I say? And so you understand," he said, grinning wider, "I'm not gonna feel the least bit guilty for this, either."

In one unhurried move, he backed her against the wall, kissed her till he wondered that the hotel's smoke detectors didn't go off.

"Night, Annie. Sleep tight." He raised his voice. "Rufus, take care of her." With that he walked away and slid the key-card in his own door. Might be a good time to catch a cold shower. He sure as hell wouldn't be going to sleep anytime soon.

Chapter Twenty-Two

When the elevator doors opened the next morning, the paparazzi surged around Annelise. They'd had her staked out, waiting for the moment of attack. She kicked herself. She'd known better. Why hadn't she ordered room service for breakfast? Dumb question. She knew why. Dottie, still excited by their adventure, had wanted to eat in the hotel's famous restaurant, and Annie had let that sway her, cloud her better judgment.

The cameras started clicking the instant she and Dottie stepped from the elevator. Dottie, smiling broadly, fussed with her hair when she saw them and gave a wonderful impression of a grande dame. Smiling despite herself, Annelise couldn't help compare her to the Unsinkable Molly Brown. A brash woman with a huge heart.

At least she and Cash had the forethought not to ride down together. She could only imagine how that would have thrilled these bloodhounds. The rumors would have flown, hot and heavy.

Rumors? Or truths? Probably a little of both.

Giving them time to get seated in the restaurant, Cash rode down on a second, later elevator, hoping to throw the photographers off the scent. No such luck. The cameramen spied him the instant the elevator door opened—almost as if they'd been expecting it. Which, of course, they had been. They'd seen the two of them last night, talking, laughing, dancing. Leaving together. She'd made a mistake there. They should have left separately.

What she wouldn't give to be back on the ranch today, currying Shadow and Moonshine instead of doing a tango with a pack of wolves.

For a split second, she read indecision on Cash's face and realized he was trying to decide whether or not he should join them or find a different table.

She took matters into her own hands. She refused to let the press dictate who she shared a table with. Waving at him, she said, "Mr. Hardeman, Mrs. Willis and I are having breakfast. We haven't ordered yet. Why don't you join us?"

Cameras whirred and clicked, following his progress to their table. Short-tempered, he yanked out a chair and sat down heavily. "What the hell? Can't Silas or Rufus put a stop to this?"

"Calm down." She spoke quietly. "Rufus is taking care of our bill and making arrangements to have our things brought down. Silas will move them along if they don't back off on their own in a couple of minutes. It's a fine line. If we're rude, they'll run a story about the uppity heiress and her lover."

Panicked eyes met hers. She patted his hand.

"If we're courteous, they'll still run a story, but it'll be angled differently. I'm afraid, though, either way, you'll probably play a rather large role in it."

"I don't care what they write," he snarled. "I want them gone."

By the time they'd ordered and the cameras were still in their faces even Dottie lost her patience. "Mind your manners, boys, and go away." She made a sweeping motion with her hand, dismissing them. "We're not doing anything newsworthy here. Eating our bacon and eggs. That's it."

"Speak for yourself, Dottie," Annelise groused, thinking about the yogurt and whole-grain cereal she'd ordered and wondering if she maybe shouldn't change it to some bacon and eggs. No, after that late burger last night, she'd best stick with something light.

Another flash blinded her.

Silas had had enough. He waded into the group. "Okay, guys, time to move on. Ms. Montjoy is having a private breakfast with friends. She cooperated with you last night, and you got some great shots. She let you take as many photos as you wanted at the fund-raiser. You've grabbed some more shots now this morning, though why the hotel allowed this, I'm not sure. I suggest you go find somebody else to pester."

"This is a public restaurant," one of the more daring paps argued.

"Yes, it is. So if you plan to check your camera, sit down, and order a meal, then by all means." He waved toward an empty table across the room. "However, if you're here to harass Ms. Montjoy, then it's my job to see that doesn't happen."

"Who's the guy?" the same reporter asked.

"What? Do I look like a Google search button?" Silas planted himself between the table and the paparazzi.

Rufus walked in, and the cameras scattered. He winked

at Annelise. "You needed the big guns." He shot a glance at Silas and jerked a thumb in his own direction. Grinning, showing a gold tooth, he said, "And that would be me."

The look Silas sent him said everything.

"I don't think you have anything to worry about, dear," Dottie said. "They can't possibly make anything out of this. Not with me here. It's not like they caught photos of the two of you alone, having an intimate, romantic, morning-after breakfast."

Annelise sighed. "Sweet, sweet Dottie. Have you ever heard of photo-shopping?"

"Oh."

"They can do amazing things with any picture. You might find yourself smiling from the top of a camel."

"I don't like camels. They spit and growl. I saw one at the zoo. Mean things."

Cash hooted. "Oh, Dottie, I love you."

"What?" Red-faced, she said, "I know Annie was only using that as an example." She took a bite of toast. "Eat your breakfast and be quiet."

* * *

The trip home was uneventful. Once he was in the air, headed back to his ranch, Cash literally felt a weight lift off him. When he and Annie had talked before about her life, he'd commiserated with her, making inane remarks about understanding.

What a load of bull that had been. After less than twenty-four hours, he'd about caved under the intense pressure. Left to his own devices, he'd have plowed a fist into one of the noses that stuck itself in Annie's business.

Rufus and Silas had followed them to the airport and

saw them off. He supposed they were on a plane headed to Boston.

No such luck.

After they landed, he loaded the women and their luggage into his truck, stopped at Sadler's while Dottie picked up a few things she needed, then headed for her house. Who sat waiting for them on her front porch? None other than Rufus and Silas. They looked as out of place as a vampire on the beach at high noon.

He pulled into the drive and got out, slamming his door. Walking around, he opened the doors for Annie and Dottie and helped them out.

"What are you guys doing here?"

"Our job."

"We don't need you."

"Don't want to argue with you, Mr. Hardeman, but that's really not your decision to make. You're not our boss. We've been hired to keep an eye on Ms. Montjoy, and that's what we'll do."

A muscle ticced in his jaw. Turning his back on them, he said, "Dottie, I'll have one of my guys bring your car in for you."

"I appreciate that." She stood on tiptoe, brushed her lips over his cheeks. Then she turned and wrapped Annie in a hug, kissing her, too. "I had the most wonderful time! I can't wait to call Cora Mae and Tilly and tell them all about it."

She giggled. "I think I'll invite them over for some iced tea and cookies. Show them my dress and some of the pictures I took. They'll both be peacock-green with envy."

"I'm glad you had fun." Annie kissed her back. "And I think you're right. You should give your friends a call. Keep the celebration going." She turned to Cash. "If you'll give me a minute to change, I'll ride out to the ranch with you. I left the Harley at Whispering Pines yesterday."

"You don't need to do that, Annie. You have to be tired. One of the guys can bring your bike in, too." He glared at the muscle-bound bozo carrying Dottie's suitcase inside for her.

Silas scooped up Annie's. "Where to?"

"Upstairs. Just set it on the landing. I'll take care of it from there."

He nodded and picked up the case as though it weighed no more than a microchip.

Annie turned her attention back to Cash. "I want to go with you. I need to work today. And you know, with the picnic tomorrow you can use another set of hands."

"Look, Annie." He blew out a breath, took those hands in his, not quite sure how best to approach this.

She beat him to the punch. "Oh, no, you don't. Don't you dare even consider it."

He read temper in her beautiful blue eyes.

"You think you're going to start treating me like Annelise the heiress, instead of Annie the ranch hand?" She jammed a finger in his chest. "No way, buster."

He laughed and slid his sunglasses onto the top of his head. "You are something else, Ms. Annelise Montjoy."

"That would be Annie to you, Mr. Hardeman."

And thank God for that, he thought. Annelise might be out of his league, but Annie wasn't. He could touch Annie. Kiss Annie. Maybe, just maybe, he could find a way to keep Annie around a little longer.

"Okay, then. Go get your wrangling duds on and stop wasting time. We've got work to do."

* * *

Rufus and Silas followed them to the ranch, staying a couple of car lengths behind. Cash figured he might as well come to terms with it. And that meant no more trips to the pond for skinny-dipping. He could have cried.

"If you don't mind, I need to make another stop in town, Annie."

"It's your dime, boss."

"Funny." He checked his rearview mirror. The black Olds trailed behind.

Her boss. Right. He doubted anybody would ever truly be the boss of Annie. She was a strong woman. Now that he'd had a taste of her world, seen her navigate it, he realized exactly how much determination it had taken for her to make this trip to Texas. She'd risked some serious ire. Some major consequences.

Yet she'd had the guts to do it. She'd ignored the wrath of her family, the threat to her own safety.

And she'd done it because of love.

What would it be like to be on the receiving end of that love?

"Cash?"

"Hmmm?"

"Where'd you go? I asked what you had to do—twice."

"Sorry. Guess I got lost in my thoughts. I was making a mental list of everything we need to finish up before tomorrow." He swore his nose grew with the lie. "I want to stop by the newspaper office. Mel ordered some fliers for me, and I need to pick them up."

Several people walked along Main Street, and he and Annie waved to them. Luke and Marcy, who ran the town's only preschool, stood outside Sally's, no doubt ready for an early lunch—one that, since it was Saturday, wouldn't include peanut butter and jelly sandwiches.

He pulled up in front of the *Maverick Junction Daily* office. "Want to come in?"

"No, I think I'll sit here and close my eyes for a minute."

"Okay, be right back." He hopped out, noting the Olds idling several parking spaces away. She'd told him the truth. It would be hell to try to sneak away for a roll in the hay with them shadowing her. A guy could lose interest pretty fast, he supposed.

He looked at it as more of a challenge. A dare.

When he stepped into the office, the smell of paper and ink welcomed him.

"Hey, buddy," Melvin said. "Thought you might stop by today. Got your fliers for you."

As he hunted beneath the counter for them, he said, "In case you're interested, some PI came by this morning before I barely had the door unlocked. Asked all kinds of questions about you." He set the box of fliers on the counter. "What'd you get yourself into?"

Cash saw red. This was because of his relationship with Annie. Somebody snooping into his business, and, so, in a roundabout way, into hers. "I'm not into anything. And I hope to hell that's what you told them."

Mel held up a hand. "I gave the man nothing. Nobody else in town did, either. You know how it works. I can beat up on my brother, but nobody else better lay a hand on him. Same goes with you." He paused. "Got some interesting pictures over the UP wire service this morning."

His stomach dropped.

"Who'd have guessed that new hire of yours was an oil baron's grandkid? A Montjoy at that. And I, for one, would never have suspected you were so light on your feet. A regular twinkle toes. The shot of the two of you on the dance floor is priceless."

He tossed a copy of it on the counter.

Cash stared at it, traced his finger over Annie. She was beautiful. Gorgeous. And in his arms. How the hell could he be mad about that? *Eat your heart out, world.*

He shrugged. "She warned me. I suppose every newspaper in the state's gonna run this."

"That would be my guess."

"You're not, are you?"

"Hell, yes. Figure I'll sell a record number of papers today. I'm running off extras. Might even feature another one tomorrow to boost sales."

"Bloodsucker."

"Hey, pal, it's news. Local interest stuff. Everybody in town's interested in what you do when you fly off to the Big D." He took a drink from the mug beside him. "Brawley was there, huh?"

"Geez! What'd they do? Send you a blow-by-blow of the night?"

"No, but if you'd like to provide any of the missing details—" One look from Cash and he held his hands up in surrender. "Just saying. Free press at its best."

"Yeah, yeah." Cash rubbed a hand over his chin. "Brawley might come to the barbecue tomorrow. I'm not so sure you're still invited, though."

"Sure I am. Wouldn't be a picnic without me."

"No pictures."

"Wouldn't think of it."

"Right."

"Brawley's date looked pretty hot, too."

With an evil grin, Cash leaned over the counter and whispered, "Dallas Cowboy Cheerleader."

"Oh, man." A look of envy flitted across Mel's face. "She as hot as she looks in the photos?"

"Hotter."

"He always did have all the luck. You tell him Doc's thinking of retiring?"

"Brawley's not interested in coming back to this one-horse town. Rachel the cheerleader's words, not mine. Believe it or not, he likes the slick city life."

"Where'd we fail him, Cash?"

"I don't know. Might be those Dallas cheerleader outfits."

He paid for his fliers and walked back to the truck, watching Rufus and Silas watch him. A private eye investigating him? If that didn't take the cake. When the guy found out how boring Cash's life was, he'd back off soon enough.

Unless he found out about Grandma Vivi and the will. Shit!

As he opened his truck door, he tried to throw it off. Annie didn't need any more pressure or guilt, and she'd carry a load of both if she knew.

*   *   *

The bodyguards stayed in the car when they arrived at the ranch. They parked where they had a good view of the comings and goings, but stayed out of everyone's way.

Good thing, Cash thought, or he'd have run them off. As if Annie needed a bodyguard here on the ranch. Geez, Louise. Staubach, tongue hanging out, had barked and jumped up on him the second he'd stepped out of his vehicle.

"Hey, boy, you'd think I'd been gone a year instead of one night." He ruffled the dog's head and scratched between his ears. Then he threw a stick, and his pet ran after it in fits of doggy glee.

"Hey, son. Have a good time?" His father tipped his hat at Annie. "Welcome home."

Cash saw the burst of happiness before Annie had a chance to rein it in. His dad had said exactly the right thing.

"Got a lot going on today," he added.

With that, the workday began.

She'd been right about coming in to work today. They needed her. With the preparations under way for the barbecue, every hand on the ranch was busy. Rosie, her salt-and-pepper hair secured in a bun, ran around giving orders in a style that would have put General Patton to shame. She knew what she wanted and expected it would be executed exactly as she said.

And that's exactly what happened.

Yet Annelise realized the men weren't scurrying to do her bidding out of fear, but from love. When a table didn't end up exactly where Rosie wanted it, she cuffed one of the younger ranch hands, who turned and gave her a big smile and a peck on the cheek. Laughter rang out, loudly and often.

Annelise had never seen anything like it. Huge sheets of plywood spread over sawhorses to form tables. Benches appeared out of nowhere for seats. A huge fire pit was cleaned out and filled with wood, ready for action. Wind chimes and bells hung from trees. And everywhere, red, white, and blue streamers fluttered in the breeze.

Oh, she'd attended similar events. But she'd never, ever seen what happened behind the scenes. The timing was always impeccably planned so she arrived only once everything was perfect. She discovered she liked this part best.

She'd unloaded a bale of hay from the back of a pickup when her cell phone rang. She dug in her pocket and glanced at the display screen. Thelma Hanson. Her heart ratcheted up to fifth gear.

"Hello, Thelma?"

"Yep, it's me. I talked to Cornelia, and she's agreed to meet you tomorrow morning, nine o'clock. She said don't be late."

"Cornelia. Is that my aunt's name?"

"Yep." Thelma gave Annie directions to the house, then said, "Don't get all stirred up now and go in there like a kid heading into a candy store. This ain't no family reunion. Them's my words, not hers. She's a mite fancier than that. Still and all, I'm telling you, things might not go quite the way you're hoping. She's not near as excited as you about this. Can't see what any of your family's business has to do with her after all these years."

Even with Thelma's warning, Annie practically floated to the barn. Tomorrow morning, she'd meet her great-aunt.

Cornelia.

Chapter Twenty-Three

Every person Annelise bumped into reminded her to be at the ranch early tomorrow to get the most out of the day. She smiled and assured them she would be. Truth, though, she might not make it at all. She had something far more important to do.

She had to talk a complete stranger into helping her. Had to plead her case to her grandfather's long ignored half sister and talk her into being tested for a bone marrow match.

Annelise tossed another hay bale to the ground and wiped the sweat off her forehead with the back of her gloved hand. It had turned out to be so much easier than she'd ever dared hope to find her great-aunt. Cornelia. Anyone could have found her—if her grandfather had let them. But he hadn't. Even if she could convince this stranger, this relative, to help, he might still refuse.

"Let me give you a hand with those." Cash came up behind her and hopped up into the back of the truck. He tossed the rest of the bales over the side in no time flat, then helped her lift them in place. Rosie wanted to use them for seating.

"Thanks." She closed the tailgate and took off her gloves. "I might not make it till later tomorrow." She explained the call she'd had from Thelma.

"You want company?"

She shook her head. "No. This is where you need to be. You can't give a party, then not show up. Besides, I think it might go better with only the two of us."

"You're probably right." He kissed her cheek. "Let me know if you change your mind." He started to walk away, then stopped and turned back to her. "Hey, were you still going to stop by tonight to show Rosie the pictures from last night?"

"Yes. I'll go home, grab a quick bath and change, then come back. She promised me dessert."

"Then you're one lucky lady. Need anybody to scrub your back?"

She looked around quickly, but no one had been close enough to hear. "Shame on you."

He laughed and headed to the barn.

*   *   *

Feeling remarkably better after she'd cleaned up, Annie pulled her bike up to the main house. From her saddlebag, she retrieved the photo album the event planner had presented her that morning, then strolled up the walk. It was a beautiful summer evening. Crickets chirped close by, and she heard a horse neighing in the stable, the lowing of cows farther away. The temperature had backed off enough to make her reasonably comfortable in her shorts and tank top.

She felt at peace—even though Rufus and Silas had pulled in behind her. There was something about this place.

The front door stood open, the screen letting in the relatively cooler breeze. The scent of cinnamon and fresh-baked apple pie wafted out to her.

Annelise knocked on the door, and that sense of well-being disappeared when Vivi answered it, her hair disheveled, her blouse partially unbuttoned. She looked well and thoroughly mussed.

"Hey, Annie. I was upstairs welcoming Cash home. I missed him last night."

Annie literally felt the blood drain from her face. Oh, God, had she been a complete fool to believe Cash when he'd told her there was nothing between him and Vivi?

Even as she was trying to talk her feet into fleeing, Cash came down the stairs, his hair still damp from a shower, buttoning his shirt. "Annie, come on in. I'll tell Rosie to put the pot on."

"Maybe you shouldn't," she said through bloodless lips. "I don't want to interrupt anything."

Vivi draped an arm around Cash and curled into him. He stepped away, frowning. "What's going on?" His gaze moved from one woman to the other.

Trailing her long red nails over Cash's arm, Vivi said, "Think I'll run upstairs and freshen up."

Still in the doorway, keeping her voice low, Annie said, "I know we never made any promises, Cash, but aren't you the man who said when you slept with someone, you wanted to be the only person in her bed?"

Cash's eyes turned hard. "I did."

"Does that only work one way? There's no reciprocity? Have things changed between you two?"

He jerked his thumb at the stairs. "Is this about that little display of Vivi's?"

She said nothing.

A muscle ticced in his jaw. "What'd she do? Tell you she and I were upstairs in the sack?"

She felt empty, half-sick.

"Come on, Annie. You're smarter than that. She staged this, hoping for exactly the response she got."

Still she couldn't bring herself to say anything.

He thumped the doorjamb with the side of his fist. "Oh, for Pete's sake. I intended to grab a quick shower at the stable, but I realized I didn't have any clean clothes there. I always keep some upstairs." His brow rose. "In the spare bedroom. I didn't want to spend the evening with you smelling of horse and sweat."

"I want so badly to believe you."

"Then do. It's as simple as that." He held the door open for her. "Come on in. Did you bring the pictures?"

"Yes, I did." Her voice still sounded chilly, but she couldn't help herself. And she couldn't believe she'd let Vivi get under her skin like that. Not again. Cash was right. She did know better.

She'd never considered herself a jealous person, but the thought of Cash and Vivi— Well, she wouldn't think about it anymore.

They walked back to the kitchen, where Rosie had perked a fresh pot of coffee and had a warm apple pie, minus one piece, sitting on the counter.

Hank was there, too, a cup of coffee and the missing piece of pie already in front of him.

"Hank. Didn't realize you were down here."

"I came while you were upstairs." He poked at the pie with his fork. "Promised Rosie I'd come try this out, make sure she wouldn't poison anybody with it tomorrow."

"You old coot." She swatted him with a dish towel. "Don't know why I put up with you."

"'Cause I'm irresistible."

"Irresistible in a pig's eye." She fetched two more cups. "I noticed the boys are still following you around." She pointed down the hall to outside. "You think they might want some pie and something to drink?"

"Rosie, that would be very nice of you. I'm sure they'd love it."

She cut a couple of huge wedges and poured them iced tea. She and Hank carried it out to the bodyguards while Annelise and Cash settled in at the table.

"They make a nice couple," Annelise said.

"Rosie and Hank? Yeah, they do. They dated before she married his friend, a friend he introduced her to. A few years after she was widowed, they finally quit pretending they weren't in love. Good thing, too, because they belong together."

"Some people do." She glanced up, caught Cash's intense gaze.

The screen door opened and Hank and Rosie came back in.

"They certainly are big boys," Rosie said.

"That's why her daddy hired them," Hank growled.

Staubach dragged himself up from the rug in front of the back door and plopped down at Cash's feet. Two minutes later, his snores serenaded them.

They sat around the table, enjoying themselves over pie and photos. "Dottie looks stunning," Rosie said. "This dress is fantastic."

The sound of heels on the hardwood floor preceded Vivi.

She stopped in the doorway to make her grand entrance, then sauntered into the room.

"Well, well. Looks like the gang's all here." Pulling out a chair, she sat down at the table and grabbed Cash's coffee.

"Make yourself at home," he said.

"Don't mind if I do, especially since it'll legally be mine real soon. I talked to my lawyer today. He tells me you're willing to let things stand."

"Cash?" Annie asked.

"Never mind," he said. "Nothing for you to worry about."

Vivi's brows arched. "Haven't you told her?"

"About what?" Annie laid down her fork.

Rosie bristled and slapped another cup of coffee on the table in front of Cash. "Want a piece of pie, Vivi?"

"No, I don't." A cat-ate-the-canary smile on her face, she said, "Vivi's Valley has a nice sound to it, don't you think?"

"Cash?" Annelise asked again. "What's going on?"

"Yes, Cash, what's going on?" Vivi parroted. "Changing your mind? Thinking you might want to hang on to Whispering Pines? I know." She clapped her hands. "You're planning to use our Annie here as your ace in the hole, aren't you? Are you going to propose first, make sure she's all roped and tied before you spring the terms on her?"

Annie's cup clattered to the table, sloshing liquid over the rim.

"Damn you, Vivi." Cash went rigid.

She took another sip of her coffee, eyeing Cash over the cup's rim. Then she focused on Annelise.

"Didn't he tell you he's got a birthday coming up in a few months? A real important one. His thirtieth." She played with her top button. "Thing is, Cash here always figured Whispering Pines would be his one day. Then his granddaddy and I got hitched. By rights, the place should be mine free and clear. But that Leo. He liked to mess with things. Wanted Cash here married and making babies."

"Vivi, that's enough."

"Oh, but she hasn't heard the best part, sweetheart." She took a bite of his pie, licked her obscenely red lips. "See, Leo put a codicil in his will. If Cash is married by the time he turns thirty, he inherits. If not, half the ranch comes to me."

She played with the wedding ring on her finger. "Didn't seem as if much was going to happen. Then you came riding into town on that big Harley of yours and the sky opened up for Cash. The answer to all his prayers. He can marry you, save the ranch, and, no doubt, share your wealth. Hell of a deal for him." She leaned toward Annelise conspiratorially. "Think he's afraid you might put up a fuss at being used as a pawn, though."

"I'm not using her. I'm not marrying her."

Annie felt like she'd been knifed in the stomach. She couldn't draw in enough breath. She didn't expect marriage. Had never expected it. And, contrary to what Vivi said, Cash had made no moves in that direction. In fact, he'd been very up-front about not wanting anything long-term. Still, to hear him announce it in such an ugly snarl hurt. Badly.

That she might have been considered as a pawn in this game, no matter how briefly, hurt worse. To be used for money, hers or someone else's—unforgivable. This is what Cash meant over dinner the other night when he'd said Vivi viewed her as competition.

"Excuse me. I think it's time I left." Grabbing her purse from the counter, she stood. "Keep the pictures, Rosie. You can look at them later." She hurried from the house, the screen door banging shut behind her.

It creaked open again as Cash followed her out onto the porch. She heard his sigh.

"Annie—"

"You could have told me, Cash."

"I didn't figure it had anything to do with you. You had enough problems of your own to deal with already."

"That's an excuse, and you know it."

He had the good grace not to deny it.

"When I think how mad you got at me when you learned who I really was. All that moral outrage about keeping secrets." She stomped her foot. "And you," she stammered. "You had one of your own. One that involved me. One that, even after everything that's happened between us, you didn't trust me enough to share."

"It has nothing to do with trust."

She slapped a hand on his chest. "Now you're going to stand there and lie to me?"

"I'm not—"

"Don't. Don't say anything else. I won't believe you. Anything we might have had shattered in there tonight." She tipped her head at the house. Her voice lowered. "You hurt me."

"I didn't mean to."

"Somehow that doesn't seem to matter right now."

He reached for her hand, but she smacked his away.

Looking up at the stars, he blew out a huge breath before he met her eyes. His head hurt. "Annie, our worlds are way too far apart. This thing between us. It can't work. And I told you before. I'm not ready for marriage."

"Even if it means—"

"Yes." He nodded. "Even if it means I lose this."

"How odd," she said. "My grandfather forbid this search for his half sister, and neither my mom nor dad would even consider going against his wishes. Grandpa has threatened to disown me if I don't leave off this hunt and come home. I'm not about to do that."

She looked him dead in the eyes. "So, Cash Hardeman, it looks like you and I are both likely to find ourselves out on the street. And alone."

* * *

Night had fallen. Her single headlamp cut a swath through the darkness. She breathed in deeply, trying to rid herself of the anger. The lights from the Olds shone dimly in her rearview mirror, reminding her that Rufus and Silas were there, but they stayed farther back than normal.

It just kept getting better and better, she thought bitterly. She slowed, leaned into a curve, then sped up again. Her eyes moved across the landscape, on the lookout for wildlife.

Who was Cash Hardeman? The man had a lot of hidden corners. And he was determined to deflect any light that might try to shine on them, exposing them and himself to her.

God knew, he could be both sweet and gentle. He'd certainly helped her out more than once, but that might only have been a Good Samaritan complex kicking in. He'd certainly been gentle when they'd made love. But then maybe he'd had an ulterior motive.

Had he, even then, been contemplating using her to gain the ranch? Or was he telling the truth now? Had the two not had anything to do with each other? She couldn't think clearly.

She'd watched him with Rosie, with Hank, with his parents, though, and knew he was capable of love.

But not with her.

Love? Her throat tightened, and the asthma she'd thrown off in middle school threatened to return. She heard a wheezing sound as she took a breath.

Calm down, she told herself. You can't change anything. Get home, turn on some music, maybe have a glass of wine. A nice long soak. She was loving that tub more and more. It put the best of therapists to shame.

Then the memory of her and Cash sharing it rushed over her, and she choked back a sob.

It was no good. She had to let it go.

She had to remember the reason she was here. She'd talk to Cornelia and convince her to go back to Boston with her. Back to her family.

Everything would be all right.

If Cornelia was a match.

If she could put a certain cowboy out of her mind.

If…

Chapter Twenty-Four

Her nerves throbbed. Her head ached.

Annelise had spent a miserable night, tossing and turning till the soft light of dawn came through her bedroom window. Sleep had refused its refuge, and in the night's dark hours, her mind ricocheted between the pain of walking away from Cash and the unnerving prospect of finally meeting her aunt.

The already-hot Texas sun beat down on her as she laid her helmet on the Harley's seat. She prayed she could get through this. Prayed she could find some way to convince the woman who stood quietly studying her to help.

Cornelia Whitney was not at all what Annelise had expected. She'd assumed this woman would be a carbon copy of Thelma. What was it Cash had said about assumptions? They'd bite you in the butt.

She pushed the thought away. Pushed any and all thoughts of Cash to the back of her mind. She couldn't afford to think about him right now.

The woman who waited in the doorway of the cheerful yellow bungalow was elegant and smartly dressed in a well-fitting pair of white dress slacks and a loose, flowing blue and white top. Her gray hair had been done up in a Gibson girl do. Other than simple pearl earrings, she wore no jewelry.

Trim and petite, she stood a good five inches shorter than Annelise. But her eyes. Looking into those cool blue eyes was like staring at her own in a mirror.

"Miss Whitney, I'm Annelise Montjoy." She extended her hand.

"I know who you are. I can see it in your face. What I don't know is why you're here."

Direct and to the point, Annelise thought. A short Katharine Hepburn.

She moved aside. "Come in. No need to forgo good manners."

Annelise stepped into a cozy living room. Devoid of most of the frou-frou that so often filled older people's homes, this one had wall-to-wall, floor-to-ceiling bookshelves filled with literature. She crossed to them and ran a hand over the spines.

"These are wonderful," she said, turning to Cornelia.

"Yes, they are. Books are my true love." She perched on the edge of a Windsor chair. "Would you like something? Perhaps tea or coffee? Cookies?"

"No, thank you." Annelise walked over to an obviously well-loved sofa and sat. "You asked why I'm here. It's because of my grandfather, Vincent Montjoy."

She watched the woman's eyes, so like her own, for any sign of recognition and saw nothing.

"Are you aware of—" She hesitated, not sure now that she was here exactly how to handle this. She'd rehearsed the scene in her mind a thousand times. Nothing, though, was as she'd expected. Reality seldom was.

"Am I aware your grandfather and I share a father? Yes, I certainly am. My middle name is Montjoy. My mother didn't want me to forget where I came from."

"Oh." Annelise clasped her hands on her lap. "My grandfather, your brother—"

"My half brother."

"Yes. Your half brother. He has leukemia and needs a bone marrow transplant. Without it, he'll die." There, she'd cut to the chase and laid it out, unemotionally.

Cornelia studied her for several long seconds. "I invited you here because Thelma asked me to talk to you. But I want you to know I wouldn't have otherwise. Thelma's a wonderful woman with a big heart." Her hands moved to the arms of her chair. "I wrote to your grandfather once. The letter came back as undeliverable. He wanted nothing to do with me, his father's dirty little secret."

"I'm so sorry."

"It's not your place to be sorry. You've done nothing wrong." Her fingers tightened on the chair arms. "Your grandfather did, though. He turned his back on me as his father had. As *my* father had. So the question becomes, why should I help him now?"

"Because . . . because you're a good person."

"You don't know that. You don't know me."

Annelise stared up at the ceiling, then brought her eyes back to the matching ones across the room. "I've thought about this so much. Thought I was ready. That I knew exactly what I'd say when we met." She held out her hands, palms up. "Now that I'm actually here, Ms. Whitney, I don't have a clue."

"Call me Nelly."

Annelise smiled. "Nelly. I know you've probably had a hard life. A lot harder than my grandfather had. I also know you don't owe him anything. You don't owe our family anything."

Her smile faded. "But I'm begging you. Please, help us. If you'd agree to be tested. You may not even be a match. If you're not, then we're done. I go back to Boston and spend what time I have left with my grandfather. You go back to doing whatever it is you do here in Texas."

She stood, unable to sit any longer. "If you are a match, though, I've got to believe you'd do this for a stranger. If some young child needed your bone marrow, you'd give it to him. I know you would. Anybody would. I'm not asking for a kidney or part of your liver. Your bone marrow will replenish itself. In a matter of days, you'll be as good as new, and my grandpa will have a chance at gaining his life back. You might hold my grandfather's life in your hands."

"I don't want that responsibility. I never asked for it."

"I understand that. But like it or not, Vincent is your brother, your half brother. You shared a father. Neither of you had any choice in that or how it played out. In this, you do have a choice."

"I hear you rode all the way from Boston on a Harley."

"I did."

"Does your grandfather know you're here?"

"I believe he does now."

"He's none too happy about that, is he?"

Annelise breathed deeply. "No, ma'am, he's not. He's ordered me home."

"I can't imagine what you hoped to gain by coming all this way to see me. It doesn't make any sense. Why didn't you simply call me?"

"Because you would have said no."

"I can say no to your face as easily as over the phone."

"Maybe. But I'm hoping you won't, because I love Vincent Montjoy. I love him," she repeated. "It breaks my heart to see this wonderful man, a man who's always been so strong, brought down low and knowing there's a chance—a slim chance—but a chance nonetheless, that we can save him. That *you* can save him. You're his only hope."

Cornelia got up and walked to one of the bookshelves. "I studied English literature in college. Your great-grandfather took care of Mother and me financially. But he broke both our hearts when he left."

She turned to lean against the shelf. "My mother died the year I went off to college. When I graduated, I didn't come back to Lone Tree. There was nothing for me here. Or so I thought.

"He bought this house for us. I suppose I should be grateful for that. Over the years, Thelma and I have kept in contact, and she helped me. I paid for the maintenance, and she saw to the actual hiring of the work for me. She's a good friend. I spent most of my life in England and didn't come back until several years ago."

"England. Is that where you collected the beautiful tea cups?" She nodded toward the china closet brimming with them.

"Some, yes. Everywhere I travel, I buy one. Most are from antique shops, some from friends who find interesting ones for me."

She picked up a porcelain music box and wound it. Carousel horses circled while "Let Me Call You Sweetheart" rang out in tinny tones. "My father bought this for me on my fourth birthday. When we walked down the street, hand in hand, I was somebody. My daddy was a very important man."

Annie's heart sped up. She was no longer dealing in abstracts. And Driller Montjoy had apparently not neglected his daughter. He'd also not been very discreet. And that must have wreaked havoc at home.

"I remember him as if it was yesterday." Cornelia replaced the music box. "I have a picture of him. Would you like to see it?"

Annelise nodded.

Her great-aunt opened a cedar chest tucked into the corner of the room and drew out an old, faded album. "This was my mother's. She began working as the Montjoy's housekeeper, you know, then saved the rascal's life when he had appendicitis."

Annelise nodded. So Cornelia's mother was the nurse she'd read about. A shared near-death trauma. A bond formed. Was that what had started the romance?

Cornelia opened the album, a far-away, rather dreamy look on her aged face. She turned to a picture of her mother and held it out for Annelise to see. "This is my mother, Kathleen Whitney."

Slowly, she turned the page. "And this is my family. Your great-grandfather, my mother, and me. It was taken on my birthday. The day he gave me the music box. The dress had been a Christmas gift, red velvet with tiny white bows on the skirt. It was my last birthday with him. A week later, he moved his *real* family, his legal one, to Boston. I never saw him again."

There was pain in her voice, pain Annelise couldn't ignore. She placed her hand over the older woman's and was pleased when she didn't pull away.

But she didn't offer an apology. Cornelia had made it more than clear she didn't expect one from her.

Why then did she want one from her grandfather?

Because he'd rebuffed her. Hadn't been willing to open any line of communication with her. Annelise thought she understood that.

Hadn't she been hurt to the core last night when she'd realized Cash hadn't been candid with her? And Cornelia's hurt went back a long way, had festered all these years.

"Vincent was only nine when they moved away," she said.

Cornelia nodded. "I know."

"Surely you don't blame him."

"Not for that, no. Father uprooted him and took him away from his friends, from everything he loved. I felt sorry for him for a while."

"Then he rejected your peace offering."

"Yes. And that was when I closed my heart to him."

Oh, Grandpa, Annelise thought. *You so blew it.*

"Is there anything I can say, anything I can do to change your mind?"

"I'm afraid not." The expression on Cornelia's face, in her eyes, showed compassion but also determination. She stood. "I know you came a long way to talk to me, but I can't help you."

"You *won't* help me. My grandfather."

"As you will. That chapter of my life is closed. I don't wish to reopen it. For any reason."

"But a good man will die." Annelise had to try once more. "He was only a little boy when all this happened. It had nothing to do with him. You know that."

"He had his daddy to put him to bed at night. I didn't."

"Please. You can't hold that against him."

Cornelia dropped her head. "I don't. I shouldn't have said that." She walked to the door and opened it.

Annelise wasn't ready to leave. "Nelly—"

"No." Her grandfather's only hope shook her head. "I

really am very sorry. I hope to live the rest of my life right here in this house in solitude and peace. I want to read my books. Have tea occasionally with Thelma. If I come forward to do this, the press will find out about me, and none of that's going to happen. It would change my life. Again.

"The Montjoys turned their backs on me and my mother years ago. 'What a man sows, that shall he and his relations reap.' Clarissa Graves. A wonderful British poet."

Annelise stood, moved to the door to stand beside Cornelia. "I didn't know my great-grandfather, Nelly. Your father. I can only say he appeared to be human. He had flaws like the rest of us."

When Cornelia opened her mouth to speak, Annelise said, "Wait, please. Hear me out. Does that mean what Driller did was right?" She shook her head. "No, of course not. He cheated on his wife. He left two young children to pay for his sins. But someone has to be willing to break that chain of hurt and wrong. I had hoped it would be you."

"I tried. Your grandfather refused my entreaty. I took the first step. I won't take another."

"I understand." Annelise opened the screen door and stepped onto the porch, fighting back tears. She'd failed. Through an emotion-tight throat, she said, "I appreciate you taking the time to meet me. I know this hasn't been easy for you."

"Wait." Cornelia touched Annelise's arm. "Do you have a picture of your grandfather? Something recent?"

"Yes, I do." She withdrew a photo from her purse. "It was taken just before he got sick." She handed it to his sister. "Keep it, please. I have more."

Without another word, she left the way she'd come. This time, though, there was no hope, only despair. Her grandfather's last chance had died. As he would.

She didn't stop the tears but let them fall, swiping at them only when they clouded her vision.

After she turned onto the main road, she pulled off to the side, removed her helmet, and indulged in a good cry. Her chest felt tight, her heart heavy. Resting her elbows on the bike's handlebars, she laid her forehead in her hands.

Alone for the first time in days, she gave in to despair. Rufus and Silas, after a good deal of cajoling, had allowed her to go the last mile to Cornelia's unattended. Coming clean with them, she'd explained the importance of the meeting. She didn't think showing up with two bodyguards would improve her chance of success.

Now she realized it hadn't mattered. Cornelia Whitney had agreed to speak with her, but her mind had already been made up. Past hurts offset anything Annelise could say.

Any hopes she'd harbored of a great-aunt who would accept her and help her had been dashed. Thelma had been right. Today had not been a family reunion.

Wiping her eyes, she blew her nose and buckled her helmet back on. Nothing to do now but go home. To Boston. She'd make the most of whatever time her grandfather had left.

What she didn't intend to do today was attend a celebration. It might be the country's independence day, but she had nothing to cheer about. No fireworks for her today. An explosion, yes. One that had destroyed all her dreams.

Her hope of helping Grandpa had gone up in smoke. Any relationship she'd thought was in the making between her and Cash had ended last night.

She waved at her bodyguards as she roared past and watched in her rearview mirror as they pulled in behind her.

As she rode, her mind kicked into high gear, planning details, mentally composing a list of to-dos. She'd go back to her apartment and pack. If she was lucky, she could catch a plane out of Austin tonight or tomorrow. She'd have her Harley shipped back to Boston. Either Silas or Rufus could stay behind to deal with that. The other could fly home with her.

Dottie. She'd grown to love her landlady. It broke her heart again to think of leaving her, of saying good-bye. And Hank. And Rosie. Sally and Oliver. Paco. Maggie.

Maverick Junction, Texas, had very quickly become part of her. What she'd learned and experienced here had changed her forever.

Tears spilled again when she thought of life without Cash in it. He'd awakened a part of her she'd never known existed. Well, with enough time and effort, she'd get over him.

In a trillion years or so.

Chapter Twenty-Five

Annelise jotted the information on a notepad, then stretched. Her muscles ached, not from overwork but from tension. She'd managed to confirm a flight from Austin into Boston's Logan International first thing tomorrow morning. Rufus would drive her and Silas to the airport, then stay behind to tie up loose ends here. He'd leave the Olds they'd rented at the airport's car return when he flew out later.

Now that she had her plans firmed up, a sense of lethargy set in, and she wandered into her bedroom. Her beautiful bedroom. One she'd painted and decorated herself. Dropping onto her bed, she took a moment to commit it to memory. She'd come here with such high hopes.

The learning curve in Maverick Junction had been steep and the price high. But she couldn't for one second regret the experience.

She could wish it had turned out differently, yes. But she wouldn't give up her time here for anything.

Exhaling loudly, she shook off the listlessness and went to her closet. The first time she'd seen it, it had seemed so small. Now, it seemed perfect. Everything she needed fit. She'd miss even this.

Taking her few pieces of clothes from the closet, she began to pack. She couldn't bear to leave Maggie's beautiful clothes behind. She ran a hand over the dress she'd worn in Dallas, held it to her, and moved to the slow music in her head. What a magical night.

And now, everything had fallen apart.

Her mind refused to quiet. *Come see me, Cash. Talk to me. Tell me this was all a huge mistake.*

But the apartment remained silent. No quick rap at the kitchen door announced his arrival. He didn't rush in to scoop her up in his arms and tell her he loved her.

Loved?

Oh, God. She covered her face with trembling hands.

She loved him. Had tumbled down the rabbit hole—cowboy boots and all.

Her stomach knotted. When had that happened?

She sat down on the edge of her bed. She was in love with Cash. *She loved him.* Loved his ranch, his ugly dog. Loved everything about him. And tomorrow morning she'd get on a plane and leave him behind. Forever.

Because he hadn't been honest. Even as he held her close. As he made love to her, first by the pond, then at his house. He'd chewed her out for keeping secrets while holding on to his own.

What if she stayed?

No, whatever else she might be, she wasn't a glutton for punishment.

Cash's words from last night replayed in her head. *This thing between us. It can't work.*

He'd made himself more than clear. No room for misinterpretation there.

She had no choice. Picking up the top, she stared into her tiny closet, at her jeans and T-shirts. They showed more than a little wear from working in them. A couple of shirts were stained. She wadded those up and threw them in the wastebasket.

Her gaze landed on her cowboy boots. She wouldn't need them in Boston. She thought of the night she'd bought them, remembered how wonderful and new shopping with Cash had felt. Even if she never wore them again, she couldn't leave the boots behind.

The banging on her door startled her.

What the heck?

She dropped the shirt she was folding onto the bed and hurried, barefoot, to the kitchen. Through the window, she saw one very angry cowboy on her landing. Had she conjured him?

He barged in, not waiting for her to open the door. "What the hell are you doing? Is this about last night?"

"What?"

"You're supposed to be at the ranch."

"I told you I might not make it."

"Your errand is finished."

"I've decided not to go."

"So, what? You're going to sit up here in this hot apartment and pout? I upset you last night. Got that. Still, that's no reason to pull this little stunt. A lot of people are upset you're not at the picnic."

"A lot of people? And who exactly would that be?"

His jaw tightened. "Me, for one."

"Why?"

"Because I—I care about you, Annie."

He cared about her. That was the best he could do. And it wasn't good enough. Despair settled in her stomach.

He hesitated. "I told you I was sorry."

"Not everything's about you," she said.

"Maybe not, but—" He ran a thumb along her cheek. Tipping his head, he took a good long look at her. His brow creased. "Annie? What's wrong?"

She looked a mess, and she knew it. While she'd been in the bathroom, she'd caught a glimpse of herself in the mirror over her sink. Her eyes were swollen and red, her cheeks flushed.

Not trusting herself, she pulled away. "It has nothing to do with you."

"Your grandfather? Is he worse?"

The concern in his voice was her undoing. Her heart, which she'd thought broken before, crumbled in a thousand shards.

"No. Not that I know."

"She won't help you."

"No." Despite her best intentions, the tears started again. "She's going to let him die."

He pulled her in, buried her face in his chest, and held her tightly. "I'm sorry, darlin'."

Between sobs, she said, "She's going to let him die. She won't even get tested."

"How about if I go talk to her?"

And he would. He would do that for her. That knowledge only made her cry harder. She was going to lose them both, her grandpa and Cash.

"Annie, I don't know what to say. What to do."

"Don't say anything at all. Make love to me, Cash."

"Annie—"

"Please."

"I should say no, but I can't." He carried her into the bedroom, then stopped. "What's this?"

She'd forgotten. Clothes were strewn across the bed, some folded, some tossed haphazardly. She couldn't tell him she was leaving. Not yet.

Double standard? Yes. She'd been angry because he hadn't told her everything, and now she was holding back. Again.

She'd tell him later. Why ruin today for him any more than she already had?

"I decided to clean my closet." With a sweep of her hand, she brushed the clothes to the floor.

About to argue the point, he gave up when she closed the distance between them and kissed him. All the passion, all the hurt, the anger, the need, poured from her to him.

Within minutes, their clothes joined the ones scattered across the floor. Naked, they fell to her bed. She needed one last time.

Cash didn't disappoint.

* * *

Freshly bathed, hair brushed and makeup reapplied, and dressed in a pair of Sadler store bargain-barrel shorts and an Armani original top she'd brought with her, Annelise walked down the stairs ahead of Cash. The back door to Dottie's opened, and Rufus stepped out.

"Ms. Montjoy." He nodded. "Everything okay?"

"Yes. I've decided to go to the barbecue after all." After a moment, she said, "You know, while we're here, I'd prefer you and Silas call me Annie."

Rufus looked almost offended. "Ms. Montjoy—"

"Annie. Otherwise the two of you will stick out like a sore

thumb. We don't want to call any more attention to you than we need to. Right?"

"Yes, ma'am."

She laid a hand on his arm. "Everyone here knows me as Annie."

"Yes, ma'am." He shuffled a foot. "Ms. Willis is ready to leave for the party. Do you mind if we give her a ride?"

"Not at all." Annelise stopped, looked at the Caddy, at Staubach waiting patiently in the backseat, his tongue lolling out. She turned to Cash. "She could ride with us."

"You feeling the need for a chaperone again? Kind of late for that, don't you think?"

Mortified, she shot a quick glance at Rufus.

"Yes, she can." Cash chuckled. "Let me run in, see if she needs help with anything."

He came out carrying a platter of cookies with Dottie trailing in his wake. Today she wore hot-pink capris and a pink and white polka-dotted blouse. Pink sandals sporting huge rhinestones finished off her outfit.

"You look wonderful, Dottie."

"You don't look half-bad yourself, sweetie. That top is the exact color of your eyes." Dottie studied her, then Cash. "You looked awfully pale when you came home this morning, Annie, but I see you got your color back."

A blaze of heat rushed from her toes to the top of her head. Cash threw his head back and laughed till she elbowed him in the ribs.

"Ouch! Careful, darlin'. Don't want to make me drop the dessert."

"I'll dessert you," she muttered.

He leaned in close and whispered, "I think you already did."

Deciding discretion was, indeed, the better part of valor, she slunk off to the car.

* * *

Things were in full swing when they pulled into the yard, and Annelise was suddenly very glad she'd come. She said a prayer of thanks that Cash had driven to her apartment to collect her, then a second one that she'd have today with him and all these others who'd come to mean so much to her.

Determined to make the most of this gift, Annelise fought to put her hurt aside. She hadn't saved her grandfather. She hadn't won Cash's heart. And so hers would ache. But for today, she'd do her best to ignore it.

Forcing a smile, she helped Dottie out of the backseat. Staubach bounded out after her.

Some of the hands had thrown together a band, and the music practically flowed from their fiddles, guitars, and a rather beat-up drum set. Paco, showing off a remarkably good voice, stood in an old hay wagon pressed into service as a stage and sang about cheating hearts. A few couples two-stepped on the makeshift dance floor they'd created the day before.

Neighbors and friends came up to them as they made their way with the cookies to several tables already groaning under the weight of the delicious-smelling food Rosie and the girls had prepared.

No one should go hungry, Annelise thought, even as a calorie counter cranked up in her mind.

Some of the townspeople nodded at her but seemed hesitant to approach. Even Cash introduced her with more deference than he had in the past.

"See," she hissed. "This is exactly why I didn't tell you about my so-called *pedigree* sooner. Don't treat me any differently than you did before you knew who my grandfather was. I'm the same woman who's been mucking out your stalls."

"The hell you are."

She put a hand on his shoulder. "Yes, I am."

"Fine. You are."

Austin, his nephew, ran up to him, a football cradled in his arms. "Throw me some, Uncle Cash?"

"You bet."

She sat down on one of the hay bales, her foot tapping to the beat of a Trace Adkins song. Her heart beat way too fast. Seeing Cash surrounded by his family, she realized how small hers was. If she lost her grandfather...Melancholy settled over her again.

She'd hoped against hope to stumble across her before-unaccounted-for aunt. She had. She'd prayed that aunt could save her grandfather. She wouldn't.

And Cash. He'd be furious come this time tomorrow when he realized she'd skipped town.

Well, it couldn't be helped. There was no other way. She couldn't stay knowing she loved him, that he couldn't love her back. And she needed to spend whatever time was left with Grandpa.

Her head jerked up as a new voice joined the band. Deep and rich. Cash stood on stage in front of the mic, singing about the wonder of love.

She couldn't bear to listen. Standing, she wandered over to the horses. Several of them had been decorated for the Fourth with red, white, and blue ribbons braided into their manes and tails. Blankets made to look like the American flag draped over their backs. Old Molly even wore an Uncle Sam hat perched jauntily between her ears.

A couple of the hands were giving kids horseback rides, and parents with cameras stood by the board fence capturing it all for posterity.

One little girl, about three years old and cute as a button

in her red, white, and blue outfit, stood in the middle of the paddock crying. She wanted to ride but was afraid to get on alone.

Out of the corner of her eye, Annelise saw Cash coming toward them. One foot on the middle rail, he vaulted over the fence. Mounting a horse with a flag painted on its side, his hat tipped low over his eyes, he held out his arms. One of the ranch hands lifted the little girl into them. Cash slowly guided the horse around the outside of the paddock. With the little girl now grinning ear to ear, he stopped by her parents so they could get their picture.

Oh, boy, Annelise thought. And the storm within grew wilder.

* * *

Cash watched Annie walk away. He finished his loop around the ring, then handed the pigtailed little girl down to her mother.

"Thanks, Cash."

"No biggie. Can't have her growing up afraid of horses." He dismounted, patted the mare's muzzle, and tossed the reins to one of his men.

His sister was waiting for him when he jumped the fence. "Hey, Cash." She locked an arm through his. "You know I've always wanted what's best for you, little brother."

"Uh-oh."

"What do you mean, uh-oh?"

"Any time you start out like that, I'm in trouble."

"Not this time. Not necessarily you, anyway." She patted his hand. "First, though, I want to say I think you've found a real treasure."

His brows wrinkled.

"Cash, anybody with half a brain knows you and Annie are getting real serious about each other."

He tried to pull away, but after wrestling two kids around, his sister had grown some muscle. Without making a stink about it, he had no choice but to stay armlocked with her.

"I saw the pictures Mel ran." She slapped at him. "Don't go making that face. I caught the two of you on AOL and *Entertainment Tonight*, too."

"What?" Now he did break loose.

"Annie's big news, bro. I also believe she's that someone special who's been missing in your life."

"You don't know what you're talking about, believe me."

"Have you done something to screw this up?"

"No." He kicked a dirt clod. "Yes. Maybe."

"What's wrong, Cash? What did you do?" Her eyes narrowed.

"I can't go into it now."

"You don't *want* to go into it now."

"That's what I said."

"Did you take Annie to the pond?"

He stood stock-still. "What?"

"You heard me."

"How the hell do you know about that?"

His sister's eyes filled with pain. "Did you two go skinny-dipping?"

Mouth set in a tight line, he said, "I'm not gonna discuss this with you."

He started to walk away, but her next words stopped him dead in his tracks. "Did you take pictures, Cash?"

Madder than he could ever remember being, he whirled on her. Anger exploded inside him. "Pictures? What in God's name are you talking about? If you've got something to say, Barbara Jean, I suggest you spit it out because right now you're pissing me off. Royally."

She took a deep breath. "Lower your voice."

"I damn well—"

"Will listen to me." She threaded her arm through his again. "Let's take a walk."

She started around the side of the barn, practically dragging him with her. He was mad enough to spit nails. Once they'd put a respectable distance between themselves and the other partygoers, she said, "Cash, just before we came, I was messing around on the computer. I Googled Annie."

He opened his mouth but, seeing the disquieted expression on her face, shut it.

"I wasn't prying. I was simply bored and wasting time till we left for here." She hesitated, and he saw tears in her eyes.

"Babs? You're scaring me."

"Oh, Cash, I don't know how to say this. I'm so sorry." She grabbed his hand. "There's a video of Annie on YouTube. She's at the pond. Naked."

He felt light-headed, as if every ounce of blood had drained from him. Then just as quickly, it all rushed back and heat flooded him. He'd murder the bastard, whoever he was, that had done this. His hands balled into fists.

"You think I'd do that?"

"No. I don't. But I had to ask. Just in case you were fooling around. Made a video for the two of you." She shrugged. "People do that."

"We didn't."

"It's posted by a Gwen Garrison."

"Gwen Garrison?"

"You know her?"

"No."

"It's not an account you set up under another name then?"

"Why in the hell would I do that?"

"Don't bite my head off. I didn't do anything. But you should check her out. In the meantime, you need to tell Annie."

"I will. But not right now. She's dealing with a hell of a lot." He gave a quick-and-dirty rundown on Annie's meeting with her aunt. "I need a minute, sis. Will you keep an eye on things?"

"Sure." She stood on tiptoe and kissed his cheek. "You know I love you."

"I know."

"You want some advice?"

"No."

Barbara Jean's eyes filled with fire, and he knew he was going to get it anyway.

Her brother-in-law's triplets saved him.

Rosie had decided to put together a candy table for the kids. A kind of trick-or-treat thing on the Fourth of July. She'd set out pretty dishes filled with taffy and penny candy. Tall glass containers full of old-fashioned red, white, and blue–swirled lollipops, ribbon candy, lemon and orange candy sticks begged to be raided.

The Rawlins boys were doing exactly that. Grabbing handfuls of the candy, they hurled it at each other—until his sister reached them. Barbara Jean caught two by the arms and scissored a leg around the third, trapping him.

Cash watched her deft handling of the situation and gave her major kudos. And it hit him square between the eyes. This might be the last Hardeman Fourth of July barbecue at Whispering Pines. Once Vivi was half owner...

Over a sinking stomach, he glimpsed Ty Rawlins threading his way through the crowd. At thirty-two, the guy had his hands full. Because he'd gotten married.

Married. Like he'd be if he agreed to Gramps's terms. Hell of a reason to go into marriage, though. Still, the weight of it dropped on him all over again, the impact as massive as that of a piano falling from twenty floors above.

What if Annie was the one walking down the aisle beside him?

He ran a finger under the collar of his suddenly too tight tee.

She wouldn't be. Period. And when she found out about the YouTube fiasco...

Could things get any more screwed up?

His gaze shifted back to Ty. He'd been happy in his marriage. Very happy. Until Julia's heart had given out. Now he was a widower, raising three kids alone. Wouldn't he have been better off if he'd avoided it all? Hadn't married Julia?

Ty reached the boys and, laughing, they dove at him, sticky fingers and all. The look on his friend's face gave Cash pause. No. In this case, Ty wouldn't have been better off. He'd loved and been loved back.

The triplets, full of mischief, spoke of that love. He doubted Ty, a hardworking rancher, would have it any other way.

His throat bone-dry, Cash grabbed a cup of Rosie's homemade lemonade and drank it in two gulps. Despite the giant fans he'd set up, the day was a scorcher. Fourth of July. What could you expect? Squinting, he stared up at the sky. Blue stretched forever, with nary a cloud in sight.

Inside his head, though, a storm of gigantic proportions raged. Trying to collect his thoughts, he slipped into the barn, into the quiet of Hank's office. Locking the door behind him, he Googled Annie. When the YouTube video popped up, his curses rent the air. The shots were grainy and out-of-focus but, no doubt about it, it was Annie. Naked as the day she'd been born, laughing and splashing around in the lake.

Shit!

Nothing he could do would make this right. He'd talked her into shedding her clothes. Assured her they were alone.

Another thought pushed its way into his head, and he kicked the desk chair, sending it crashing to the floor. If the bastard who'd taken this shot had been there while they'd been in the pond, had he stayed around for part two?

Oh, God. What had he done? What if someone had captured them making love? It had been Annie's first time. She'd be devastated.

She'd never forgive him.

He flipped open his phone. A video like this, made without consent, had to be illegal, and by God, heads would roll.

It had been posted that morning, so hopefully not many had seen it. And nobody else would. Time to call in some favors.

* * *

By the time he stepped back into the sunlight, the clip was history. He could only hope no one had downloaded it or made a copy.

Regardless, the damage was done, and he had to tell Annie.

Something like this would be tough to get through in the best of times, and, boy, they were a long way from that. Yeah, they'd made love this morning, but it had been more an act of desperation than love. He seriously doubted the two of them could jump another hurdle. His heart physically hurt. He couldn't bear to lose her.

Damn it, he'd let her down. He'd promised her sanctuary at the pond.

What bottom-sucking scum had been there watching them?

He seriously doubted it was Gwen Garrison. According to the friend he'd called for help, Gwen was an eighty-year-old great-grandmother in Michigan. Somebody'd hacked her account.

He scanned the crowd. Was the Benedict Arnold here among his family and friends? Enjoying his hospitality? Eating his food? Dancing? He scrubbed his hands over his face.

Nothing else he could do right now. He'd have to suck it up and put on his party face. Otherwise Annie'd guess something was wrong.

Seemed everyone else was having a good time, though. Nobody'd hit the keg too hard yet, so nothing to worry about there. The smell of spit-roasted beef teased his olfactories and made his stomach rumble.

He started toward the food table but stopped dead in his tracks as he walked past a group of his hands.

"Naked. Absolutely naked," he heard one of them say.

With a snarl, he turned. "Who said that?"

Norm swallowed hard. "I did, sir."

Cash's last remaining vestige of sanity gripped him around the throat and shook him. "What were you talking about just now?"

"Chicken wings."

"Chicken wings?"

"Yes, sir. Bear likes his in garlic butter, and Chris says they need to be smothered in the hottest sauce you can find. I like mine naked. Not a blessed thing on them—except salt and pepper, of course. Lots of salt."

Cash called himself every kind of fool.

"You okay?"

"Yeah. I am." He let out the breath he'd been holding. "And I agree with you, Norm. That's how I like mine, too. Excuse me. Got to go give my mom a hand." He walked away kicking himself for being an idiot. He'd fully intended to rip out Norm's heart first and ask questions later.

Guess he didn't have himself in hand yet.

He walked to the edge of the pasture.

As always, he'd invited his Little League team. They were on the field, whooping and hollering and having a grand time. Rufus, as third-base coach, waved a runner on, while Silas squatted behind home plate playing umpire. And right in the middle of it all was Annie. Surrounded by his team and his family, she held a baby on her hip while pumping a fist to cheer on the runner. She was positively radiant. Beautiful beyond description. Her smile could have lit the field at night.

Oh, yeah. He could come home to that every day.

Totally at ease, she was unaware of a thirty-second video intent on destroying her world. He needed to stay clear of her till he could make sense of things. Till he decided how to tell her.

Vivi chose that moment to sashay past, winking at him over her shoulder, and his jaw tightened.

Again, he wondered what his grandpa had been thinking. Hell, what had *he* been thinking just a little while ago? Marriage?

He didn't find the institution itself horrific. What he found mind-boggling was the idea of being forced into it in a set period of time. Marriage was something two people entered into because they loved each other, not something you dove into because you had a deadline and had to grab the first girl you bumped into.

It would be like running bare-assed naked from something, forced to pull the first piece of clothing off a laundry line, then having to wear it all day whether it fit or not. You could end up riding the range in a pink bathrobe.

He didn't intend to do that grab-bag choosing with his life partner. Grandpa and Grandma Edith had been happy. His mom and dad were happy. His sister Babs was happy in her marriage. He wanted to be happy, too, and he seriously doubted he could pull that off if he simply picked a mate because the calendar was running down.

The big countdown.

Heck, if he needed to pick a mate by the calendar, maybe he'd better run into town for the latest *Playboy* magazine. He could find out who this month's babe was and marry her. The babe of the month.

He glanced across the field, saw Annie walking toward him, and his mouth went dry.

Playboy babes were overrated.

Chapter Twenty-Six

Despite the fact that Cash had all but dragged her here, despite what she had to do tomorrow, Annelise couldn't ever remember having a better time. Stopping in front of one of the fans, she let the breeze play over her.

Cash leaned against a fence post. A long, tall Texas cowboy. A great-fitting pair of jeans, cowboy boots, and a Stetson. Whew! She grew warmer, even in front of the fan. Real men and big belt buckles.

He bent down to help a small child over the fence, and his hat fell off. He scooped it up and slapped it against his thigh before setting it back on his head, shadowing his eyes and hiding his expression.

Still a little miffed with him, she veered off in the direction of the food table. Rosie could use some help. It was time she took a break and enjoyed the day.

Hank beat her to the table, and Annelise watched the red bloom across the housekeeper's cheeks. Even after years together, years of sitting in the kitchen eating pie, they sparked each other. The two were still sweethearts.

Annelise went to the opposite end of the table and cut a coconut cake into individual serving sizes. She plated a few pieces, making it easier for people to handle.

At the other end of the table, Hank asked, "Want to dance?"

"I can't, you old fool," Rosie said. "I'm busy."

"I'll wait while you finish up whatever it is you're doing." He waited all of three seconds. "Want to dance?"

Rosie rested her hands on her ample hips. "You hard of hearing?"

Hank grinned. "Nope. Just ain't heard the right answer yet."

Annelise laughed. "Go on, you two. I've got this covered."

"There you go," Hank said. "That song they're singing reminds me of our senior prom. We danced all night." He swung Rosie out onto the dance floor.

Annelise was still smiling when Maggie came up beside her. "They make a cute couple."

"Yes, they do."

"You and Cash looked pretty good together, too."

Annelise frowned.

"Don't give me that look." Maggie grinned. "I saw the two of you dancing. On TV. I love the gossip shows."

"You wouldn't if you found yourself featured on them."

Maggie scrunched her lips in thought. "You know, I'm not so sure of that." She picked up a brownie, took a bite, and rolled her eyes in appreciation. "You looked so gorgeous, Annie. And my dress. It's splashed all over the news. I can't thank you enough for putting my name out there, telling everyone I designed and made it. I have to keep pinching myself to prove it's all real and that I didn't dream it."

"Have you had any calls?"

Maggie hugged herself. "Yes. I have a couple orders." Her grin grew bigger, then disappeared. "I saw Brawley Odell was there, too, with some plastic-looking woman hanging all over him."

"A Dallas cheerleader."

"Figures. He always was too good for the rest of us."

Oh, ho. Something going on here, Annie thought.

Then Maggie caught Annie's hand. "Come on. The table can take care of itself. Let's get some watermelon."

So Brawley Odell thought he was too good for the rest of *us*. Had Maggie included her in that group? And why should that make her feel almost giddy? Yet it did.

Before they could head off in search of the watermelon, though, Maggie's grandfather muttered, "My toast burned pretty near to a crisp while she sat glued to that TV, watching you and Cash at the shindig the other night. Could have sworn I saw Dottie Willis there, too."

"You did, you old geezer." Dottie came up behind him.

"Gotta hand it to you, woman," Fletch said, "you were a sight for sore eyes in that pink outfit, even if my granddaughter didn't make it."

"Flattery, Fletch. Flattery." Dottie scooped up two pieces of apple pie, and they left the food table together.

While Annelise and Maggie enjoyed a piece of juicy watermelon, Doc Gibson came over to them.

"Hey, Maggie. Annie, how's that little filly I treated the other day doing?"

"She's almost as good as new."

"You sure look different than the last time I saw you, Annie," another male voice said.

She turned to see Brawley Odell.

"Brawley, how are you?"

"I'm good." He kissed her lightly on the cheek. "Doc and I have been sharing vet stories. City people are crazy when it comes to their pets." His eyes moved from her to the woman beside her. "Maggie."

"Brawley." Her green eyes frosted over. "I need to check on Grandpa. Excuse me."

Annie stared after her new friend. What had just happened? She turned back to Brawley, saw his eyes had taken on the same coldness.

She decided not to ask. Some things were better left alone. Her phone rang. "I'm sorry, but I have to take this."

Walking toward the barn, she answered. "Thelma?"

"Cornelia called. She wants to talk to you again."

"She does?" Hope fluttered in her stomach.

"Said so, didn't I?"

"Yes," Annelise stuttered, feeling chastised. Thelma put the fear of God in her.

"Can you stop by her place tomorrow around nine?"

"Yes, I can."

"Good." And the phone went dead.

Slightly bemused, she rubbed at her forehead.

"Headache?" Cash asked.

"I don't know."

He frowned. "How can you not know if you have a headache? I've got aspirin in the barn."

"Yes, that's probably a good idea." She caught his hand in hers. "You've been avoiding me for the last hour. What's wrong?"

"Nothing," he answered quickly. "I've been busy playing host, that's all."

"Hmm." Something was off. She knew it as well as she knew her own name. He was distracted looking, as though his mind was a million miles away.

"Who was on the phone? Who upset you?"

They walked into the shade, and Annelise squinted after the bright sunlight. The barn felt cool. She followed Cash to the back where they kept the first-aid kit.

"Thelma, but she didn't upset me. She...Cornelia wants to talk to me again."

Digging in the kit for aspirin, Cash looked up quickly. "That's good, isn't it?"

She nodded. "I think so. Yes."

He got a bottle of water from the small fridge. "Here you go."

She took a couple tablets and washed them down.

Cash reached out and caught her empty hand in his. He pulled her to him, ran his hand over her back. "Don't be mad at me. Please."

"I'm not."

He drew away and gazed down at her, skepticism in his eyes.

"I'm not really mad."

"Miffed?"

"A little."

"Hurt?"

"Yes."

"I'm sorry I didn't share. Especially after I got angry when you didn't." His eyes clouded.

Unease stirred in her. "Anything you need to tell me?"

"Why would you think that?" He sounded defensive.

"A feeling, that's all."

He shook his head. "Today's for celebrating."

She said nothing, but snuggled against him. They were a mess. Guilt about tomorrow's plans nagged at her. Plans that, after Thelma's call, she'd have to change, she realized. She wouldn't be hopping on that plane after all.

He kissed the top of her head. "I'll tell you what's not okay, though. All those other guys making moon eyes at you and stealing your dances. I think every man here is smitten with you."

"Smitten. I like that word." She wrapped her arms around his neck. "So let's dance."

A song about loving in the moonlight filtered through the open door, and they slow-danced right there in the hay, with only horses for an audience. She laid her head on his chest and relaxed into the moment. The hand he placed on the small of her back threatened to brand her right through the cotton of her shorts.

But then he didn't want to brand her, did he? Didn't want to make her his. A sigh escaped, and Cash tightened his arms around her.

What was she going to do with this cowboy? Where would they be if it wasn't for his grandfather's will? Did that have him balking at commitment? Did he feel hedged in?

Why was he so edgy today, though? A casual observer would see a laid-back, easygoing Cash. But she knew him too well. Knew that attitude was a façade today. He was wound tighter than a seven-day clock.

Of course, she wasn't in a much better position.

"We'd better get back outside." She threw him a grin and headed toward the door. "People are going to talk."

He snagged her hand. "Wait, Annie. You were right. There is something I need to say. Something we need to talk about."

She started to make a flippant remark until she saw the absolute dejection on his face.

"I was going to wait, but it's best you know."

"Know what?"

Before he could say another word, all hell broke loose.

With all the fanfare of visiting royalty, a cavalcade of black limos, kicking dust in their wake, made its way down the long drive.

The music stopped, the dancing stopped, the clatter of silverware on plates stopped. Conversation ceased as all eyes turned toward the newcomers.

Annelise groaned as she watched from the barn door. Her worst nightmare had come true. Her family had arrived in Maverick Junction.

"I think our conversation's going to have to wait, Cash."

He nodded.

The cars stopped and uniformed drivers hopped out to open doors. Two bodyguards exited the first car. After a quick visual, they opened the door again. Her father, dressed in a dark blue suit and tie and a pair of his favorite Italian shoes, stepped out. His dark hair, now gone gray, was cut close to his head.

He turned to help his wife out. Georgia Montjoy, tall and in great shape, made quite a statement in a perfectly tailored, pale yellow silk suit and six-inch heels. They'd both die of heat inside half an hour, Annelise thought. And the shoes. The first time her mom stepped on a cow paddy in those— Well, it should be interesting.

Her cousin Sophie, her mother's hairstylist, and another bodyguard exited the next limo.

When she saw who climbed out of the third, she groaned. By this time, Cash stood behind her, a hand on her shoulder. "Your family?"

She nodded silently.

"So who's the guy in the last car? The one who made you whimper."

"I didn't whimper."

"Yeah, you did."

"You're wrong. And that would be Douglas DeWitt."

He stepped to her side and slid an arm around her in what she assumed to be a show of unity. God bless him for it, because she'd need support.

"That the Douglas DeWitt your folks think you should marry?"

"Yes."

His hand tightened on her waist, and she felt him stiffen.

"Isn't that a little archaic?"

"A lot archaic," she agreed. "And very much a part of my life."

"You're not who you were when you left Boston, Annie."

No, she certainly wasn't. No longer the pampered, sheltered, and very naïve woman she'd been, she was also no longer a virgin. And she was far closer than she'd ever been to knowing the real her, knowing what she wanted from life. Understanding that was the man beside her.

"Cash, promise me one thing."

"What's that?"

"Don't let them kidnap me."

His brow arched practically into his hairline.

"I'm serious. I can't go back to Boston yet. They'll have no compunction about strong-arming me, and I have to talk to Cornelia again."

"In that case, darlin', I promise."

And he would, she realized. Cash would willingly step in and run interference for her with her family. That gave her a warm feeling that had nothing to do with the smoldering Texas sun beating down on them.

She felt protected, but not in the smothering way of bodyguards and security systems. He had her back.

Together, they went to meet her parents.

"Annelise, honey. God, I've missed you." Her mother

wrapped her in a genuine hug, then stepped back to look at her. "What are you wearing?"

"The same thing I wear every day here. Well, not exactly. I dressed up a bit today. After all"—she waved a hand to take in the festivities—"we're celebrating the country's birthday."

She ran a hand over the Armani suit's sleeve. "You're the one who'll have trouble with the dress code. You're a bit overdressed. And the shoes. They're going to give you a problem."

"I'll be fine, honey." Georgia patted her daughter's cheek, smoothed the dark hair so unlike her own blond. "I always am."

Her father, stocky at five-eight and pushing two hundred, scooped her up in a bear hug.

"Daddy!" She threw her arms around his thick neck. "I've missed you."

Her father held her tight. "We've missed you, too, sweetie. I ought to take you over my knee for putting us through this scare."

Annelise laughed. "You've never done that, and I can't imagine you'd start now."

He sent her a stern look. "You've never deserved it before now."

"Touché." She took Cash's hand. "Daddy, Mom, this is Cash Hardeman. He ... Whispering Pines is his grandfather's ranch. He's running it."

The men shook hands, then Cash turned to her mother. "Mrs. Montjoy, I see where Annie gets her looks."

Her mother patted his cheek. "Annelise, I think I like this boy."

By now, her cousin Sophie and Douglas had joined their group. Annelise made introductions. Around them, the festivities picked back up, but she was aware of the eyes still watching them. Curiosity was a powerful force, and the Montjoys' showy entrance had created lots of it.

Leave it to her folks to grandstand. No simple slipping in for them. Oh, no. Everyone knew they had arrived.

Douglas caught her hand in his and raised it for a kiss. Beside her, she felt the heat emanate from Cash.

"I've missed you," Douglas said.

"It's been awhile, hasn't it?" Annelise withdrew her hand and barely restrained herself from wiping it on her shorts. She craved a cold drink.

DeWitt, usually cautious, ignored Cash. "I saw the photos of you and what's-his-name here in Dallas. Actually, I saw quite a lot of you." He smirked.

Cash's eyes went hard.

Annelise said a prayer for Douglas's soul as Cash shifted. "I—"

"The name's Cash Hardeman, DeTwitt."

"The name's DeWitt."

"Yep. Got that, Twitt."

"You're mispronouncing it deliberately to provoke me," DeWitt said between clenched teeth.

"Is it working?"

Douglas, in his city clothes, his expensive TAG Heuer watch prominently on display, made a disgruntled sound beside her. "I don't understand you, Annelise. You're looking at that man like you want to crawl in bed with him."

"That man?" Cash turned his head to the right, the left, then swiveled on his heel to look behind him. He pointed at his own chest. "Are you talking about me?"

"Why don't you take a hike, Hardeman? Annelise and I have things to discuss."

Cash slipped an arm around her waist. "My place is right here beside Annie."

She could have kissed him.

"He calls you Annie?"

"Does that offend you, Douglas?" she asked.

"Offend me? That's too mild a word for what I'm feeling right now. Have you forgotten who you are?"

"No. I haven't. I've *remembered* who I am."

He huffed. "Whatever that's supposed to mean."

"It means I'm following my heart. Finally."

"With a cowboy?"

Cash stiffened beside her. "You a photographer, DeTwitt?"

A strange expression crossed Douglas's face. "That would be beneath me, wouldn't it?"

"Depends on the type of photos you take." Cash nudged his hat back from his forehead. "Then again, snakes crawl pretty close to the ground."

Annelise cocked her head. "What am I missing here?"

"Want to tell her, Douglas?"

"Tell me what?"

"Nothing. He's crazy," Douglas shot back. "And you've obviously lost your mind, too, Annelise."

His doggedness surprised her.

"On the contrary. I think I've found it."

"What about us?"

"Us?" She kept her voice down, her expression neutral. "There never was an us."

"There were expectations."

She almost laughed. "Oh, Douglas. Yes, those expectations. Exactly what I told Cash I was escaping from while I was here." Her voice softened. "I don't want to be mean, and I certainly don't want to hurt you, but the only expectation between us was a warm body on the other's arm at public events when either of us needed one. You know that."

"Maybe I've changed my mind. Maybe I want more."

When he reached for her, Cash made a sound, not unlike a feral growl.

Annelise shook her head at him. "You only think that, Douglas, because someone else is playing with your toy."

He frowned.

Vivi sauntered up to them, and for once, Annelise was happy to see her. "Hello. I'm Vivi Hardeman." She held out a hand to Douglas.

"Yes, Douglas, let me introduce Cash's grandmother."

Vivi's head whipped around.

If looks could have killed, she'd have been dead on the spot. But she'd have died happy.

*　　*　　*

Annelise sat at one of the tables, listening to her family and enjoying them. Her parents liked Cash and wandered over to join him at the makeshift bar. She felt a little nervous about how well they were getting on.

It should have settled her. But it didn't.

Douglas had followed Vivi off to God-knew-where after telling Annelise the two knew each other—sort of. Vivi had contacted him after she'd learned Annelise's true identity, and they'd been e-mailing back and forth. Turned out it had been Vivi who'd invited him to the barbecue. She was the reason he'd come to Texas with her parents.

That made her extremely anxious. What did the two of them have in common besides her and Cash?

Vivi wanted the ranch, and no doubt she'd do whatever it took to reach her goal. Annelise didn't envy Cash's having to deal with her. And on top of his grandfather's death. What a shame.

Had Vivi been afraid she and Cash were getting too

close? If the objective had been to get her and Douglas back together, that plan had flopped.

Couldn't she see Cash's reluctance to commit? Had she wanted Douglas to remind Annelise what she'd be giving up by settling for Cash, in case marriage was on her mind?

It was. But not to Doug. Her gaze drifted back to where Cash stood at the bar.

She smiled as another thought struck her. Maybe, just maybe, she'd been looking at this all wrong. Maybe Vivi'd set Douglas up as *her* next mark. Younger than Cash's grandfather and every bit as wealthy. And a slap at Annelise's pride, stealing what she thought was hers.

Oh, she hoped the two would get on like gangbusters. They deserved each other.

Douglas was pompous and arrogant, his hair too styled, his outfit too—intentional, his face and hands too soft. Picking up a pencil probably constituted the most physical labor he'd ever done and ever would do.

She remembered the feel of Cash's hands on her, the calluses, the muscles that played in his arms and back, and nearly sighed out loud.

If nothing else came from this sojourn, she'd learned a valuable lesson. She'd nearly settled for less, was worth more. Cash had shown her that.

"You're a million miles away, Annelise." Sophie put down her fork. "Are you okay?"

"I am. Yes. I'm so glad you came along." She took her cousin's hand. "We don't get to spend enough time together now that they're not sending us off to summer camp."

Sophie laughed, her short blond hair catching the sunlight. "Those were the days, weren't they?"

"Yes. A pity we didn't realize it."

"That cowboy of yours. I'd go to camp with him any day

if he wasn't already taken." She shot Annelise a look. "Fill me in, cuz."

Annelise floundered, unsure how to explain the relationship between herself and Cash. She gave a bare-bones outline of her time with him, leaving out her feelings, his feelings, the magic.

Sophie only smiled. "There's so much more, but I can wait. You'll talk. I have my ways."

Annelise laughed. "I know that for a fact."

"You do understand they brought me along to talk some sense into you. To be the voice of reason. I'm not going to, of course. Personally, I think you're doing the right thing. It's a shame nobody else has the courage to fight for your grandfather's life." She took another bite of Rosie's potato salad. "You know, she could make a fortune on this in Chicago."

"She could make a fortune on her cooking anywhere. But she likes it here."

"That I don't quite understand. I feel like a fish out of water." She studied Annelise. "You like this whole ranch scene, don't you? The cows freak me out. All that testosterone running around on hooves with those big horns." She shuddered. "Not my thing."

She grabbed Annie's arm. "Who is that?"

Annie searched through the crowd to see who she was looking at. Then she smiled. "The scenery doesn't get much better, does it?"

"The man is gorgeous in capital letters. Do you know him?"

"Not well. He's Cash's sister's brother-in-law."

"What?"

Annelise laughed. "I know. It's confusing. He was married to Cash's sister's husband's sister."

"You make my head hurt." She halted. "You said was. Did his wife leave because she couldn't handle the ranch? Did she hate all these animals, too?"

"No." Annelise sobered. "She died."

"Oh, my, gosh. That's so sad. Did they have any children?"

"Three boys. Triplets."

"Three boys? Him?" She grinned, then shrieked as a glass of cherry soda landed in her lap. Her white silk lap.

"Oh, Jonah. Look what you've done!" Ty Rawlins grabbed a pile of napkins and knelt to sop up the mess on Sophie's lap.

Sophie's cheeks turned as red as the cherry soda. "Why don't you give me those? I'll do it."

By now, Ty realized exactly where he was dabbing and the tips of his ears turned scarlet.

Annelise watched it all with horrified amusement.

"I'll have your outfit cleaned. I promise. Or buy you new," Ty stammered. "God, I'm so sorry." He shot his son a dark look.

"It's okay. Honest," Sophie assured him. "No harm done. It's a picnic."

"I don't know. Cherry soda? That's going to leave a stain."

"Don't worry about it."

"I'm hungry, Daddy." Jonah pulled at his dad's arm. "When can I eat?"

"Go." Sophie laughed. "Feed him."

"You're sure?"

"Positive."

While Sophie patted her lap, Ty sat the boy down and fixed him a plate of food. The other two quickly joined them.

Sophie stared at them, dumbfounded. "They all look exactly the same."

Annelise nodded. "Triplets."

"How do you tell them apart?"

"I don't. But since the cherry soda kid is Jonah, one of the other two is Jesse and one is Josh."

"Boy, does he have his hands full. I wouldn't wish that on my worst enemy."

They watched as Ty patiently filled the other two plates with exactly the right foods for each child.

"The man's good," Sophie whispered to Annelise.

"Yes, he is."

Just as Ty turned back to her and Sophie, one of the boys let out a howl. Staubach sat by the table, a stolen plate at his feet. Clamping his mouth around a hot dog, he hightailed it across the field.

From the escalating tears, the missing hot dog belonged to either Jesse or Josh. Annelise hadn't a clue which one.

Ty sighed, picked up the crying triplet in one arm, and moved back to the table to fix another dog.

"You'd have to be a plate short of a setting to get mixed up in that situation," Sophie muttered.

* * *

Her parents and ensemble headed off to Austin for the night. They'd fly back to Boston in the morning.

So should she, but, in a stolen moment, she'd canceled her flight. The meeting with Cornelia took priority over everything else. She was afraid to let herself even hope Nelly might have changed her mind. Might help Grandpa.

As her mother hugged her good-bye, she put her mouth close to Annelise's ear. "This one's a keeper, honey. He's also a man. A real man. Be careful. But don't screw it up."

Startled, Annelise stared at her mother.

"I mean it, dear. Cash Hardeman is a good man. You could do a hell of a lot worse."

"I thought you liked Douglas."

"The man has no backbone. And did you see him with that made-up blond bimbo? I mean the two practically drooled over each other."

Annelise couldn't help it. She laughed. "That blond bimbo is Cash's grandmother."

"Excuse me?"

"It's a long story, Mom. One I'll share with you in front of the fire on a cold Massachusetts evening."

She kissed her father and Sophie and wished them a good trip. It had been fun to have them here today. Then she turned to Douglas and shook his hand. "Good-bye, Douglas."

"Well, it's not really good-bye, is it? I mean, it's more like see you later."

"No." Annelise met his eyes. "It's good-bye."

"You can't be serious."

"Oh, but I am. Everyone's in the car. You'd better get in before they leave you out here in the wilds with the coyotes and rattlers."

"This isn't a very pretty side of you, Annelise."

She shrugged and strolled away, straight into Cash's chest.

He put his hands on both her arms and steadied her. "Have a good day?"

"I did. I really did. I can't remember the last time I had so much fun. I'm glad you dragged me here."

"I'd have hog-tied you if I had to."

"You wouldn't have."

Mischief danced in his green eyes, and she decided not to pursue it.

"Thank you. For me and my family. It was nice of you to make them feel so welcome."

"I like your family. I hadn't meant to. I was prepared to dislike them for what they've put you through, but they're not what I expected."

"They're good people."

"And they love you."

"Yes, they do."

"You know, Annie, for a city slicker, you're okay. Your cousin Sophie? Boy." He shook his head. "Doesn't take more than a grasshopper to scare her."

"She's concerned about the testosterone levels in the bulls."

"What about you? You afraid of a little testosterone?"

She rose on tiptoe and kissed him. "Not on your life."

Chapter Twenty-Seven

Annelise woke up to the ringing of the phone. Checking the caller ID, she groaned. Her grandfather. And she hadn't even had a cup of coffee yet.

"Hello, Grandpa."

"Annelise? Did I wake you?"

"Yes, but it's time for me to get up anyway. You sound good."

"I'm feeling good."

She squinted at her clock, considered the time difference. "Why are you up so early?"

"Don't sleep much anymore."

"I guess not." She staggered to the refrigerator and snagged a Coke. The caffeine in it would have to do for now. Taking a long swallow, she listened to him tell her what a great time her parents had had yesterday.

"When your dad phoned last night, he said the man who owns the ranch quite impressed him. Cash Hardeman."

"He's a wonderful person." She thought of how impressive he'd been last night after he'd driven her home. No wonder she was exhausted this morning. The man had worn her out. She smiled. Unlike Sophie, she thoroughly enjoyed a good dose of testosterone.

Her smile faded. Despite all that, he still hadn't told her he loved her, and she understood he wouldn't.

"That's really not what I called about though."

Uh-oh. Here it came. She'd been expecting this.

"I understand you found, um, you found, well, my father's other child."

"Your half sister, yes. Her name is Cornelia Whitney."

There was a beat of silence. "If I recall correctly, I expressly forbid you or anyone else to search for her."

"Yes, Grandpa, you did."

"Yet you went behind my back and tracked her down."

She steeled herself. This was where he'd disown her. The money? Unimportant. Her grandfather's love? Beyond price.

"Yes, I did."

"Annelise, do you understand what you're doing?"

"I'm trying to save your life."

"Even if I don't want you to?"

"Even if."

Again, silence. "I don't want anything to do with that part of my life. I've tried for over sixty years to put it out of my mind, and now here you are dredging it all back up again."

"I'll apologize for that."

"But not for the rest."

"No." Her heart sat in her throat. She put down the Coke, afraid she might be sick.

"I haven't ever talked to anyone about this, not even your grandmother, God bless her soul."

"Maybe it's time, Grandpa." She held her breath.

"Maybe it is." With that, he started his tale, and she took a shaky breath and listened.

The birth of Cornelia had changed her grandfather's life. When his mother found out about Driller's affair, she'd insisted they leave Texas, and so they'd picked up everything and moved to Boston.

He'd lost his home, all his friends.

"Grandpa, it wasn't Cornelia's fault. In truth, she was as much a victim as you. She grew up without a father. Grew up wearing the stigma of illegitimacy."

Annelise realized she'd stumbled into a whole family dynamic here that she hadn't considered. She'd been concerned for her grandfather's health and hadn't taken into account the emotional toll this had taken on him and Cornelia over the years.

"I saw them, you know. One day I was in town with some friends. My mother had given me a quarter. Quite a lot in those days. I think she wanted me out of her hair for a while.

"Fletch, Tommy, and I came out of the general store, eating licorice sticks, and there they were. My father and her. Holding hands." His voice thickened. "She was holding my daddy's hand. He'd never walked down the street like that with me. Never held my hand."

"He hurt a lot of innocent people with his carelessness," Annelise said quietly.

"Yes, he did. Nothing was ever the same after that, after he paraded his love child in front of the town. It didn't take any time at all for the gossips to tell my mother." He sounded bitter. "We moved East to get away from it, but my family never healed. I never once saw my parents touch each other after Texas, not even casually."

"Grandpa—"

"I didn't share this so you'd feel sorry for me," he said gruffly.

"I understand that." She blinked back tears. "But don't you see? If you refuse to take a chance at this, you're letting him hurt you and everyone who loves you all over again."

"Humph." After a second, he asked, "How much does this woman want? What's it going to cost us for this blood test?"

Annelise closed her eyes, praying he was softening. "Cornelia hasn't agreed to do it yet."

"That's because she's waiting to see how much of the Montjoy fortune she can steal."

"I don't think that's the case," Annelise said. "To be perfectly honest, though, if she can save your life, it would be worth every penny we have."

"Easy for you to say."

She made a face, even though he couldn't see it.

"Well, it is. You haven't yet put in the hours I have. I've worked hard for that money. My son and granddaughter deserve it, not some girl born out of an adulterous affair. I've lived a good life. Maybe my time has come."

"That's just plain stupid, Grandpa. And you're not stupid. That might be the line you're feeding everyone else, but it won't work with me."

He made a noncommittal sound.

"I met Fletch."

"You did? How is he?"

"His granddaughter's the one who designed my dress for Dallas."

They chatted about his old friend for a few more minutes before Annelise said, "I have an appointment with Cornelia this morning. I'll call you back after I talk to her, okay?"

"I'd rather you didn't do this, honey."

"I'd rather I did."

She waited out the silence.

Finally, he said, "Okay. I'll talk to you later then. I love you."

"Love you, too, Grandpa."

She hung up the phone and cried, her emotions all over the place. She'd been prepared for the worst. For his anger. For him to turn his back on her. Instead, he'd told her he loved her and had given his implicit approval to this venture.

The ball was in her court.

* * *

"Annie? You here?"

Her heart skipped a beat at the sound of Cash's voice.

"In the bathroom. I'll just be a second." She draped her towel over the side of the tub and slipped into her robe. "I was getting ready to meet Cornelia."

"Have you got a few minutes?"

"I've got plenty of time." She smiled at him as she stepped out of the bathroom and moved to the counter. "Want some coffee?"

He shook his head.

"You look awfully serious."

"Can I sit?" he asked.

"Sure. Does this visit have anything to do with yesterday? When you said we needed to talk?"

"Yeah."

She took the chair across from him, drawing the robe more tightly around her when he closed his eyes and rubbed his hands over his face. "Cash? What's wrong?"

"Oh, sweetheart, I'd rather take a whipping than have to tell you this." He blew out a huge sigh.

"I'm a big girl." Still, her palms grew damp.

"Yeah, I know you are. But that doesn't make it any easier." Legs stretched out in front of him, ankles crossed, he told her about his conversation with his sister. What he'd found when he went online himself.

She felt herself pale. Her stomach churned. "How could this happen?"

"I don't know."

"You promised me we were safe there."

"I know I did, and we should have been."

Her mind raced, trying to make sense of what he'd said. "You saw the video?"

"Yes."

"How bad was it?"

"Shit!" He jumped up, paced the small area. "You were naked, okay? But you were in the water. You were only exposed from the waist up."

A small groan escaped her.

"The footage was really bad quality. Grainy. Out of focus."

"But I was recognizable?"

He nodded.

"A professional didn't take them." Her chin trembled. Hurt ripped through her, a sense of violation. She met Cash's eyes. Felt her world come apart even as she said, "You were playing with your phone that afternoon."

"Yeah, I was. So?"

"It has a camera."

His jaw set in a hard, tight line. "If you're even hinting at what I think you are, we're done, Annie."

Hot tears sprang to her eyes. "No one else was there, Cash. You said yourself we were in the middle of nowhere. Alone. That no one else was around."

"Yep, I did. So tell me. Exactly how stupid and lowlife would I have to be to take pictures of you—and put them out there for every sicko in the world to watch?"

She flinched. "I don't know." She swallowed the huge lump in her throat. "How dumb would you have to be?"

He swore and, picking up a book from the counter, threw it across the room.

She jumped. "Stop it!"

A muscle ticced in the side of his face. "Annie, you don't want to do this. You don't want to go where you're headed."

She wouldn't back down. "Then give me a better answer. An option."

"Like hell I will. It's a question I shouldn't have to answer. One that never should have been asked." He reached for the door handle. "I obviously don't know you at all nor you me."

"Don't you think it's strange?" she asked. "Two of us were there. Two of us were naked. Yet you're not in a single frame. Why is that?"

"I have no idea, other than you're the big money item."

She pinched the bridge of her nose. "The stockholders. This will be disastrous." For the second time that morning she thought she might be sick. "My grandpa will see those pictures. My mom. My dad. Oh, God." She put her head in her hands and dropped into a chair.

He started toward her.

"No. Please. Don't touch me. Not now." She shook her head, and he stayed where he was.

"You asked me what my mom would think about pictures of us," she said quietly.

"At the fund-raiser, damn it. You know that's what I was referring to."

"Do I?"

"I don't think your family saw them. Nobody else will, either."

"What?"

"The clip's been removed."

"How?"

"I made a couple calls. It's illegal to post stuff like that."

She nodded but said nothing.

"You had my phone, Annie. You borrowed it to take a picture of Dottie. Did you see a video of yourself at the pond?"

"I didn't look."

"Would I have been stupid enough to have left it with you if there were any there?"

"You could have downloaded them already, then deleted them from your phone."

"Oh, for— If you honestly think I'd have ruined that special moment by taking pictures—and then posting them on YouTube..." He spread his hands wide. "If you don't trust me on this, there's nothing here, darlin'."

She sat silently, staring at her folded hands.

He stood unmoving for a full minute. Then he turned on his boot heels and left, slamming the door behind him so hard the window rattled.

Annelise laid her head on the table and let the hot tears come. Hurt and shame, heartbreak and doubt raced through her.

How many people had seen her splashing and playing naked in that pond?

Please, God, she prayed. Let that be the only video to surface. If whoever had taken it had stayed to take another of her and Cash when they'd made love, she wouldn't survive it.

But then, Cash's hands had been pretty busy at that point. He'd been way too busy to take pictures.

Except, deep-down inside, she didn't believe he'd done this. Even as she'd accused him, she'd known he was innocent. His mother had raised him too well. He was too much the gentleman.

He *cared* for her.

And still she'd accused him. Hurled those horrid words at him.

He'd never forgive her for that. Nor should he. A relationship had to be built on trust. And she'd certainly shown a lack of that.

If he didn't do it, though, who had?

The conversation between him and Douglas came back to her. Cash had asked him if he was a photographer. That was after Douglas's comment that he'd seen lots of her. She'd assumed he'd meant lots of photos, but he hadn't. He'd seen the video and rather than tell her about it, he'd taunted Cash.

Douglas hadn't taken the video, though, either. He'd never have subjected himself to the ride it would take to reach the pond.

Somebody *had* made that ride, though.

* * *

Cash wanted to beat something. Somebody. God help the vermin when he got his hands on him.

When Annie accused him of being the one who'd taken the video, it had hurt as badly as if someone had skewered him on a sword, then twisted it. He couldn't believe she had so little trust in him.

Now, as he muscled the Caddy along the two-lane back road, he fought the fury inside him, fought to get past it to reason.

She'd been caught off-guard. He realized that. Her accusations had been knee-jerk. There was no way she'd truly think he'd do that to her. He had to believe that. Still, her words had hurt like hell.

And Babs had asked him the same question.

Under the circumstances, he supposed that was only natural. It sure didn't sit well, though.

Only sub-human slime took pictures like that.

He remembered Mel telling him about a PI who'd been in town asking questions. Had he done more than that? The timing didn't fit, though. He'd come into town the morning after the fund-raiser. After they'd been out together in public. After the pond.

So who, then?

None of his ranch hands. He would swear on a stack of Bibles he didn't have anybody on his payroll capable of doing that.

Douglas had seen the video. The bastard. When he'd made that comment yesterday, Cash had wanted to throttle him. Wanted in the worst way to wipe that smirk off his ugly mug. Annie, thank God, hadn't understood what he was talking about. No doubt, though, she'd put two and two together now that she had the facts.

The idea of DeWitt sitting at his computer, drink in hand, and playing voyeur made Cash see red. Anybody who'd get a kick out of that was just plain sick.

DeWitt hadn't taken the pictures, though. As much as he'd like to punch the guy's lights out, it wouldn't be for this. He'd hadn't been anywhere near Maverick Junction that day. A couple of calls had verified he'd been in Boston.

Thank God Babs had been fooling around on the computer and found it. According to his contact, the clip had only been up for two hours. Even one second was too long, but it sure as hell could have been worse.

He'd scratched the paparazzi off his list of suspects right

away. With the cameras and lenses they used, the quality would have been far superior. Most telling, though? It had been on YouTube, and those guys didn't give anything away. If one of them had taken the video, they'd have been able to retire for life.

He thought back to that day. The ride. The picnic lunch Rosie'd packed.

The spat he and Vivi had on the porch when he refused to take her along.

And he knew.

Damn her hide. This was Vivi's style. Spiteful and childish.

* * *

It had taken every bit of courage Annelise had to leave the house. All her resolve to pull herself together. This meeting was bigger than her shame, though. Bigger than her disappointment—both in whoever had filmed her and in herself for the way she'd treated Cash.

Yesterday had been so wonderful. She'd started to rethink her plan to go home, her need to turn tail and run. Didn't she owe him another chance? Maybe she could travel back and forth between Boston and Texas. Split her time between Grandpa and Cash.

Her behavior this morning, though, had destroyed all hope. *She* didn't deserve another chance.

Caught up in her thoughts, she nearly missed her turn.

Cornelia Montjoy Whitney was sitting in a rocker on the front porch when she pulled up.

She turned off the truck, the one Cash had lent her yesterday—before she'd been so awful—took a deep, deep breath, and climbed out. "Good morning, Ms.—"

"Nelly, Annie. Please. Do an old woman a favor and call me what my friends do. After all, it appears we're family."

She blinked back tears. With the mood she was in it wouldn't take much to send her off on another crying jag. "Yes, Nelly, we are." She stopped short of the porch and put her hands in the pockets of the capris she wore.

"I spoke with my grandfather this morning."

"How is he feeling?"

"Good. He's having a good day."

"Did he ask how much I planned to extort from him in exchange for my bone marrow?"

Annelise's eyes widened. She opened her mouth but closed it without saying anything.

Nelly surprised her by laughing. "He did. It's all over that pretty face of yours. I hope you set him straight—and that you never try to play poker for a living." Her smile faded. "I sincerely hope after our talk yesterday you don't think that of me."

"No, ma'am, I don't, and I told my grandpa that in no un-certain terms."

"I'll bet you did." She picked at the skirt of the simple cotton dress she wore today. "I've been studying Vincent's photo. The one you gave me."

Nelly sat up a little straighter. "I can't call myself a Chris-tian woman anymore if I refuse to do this. I've followed your grandfather in the news. He's done our father proud." Her voice trembled slightly. "You're right. I shouldn't hold his father's sins against him. He was no more to blame for what happened than I was."

Annelise held her breath. Could it be? Would Cornelia agree to help?

"I see you didn't drive that big bike here today."

"No, Cash lent me his truck."

"Good. Then I suppose you won't mind driving me into town. I called Doc Wilson at his house last night." She shot a look at Annelise. "Doc Wilson treats people, not horses. He promised to fit me in today. Let me get my purse, and you can drive me in for this blood test you're so set on. We'll see what happens from there."

Grinning, Annelise rushed up the porch stairs and grabbed the oh, so reluctant aunt of hers in a huge hug. "Thank you. Oh, thank you so, so much!"

Driving into town, dust billowing behind them, Rufus and Silas at a discreet distance, Annelise said, "Please don't hate my grandfather."

"Why would I hate him?"

"Well..." Annelise shrugged.

"Because he had my father?" Nelly asked. "Because he carried the Montjoy name?"

Annie glanced at her. "Yes, I guess."

"I don't hate him. I knew my father loved me. Deep down inside, he loved me." She twisted the catch of the purse on her lap. "I think, though, that Vincent doesn't like me very much. Otherwise, he wouldn't have sent my letter back."

"He saw you with his father, you know." And Annelise told the older woman the story her grandfather had shared with her that morning.

Cornelia sighed. "Driller hurt us all."

Chapter Twenty-Eight

The screen door banged shut behind Cash.

"Vivi? You here?"

Rosie peeked her head around the kitchen door. "What's wrong with you?"

"Why don't you take a pitcher of iced tea over to Hank? Sit down at the picnic table behind the barn and shoot the breeze with him a bit?"

"But I've got—"

Temper, barely controlled, wrestled to escape. "Is she up there?" He jerked his chin at the second floor.

"Yes."

"Great. The two of us need to have ourselves a talk. And I need you to leave the house for a bit."

"Cash, I've never seen you like this. You're not going to do something you'll regret?"

"My only regret, Rosie, is that I didn't confront her months ago." He looked into her frightened eyes. "I won't touch her."

Rosie walked down the hall to him and laid her hand on his arm. "I know you won't. You're a gentleman through and through."

"Sure wish others were as convinced of that as you are."

"You talking about Annie? You two have a misunderstanding?"

"More than that. Way more than that."

"Fix it."

"I wish I could. Now skedaddle, will you?"

"Believe I'll just go out the front door here. Hank's always got cold soda in the fridge over there."

"Thanks."

She patted his arm and left.

"Vivi!"

"Geez, Cash." Her voice floated down from upstairs. "You could raise the dead with all that bellowing. What's wrong with you?"

"Come down here."

"I don't want to."

"Then I'll come up there."

"I'm not dressed."

"Really? Well, then, how about I bring my camera along? See if I can get some photos or maybe a video. You can show me how to post them on YouTube."

When she didn't answer, he asked, "Cat got your tongue?"

"You're—you're—"

"I think pissed is the word you want." He ran his hand along the old oak banister. "You messed up, Vivi. Big time."

"I don't know what you're talking about."

"Yeah, you do. Did DeWitt help you?"

"I repeat, I don't—"

"That's okay. You don't want to tell me, fine. You can

take all the heat yourself. What you did was illegal." He hesitated. Hated to ask. Had to know. "Do you have any other videos or pictures?" He held his breath.

"I don't know what you're talking about." Her voice was petulant.

"Damn it, Vivi. Do you have any more?" He pounded his fist on the railing.

"No! I left right after—I mean—"

He wet his lips, relief flooding him. "You listen, and you listen good. If *anything* else surfaces, I'll see you rot in jail."

When she remained silent, he said, "My last offer is still on the table. You sell me your interest in the ranch at that price and go away, and I won't have you arrested."

"You and Annie are used to doing that, aren't you? Throwing your money around. Getting your own way."

"Vivi, you're the one who stepped over the line here. You violated—in the worst way possible—Annie's privacy. I don't make a habit of throwing my weight around, but this time? I'll make an exception. Thing is, though, this offer's only good for five minutes, and the clock's ticking."

Chapter Twenty-Nine

This should have been one of the happiest days of her life. She and Nelly, who'd turned out to be a near-perfect match for her grandfather, were flying back to Boston. Her wildest expectations had been met.

Yet as the tires hummed along the pavement, Annelise stared out the window at the passing scenery and saw nothing. This ride to the airport was the longest of her life. Cash had insisted on driving them, but now he sat behind the wheel moody and silent.

She wanted to scream and rail at the dispassionate strangers they'd become. The last real conversation they'd had had been over the phone. He'd told her Vivi had taken the video and then sent it to DeWitt, who'd uploaded it to the Internet using a hacked account.

Cash and she had agreed that the publicity would outweigh any good that could come of pressing charges, and that had been that.

Annelise had spoken to Rosie a few times while they'd

waited for the results of her aunt's blood test, but she'd made excuse after excuse, fabricating reasons she couldn't see Cash. Though it had broken her heart, she'd even quit going to work at the ranch.

She and Cash simply weren't made for each other. It had nothing to do with her money or social status. He had all that, too. Maybe not to the extent she did, but he and his family were far from paupers. Their family name was on the Who's Who list in Texas.

And the problem between them had nothing whatsoever to do with physical compatibility. They were totally in sync on that level. The man made her body sing.

Emotionally, though, they were total opposites. Yin and yang.

Her stay in Maverick Junction had taught her just how much she wanted someone to love, someone who loved her. A partner for life. Someone who would trust her. Whom she could trust back. They couldn't quite seem to get there. Not enough for Cash to move beyond the caring and into loving. Not enough to want her by his side for life.

As they turned into the airport, she said, "Drop us off at the curb, Cash. There's no reason for you to park."

"I'll help you with your luggage."

"A porter can do that. And Silas is with us."

"Okay."

He slid the SUV to the curb and hopped out, rounding the hood to open her door. But he didn't take her hand to help her out. Silas helped Cornelia from the backseat, then moved to the rear to unload their luggage.

"We need to talk, Annie."

"Cash—"

"Silas," Cash said. "Do you mind dealing with that and helping Nelly inside? I need a minute with Annie."

The two men exchanged looks.

"You got it," Silas said. "I'll be right inside, Ms. Montjoy."

She nodded. When she turned back to Cash, his eyes searched her face.

"Annie, I know you need to go home. I understand that."

He hesitated, and she saw uncertainty in his eyes. Cash, who always knew what to do, what to say, was at a loss. She wanted to touch him. Didn't dare. She'd break into a thousand shards.

"This is more than that, though, isn't it?" he asked. "This is good-bye."

Unsure of her voice, she nodded.

"Why?"

"We've been through this. There're a myriad of reasons. I need more. More than you want to give me. Thanks to you, I understand I deserve more. You taught me that."

"Annie, I—I care about you."

"I understand that, Cash. And even knowing that, I didn't trust you when I should have. I knew deep-down you hadn't made that video. And still, I accused you. I let us both down."

"Because I didn't give you reason to trust. I'll make it up to you."

Tears shimmered. "Oh, Cash." Her voice broke. "I can't do this."

"Don't leave me, darlin'."

"I have to. I love you, Cash." She saw the shock, the surprise. "I know you don't love me back. I understand you can't. I don't understand why, but that doesn't really matter, does it?"

"I don't want you to leave."

With a sad smile, she raised her hand, brushed it along his stubble-rough cheek. "Good-bye."

With that she turned. Self-preservation had her nearly running into the terminal. She made herself move forward; she didn't dare look back. If he was still there, she'd go to him. Settle for whatever he could give her until he decided to move on.

He'd made it more than clear, over and over, that he wasn't ready to make a commitment. She couldn't go on without one.

*   *   *

Half an hour later, the pilot gave Annelise a thumbs-up, and the engines roared to life. Within minutes, their private jet lifted into the air.

Face pressed to the window, she watched the buildings grow smaller and smaller. Was he staring up at the sky, waiting till the plane disappeared from sight? Or had he turned the minute she left, eager to get back to the ranch, to his life?

He'd think about her. She knew he would.

And yet her cowboy hadn't been able to pull the trigger. He couldn't make promises. He'd said he cared for her. Not enough, because while she hadn't been looking, she'd fallen head over heels in love with him, and she wanted to be loved right back. She refused to settle for less.

His grandfather had sure botched things with that will and the Vivi fiasco.

Cash couldn't see beyond it. Couldn't recognize love because all he could see were the chains of obligation.

So, somehow, someway, she had to pick up the pieces and move on. Work around this gigantic hole he'd left in her heart.

Annelise picked up her phone and called her grandfather. "We're in the air, and we'll be in Boston by noon."

"I'll be right here waiting for you," he groused.

The confinement had been hard for him. Once Cornelia had been deemed a match, he'd had to go back to the hospital. Back to solitary confinement, as he put it. In order to receive his half sister's marrow, his own had to be destroyed with chemotherapy and radiation treatments. They couldn't mix the good with the bad.

But that left him lacking an immune system and susceptible to any and all germs. So, his new home was in a sterile hospital room in the isolation wing.

"I know this is hard for you."

"They've killed my white blood cells. If Cornelia doesn't come through..."

Annelise heard the fear in her grandfather's voice.

"She's not going to change her mind, Grandpa. She's right here with me. I'll see you soon. Love you."

"Are you ready for lunch, Ms. Montjoy?" Hilda, their flight attendant, stood with a tray for her.

Too worked up to be hungry, she declined lunch. "Why don't you give mine to Silas? I'm sure he'll be able to handle a second one."

Hilda set it beside him. "If you change your mind, I have cheese and fruit, chips, whatever you'd like."

"Thanks." She sipped her coffee. "Do you need anything else, Nelly?"

"Oh, no. This is wonderful. I've never flown on a private jet. I believe I could get quite used to it."

"I'm going to take a short nap if you don't mind."

"Not at all. This has been a difficult morning for you."

Annelise closed her eyes. Difficult? Now there was an understatement.

As badly as she was hurting, it was worse because she knew she'd hurt him, too. Ironically, Cash was the vulnerable one. So much more vulnerable than she. She'd learned to protect herself emotionally from a very young age. Early on, she'd blocked herself from the negatives the press threw her way, from the mind-boggling expectations that, in all honesty, were mostly self-imposed.

Cash had never learned to do that. Hadn't needed to.

She imagined the whole YouTube mess had actually been harder on him than on her. And yet he'd handled it. For her.

He'd taken care of her. A single tear dripped from her chin to her hand.

Half-asleep, she let her mind drift. Remembered.

Her first impression of Maverick Junction. A dusty little town with no soul. So wrong.

Sally's Place and that first long drink of iced tea.

Cash walking through that door, his long, lean body creating a hunger the second she saw him.

Big-hearted Dottie, in her pink outfit, welcoming her with milk and chocolate-chip cookies right out of the oven.

The sun kissing her naked body as she and Cash lay together by the pond.

Snuggled beside him under the stars at the drive-in, Staubach snoring in the backseat.

Dancing with Cash in Dallas, his hard body pressed close to her own.

Cash holding the young girl on the horse.

Annelise drifted off to sleep, not waking till the wheels of the plane touched down.

She was home.

And she'd never felt more alone.

* * *

Cash banged the door shut behind him so hard that Staubach started barking. "It's okay, boy." He reached down and patted him.

It had been three days since Annie'd left. He'd never been more miserable. He'd figured once she boarded that plane, he'd drive home and get on with his life.

He'd miss her, sure, but he'd move on. Problem was, it wasn't happening.

He tried feeding himself a good dose of reality, telling himself that his and Annie's lives had no common ground. She belonged to a family dynasty, for God's sake. Annie— an oil baroness. Why would she even consider being with somebody like himself? A guy who worked hard every day, who enjoyed working hard every day.

There was no way Annie'd ever marry him—if he asked her, of course. Big assumption there, that he was ready to tie himself down.

Hell, even if she did agree to take him on, he couldn't live her life. He didn't want to even try. He couldn't spend his life in suits and tuxes, always looking over his shoulder for the press, careful not to commit some major faux pas.

And she sure as hell wasn't about to give that up to live his ranch life in Maverick Junction. Nor could he ask her to.

So there you go. He and Annie were over. And admitting that was like sticking a fork in his eye.

A beer in one hand and a bag of chips in the other, he kicked back in his recliner. After a couple of long, cool drinks, he set his Lone Star on the end table and picked up the remote.

He'd watch some TV. Maybe the Rangers were playing a little ball tonight.

They weren't.

Cursing himself, calling himself every kind of fool, he clicked on his DVR.

And there was Annie staring out at him.

The press met her at the airport. The story had all the makings for good drama—her sick grandfather, the long lost relative, Annelise rushing home to his bedside with the answer to all their prayers.

Why he'd recorded it, he hadn't a clue. None that he'd 'fess up to, anyway, even to himself. Why he watched it every night, over and over, he couldn't say.

Or refused to.

It grew dark outside, but Cash didn't bother to turn on any lights. There was his Annie, all decked out in her designer duds, looking for all the world like the heiress she was. Like one of the fairy princesses in his niece's storybooks.

And damned if the Twitt wasn't at the airport to greet her. The guy had more guts than brains. He knew he'd been found out, and he'd still showed up. Cash ground his teeth. When DeTwitt reached for Annie's hand, she avoided it by digging into her purse as if searching for something. No doubt the two would have words later. Annie'd lay him out good.

"Keep your hands to yourself, you lout," Cash grumbled, "or I'm gonna have to cross the continent to punch out your lights."

"Speaking of lights."

His mother flipped on the overhead, and he blinked, swore.

"Boy, for somebody who doesn't care—"

He jerked out of his chair. "I didn't hear you come in."

"I figured as much." She studied him. "You look like hell, son."

"I feel like it, too. How about that?"

"Don't bite off *my* head. It's not me you're mad at."

Hands jammed in his pockets, he said, "Okay. I'll play. Who am I mad at?"

"Yourself, of course."

His mother moved into the kitchen, and he trailed after her. As she started stacking dishes and loading them into the dishwasher, he said, "Mom, you don't have to do that."

"No, I don't. But I am your mother. I love you. And it's about time we had a talk."

"A talk? About what?"

"About that stupid old fool who fathered *your* father."

"You want to talk about Grandpa?"

"Good." She tipped her head at the bottle in his hand. "I see you haven't had so many of those you can't think."

"This is my first one."

"And it needs to be your last. You have a lot to do. Your dad and I will babysit Staubach. I'll take him with me tonight."

Now he was totally confused. "Why does Staubach need a sitter?"

He pulled out two chairs and dropped into one. "Quit fussing over there and come sit down. You've lost me. What does any of this have to do with Grandpa?"

Then he narrowed his eyes. "Does Dad know you're here?"

"As a matter of fact, he does. I'm here with his blessings. He agrees with everything I'm going to say to you."

He shrugged and tipped back in his chair.

"Leo never could stay out of anybody else's business," his mother said as she sat across from him. "Don't get me wrong. I loved the man. He was like a second father to me. But we all know it was a mistake when he married Vivi and an even bigger one when he added that codicil to his will.

He wasn't thinking clearly anymore. We should have been on top of that. And we weren't."

"That's—"

"Quiet."

When his mother used that tone, he always did whatever she asked. Now was no exception.

She leaned her elbow on the table and rested her chin in her hand. "Annie is the one, baby. I knew it the second I heard you say her name. When I saw the two of you in the stables after your ride, any doubts I might have had disappeared."

He opened his mouth. She held up a hand, and he closed it again.

"You two are meant for each other. Don't let her slip away because of Grandpa Leo."

"It has nothing to do with him."

"Oh, come on, Cash. I didn't raise a dummy. Of course it does. You're thinking you would never have considered marrying your Annie if Gramps hadn't added that stupid stipulation. You've talked yourself into believing marriage is on your mind only because of that artificial deadline. That's been settled now, and Vivi is gone. But you're still sitting here in the dark, thinking about Annie. Missing her. So none of those arguments are valid. Your father and I watched you and Annie when you were anywhere near each other. What we saw on your faces was real. It's time you put your grandfather's foolishness to rest and pop the question."

He got up and walked to the window.

"Answer one question for me, Cash."

"Okay."

"Do you love her?"

Without turning around, still staring into the darkness, he said, "Yes."

"Have you told her that?"

"No."

"Then you'd better get packed. Sounds to me like you need to make a trip to Boston."

He stayed at the window, listened as she called to Staubach, and heard the door close behind his mother and his dog.

The woman was a steamroller. And she was right. His mom always had been.

He rested his forehead on the windowpane. No doubt Annie'd say no, but no guts, no glory. He had to take a final shot at talking her into a life with him. On her terms.

She liked the city? Fine. There were plenty of things he could do besides ranching. He had a college degree, a fairly sharp mind, and a burning desire to be with Annie.

If that meant living in Boston, then that's where he'd hang his hat.

Chapter Thirty

Annelise, her parents, and Nelly, along with three of her grandfather's nurses, stood at his bedside, singing happy birthday. The nurses had brought him the traditional birthday cupcake since the transplant marked a rebirth.

He beamed and took a small bite. "It's the first day of the rest of my life. A life I'll have because of you, Nelly." He looked at his half sister and then at his granddaughter. "And you, Annelise. You're a stubborn one. And today, I'm thankful for it."

She gaped at him. "You're calling me stubborn? Have you looked in the mirror lately?"

Everyone laughed.

He took her hand in his. "So. I understand you met a boy out there in Texas. Your mother told me he's quite the catch."

"I don't think that's exactly what I said," her mother corrected.

"Still, it's what you meant," he said. "Your father was impressed with him, too. Said he has a good business head on
his shoulders."

It hurt. Talking about Cash was like sticking a pencil in a
fresh wound.

"Cash Hardeman is as fine a young man as they come,"
Nelly said. "I've known his family since, well, since his
grandpa was a young boy. And I do mean boy, in this case.
Calling Cash a boy— Well, doesn't really tell the tale, does
it, Annie?"

Annelise wet her lips. "No. He's a man." Her chest felt
asthma-tight.

"So why aren't you with him?" Her Grandpa practically
bellowed.

Annelise gaped. "Because...because I had important
things to do here."

"Why didn't you bring your fellow along?"

"Grandpa." She toyed with an earring. "First of all, he's
not *my* fellow. Second, we're like, I don't know. Champagne
and bottled beer...city and country. We live in completely
different worlds." She ducked her head. "Besides, and this is
probably the biggest reason, he's not interested in me. Not
really."

"Then why'd he follow you all the way to Boston?"

"What?"

Grandpa tipped his chin toward the window that faced
onto the nurse's station. "That the young man out there in
the cowboy hat? The one you're not pining for?"

She followed his gaze, and there stood Cash. He looked
tired. He looked wonderful. He looked right at her.

Her breath caught.

Cash crooked his finger in a come-here gesture.

She turned to her grandfather.

"Go." He made a shooing motion. "Get out there and see what the boy wants. He certainly is a tall one."

"Yes. Yes, he is."

"Should make some wonderful grandbabies."

She laughed and rushed out to Cash. "What are you doing here?"

He shook his head. "Questions later. First, this. I need this." He ran his thumb over her lower lip. Then he took her hand in his, lifted it, and kissed her fingers, the palm of her hand. Dipping his head, he kissed her neck below her ear.

"I love when you wear your hair in a ponytail. Love the way it bares your neck for me," he whispered.

"Cash—"

"You know one of the reasons for a hat like this?" He touched a finger to the brim of his Stetson.

She shook her head. "No, but I think you're going to tell me."

"Darned right. It hides us from prying eyes when we do this." His lips claimed hers, and she lost all rational thought. When he lifted his mouth from hers, she felt light-headed and more than a little dizzy.

"I had to come, Annie. I had to be here with you today. It's a special day for your family." He grinned crookedly, his dimples deepening. "My mom stopped by last night and chewed my butt good."

"Why?"

"Because I wasn't behaving like a Hardeman."

She frowned in confusion.

"Hardemans fight for what they want." He took her hand again and played with her fingers. "I know I'm not in your class, Annie. I'm not gonna poor-mouth my family. We're comfortable. More than. We have a nice operation in Texas. We raise horses and run beef cattle, and we do very well at it.

"But my name doesn't have a pedigree after it. It's not going down in any history book. I can guarantee there'll be food on my table every day, but I won't be eating that food off Limoges or Lenox china or whatever the hell kind you're used to." He stopped, took a deep breath, and planted his hands on his hips. "And that's the way I like it, Annie. The way my family likes it."

"You think that matters to me, Cash? That I care about my china? Did you pay attention to what I set on my table? Mismatched thrift store plates. And I loved them, more than any designer plates I've ever eaten from."

"I know. And despite all the reasons we shouldn't work, I believe we do." He cupped his hand under her chin, tipped her head up so their eyes met. "Because of that, today's a special day for me, too." Grasping her hand a little tighter, he stared into her eyes. "Marry me, Annie."

Annelise's heart leaped to her throat. Right there in the hospital, with her dressed in a sterile gown and little blue booties, her cowboy was proposing to her. Words refused to come.

When she said nothing, he removed his hat and raked his fingers through his hair. "I didn't mean to do it like this. I hadn't planned to do it here. You deserve moonlight and romance. A big production. The whole shebang. But I couldn't wait. When I saw you in there— You're so damn beautiful. And I've missed you. I've been so lonely without you. It's like the best part of me hopped on that plane in Austin and flew away."

He sighed. "I love you, Annelise Montjoy, and I always will. Marry me?"

"You love me?"

"Wait. Before you answer. I've got more to say." He held up a finger. "Marry me, but not because of my grandfather's will. My mother was right last night. I let the codicil, the whole deadline thing play with my head. I convinced myself I was only thinking of marriage because of it. But that's not true. I want you, Annie. I want you to be my wife. Grandpa had his Edith, his sunshine. His reason for living. I've found my Annelise."

She started to open her mouth, but he held up a hand.

"One more thing."

"Boy, for someone who's in a hurry for an answer, you sure have a lot of qualifications."

He let out a half laugh. "That's because I'm scared to death you'll say no. I want everything up-front. No surprises."

"Now you sound like a lawyer."

"I know. I'm blowing this, aren't I?"

She simply smiled at him.

"Okay, here's the one last thing." He took her hand again. "I don't care where we live. As long as we're together, it's the right place. Vivi's gone. She sold me her half."

"Seriously?"

"Seriously."

"That's why you didn't need to press charges." Annelise grinned. "You blackmailed her, got your own justice."

He grimaced. "Blackmail is a strong word. I may have used what happened as leverage, but I didn't blackmail her. That said, I can sell the ranch if you want, or my father can oversee it."

"You'd give up Whispering Pines for me? You'd leave Texas and live here in Boston?"

"If that's what you need."

"It isn't. I need *you.*" She laid a hand on the side of his face. "I want everything that comes with you. I love you, Cash Hardeman, and I always will."

"So, come on, darlin'. Tell me you'll marry me."

"Without any reservation. My answer's yes. Yes, yes, yes!"

He hugged her to him, grinned ear to ear, and let out a long breath. Reaching into his jeans pocket, he pulled out a jeweler's box. Opening it, he took out a beautiful diamond and blue topaz ring and slid it onto her finger. "It reminded me of your eyes."

"Oh, Cash. It's beautiful."

"So are you." He cradled her head in his hands and kissed her, long and deeply.

From both inside her grandfather's room and behind them at the nurse's station, they heard clapping. She held up her hand and circled so everyone could see the ring.

Then, holding hands and laughing, the two bowed to their audience. Cowboy boots and champagne flutes. Together, they could have it all.

See the next page for an excerpt from

Nearest Thing to Heaven

Chapter One

Not fair!"

Sophie London leaned her head against the icy window-pane and stared out at the gray Chicago skyline. Fingering the amethyst in her pocket, she tried for the billionth time to rationalize away her fear of flying. The mere thought of hopping on a plane made her palms damp.

And now this weather.

The timing couldn't be worse. Sighing, she sipped from her mug of cocoa.

Mother Nature, who'd either gotten up on the wrong side of the bed or suffered from a major case of PMS, was throwing herself one monstrous, rip-roaring tantrum. During the course of a single hour, the sun had disappeared and left behind a low, ominous cloud cover. The temperature had dropped almost twenty degrees.

A mix of snow and rain spit against the glass. Wonderful. Even tucked away in her fourth-story apartment, Sophie swore she could hear the slush on the sidewalks contracting and solidifying to ice. No doubt about it. Her taxi ride to O'Hare would be a slip-sliding, horn-honking nightmare.

Only mid-November and already the temperature had dipped below freezing. Dirty snow and boot-soaking slush blanketed the sidewalks. Frigid gusts of wind, intent on seek-and-destroy missions, whipped off Lake Michigan and zeroed in on already bitterly cold pedestrians unlucky enough to be out and about.

By tomorrow, none of this would matter, Sophie reminded herself. Because this afternoon, nerves or not, she fully intended to be on a flight headed to Texas, sipping a glass of wine, and eating the last of her carefully hoarded birthday stash of Godiva chocolate!

That is, if the worst of the weather held off long enough. Otherwise, she might experience the blizzard from inside a 747 stranded on the tarmac.

No. Don't even go there.

Think positive, Sophie. Think positive. She breathed deeply and turned her back on the ugly outdoor scene. From her stereo, Enya's ethereal voice surrounded and relaxed her. The lavender, grays, and creams of her bedroom did the rest. How could she stay upset inside this feminine, restful retreat she'd created?

A glance at the clock had her stomach dropping. Oh, my gosh! If she expected to make her flight, she'd better hustle. And being on that plane when it took off wasn't optional. She had a wedding to attend. She could only thank God it wasn't hers.

Annelise Elizabeth Katherine Montjoy, her cousin and BFF, was tying the knot. Marrying a cowboy. An honest to God cowboy. Sophie still couldn't quite wrap her head around that.

She'd better, though, because, inside of twenty-four hours, she'd be in the middle of a fitting for her maid-of-honor dress. And that cowboy would be the groom.

So…back to clothes. Hanger by hanger, Sophie studied the ones in her closet, an eccentric mix of beautiful vintage pieces and quirky thrift store finds. What should she take to Maverick Junction, Texas? Not white silk. Been there, done that. Like an idiot, she'd shown up in exactly that for a Fourth of July barbecue at the Hardeman ranch.

That memory brought to mind the handsome cowboy whose kid had dumped his cherry soda in her white-silk lap…and the way said cowboy had tried to wipe it clean. Whew! Maybe she should stick her head out the window and cool off.

Ty Rawlins. So hot she could almost forget he cowboyed for a living. The man was something else. Yeah, and wasn't that the truth? How about starting with the fact he had three-year-old triplets? Boys. Didn't that cool a gal off faster than any Chicago winter. Yikes. Added to that, he was a widower to boot. A woman would have to be beyond insane to jump into that mess.

Insane? Her? No. Behind on the deadline for her spring line of greeting cards? Definitely.

And if she didn't meet that deadline, she'd also find herself behind on her mortgage—and out on her butt on that ice-covered sidewalk.

But all that would have to be sidelined till after the wedding. Right now, she couldn't do a thing about it, so why fret.

Pushing the worry aside, Sophie grabbed clothes and stuffed them willy-nilly into her bag. She opened drawers and pawed through them, pulling out everything she might need and dumping it in her suitcase. Enya had to travel with her, so she grabbed her mp3 player and added it to her bulging carry-on.

Her beautiful bedroom looked like a hurricane had ripped through. Well, that, too, would have to wait. She'd put it to rights when she returned.

Or was leaving it like this tempting fate? Her fingers found the amethyst in her pocket, ran over its smooth surface. No time. She had to go.

Satisfied she'd done all she could, she slung her carry-on over her shoulder, zipped her large case, and, with one last look around, rolled it out to the living room. She had one hand on the doorknob when her phone rang.

Without thought, she answered—and instantly regretted it.

Nathan.

"Hey, beautiful," he said. "What are you up to?"

Her stomach dropped, and she leaned against the door. When would she start checking caller ID? This is exactly what it was for! Next time, she promised herself. But for now, nothing she could do but suck it up and deal with him.

"Actually, Nathan, you just caught me. I'm heading out the door as we speak. I'll be gone for a couple of days."

"Business?"

"No."

"Want company?"

A low-grade headache took root. Her neck and shoulder muscles tightened, and she wet her lips. "No, I don't."

She hated that he forced her to walk so close to rude.

"Where are you going?"

"Away."

Uncomfortable silence fell between them.

"You can't even tell me where you're going?" Petulance seeped into his voice.

She closed her eyes and breathed deeply. "Nathan, we've had this talk before."

"What talk?"

Okay, now he was being deliberately obtuse. "Look, I have a plane to catch."

"What talk, Sophie?" His voice had lost the wheedling tone and taken on a harder, demanding quality.

Thirty seconds more and she'd have been out the door. No, he'd have called her cell if she hadn't picked up...and she'd have answered that, too, without checking.

"This isn't a good time—"

"It's the perfect time."

"Okay." Resolve squared her shoulders. "We decided this wasn't going to work. That we both needed to move on with our lives. Separately."

"*You* decided."

Her pulse kicked up a notch. She hated confrontation, but she couldn't give in on this.

"Fine." Her carry-on slid off her shoulder, and she hitched it back up. "You're right. *I* decided."

"I figured by now you'd have changed your mind."

Oh, boy. This had been hard the first time—and the second and third times. She so did not want to rehash it all again. Why couldn't he simply accept they were done?

Actually, they'd never really started. Nathan Richards was gorgeous, successful, and, at first blush, personable. They'd dated a couple of times and had fun. Then he became possessive. Very possessive. He started showing up at her door. At the grocer's. At the theater.

Truth? He spooked her.

"I haven't changed my mind. I'm not *going* to change my mind. Good-bye, Nathan." She hung up, a plan forming in her mind.

The newlyweds would leave for their honeymoon right after the wedding, so the apartment Annelise rented would be empty. It might not be a bad idea to stay in Maverick Junction a little longer than she'd originally intended. Give Nathan a chance to deal with reality and her time to work undisturbed on her spring line.

Letting her bag drop to the floor, she moved to the window. Scooping up her pots of herbs and lavender, she walked across the hall to her neighbor's.

Dee was at work, so Sophie set the plants in the hallway outside her door. Rushing back into her apartment, she scrawled a quick note.

> *Take care of my babies for me, Dee? Might be gone a little longer than expected. Thanks so much! You're a doll!*
>
> *Love, S.*

She propped the card against the pale blue pot of English lavender. Okay. That was taken care of. Her plants wouldn't wither and die while she was gone. Hands on her hips, she chewed her lip and studied the single piece of luggage at the door. It wouldn't be enough. Not with her change of plans.

She dashed back to her bedroom, dragged another suitcase from beneath her bed, and flung in random clothes. Tugging it behind her, she hurried back to the living room. Better. Now, if she decided to stay in Maverick Junction, Texas, a bit longer, her plants would survive and she'd have clothes to wear without doing laundry every other day.

The heat kicked on, reminding her to adjust the thermostat before she left. Had it really only been a couple of months earlier she'd been running the air conditioner? This summer had been a scorcher, and she'd practically lived on Lake Michigan in her little sailboat.

Winter had come roaring in early, teeth bared. Only a few weeks into colder weather, and she was tired of it already.

This wedding might be exactly what the doctor ordered. Time and space should cool Nathan's heels while sunshine and warm weather cured her sudden lack of creativity.

Speaking of... She slid her laptop into its case. If she expected her muse to stir, it might be best to have her work tools with her.

Without giving herself time for second-guessing, Sophie turned off the lights, locked her door, and headed for the elevator. Unconsciously, her hand slipped into her pocket to rub the amethyst again.

As she let herself out of the building, she cautiously glanced up and down the street. She wouldn't have put it past him to have called from right here on her doorstep.

No Nathan in sight.

About the Author

Lynnette Austin loves Starbucks, Peppermint Patties, and long rides with the top down and the music cranked up! One of the great things about writing is that daydreaming is not only permissible but also encouraged. She grew up in Pennsylvania, moved to New York, then to Wyoming, and presently divides her time between Florida's beaches and Georgia's mountains. She's been a finalist in RWA's Golden Heart contest, PASIC's Book of Your Heart contest, and Georgia Romance Writers' Maggie contest. Having grown up in a small town, that's where her heart takes her—to those quirky small towns where everybody knows everybody...and all their business, for better or worse.

You can learn more at:
AuthorLynnetteAustin.com
Facebook.com/Lynnette-Austin
Twitter: @LynnettAustin

Fall in Love with Forever Romance

MISTLETOE COTTAGE
By Debbie Mason

The first book in a brand-new contemporary series from *USA Today* bestselling author Debbie Mason! 'Tis the season for love in Harmony Harbor, but it's the last place Sophie DiRossi wants to be. After fleeing many years ago, Sophie is forced to return to the town that harbors a million secrets. Firefighter Liam Gallagher still has some serious feelings for Sophie—and seeing her again sparks a desire so fierce it takes his breath away. Hoping for a little holiday magic, Liam sets out to show Sophie that they deserve a second chance at love.

Fall in Love with Forever Romance

ONLY YOU
By Denise Grover Swank

The first book in a spin-off from Denise Grover Swank's *New York Times* bestselling Wedding Pact series! Ex-marine Kevin Vandemeer craves normalcy. Instead, he has a broken-down old house in need of a match and some gasoline, a meddling family, and the uncanny ability to attract the world's craziest women. At least that last one he can fix: He and his buddies have made a pact to swear off women, and that includes his sweetly sexy new neighbor...

THE BILLIONAIRE NEXT DOOR
By Jessica Lemmon

Rachel Foster is surviving on odd jobs when billionaire Tag Crane hires her and whisks her away to Hawaii to help save his business. As things start to get steamy, Rachel falls for Tag. Will he feel the same, or will she just get played? Fans of Jill Shalvis and Erin Nicholas will love the next book in the Billionaire Bad Boys series!

Fall in Love with Forever Romance

HEATED PURSUIT
By April Hunt

The first book in a sexy new romantic suspense series from debut author April Hunt, perfect for fans of Julie Ann Walker, Maya Banks, and Lora Leigh. After Penny Kline walks into his covert ops mission, Alpha Security operative Rafe Ortega realizes that the best way to bring down a Honduran drug lord and rescue her kidnapped niece is for them to work together. But the only thing more dangerous than going undercover in the madman's lair is the passion that explodes between them...

SOMEBODY LIKE YOU
By Lynette Austin

Giving her bodyguards and the paparazzi the slip, heiress Annelise Montjoy comes to Maverick Junction on a mission to help her ailing grandfather. But keeping her identity hidden in the small Texas town is harder than she expected—especially around a tempting cowboy like Cash Hardeman...

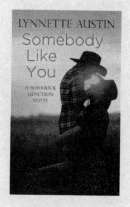